Lynne Graham was born in Northern Ireland and has been a keen romance reader since her teens. She is very happily married, to an understanding husband who has learned to cook since she started to write! Her five children keep her on her toes. She has a very large dog, which knocks everything over, a very small terrier, which barks a lot, and two cats. When time allows, Lynne is a keen gardener.

Michelle Smart's love affair with books started when she was a baby and would cuddle them in her cot. A voracious reader of all genres, she found her love of romance established when she stumbled across her first Mills & Boon book at the age of twelve. She's been reading them—and writing them—ever since. Michelle lives in Northamptonshire, England, with her husband and two young Smarties.

THE KING'S CHRISTMAS HEIR

LYNNE GRAHAM

PREGNANT INNOCENT BEHIND THE VEIL

MICHELLE SMART

MILLS & BOON

First published in Great Britain 2022
by Mills & Boon, an imprint of HarperCollins*Publishers* Ltd,
1 London Bridge Street, London, SE1 9GF

www.harpercollins.co.uk

HarperCollins*Publishers*
1st Floor, Watermarque Building,
Ringsend Road, Dublin 4, Ireland

The King's Christmas Heir © 2022 Lynne Graham

Pregnant Innocent Behind the Veil © 2022 Michelle Smart

ISBN: 978-0-263-30097-0

09/22

THE KING'S
CHRISTMAS HEIR

LYNNE GRAHAM

MILLS & BOON

For my daughter Rachel and her unswerving support

PROLOGUE

THE SNOW WAS falling in a blinding blur that ensured that the hiker couldn't see more than a foot ahead of him. He was colder than he had ever known it was possible to be, which didn't say much for his top-flight protective gear or the countless ski trips he had enjoyed since childhood. Those experiences had convinced him that he was a tough mountain man capable of handling anything that the weather could throw at him.

Too late now to realise how imprudent he had been, he acknowledged grimly. Vittorio's illness had knocked him for six and his brother's demand that he go off and live his own life while he suffered had almost sent him off the rails. He was neither impulsive nor foolish, but he had *needed* solitude to accept both Vittorio's diagnosis and his wishes. In the grip of terrible grief, he had scorned the trappings of his world: the bodyguards, the five-star accommodation and private jets. That lifestyle attracted attention like a flashing neon light, and he didn't want that. It had not once occurred to him that going fashionably off grid could endanger him. Innately confident, he had seen himself as mature and invincible. He had even argued about making a monthly phone call home, ostentatiously ditching his phone before his departure. He was twenty-seven years old…how mature had either of those decisions been?

Now that he was lost and likely to die of exposure such trivial concerns seemed a million miles from his current daunting reality. His confused, self-critical thoughts were drifting, blurring, his steps no longer sure in the heavy snow. Hypothermia, he guessed abstractedly, hitching his rucksack, which seemed to grow heavier with every second. In an abrupt movement, he began to struggle free of its weight and as he stepped forward again, feeling much lighter and freer, he caught a glimpse of lights and stared in disbelief through the falling snow at the small outdoor tree illuminated with a colourful string of lights. There was a house with a garden at the foot of the hill. He didn't like Christmas. Indeed, he had never enjoyed Christmas, but that evidence of civilisation had never been a more welcome sight. As he descended the steep slope with the haste of impatience, he lost his footing and skidded into a fall that made him shout. He fell backwards, struck his head a glancing blow on a rock and knew no more…

CHAPTER ONE

Two years later

HIS MAJESTY, KING GAETANO of the European country of Mosvakia, paced by the window of his private office as he awaited the arrival of his best friend and legal advisor, Dario Rossi.

Dario had phoned him to tell him that the investigation agency had finally found *her*, and Gaetano was eager to hear the details. Not because he was particularly interested in what his estranged wife might be doing or where she was living, he assured himself, but simply out of natural human curiosity.

Although there was nothing particularly natural about the predicament he had got himself into just over two years earlier, he conceded sardonically, his lean, darkly handsome face tense with scornful recollection. While suffering from temporary amnesia, Gaetano had managed to marry a woman he had known for barely six weeks, a woman whom he knew virtually nothing about. Gaetano, prior to that act of inexplicable insanity, had been a playboy prince, notorious for his affairs and dislike of stuffy conventions such as getting married and maintaining a royally respectable low profile. So, what the hell had come over him after that accident in the mountains?

Two years on, Gaetano was still struggling to answer that baffling question. And to underline the obvious mistake he had made in marrying the woman, his bride had *deserted* him at dizzying speed. Gaetano, the son of a mother who had abandoned him as a toddler, had little sympathy for lying, disloyal women who walked out on their responsibilities. That he should also have married the same sort of woman infuriated him and it only emphasised how unsuitable the wife he had chosen had been. Most particularly a woman who had told him she loved him only hours before running away from him when he had needed her the most.

Mosvakia was a small country on the Adriatic coast, which had been in meltdown for the first year of Gaetano's return home. Vittorio had had leukaemia but instead of the long slow decline he had envisaged, Gaetano's older brother had died very suddenly from a heart attack. There had been no time for the careful training and transfer of power that Vittorio had planned for his little brother, no time for final goodbyes either.

Even worse, there had been neither the space nor the privacy for Gaetano to grieve or freak out about the huge responsibility of the throne that had become his without warning. Gaetano had had to bury his personal feelings deep and keep it together for the sake of the Mosvakian people. Wild ideas like abdication had had to be firmly squashed when the streets had filled with candle-holding crowds mourning his brother's demise.

Loyalty and respect for Vittorio's dutiful example had gripped him hard.

He had toiled through the endless weeks of official mourning, the solemn state funeral rites and his own subsequent coronation like an automaton, simply making the speeches and performing the duties that were expected of him in his new and unfamiliar role as monarch. Like the rest of Mosvakia, Gaetano had still been reeling in total shock because Vittorio had been the brightest jewel in the Mosvakian crown and an impossible act to follow.

Furthermore, nobody had *ever* expected Gaetano to follow his sibling and end up as King. He was the second son, born from their father's brief second marriage, the literal spare to match the heir. Twenty years older than Gaetano and already having ruled for almost as long, Vittorio had married at the age of forty. Everyone had assumed that an heir would arrive quickly after his marriage to Giulia, only sadly, that long-awaited event hadn't happened, and then poor Vittorio had fallen ill.

Only months into Gaetano's reign, senior courtiers had begun to hint that Gaetano should now consider finding a bride. He had thought about the runaway wife who nobody but Dario knew he had, and he had duly redoubled his efforts to trace her and get a divorce. She had been impossible to find, with no social media presence.

Suddenly, memory sliced in like a shot of lightning to throw his rational thought processes into chaos. He remembered a tiny woman with a mass of strawberry-blonde hair and huge aquamarine eyes that dominated her delicate freckled face, a woman standing in front of a Christmas tree covered with multi-coloured lights. She was smiling, always smiling at him as though he lit up her world. His first sight of her and then the images and the remembered jumble of thoughts became distinctly cringeworthy. Why? Unbelievably, Gaetano, the heartbreaker and sexually unfettered cynic, had developed a severe case of insta-lust or insta-love, whatever people called that overwhelmingly immediate desire to possess another human being body and soul.

Gaetano blinked and gritted his teeth hard, annoyance flashing through him that those disturbing, illogical memories could still infiltrate his brain when he relaxed his guard even for a moment. Even two years on, she had left a mark on him that, it seemed, nothing could fully eradicate, and it outraged his pride. He turned with relief when a knock sounded on the door and Dario strode in clutching a file and looking nothing short of triumphant.

'At last!' Dario proclaimed, slapping the file down on Gaetano's desk, a tall, rangy male with a neatly clipped beard and a ready smile, a close friend since childhood. 'Now we can sort out that little problem of yours and return your life to normal.'

Gaetano frowned at that choice of words. 'Regrettably, my life's never going to be normal again.' As soon as he voiced that absurd truth, he raised a lean brown hand in a gesture of immediate apology. 'Forget I said that. I know that I should be grateful that our people have accepted me so readily in Vittorio's place.'

'Don't apologise for admitting that you never wanted the throne. You weren't trained for it, and you don't enjoy the pomp and ceremony in the same way as Vittorio did. And don't look at me like that, I was *not* criticising your beloved brother,' the lawyer declared. 'I merely want to point out that Vittorio was by no means perfect.'

'He was a good king,' Gaetano cut in defensively.

'He was an introvert, and you are an extrovert. You excel at diplomacy, and you single-handedly rescued the crown estate from bankruptcy years ago. You are and were very different men with divergent strengths. Stop comparing yourself to him,' his old friend chided quietly. 'If it's any consolation, my wife thinks women prefer you because you're so handsome and I know that's a very silly comment on a serious situation, but it should at least make you laugh.'

'Carla often makes me laugh,' Gaetano responded with his flashing smile, even white teeth bright against his bronzed skin. He swallowed the urge to point out that he had been unable to enjoy his friends' company over cosy suppers in recent times because his new status made such casual outings almost impossible to arrange or enjoy.

Bodyguards and police now surrounded him wherever he went. His attempt to lessen that security presence and reduce the long list of rules he was supposed to follow for his own safety had been unwelcome. Having lost his grandfather to the sea, his father to a car accident and now a third king to ill health, the Mosvakian government currently viewed royals as extremely fragile beings in constant danger. And now that there was only *one* royal-born left? Everyone was scared that some random act of fate or violence could kill off

Gaetano as well, especially when he had no heir to follow him.

As Gaetano leant back against the edge of his desk
to study the file, silence fell. Dario ordered coffee while
Gaetano rapidly scanned the initial listed facts, but he
ended up staring at the single photograph on offer instead. It wasn't a very good photo, depicting as it did
a young woman bundled up in a padded jacket against
the wintry cold, a braid of reddish blonde hair escaping from the hood and only a slice of her pale freckled
profile visible.

'She's…she's signed up for further education
classes?' Gaetano breathed in surprise, his attention
still locked to the photo.

'Yes, she mostly studies online. The two of you really
didn't talk very much during those six weeks, did you?'
the lawyer murmured. 'When you met Lara Drummond,
she was working as a house-sitter.'

'She told me that she was a waitress and a cleaner!'
Gaetano objected, his strong jawline clenching.

'That wasn't a lie. She's currently working evenings
as a cleaner. I imagine she will be eager to agree to a
quick divorce if you offer her a decent settlement,' Dario
opined with cynical conviction.

'She's *not* a gold-digger!' Gaetano bit out defensively.
'If she'd wanted money, she would scarcely have run
away from me and my jet-set life!'

'Gaetano… I'm your lawyer as well as being your
friend. My primary goal is to protect you. You married
her without a prenup and because of that she could ask
for the shirt off your back and get it in a British court,'
Dario warned him worriedly. 'But as things stand, *she*

left *you*. You have lived apart for the requisite two years and a no-contest divorce is straightforward.'

Gaetano nodded in silence, struggling to get a grip on the emotions simmering up inside him, emotions he had successfully managed to suppress for most of his life. He was convinced that letting his emotions loose was what had plunged him into trouble in the first place. He hadn't known who he was when he first met Lara and his amnesia had made the most of that new exhilarating freedom to do and say as he liked. Without the restraints imposed by his birth and conditioning and the depressingly constant presence of the paparazzi, Gaetano had become a much more innocent, vulnerable version of his true self and he had allowed his emotional intensity to control him.

He was appalled by that truth and determined never ever to make such a mistake again. Vittorio had fallen in love several times with the wrong women before he finally married Giulia, a woman whom he'd loved only as a friend. Gaetano had grown up watching his brother get his heart broken, witnessing for himself how many gold-diggers and social climbers were willing to lie and cheat their way into Vittorio's life and pretend to be something they were not.

'Yes, a divorce should be straightforward. Of course, that is assuming that there is no chance that Lara Drummond's child could be yours?' Dario prompted, that question startling Gaetano out of his reflections.

'She has a *child*?' Gaetano exclaimed, incredulous at that news, stalking over to the window with the file and turning his back on his friend to read it again.

Lara had had a little boy but, as his birth certificate had yet to be tracked down, the investigation team could only make a rough guess at his age. *Eighteen* to *twenty-four* months? Gaetano counted dates inside his head, and he did it so painfully slowly that nobody would ever have guessed that he was gifted in the mathematical field.

'Evidently your runaway wife has not been living the celibate life in the same way that you have been,' his friend pronounced in a rueful undertone. 'It may well transpire that she was pregnant when you first met her. But no matter, it is, hopefully, another reason why she may well be happy to regain her freedom. The only evidence of a male in her life, however, is her landlord, who appears to be a friend.'

His strong jawline clenched like a rock, Gaetano swung back to face the other man. 'A *friend*?' he derided.

'The agency cannot be more precise because the landlord is a soldier deployed abroad and nobody has actually seen her with him.'

'But she's living in *his* house.'

'It was originally his parents' home and his sister lives there with her as well,' Dario slotted in wryly. 'So, no proof of anything untoward that could be useful to us.'

'You have my gratitude for keeping this business-like,' Gaetano breathed, running a restive set of long brown fingers through his cropped black hair while resisting the temptation to smash a frustrated fist into the wall.

'You knew her for six weeks and you weren't exactly in your right mind during that time. I assume we can now proceed as planned?' Dario studied him expectantly.

Gaetano's dark as midnight gaze narrowed. 'No. I want to see her first…when I'm *in* my right mind. I want to know how I react to her now.'

'For many reasons that would be unwise,' his friend warned him, frowning. 'The press could catch on. You did nothing wrong in marrying her, but I know you would prefer that connection to stay out of the public domain. You could also meet her again and—'

'I'm not going to fall down the same rabbit hole a second time!' Gaetano scoffed with a contemptuous curl of his expressive mouth. 'I intend to see and speak to her without turning it into a confrontation. Have a little faith in me, Dario. I'm not a complete idiot. I know I need this divorce, but I also have to move past what happened with her and I don't think I can comfortably do that without seeing her one last time.'

Unaware that the life she had carefully rebuilt after getting her heart smashed to smithereens was about to crash into a major obstacle, Lara stepped out of the shower with a smile and began to dry her hair. She loved Saturday mornings because Alice gave the children breakfast, and she got a lie-in before taking the kids to the park. Sundays it was Lara's turn to rise early and look after their little monsters. She crammed her mass of strawberry-blonde hair into a clip at the base of her skull. It felt heavy and she frowned.

Maybe it was time to get her hair cut to a more manageable length. It was sentimental to think of her grandfather smoothing her braid and admiring how long her

hair was getting. But it was downright suicidal to remember long brown fingers feathering through her hair
on a pillow and telling her how silky and soft it was. A
sharp little pain pierced her chest as self-loathing set
up shop inside her again. Gaetano was impossible to
forget. As far as experience went, she had gone from
zero to sixty with Gaetano the instant she laid eyes on
him. Messy black hair in need of a trim, strong jawline outlined in black stubble, eyes as dark as pitch, set
deep below strong brows. So handsome he had made
her pinch herself to check that she wasn't dreaming.

But in reality, she *had* been dreaming, Lara reminded
herself doggedly, because only in a silly girlish dream
would a guy like Gaetano have truly fallen in love with
her. Little ordinary Lara, the world's most natural wall-
flower, the sort of girl whom most people overlooked
and forgot. She lacked the hooks that attracted male
attention. She was no good at flirting and her curves
were of the modest variety. There was nothing exciting about her, nothing that made her stand out from the
crowd and yet, for the space of a magical six weeks,
Gaetano had made her feel like the most beautiful and
desirable woman in the world.

And when he had emerged all at once from his loss
of memory? Lara shivered and crammed those recollections back into the mental locked box where she kept
all such damaging, hurtful things. Dwelling on the bad
stuff didn't change anything or indeed ease the hurt of
those experiences. And Gaetano had hurt her so badly
that on one level she knew that she would never recover from their brief marriage. That was what hap-

pened when you thought you had found 'perfect' and then it all suddenly fell apart in your hands.

Gaetano had made her feel wanted and necessary to someone else for the first time in many years. He had valued her when others had not, he had *seen* her while others ignored her, not least her adoptive mother. His apparent love for her had seduced her into capitulating fast to his attraction, plunging them both headfirst into a whirlwind marriage. It was little wonder that she had run off once he'd emerged from his amnesia and regretted their relationship. Nor could she have borne telling him about their son because if he didn't want her or to be married, why would he want a child from his mistake?

Clad in worn jeans and a sloppy sweater to fend off the winter temperatures, Lara ate her toast standing while Alice's five-year-old daughter, Iris, fought with Lara's son, Freddy, over the bike. The bike belonged to Iris, but Freddy, who wasn't dexterous enough as yet to ride it, loved to sit on it and ring the bell. He pinned big dark expectant eyes on his mother, a guilt trip in a single glance. Freddy was a total drama llama, given to fiery tantrums and sobbing meltdowns. His intensity fascinated Lara, who had a quiet, calm nature, but it also reminded her painfully of his volatile, passionate father. Iris took the bike and Freddy flung himself down and sobbed noisily.

'If you want my advice,' her friend and one-time stepsister, Alice, whispered at her elbow, 'you won't take the bike with them to the park today.'

'He can't ride it anyway. He has to learn.' Lara knew that her son would only shout and scream louder if she tried to lift him off the floor. 'It's not fair to deprive Iris of her bike.'

'He is *so* stubborn,' Alice remarked in wonderment as Freddy kicked his feet and screamed while Iris wheeled her bike out to the small hall before walking back to try and comfort Freddy. She was a kind little girl, well aware of the fact that Freddy was still a baby. Freddy, however, was a pretty tall and sturdy toddler in spite of the reality that he was still only sixteen months old. He looked much older than he was because of his sheer physical size.

'He's a handful and no mistake.' Alice sighed, a tall, elegant brunette with blue eyes and long hair in a ponytail.

'Auntie Lara…?' Iris danced in the doorway, her energetic little body raring to go. 'Can we go now?'

Freddy stood up, tears magically dried as his mother helped him into his coat and buckled him into the pushchair. When Iris ran off to the swings at the park, Lara unclipped her son and lifted him onto the baby slide. He threw up his arms with pleasure as he whizzed down the slide. He stumbled clumsily off at the bottom to run back to her. He couldn't manage the steps on his own yet and it annoyed him when he saw other children climb alone, but then the other children were all older and steadier on their feet.

As Freddy ran over to watch Iris on the swing, Lara followed, thinking about the coffee she would treat herself to once the kids had had enough. Life was so busy that she truly valued her rare moments of relaxation. Alice worked from home as an accountant and the two women shared childcare, although Lara was very aware that at present Alice was doing more than her fair share because Freddy was not at school like Iris in the mornings when Lara slept, and he required more attention.

Lara was very fond of Alice and her brother, Jack. Although Lara's mother had divorced the twins' father after only eighteen months of marriage, Lara had stayed in touch with her step-siblings. She was still grateful that they hadn't blamed her for her mother's change of heart and their father's misery. Of course, they were well aware now of how many different partners Eliza Drummond had loved and left, and of how Lara had been forced to take refuge with her grandparents when she was sixteen because she had begun to feel threatened by her mother's boyfriend. To say the least, Lara had had a colourful upbringing, although her early years had started out quiet, secure and happy.

She had been adopted as a newborn baby by Stewart and Eliza Drummond. Her father had been a doctor and she had adored him. Tragically he had died from an aneurysm when she was nine and her adoptive mother had subsequently made some very bad decisions. Devastated by her husband's death, Eliza had flailed around like a boat without a rudder, her only goal seemingly to find a man to replace the one she had lost. Unfortunately, she had found more bad than good men. The bad ones had stolen her money and beaten her up and the good ones had bored her. Alice and Jack's father had been one of those rare, good men.

It was a long time since Lara had seen her mother. At sixteen she had moved in with her grandparents, her late father's mum and dad, and while living with them she had begun catching up on her education. As far as she knew her mother, who ran a bar in Spain, had not returned to the UK in recent years. Eliza didn't stay in touch with her adopted daughter. Lara's return to the UK seemed to have killed any further interest the older woman might have had in her. The hurt caused by that lack of interest was a familiar theme in Lara's life.

'Of course, you're adopted…it's not the same,' her father's sister, her aunt Jo, had once declared with a fatalistic shake of her head. 'You're not really related to the rest of us at all and we can't help remembering that because you don't look remotely like any of us. It's a shame my brother died, because he really did think of you as *his* daughter. I'm sorry you lost that relationship.'

Lara had often been desperately sorry on that score as well but there was no point crying over spilt milk. Now that she was also a parent, she had tried to leave her childhood disappointments behind her and move on.

As she took the children to feed the ducks, she noticed a man walking down the path on the far side of the lake. He was unusually well dressed for the park, clad in a dark formal overcoat worn over what looked like a suit underneath. He walked very upright with the easy confident glide of a predator and Lara froze, momentarily tense because even from this distance the man reminded her just a little of Gaetano, who had likewise possessed that almost feral grace of movement. This guy was also very tall and well built, with black hair and a bronzed complexion that spoke of warmer climes, but he wasn't close enough for her to get a better look at him.

Of course, it couldn't be Gaetano, she scolded herself irritably. What would the King of Mosvakia be doing in a small run-down urban park? Even less would he want to run the risk of being associated with her, the very ordinary woman he had mistakenly married! She had been a *huge* mistake on Gaetano's terms, Lara made herself recall. The colour that the breeze had stung into her cheeks disappeared as she remembered the last day she had seen him two years earlier.

'I married you… I actually *married* you?' Gaetano had realised in absolute horror, looking at her as though she must somehow have tricked him into becoming her husband, his recoil from the concept of being married to her etched in his shaken features as he studied her. 'What the hell have I done?'

'We'll deal with that problem later,' his friend and sidekick, Dario, had interrupted with smooth impatience. 'Right now, it's not important. What *is* important is that you come home to Mosvakia to recover from your ordeal. We've been worried sick about you for weeks!'

Lara remembered how it had felt to be lumped in as part of Gaetano's 'ordeal', her tummy clenching on a nauseous wave. She gathered up the kids and walked over to the coffee van. Of course she hadn't informed Gaetano about the fact that he had a son. That would have been very bad news on his terms when he didn't even want Lara as a wife. And why would he?

There had been a time when she had stalked Gaetano on the Internet, hungrily absorbing every photo and atom of information, but the drip-drip effect of reading about his many, many affairs had soon cured her of that weakness. She had soon learned that the man she had married had a raunchy background with the models, actresses and socialites who had shared his bed. Seemingly, Gaetano had had no serious relationships in his past. He had pursued sex, rather than love, and none of his affairs had lasted long. In short, he was not the man she had fallen madly in love with, not the man she had happily married. He was, in truth, the 'Playboy Prince' he had been dubbed by the press.

Collecting her coffee, Lara sat down on one of the battered old chairs beside the van and watched Iris and Freddy chase a ball. Freddy fell over a couple of times and Iris dragged him up. She was a terrific big sister. Lara had often wished that she had had a sibling. Occasionally she had thought about the fact that she was adopted and that she might have blood relatives somewhere in the world, if only she had the guts to look into her back story. Unfortunately, the many hurts and let-downs meted out by her adoptive family had made her reluctant to risk inviting more disillusionment and disappointment into her life.

Across the grass lay the wooded area of the park and as she sipped her coffee she saw men emerge from below the trees and wondered what they were doing. They had a serious, professional look about them and she thought they might be police. Were they searching for someone? Their presence spooked her, and she glanced at the kids, ready to take them home even though she hadn't yet finished her coffee. Somehow, her usual relaxation in the winter sunshine was absent.

'Lara...?'

It was a voice Lara had believed she would never hear again, dark and deep, overwhelmingly male. But then almost everything about Gaetano was overwhelmingly male, she conceded as she sat there hunched, virtually afraid to lift her head because she was convinced that she was suffering some kind of auditory hallucination. Thoughts about Gaetano had overloaded her self-discipline and raised her anxiety level, she told herself irritably.

On that thought she looked up and was totally stunned when Gaetano settled down into the rusty weathered chair opposite her, his brilliant dark eyes locked to her, black lashes a thick canopy over his piercing gaze. It was those eyes of his that got to her every time. Dark, hypnotically compelling and potent. Beneath his weight, the rickety chair squeaked in protest. He was six feet four inches tall with the wide shoulders and lean hips of an athlete. He was still breathtakingly beautiful. Her mouth ran dry, her lungs compressed, butterflies fluttered. An unwelcome tightening in her pelvis made her stiffen even more as her breasts pushed against the lace of her bra in concert.

Lara's hair was loose and tumbled round her shoulders, the strawberry blonde waves tossed by the breeze and framing her delicate face. She was not a beauty, Gaetano told himself, yet when he looked at her, he still couldn't take his eyes off her. Either she was impossibly pretty in her delicacy or simply incredibly sexy. And covered from head to toe in jeans and an unflattering padded coat, how the hell could she be sexy? Everything about Lara was natural and unstudied, from the freckles scattered across her nose to the sensible clothing she wore. She was quite unlike any woman he had ever met before and that was probably what had drawn him in.

And yet she *was* sexy, Gaetano acknowledged grudgingly, his attention lingering involuntarily on the full pink pout of her lips and the brilliant blue of her eyes. As his trousers stretched taut at the groin with an arousal he could barely credit, he tensed, flashes of memory returning to haunt him as they so often did in the dark of the night in his empty bed. Skinny but curvaceous, he recalled, so skinny he had tried to feed her up until she had confessed that she never ever put on weight. She was wild and impossibly sweet in bed, so receptive to his every move he hadn't been able to keep his greedy hands off her.

'You have five minutes with her before there's a risk of press intrusion,' his chief security officer had warned him.

He was already three minutes into that time limit, and he had been silent. 'We need to talk,' he informed her then with chilling gravity.

Lara felt that chill, that distance in Gaetano straight down to the marrow of her bones. She remembered his warmth, his intensity, and suddenly, that clear change in him shook her. She didn't know what she had expected from him. When she had first run away from him, she had had no plan. That had been a knee-jerk response to his wounding rejection. She had had no thought of what the future might bring and no suspicion that she was pregnant.

'Yes, we need to talk,' Lara conceded reluctantly, her gaze entrapped by glittering dark eyes enhanced by the lush fringe of ebony lashes. Mesmeric eyes teeming with raw allure. She swallowed the lump in her tight throat.

Gaetano slid a printed card across the small table.

'I'm staying at this address. I'll be waiting there for you this evening. If you want, I can send a car to pick you up.'

'That won't be necessary,' she whispered, grasping the card with nerveless fingers, dragging it down off the table into her pocket. For the sake of her pride, she had to take control of the encounter and intelligence had already suggested the most likely reason why Gaetano would seek her out after so long. And if that was true, that had to mean that their marriage had been legal, after all, she reasoned numbly. On the basis of that startling enough assumption, she said tightly, 'You want to discuss a divorce, don't you?'

Gaetano dealt her a cold hard appraisal, backed by the cold hard power of his forceful personality. 'What do you think?'

CHAPTER TWO

GAETANO STRODE AWAY and only then did Lara draw breath again, sucking in the icy air like a drowning swimmer. His appearance had plunged her fathoms deep in shock. In the immediate aftermath she was annoyed that she had not been the first to acknowledge their dilemma and take charge. *She* should have contacted *him* to request a divorce, she reasoned fiercely. But that would have meant throwing Freddy into the mix and Freddy was another question altogether. She didn't want to talk about her son, but she couldn't lie about his existence either.

Strapping Freddy into his pushchair, she left the park with Iris to walk home. She would have to meet Gaetano and put their little winter idyll behind her where it belonged. And why was she so tense and worried? Gaetano had made a mistake marrying her. The instant he had recovered his memory he had immediately recognised their marriage as a mistake. Why would he be any more interested in Freddy than he was in Freddy's mother?

'Are you going out tonight?' she asked Alice when she got back to the house, because Lara didn't clean at weekends and her friend usually went out with her boyfriend.

'No. It's a hot bath and an early night for me,' Alice announced with a roll of her expressive eyes.

'You're not seeing Jamie?'

'No, he took offence when I said it was too soon for me to meet his family, so we're on a break,' her friend divulged.

'You've been seeing him for months now,' Lara remarked carefully.

'I've done the "getting serious" thing once and I'm not interested in doing it again,' her friend told her squarely.

Lara bit her tongue because she knew her friend would get annoyed if she tried to persuade her otherwise. Alice had been engaged and Iris had been a toddler when her fiancé had died in a motorbike crash. Devastated by that loss, Alice had sworn off risking her heart again.

'Well, it suits me if you're staying in because I've got to go out tonight. Freddy's father came to speak to me in the park,' Lara confided.

Alice stared at her in surprise. 'Where did he come from? I thought he wasn't local.'

'He's not but obviously he's tracked me down and he wants a divorce. I've agreed to meet up with him this evening.'

'What about Freddy?'

Lara winced. 'We'll see.'

'You should've told the guy about his son ages ago.' Alice sighed. 'Some financial support would have made your life a lot easier.'

'It can't be a coincidence that he appeared in the park I visit every weekend,' Lara fielded ruefully. 'To find me he probably had to use a detective agency, so I'm pretty sure he would've found out about Freddy at the same time. And? He didn't even *look* in Freddy's direction…not once!'

'I wish you'd tell me more than the bare bones of what happened between you.'

'He got his memory back, Alice, and he didn't want me or what I thought we had any more,' Lara pronounced curtly. 'That's all you need to know.'

It wasn't that she didn't trust Alice, only that the finer details of her involvement with Gaetano and his precise status were just a little too sensational to share. Alice would not deliberately reveal Lara's secrets to anyone, but nobody liked to gossip more than Alice once she had had a couple of drinks. It had been less risky simply to leave her best friend partially in the dark and stick to sharing only the necessary facts.

The unembellished facts, Lara reminded herself, recollection tugging her back more than two years in time.

Two years ago she had been working as a waitress in a York café and living in the bedsit above until her boss had decided to retire and sell the building. In dismay at losing both employment and home together, Lara had discussed possible future plans with her closest friend at the time, Cathy, the older woman who'd managed the craft shop next door.

Realising that Lara was at a loose end, Cathy had then asked her if she would look after her house and her pets for several weeks over Christmas while she and her husband flew out to Australia to visit their daughter and their grandchildren. Having looked after Cathy's pets before at her remote farmhouse, Lara had been pleased to accept the invitation. It would give her a comfortable breathing space in which to decide what she wanted to do next with her life and allow her to enjoy Christmas in peace and tranquillity.

The day Gaetano arrived it was snowing heavily. Lara had spent a lazy day watching festive movies with the dogs and the cats. There were no close neighbours and no passing traffic because the single-track road to the farmhouse ended at its gates. In snow the steep road was virtually impassable, and she was relieved that she had shopped for fresh food only the day before.

Behind the house, a hilly outcrop of rock ran down to the edge of the garden. She was cleaning the kitchen when she heard the shout, and the dogs began barking. The sudden noise spooked her. When she looked out of the window, she saw a man lying in the snow near the tree that Cathy always had draped in outdoor lights for the festive season. By the deep tracks in the snow, she guessed that he had tripped over the low border of shrubs that marked the garden boundary and had fallen there.

In dismay she pulled on her friend's outdoor boots and jacket, pausing only to grab up the walking stick by the door because she knew she would struggle to get an injured man into the house without help. How long would it take for the emergency services to arrive in such weather? Where had he come from? He was dressed like a walker, but it was the hardly the season for hill walking.

In the act of trying to raise himself the man slumped

down again, relieving her of the fear that he was unconscious.

'You'll freeze if you stay out in this.' Shivering, Lara shook his shoulder. 'Up!' she instructed in desperation. 'It'll take ages for anyone to come here and help and by then you might be dead from exposure.'

'You're a cheerful little soul,' her accident victim mumbled.

Relieved that he was at least well enough to be sarcastic, Lara grabbed a handful of the back of his jacket and tried to pull him, but he weighed a ton. 'Come on!' she urged.

'I hit my head…everything's spinning,' he framed.

'You can have the pity party indoors where it's warm.' Lara brushed away black tousled hair to whisper in his ear. 'Lovely fire, nice hot drink. Come on, I can't do this without your help.'

He groaned and started to raise himself again.

'Lean on me,' she told him, bending down and dragging his arm to her shoulder. 'Now…*move*!'

He moved, indeed got as far as his knees before *she* was driven face down into the snow by his weight.

Shaking herself free of snow, she rolled upright. 'Good, we're getting somewhere…you're halfway there.'

He blinked in bewilderment, snowflakes falling and clogging on the most outrageous curling black lashes. Dark, dark eyes, the kind that a woman stared at. It was Lara's turn to blink in puzzlement that such a thought should occur to her at such a time. Was she crazy?

'Here…use the stick as a support,' she pressed, pushing it into his hand, closing his clumsy fingers round it and standing. 'It's only a few yards.'

He levered himself up and swayed. 'Sick, dizzy.'

'Lean on me,' she advised, staggering when he obliged. 'Glory be, why do you have to be so big?'

'Why do you have to be so small?' he groaned, lurching forward at a snail's pace, his feet dragging. 'What height are you?'

'Four feet ten,' Lara admitted with great reluctance.

He staggered and swayed outside the back door, struggling to stay upright, and she thrust the door wide, scared to let go of him in case he went down again.

'Four feet ten,' he slurred like a drunk. 'Like a miniature person out of *Gulliver's Travels*.'

'Enough!' Lara snapped as he stumbled over the threshold and rocked like a very tall building in an earthquake. 'Over to the seat by the fire before you fall down.'

'Don't overheat me...it's dangerous with hypothermia,' he warned her.

Lara gritted her teeth as she guided his wavering steps towards the stove and pressed him down in the big fireside chair there. A sharp word from her silenced the mad excitement of the dogs careening round them. She swiped off his beanie because she had noticed a bloodstain on it and walked round to the back of the chair, tipping his head forward. He had a lot of dense black hair and she gently felt through it to feel the sizeable swelling there. There was no large wound and didn't seem to be any fresh blood. The rich musky scent of him assailed her nostrils. He smelled incredibly good.

'I think you'll live,' she murmured unevenly, still out of breath from her efforts with him. 'Are your feet wet?'

'*Sì...*'

The foreign word took her aback because he had previously spoken what she would have described as distinctly posh public-school English. 'Wet?' she pressed again.

'Yes,' he finally mumbled.

'We've got to take off anything wet that you're wearing to raise your temperature and then I'll get blankets.' Lara dropped down at his feet to tackle his boots. 'I thought these would have been waterproof.'

'Got my socks wet,' he groaned.

Lara rolled her eyes and dragged off the sodden socks, noting that he even had nicely shaped feet. She raced off to get blankets from Cathy's substantial airing cupboard. Returning to his side, she checked his waterproof jacket.

'Think we'd better get this off too…let the heat in,' she reasoned uncertainly, unzipping and unsnapping at speed.

'Are you planning to strip all of me?' he asked lazily, raising his head for the first time to look directly at her.

And, wow, that first glance froze her in her tracks because it was the first proper look she had managed to have of him, so busy had she been trying to get him into the house and then work out what best to do for him. Now the most amazing caramel-brown eyes collided with hers and held her fast. Looking away was more than she could contrive when those stunning eyes, illuminated to tawny gold by the firelight, were set in the most gorgeous masculine face. Tousled black hair tumbled over his brow to match sculpted cheekbones, an arrogant blade of a nose and a strong jawline, enhanced by a swirl of thick black stubble. His incredible bone structure was very distinctive and, she thought weakly, capable of turning any female head.

'You're like a doll,' he muttered, frowning and moving his head slightly to focus better, his lips compressing as she hovered in front of him.

'You're in pain.'

'Only a headache,' he parried, shifting his wide shoulders back and letting her tug at his sleeve to free one arm. As he spoke the dogs settled round his feet and their relaxed attitude to him eased her tension.

Lara dragged the jacket off and set it aside before checking the long-sleeved top he wore underneath. It was dry but she could feel the clammy chill of his broad chest underneath. And the realisation that she had been so busy mooning over him that she had momentarily forgotten what was most important shamed her. Shooing the dogs away, she grabbed up the blankets and carefully covered him, tucking the warm folds round his bare feet with extra care. To her amusement the dogs settled back round him again.

'I need to get you warm,' she muttered, stoking the stove to encourage a fresh burst of heat.

'It's a shame sharing body heat to chase the cold has gone out of fashion,' he murmured sibilantly.

My goodness, he was flirting with her, so he couldn't be that injured, Lara registered in disconcertion, a flush warming her cheeks. She didn't have much practice with flirting. Decent men tended to assume she was younger than she was and treat her like a kid sister. The oversexed types wasted little time trying to get her into bed, which was a major turn-off for her. The men who she deemed attractive were invariably not attracted to her.

That was why she was still a virgin at twenty-one. But that lack of sexual experience was also the result of her adoptive mother's frequent affairs and break-ups, not to mention the sleazy boyfriends who had targeted Lara as an adolescent. The way she saw it, a little restraint was an extra tool in her self-preservation box.

'You're very shy,' he mumbled thickly.

Seeing that his head was dipping lower, she shook herself free of his intoxicating effect on her and said anxiously, 'No, don't go to sleep. As far as I know you shouldn't be sleeping, not with the concussion you probably have.'

'Are you a nurse?'

'No, that's just basic first aid. I should ring for an ambulance now.'

'Don't need an ambulance, don't need medical attention. I got a knock on my head. It's no big deal.'

'Are you a doctor?'

'You're cheeky,' he sighed.

'Look, I'm going to phone the nearest neighbour for advice…she's a retired doctor. Please try and stay awake.' Dr Beresford, a keen craftswoman whom she had often met in Cathy's shop, would tell her whether or not she should call the emergency services to attend to her uninvited guest, although on such a night possibly only a tractor or a snowplough would manage to get up the road.

Moving out to the hall, she dug out her mobile phone to ring the woman.

Dr Beresford cut through her apologies for disturbing her. 'A walker?' she prompted in astonishment.

'Yes… I thought it was crazy in this weather too.

He's hit his head and has a bump on the back of it but no other injuries. I'm trying to warm him up and I'll give him tea.'

'No stimulants,' the doctor warned her. 'Does he seem confused?'

'No. Aside of a headache he seems all right but he's pretty shaky on his feet.'

'If he's not seriously hurt it's unlikely that the emergency services would fly in to pick him up. I know for a fact that they're already dealing with a motorway pile-up this evening. But I don't like leaving you alone with a strange man either. Possibly if I were to inform the police or the mountain rescue team *they* would make the effort to walk up from—'

'That's not necessary,' Lara declared. 'He's not the creepy type…and I would know.'

'Well, that's good. I wish I could say that I could call over tomorrow but with Cathy's road in such a state—'

'I'll be fine. We've got heat and food. Should I be keeping him awake?'

Having received her instructions, Lara finished the call and walked back into the spacious kitchen and living area. Her uninvited visitor had fallen asleep while the dogs snored at his feet. She decided to leave him in peace until she had made a pot of tea and some ham sandwiches. While the kettle boiled, she studied him. He really was quite ridiculously handsome, she mused, no longer embarrassed by her previous reaction to him. She was convinced that any woman would have found herself staring just a little too long at such perfect masculine features. Entirely symmetrical features, eyelashes long enough to trip on and a superbly shaped pale pink mouth set in an extensive black shadow of stubble. His deep voice, the angular strength of his jaw and his sheer size lent him a ferociously masculine quality and yet even when he had flirted with her just a little there had been nothing to creep her out.

And nobody knew more about creepy men than Lara did. Her mother had had several live-in boyfriends who liked very young girls: men with sleazy eyes who tracked her every move once her skinny body began to develop petite curves, men who got too friendly when her mother was absent, men whose hands strayed where they shouldn't, men who hovered in her bedroom door-way saying, 'Just checking on you…'

With a shiver of recollection, Lara shot out of that last frightening memory and lifted the tray to carry it over to the coffee table. Leaning forward, she gave his shoulder a slight shake to wake him as gently as possible before sitting down again.

'Dr Beresford said to only let you sleep for small stretches. I'll wake you up every couple of hours to check that you're all right.'

'Oh, joy,' he drawled softly.

'Yes, I'm looking forward to a night without much sleep too,' Lara countered gently, determined not to take any nonsense. 'It'll be rather like having a baby in the house.'

Her visitor stared back at her in disbelief.

'Do you take sugar and milk in your tea?'

'Milk, yes…sugar, no. But I don't *drink* tea,' he told her. 'I only drink coffee… I think,' he completed, less certainly, his voice trailing off as his brow furrowed as if something was confusing him.

'But coffee is a stimulant and the doctor advised against that.'

'Do we have to follow even the tiniest piece of medical advice?'

'Yes,' Lara confirmed. 'As long as you're my responsibility.'

'I'm not sure I want to be anyone's responsibility,' he framed tautly.

He didn't like being told no, didn't like restrictions, was possibly even accustomed to his looks and charisma smoothing his path in life. Lara smiled and shrugged. She poured tea into a mug and set it close to him. 'I made sandwiches. I don't know if you're hungry.'

He sipped the tea with a wince of distaste that he tried really hard to hide. He was arrogant but he had manners, she decided. She offered him the plate of sandwiches. He accepted one and she smiled again, thinking that an appetite was a healthy sign.

'I'm Lara, Lara Drummond,' she murmured.

'Lara…that's unusual,' he remarked rather than responding as she had expected with his own name.

'You can blame my mother. She was a big fan of *Dr Zhivago*.'

He gave her a blank look and she settled the sandwich plate in front of him.

'It's a film set in Russia during the first world war, starring Julie Christie and Omar Sharif,' Lara explained ruefully, because it was obvious that he didn't know what she was talking about. 'It's a romantic drama. That's where I got my name from.'

'Are you romantic?'

'Not at all.' Lara rolled her eyes at that idea after

the adolescent experiences she had enjoyed. 'What's your name?'

'Guy…' he responded instantly and then he went oddly stiff and closed his lips again, his brows drawing together in a frown.

'Guy.' It struck her as an upper-class name that was a perfect match for his posh accent. He wasn't very talkative. Of course, it could just be that he wasn't feeling well and that he was exhausted, she scolded herself as she pushed another sandwich at him, keen to drive the frown from his lean dark features.

'And you got lost,' she commented.

'Yes,' he confirmed in an odd tone of finality. 'I think I saw the tree with lights just before I fell. It feels familiar…somehow.'

'Cathy loves to put the lights out on the apple tree so that she can see it from her kitchen window.'

'Cathy?' he queried.

'The owner of the house. Well, Cathy and her husband, Brian. This is their home.'

'And who are you?'

'The house-sitter…an unofficial one. Cathy and Brian are spending Christmas in Australia and I'm here looking after everything until they come home,' she clarified. 'Let me show you to your room…'

He stood up slowly and his lashes flickered as he shifted his shoulders and his neck with caution.

'Luckily there's a room down here that you can use. I can see you're still a bit dizzy so it's best you don't tackle the stairs yet. The room's small but it's comfortable,' she confided, pushing open the door, relieved to see that the bed was already made up and that she wouldn't have to do it.

'Is there a bathroom?'

'Yes, but I'm not sure you should use the shower yet either.'

'I have a headache but that's it,' he said firmly as she opened another door across the corridor to indicate the washing facilities.

'I'll be in the kitchen. I'm going to use the sofa to-night so that I can stay within reach.'

His curling black lashes dipped low over his dark eyes, and he flashed her a slow-burning smile of appreciation that made her heart thunder in her ears and her mouth run dry. 'I appreciate all the help you've given me. Thank you.'

She stood in the hallway a full minute after he had vanished into the bathroom and then her brain kicked in again and moved her. But that smile of his, my goodness when his whole face lit up like that he was stunning. Returning to the kitchen, she tidied up, tended to the animals and settled them for the night. Shortly after that she heard Guy close the bedroom door and she expelled her breath on a hiss.

Who was he? Why hadn't she asked him where his stuff had gone? Had he lost it in the snow when he fell? Or had he simply been out rambling? If so, he could only be staying somewhere within reasonable reach but there were no houses closer than Dr Beresford's and even she was a couple of miles away. And if he did have accommodation nearby, why hadn't he mentioned it? Her own head was starting to ache with stress, and she went upstairs, donned her warmest pyjamas, gathered up her duvet and her alarm clock and went back downstairs to get as comfy as she could on the sofa.

The alarm wakened her from a solid sleep, and it took a moment or two for her to orientate herself and recall why she was getting up in the middle of the night. Sighing, she clambered off the sofa. She felt a bit cruel waking him up after the experience he had been through, and she brought him a warm drink as a consolation. She knocked on the bedroom door and waited but there was no sound within. Compressing her lips, she went in, the light from the hallway illuminating the room. She set the drink on the bedside cabinet.

He was fast asleep, his black hair very dark against the pale bedding. She bent down, steadying herself with one hand on the headboard, and shook the arm resting on top of the duvet. 'Guy?' she prompted. 'It's time to wake up…'

He stretched up a hand and found her shoulder, his dark eyes flying wide in surprise. '*Mi dispiace*…what did you say?' he framed groggily.

'I brought you a warm drink. How are you feeling?'

He slid a leg out of bed and began to rise, making her suddenly aware of how very tall he was. She stumbled backwards. As he lifted his hands as though to reassure her and stay her retreat, he caught his foot in the trailing duvet and lurched forward, knocking her off balance. A gasp of dismay parted Lara's lips as she went crashing down on the floor with him on top of her. They looked at each other, stunned by the accident, and then just as quickly Lara began to shake with giggles.

'*Mi dispiace,*' he said again.

'What does that mean?' Lara asked, her aquamarine eyes brimming with laughter at their mutual clumsiness.

'I'm sorry… I am truly sorry,' he declared, struggling to disentangle his foot from the bedding.

'It was your expression…the shock and horror!' she gasped, giggles convulsing her again.

'Stop,' he told her, raising himself up from her prone body to release her from his weight.

He was smiling now though, his shapely mouth quirking with reluctant amusement, his dark golden eyes alight as he scanned her triangular face.

'You are shockingly cute and sexy,' he muttered.

Her eyes brightened even more. 'Seriously?'

'Even in Christmas pudding pyjamas,' he conceded in unhidden wonderment, his mouth drifting down closer to hers. '*Dancing* Christmas puddings too…'

Lara couldn't breathe that close to him, but she lifted her head up to him, eyes wide, lips parting in an invitation that seemed so natural in that moment.

His breath fanned her cheek, his lips brushed hers in the briefest possible caress and a feverish little shiver of delicious response rippled through her. With a groan, he levered back from her, and she followed him by sitting up, eyes starry as she stared at him.

'This is crazy,' he breathed.

Rebellion twisted inside Lara, who had learned to repress her secret desires and always do the sensible thing. Every time, she did the sensible thing…until she leant forward quite deliberately, all tantalising, teasing femininity, and their mouths collided. It was as if one of them had struck a match and lit a firework as he eased her gently towards him and kissed her with all the unrestrained passion she had always craved and never once received from a man. The pressure of his mouth on hers was urgent, demanding, igniting a new and irresistible hunger. She had never felt that way before and she kissed him back with enthusiasm, squirming with pleasure as his tongue stroked along hers. A flood of heat surged between her thighs, her nipples prickling into tight little buds.

'Really crazy,' he extended gruffly, carefully setting her back from him and using the bed to haul himself upright again.

Only then did she become aware that he was only wearing boxers that moulded every angle of his big muscular bronzed body and the effect of that kiss on him was fairly obvious. She reddened, seized by the awful heat of embarrassment at how forward she had been. Such behaviour was so out of character for her that she was astonished by it. The ache that had stirred at the heart of her tightened, reminding her of its presence. Red as a beetroot, she scrambled upright.

'Don't know what happened there. I brought you a hot chocolate,' she muttered in a rush, indicating the mug. 'How do you feel?'

'Lousy,' he groaned, settling back on the bed and yanking up the duvet to cover himself. 'I don't think my name is Guy. It doesn't feel familiar.'

Lara was taken aback. 'But you *said* your name was Guy.'

'No. I began to say the name but when I thought about it, it wasn't there any more in my head.' He sighed. 'I'd forgotten it like everything else.'

Her eyes full of concern, Lara hovered. 'Like every-thing else?'

Guy, who wasn't sure he *was* Guy, studied her. 'I can't remember *anything*. My name, what I was doing out there in the snow alone…who I am…where I come from…there's just this great woolly blank inside my head!' he exclaimed in a frustrated undertone.

Emotion boiled like swirling dark water in his highly expressive eyes and nothing could have masked the hint of panic edging his low voice. Lara winced. 'You banged your head. You're confused and, if you can't remember now, it'll probably all come back to you by morning. The worst thing you can do is get upset about it.'

'Of course, I'm upset about it!' he exclaimed rawly.

'And the more upset you are about it, the more con-fused you will feel. Try and get some sleep now,' she urged quietly and swiftly moved back to the door.

'I shouldn't have kissed you,' he breathed abruptly. 'It was inappropriate and I apologise.'

'It was nothing, a mad thoughtless moment…that's all,' Lara replied with forced lightness of tone. 'Any-way, I did encourage you and I didn't exactly run away screaming.'

'Nonetheless—'

'Leave it there. Calm your mind and rest.'

'What am I going to do if I don't remember by morn-ing?' he groaned.

'We'll see.'

What on earth had she done? Kissing him like that when he was half naked and she was wearing her stu-pid festive pyjamas? Lara slid back under her duvet and shivered with cold and shock. She hadn't known a man could make you feel like that with a kiss. She hadn't known she *could* feel like that. Only a kiss though, she reminded herself tiredly, don't make a silly fuss about a kiss...

CHAPTER THREE

Present day

LARA SHOOK OFF those memories in haste as she changed to meet up with Gaetano. She saw no reason why she should show up barefaced and wearing her oldest jeans, looking as though she had given up on even trying to be attractive. No, she wasn't ready to be seen in that light, not when *he* was dressed and groomed as if he were about to walk into an expensive restaurant or a fancy business meeting!

As soon as she had Freddy tucked into his sleeping bag clutching his beloved toy rabbit she went for a shower and washed her hair. She had to raid Alice's cosmetics to do her face. She grimaced. She hadn't given up after her marriage imploded before her eyes, she *hadn't*! But she had had no interest in men after that humiliation and then, in no time at all, she had discovered that she was pregnant. And Freddy's arrival had changed everything. Her years of evening classes aimed at helping her catch up on the education she had missed out on had counted for nothing once she'd had to work out how to survive on her own and provide for her son as well.

Alice had saved her life by offering her a home and the two women had fallen into a comfortable groove, working around each other and sharing childcare. But Lara had had few choices when it came to how she made her living. She worked at night cleaning commercial premises because those hours of work suited her. Freddy was in bed and although Alice had to babysit, she wasn't actively having to do much. Lara operated on less sleep and contrived to spend most of her day with her son and slot Iris, who was at school, into their schedule as well. The arrangement suited both women for the present even if it didn't allow scope for Lara to aspire to more rewarding employment. That could wait until Freddy was at school and she had the freedom to consider other options. Currently, Lara worked sufficient hours to ensure that rent, food and other basic needs were covered without her having to take too much advantage of Alice's frequently offered generosity.

Having put on her dressiest outfit while scolding herself for putting so much effort into her appearance, Lara slotted her feet into perilously high heels. Alice had bought them for her the previous Christmas, mainly as a joke, saying that it was time Lara went out and painted the town red with her. Only that one night out being hit on by men who neither attracted nor interested her had put Lara off and persuaded her that she was far too picky. Nor did the idea of having to explain her marital situation appeal to her. Being possibly married without a husband left her in a kind of no man's land when it came to dating and she knew she needed to do something about that.

'You look incredible. I gather you want him to regret how he treated you?'

'It's a bit late in the day for that,' Lara contended. 'But that doesn't mean I want him to look at me and feel that his worst expectations of me have been vindicated, which I'm sure is exactly what he thought when he took me by surprise today in the park.'

Alice handed her the keys for the hatchback parked in the drive. Lara slipped off the shoes and drove off. Her heart was sitting at the base of her throat. She just couldn't credit that she was about to see Gaetano again. That brief encounter in the park already had the unreal hazy edge of a dream. No, not a dream, she decided ruefully, a nightmare. What woman wanted to lay eyes on the man who had broken her heart again? Gaetano di Santis had ripped her in two, but she wasn't the same trusting and vulnerable woman that she had been. She lifted her chin. *Game on, Gaetano!*

The satellite navigation led her to a stately home situated in its own park. Of course, he would hardly be slumming it, not a king, not a male born into generations of royalty and the luxury lifestyle that went with such status. She drove down the long winding driveway, staring at the imposing façade of the large Victorian mansion and wincing. Immediately she felt underdressed and out of her comfort zone. Stiffening her spine while telling herself off for being so sensitive, she put on her shoes, locked the car and walked across the gravel very slowly to the pillared entrance, striving not to totter in her high heels.

Two men in suits greeted her at the door and asked her who she was visiting.

'Gaetano,' she said tightly, colour lacing her pallor at having to make even that much of an explanation, and their surprised looks didn't help.

'His Majesty is working in the library,' one of them whispered to the other, their low-pitched voices seemingly part of their job.

'His Majesty doesn't like to be disturbed unnecessarily,' another voice, which was female, interposed brightly from the rear of the hall. 'Perhaps I can help?'

Lara glanced at the svelte blonde older woman, unimpressed by her welcoming smile when her blue eyes were as hard as granite. 'I don't think so...possibly I should've called ahead.'

'That would have been wise. Perhaps you could phone and make an appointment first. Usually that approach works best with someone as busy as the King,' the woman pointed out cuttingly.

Lara walked back outside, dug out her phone and the card Gaetano had given her to punch in the number. 'Gaetano?' she asked as soon as it was answered. 'I'm outside and ready to head home again. I can't get past your staff. I'll give you a count of ten before I leave.'

Lara strolled back towards the car. As she unlocked the door a lion's roar broke the evening silence. *'Lara!'*

Gaetano now stood in the porch in person, seething annoyance emanating from him in a wave, a touch of colour accentuating his high cheekbones.

'I should've phoned and told you what time I would be here *before* I left home,' Lara conceded gracefully as she walked back towards him, barely able to breathe above the nervous tension gripping her chest in a vice. 'But I wasn't expecting all this security.'

His intense dark gaze burned over her to the extent that she almost stumbled over her own feet in the grand hall.

'Allow me to take your coat,' a little man proffered, extending his hands.

Lara doffed the black wool coat she usually only wore for church, and it was carried off with the same reverence that a fantastically expensive designer garment would have commanded. Under Gaetano's incredulous scrutiny the floral dress that swirled round her knees suddenly felt incredibly tight and she shifted her feet uneasily.

Gaetano studied her fixedly. In any terminology his wife was a living, breathing doll with delicate flawless features. She was tiny and shapely with perfect legs, porcelain-pale skin and a wealth of wavy strawberry-blonde hair tumbling round her narrow shoulders. She looked amazing, not a thought that he believed he should be having in such circumstances, but it was, at least, the proof that he had not been entirely insane two years earlier when he'd promised to marry her and forsake all others. As if in evidence of his susceptibility as he noted the luscious peach of her mouth and the surprisingly full curve of her small breasts, a warning pulse throbbed at his groin and he tensed, infuriated by that response. Was that reaction really so surprising when he was sex-starved?

'What on earth are you wearing on your feet?' Gaetano demanded abruptly. 'All of a sudden you're unnaturally tall!'

Lara extended bare toes cradled in clear plastic straps, her heel raised a towering six inches by the sandal. She tilted her chin. 'Why not?' she said lightly. She had a choice of trainers, a pair of biker boots and the silly sandals. There were few options in Lara's slender wardrobe. She didn't go out much and she didn't need many outfits.

'Let's go into the library,' another voice slotted in quietly.

Lara froze, uneasily conscious of being the cynosure of every eye around them. An alien dropping in could not have commanded more attention. The security men were standing at the back, frowning. The sharp-tongued blonde was staring a perplexed hole in her. She shot a glance at the lean bearded man she recalled from two years earlier, Gaetano's protective sidekick, as she had tagged him. She tasted bile in her mouth. He was a lawyer and a personal friend. She didn't remember his name, but she did remember his shocked and hostile attitude to her.

'I'm here to see you *alone*,' Lara told Gaetano defensively.

'That's not a problem,' he responded smoothly, ignoring the frown of disapproval from his friend.

The butler, who had borne off her coat, moved forward to guide her into a side corridor and usher her into a heavily furnished Victorian library. Gaetano stepped past her and lounged back against the side of the desk, which had an open laptop on it.

'This meeting is difficult for both of us because so much time has passed,' Gaetano remarked smoothly.

'Did it not occur to you that I would need to get in touch with you?'

His cool composure bit into Lara like a blade. Inside herself she was a mess of pain and regret. She was looking at the man she had loved, and he hadn't had the decency to develop a pot belly and a receding hairline to banish her idealised memories. No, he had got even more gorgeous in a scarily sleek, sophisticated way. He wasn't the guy with the tousled black hair, stubble and jeans whom she had fallen head over heels for within days. He wasn't the guy looking to her for understanding and support when he was suddenly thrown into an unfamiliar world. He wasn't the man whom she had taught to cook and wield an axe, marvelling at his lack of ordinary practical knowledge. No, this was a guy wearing an exquisitely tailored navy suit that probably cost more than she'd earned in two years of work. His hair was perfectly styled, his jawline clean-shaven, his dark blue shirt perfectly complemented by his silver tie. The only thing she had remembered right about the guy she'd married was that he was very, *very* good-looking.

'I wasn't thinking about stuff of that nature when I left,' Lara replied flatly.

She had run in pain and humiliation as if she could somehow leave that horrible sense of rejection behind her if she ran fast enough. She had run as an animal ran, without thought or consideration. Too late she had learned that pain found you wherever you ran and that there was no escaping it.

'It has taken me all this time to track you down,' Gaetano informed her.

Was he expecting an apology? Lara gritted her small

white teeth, knowing she hadn't wanted to be found, not when it entailed standing in front of Gaetano as if she were being hauled over the coals for some dreadful mistake. Quite deliberately she settled into an armchair without being asked, sneering at her foolish younger self for not guessing from the first that such comfort and opulence was Gaetano's natural milieu. His confidence, his innate good manners, his ability to speak more than one language and wide-ranging general knowledge. All those facts should have made her appreciate that his position in society was far removed from hers. She truly hadn't thought such things as class mattered any more. But Gaetano had taught her different when he'd looked at the not-very-well-educated waitress he had chosen to marry and make his. In shock and dismay and regret.

'I wasn't even sure we *were* legally married,' she pointed out defensively.

Gaetano frowned. 'Why would you think we were not?'

A tight little laugh was wrenched from Lara. 'Don't you remember what Dario said that day? He said something about constitutional law and how could you get legally married without the sovereign's consent? So, obviously I thought that the legality of our marriage was in doubt.'

'That wasn't the case. There *is* no such law relating to the royal family in Mosvakia.' Gaetano clenched his teeth, knocked off topic by that admission of hers because he remembered little of what had been said that morning. He had been reeling with shock and grief. At one and the same time he had regained his memory and learned that his brother had died, and he was now King.

Lara nodded in silence.

'Now that you're here, however, I do see that it is best to make this encounter impersonal.'

'Impersonal?' Lara almost whispered, crossing her legs in the hope that he wouldn't realise her lower limbs were shaking. How the heck could a divorce be deemed impersonal?

A knock sounded on the door and the little man who had taken her coat appeared with a laden tray. There was much bowing and scraping in Gaetano's direction before the tray finally reached the side table and they were alone again.

Gaetano cleared his throat. '*Sì*, impersonal. After this length of time, nothing else makes sense. There should be no recriminations, no bad feelings.'

What had happened to the passionate guy who had swept her off her feet and insisted on marrying her after a mere ten days of acquaintance?

'I doubt if that is possible, but I have no wish to get into an argument with you,' Lara declared stiffly.

'We've been living apart for two years and all I require is your consent on a document to a divorce. That consent, while not strictly necessary, would make the proceedings run more smoothly.' As Gaetano spoke, he tapped a document and pen lying on the desk. 'May I ask my friend and lawyer, Dario Rossi, to join us?'

'No,' Lara said succinctly, still unable to overcome her aversion to the man who had viewed her with cool hostility while her entire world had caved in round her ears, all his concern reserved for Gaetano. And back then, Gaetano *had* been her whole world because she had never even dared to dream of finding a love like that and, having found it, she had been devastated when it had proved to be an empty illusion.

'No?' Gaetano queried in polite surprise.

'No,' Lara repeated. 'I didn't take to him at our first meeting.'

Gaetano surveyed her, noticing that she hadn't poured the coffee and marvelling at her seeming tranquillity, which was why her refusal to allow Dario to join them took him aback. She seemed as though she were a thousand miles away from him inside her head and he hadn't expected that air of emotional detachment from her, not from a woman he remembered as being wonderfully warm and caring.

'Do you have any objection to us getting divorced?' he intoned flatly.

Lara gritted her teeth again. 'No,' she asserted.

'Let me assure you that I will pay all your legal fees to the lawyer of your choice. There will also be a substantial financial settlement,' Gaetano informed her, getting back into his stride again.

'I don't want your money,' Lara told him, wondering when he was planning to get around to mentioning Freddy and also wondering if she was cutting off her nose to spite her face, as her grandmother would have quipped. After all, money would allow her to get her life in order sooner than she had hoped and build towards a better future.

'I owe you some compensation for the way our relationship played out,' Gaetano countered gravely. 'But I do also wish to thank you for the valuable assistance you gave me during the weeks we were together. Matters could have gone a great deal less pleasantly for me.'

'I wish I'd left you in the snow!' Lara retorted, and even as she made that childish statement she knew she was lying because without Gaetano, there would be no Freddy and Lara's life revolved around Freddy.

'I don't believe that.'

Her huge aquamarine eyes that were neither blue nor green and changed according to her mood flashed at him, but she compressed her lips and remained silent.

'Would you like coffee?' Gaetano was finally moved to ask in the smouldering silence. He felt curiously reluctant to let her go. On some level, he simply wanted to feast his eyes on her because, aside of the absurd shoes, she was every bit as beautiful and sexy as he recalled. He recalled other things about her as well, things he tried to bury but that often returned to him when he was alone. The way she smiled when the sun shone, the way she reached for him in the darkness, the way she laughed when he said something she deemed silly or unrealistic. And a whole host of other far more sexual recollections such as what it felt like when her tiny body clenched round his in climax, how shy she got in daylight, the ridiculous inhibitions about time, place and frequency she had harboured in the field of intimacy.

Recognising the heat building below his belt, Gaetano had cause to be grateful for the concealment of his suit jacket. Yes, she still turned him on, turned him on more than other women, but he had to walk away from that kind of temptation and do his duty. He had to have a wife and children. That he hadn't been trained to accept that sacrifice wasn't an excuse. The responsibility that had once been Vittorio's was now his and there was no point complaining about it. In the most basic sense, producing the next generation with an acceptable woman lay at the very heart of his role as monarch.

'No, thanks. I'm not staying.' Indeed, Lara was already rising from her seat, eager to be gone.

Her cheeks were pink, her striking eyes downcast as she disconcerted him by reaching for the pen and scrawling her signature on the document that Dario had given him.

'You shouldn't sign a legal document without your own lawyer at hand to represent your interests,' Gaetano remarked tautly.

'That's your world, not mine,' Lara parried in a tone of scorn. 'I don't require a lawyer to tell me I want to be free of you. You have disappointed me in every conceivable way, Gaetano.'

'I regret that you feel that way,' he breathed curtly.

'No, your only goal is that I sign this form so that you can shed any responsibility you might have for me as discreetly as possible. That doesn't surprise me but I'm angry on my *son's* behalf!' Lara countered, throwing her head back. 'He is an innocent party here and you didn't even *look* at him at the park!'

'You're trying to say that your son is also…*my* son?' Gaetano framed in open disbelief.

'He's sixteen months old, Gaetano. Who else could be his father?' she fired at him in disgust. 'But don't worry, we're getting along fine without you and we need nothing from you. Even so, your lack of even polite interest in him is unforgivable!'

With that ringing indictment of his attitude, Lara dealt him a seething look of condemnation and stalked

out of the room, down the corridor and into the hall.
'My coat?' she urged with an edge of desperation when
the little manservant appeared.

Pulling her coat on, she stomped down the steps and
across to the car. Her mobile began ringing. She ignored it and knew she would block his calls. She didn't
want to exchange another word with Gaetano. She was
too angry with him and too hurt by his indifference to
their son…

CHAPTER FOUR

THE FOLLOWING MORNING, Dario was talking in legal
mode, a habit that often led to Gaetano beginning to
tune him out while on one level he continued to listen
without engaging. They were both in shock but while
his friend reacted as a lawyer, Gaetano was reacting as
a man who had just learned that he might be a father.
His brain was in a state of freefall because Lara's claim
had shattered him.

How could he have a child he didn't know about?

How could Mosvakia have a crown prince it had yet
to learn existed?

Why the hell hadn't Lara told him that she was pregnant? He should have been involved from the start. He
should have been there at the birth of his child, and it
galled him that he had been denied that right and all
the other rights that fatherhood bestowed.

'You didn't even think there was a possibility that
the child could be yours?'

'The investigation agency assumed the child was
older and that misled me,' Gaetano murmured, refusing to elucidate on that topic further. 'We should have
waited until the birth certificate was available.'

'You will need DNA tests.' Dario was not to be silenced. 'Had I known there was the possibility that the boy could be your heir I would have advised a very different kind of approach to the mother.'

Gaetano gazed out of the window, impervious to the view. 'I didn't realise conception could be that easy. I watched Vittorio and Giulia struggle for years trying to have a child, going through all that fertility treatment…' His shapely mouth compressed, and he said no more about his brother's misfortunes in that department. But his visceral response to the concept of being a father and of that being a huge honour as well as a life-changing responsibility was steadily increasing.

His mother had abandoned him as a toddler and hadn't even thought better of that move when only months later his father was killed in a car crash. To all intents and purposes, Vittorio had become his half-brother's father as a twenty-year old. Even at that young age, Vittorio had made a real effort to be a parent to the lonely child in the royal nursery and Gaetano had loved him accordingly. Recalling that truth, Gaetano swore that he would do no less for his own child and, hopefully, he would do a great deal more bearing in mind that he was older and wiser.

'I *must* see him!' he exclaimed abruptly. 'How can I not even know my son's name?'

'You shouldn't rush into anything before there's proof.'

'Dario, stop being a lawyer,' Gaetano interrupted with a frown. 'How would you feel if you discovered you were a father purely by accident? What if I hadn't searched for Lara? What if I hadn't been able to track her down? I might *never* have known I had a son!'

'In your position, I'd hang her out to dry for this,' Dario countered. 'I understand your anger.'

Gaetano almost groaned out loud at that response. He wanted to see his child, but Lara appeared to have blocked his number. He suspected that Lara was endeavouring to ignore the destruction she had wreaked and remained in denial. *He* had disappointed *her*? Why didn't she turn that around and accept how much she had disappointed *him*?

By that evening with his patience running out, Gaetano chose to ignore Dario's dire warnings and he called in person at Lara's home. The door was opened by her friend. She was very respectful but firm in her certainty that she could not allow him to see his child without Lara's presence. Gaetano cursed the fact that he had forgotten that Lara worked nights. He rang Dario to get him to look up the file and get him the name of the cleaning firm.

'This is not discreet, sir,' Dario lamented in a studiously formal manner.

Gaetano ground his teeth together. He was *done* with discretion. He rarely lost his temper but there was a knot of rage gradually tightening inside him. That rage had had twenty-four hours to grow. Lara had stolen his child from him, deprived him of his paternal rights and denied his son the benefit of a father. For what reason would he tolerate such treatment?

'I'll be out of your way in five minutes,' the last office occupant on the floor informed Lara without even looking at her.

And cleaning while being ignored by those who did overtime was exactly how Lara preferred to work. She had learned that it was best to melt into the woodwork. Her hair was concealed by a beanie, her overall baggy enough to conceal any hint of the shape of the female body inside it. The last thing she wanted was male attention when she was alone in an almost empty office block. Her unwelcome experiences in that line from her years living with her adoptive mother had made her very cautious around men.

As the man departed, leaving her free to empty the rubbish bin and run a mop across the floor, she donned her ear buds. Soon she was humming beneath her breath while planning what she would do to keep Freddy amused the next day. Just letting him pelt round the house didn't work. He was a lively, demanding child, better kept occupied than allowed to get bored.

Gaetano strode down the corridor of the anonymous office block where his wife worked...*cleaning*. Did she enjoy being a martyr? Saying she didn't want or need his money when she was forced to do such lowly work to survive? Putting *him* in the wrong even though she had deserted him and lost herself so very efficiently? When he saw her bent down in the office, he could not initially believe that that tiny amorphous figure was Lara. She looked like a homeless person rather than a young, attractive woman. She hadn't noticed him because she was too busy listening to music and how safe was that for a woman on her own in such a place?

And then even as he thought that Lara whirled round and almost leapt in the air in fright, the hand on the mop loosening its grip and letting it drop with a clatter against the bucket as she pressed her palm against her heart instead.

'What on earth…?' she gasped breathlessly, studying him with wide disbelieving eyes.

Such exotic eyes too: the aquamarine colour of the Adriatic Sea that washed the shore of Mosvakia, that indescribable peacock-blue-green shade that he had never seen in any other face. The very first thing he had noticed about her.

'How the heck did you find me? How the hell did you even get past the security guard at the entrance?' Lara hissed furiously.

'You blocked me on your phone. Did you expect me to take that lying down?' Gaetano raked at her.

Lara dragged her beanie off with an exasperated hand, her face hot with embarrassment that he had chosen to ambush her during her cleaning shift. Wildly tossed strawberry waves fell round her shoulders and she pushed them angrily back behind her ears. 'I'm not having a fight with you, Gaetano, not here where I'm supposed to be working. I'll see you tomorrow when I am available. I am *not* available right now!'

As he stood in the office doorway, sheathed in a black cashmere overcoat and a dark grey suit teamed with a red shirt and a blue silk tie, Gaetano slashed a silencing hand in the air. It was, for Lara, a disturbingly regal and commanding gesture such as she had never seen from him before and it rather intimidated her.

'I don't care,' he shot at her. 'Last night you told me that I had a son and you seemed surprised that I didn't look at him in the park. I didn't know that he could *be* my son! And if he *is* my son, I don't even know his name!'

Lara folded her lips into a flat line. 'Naturally, since you tracked me down to the level of knowing *when* I went to the park, I assumed you also knew about him.'

'I flew out here the instant I had an address for you. The detective agency had not completed the report. I was told that there was a child, but he was estimated as several months older and I assumed that he wasn't mine.'

'Oh, for goodness' sake, Gaetano…how could he be anything *other* than yours when you were my first lover?' Lara derided in angry dismissal of that explanation. 'Keep your comforting self-delusions to yourself! I will not be insulted by that kind of insinuation because you want to put our marriage behind you as if it never happened!'

Gaetano's dark eyes were now burnished by a fiery glitter, his lean darkly handsome face still taut with tension. 'What is his name?' he asked rawly.

'Frederick. I named him after my grandfather, but I call him Freddy,' she admitted grudgingly. 'I'm afraid you're not named on the birth certificate.'

Another spear of anger pierced Gaetano's tough hide. He felt almost as though he had been written out of existence and their marriage with it. He stalked closer to her, his dark brooding gaze intense. 'Did you even think about what you were doing? About the legalities of lying on such a score? You are not allowed to rewrite my son's ancestry and deny him his father just because it suited you to do so. That is not your choice to make.'

'I thought you would want his ancestry hidden,' Lara

argued helplessly, taken aback by his vehement objections. 'You didn't want me as a wife…why would you have wanted a child with me?'

'Mannaggia!' Gaetano vented in sheer frustration, barely able to cope with his loss of temper because he had been trained in childhood never ever to lose his temper. His wild tantrums as a young child had appalled his big brother. 'We will not discuss that statement here and now,' he bit out in a roughened undertone. 'But you must see that, even were the first statement to be true—and I'm not saying it *is*—the two things are not the same.'

Lara gathered up her equipment, stacked it noisily on her cleaning trolley and moved to the next office beneath his incredulous scrutiny, which made it clear that he could not credit that she could dare to continue with her job in his presence. 'No, I don't see or accept that,' she finally replied and got stuck into her job again.

She refused to give an inch to his expectations. He might be a king but he was not *her* king. Good grief, had she broken the law when she registered her son as a single woman and claimed that she did not know the father's name? She hadn't thought about stuff of that nature during her pregnancy when her only driving motivation had been to hide and ensure that nobody found out she had ever been foolish enough to marry an amnesiac, who had turned out to be so much more than she could ever have suspected. A dark horse, indeed. And the instant Gaetano had remembered *who* he was and *what* he was, he had spurned her. Her pained ruminations as she mopped the floor in rigid silence brought her right up to the very toes of his polished and, she was certain, highly expensive shoes.

'Stop this,' Gaetano bit out savagely. 'Stop trying to ignore me! I'm not going to go away. I am a very persistent, very determined man.'

'And I am a very angry, very bitter woman,' Lara snapped, still without looking at him.

Without warning, Gaetano lifted her off her feet and deposited her gently on the side of a desk. The mop had fallen out of her hands with a clatter. 'That must be my fault, then, *bambola*,' he breathed with regret, sharply disconcerting her. 'You were not an angry, bitter woman when I met you…'

That truthful point released her fierce tension, and she was startled by the surge of prickling tears that hit the backs of her eyes because she was not a cry baby either. *Bambola*…doll…his pet name for her, a name she had believed she would never hear again, and it unleashed an anguished flood of memories inside her that hurt. 'Go away…' she told him shakily.

Gaetano trailed a fingertip across the single tear that had spilt down her cheek. 'I'm sorry I lost my temper and raised my voice.'

'We're not the same people we were two years ago.'

Gaetano almost said something sarcastic and bit it back just in time, suddenly struggling for *her* sake to be the man he had been before he got his memory back. He regretted the fact that that humbled, more hesitant version of himself had probably been far kinder and more considerate than he was, in reality. 'I don't want to hurt your feelings or you in any way,' he declared in a driven undertone. 'That's not why I'm here.'

'You're here for a divorce,' she reminded him unnecessarily.

'You sound like Dario. I don't need that right now,' Gaetano admitted with an honesty he hadn't observed in two long years, and the minute he uttered the words he wanted to bite them back because, until she had come into his life, he had never ever admitted a vulnerable moment to anyone, even his late brother.

Seated on the desk, she could not evade his eyes any longer. And for a split second she glimpsed the guy she had loved in the brooding turmoil of his beautiful dark eyes, and it anchored her a bit, made her feel more in control. She studied his lush black lashes, the perfect line of his nose, his shapely mouth in the sea of dark stubble that was beginning to shadow his jawline, and all of a sudden he seemed achingly familiar and her heart was clenching inside her chest again as though he had squeezed it.

He bent and lifted the fallen mop to set it out of his path, his distaste for the item unhidden.

'It's just a job!' she protested as if he had spoken, reading his body language with an ease that made him feel oddly naked because nobody did that around him, absolutely nobody.

'It's a job you don't *need* and that's one reason why I became angry,' Gaetano murmured fiercely. 'I am a very rich man and there is no need for you to be employed.'

'Gaetano—'

Gaetano made an exasperated zipping motion near her mouth with his finger, and she leant forward and nipped his fingertip lightly between her teeth in rebuke.

It was something only Lara would do, and he couldn't help it, he grinned and burst out laughing, all annoyance vanquished.

A little embarrassed that she had got that personal, Lara lifted her flushed face and said, 'Well, you know I can't *stand* that mansplaining thing you do when you get all serious and pompous and talk like I haven't got a brain.'

'And you will naturally agree with me that you don't need to take a job from someone who does need it to make a point. You don't need money to survive, not with me around,' he instructed, clearly not having learned his lesson yet.

'But you're not around and we're getting a divorce.'

'Forget that. As your husband I am still responsible for keeping you and my child. Quit the job here and now,' he told her.

'I can't do that. I have notice to work if I want to leave.'

Gaetano groaned out loud. 'OK, strip this back to its most basic. If our marital situation gets into the media, I don't want to be the king with a wife scrubbing floors because he is too stingy to pay his dues,' he spelled out.

'You think it might get into the press about us?' she gasped in a panicked tone.

'I can assure you that my staff will do everything possible to keep us out of the newspapers, but we can't control everything,' Gaetano pointed out drily. 'So, please let me take you home now and call an end to this charade!'

'It's not a charade…it's my life!' she exclaimed, anxiety flooding her expressive face at the prospect of change being forced on her. 'I don't want to be unreasonable, Gaetano.'

'Then don't be. You give a little, I give a little? That's how people negotiate what works best for them.'

'Is that the former hedge-fund manager talking?' Lara almost whispered. 'The guy who insisted on teaching me algebra?'

His beautiful eyes gleamed with amusement, and he ran his finger along her full bottom lip. 'Admit it. I was an extraordinarily good mansplainer.'

And she snorted with laughter and her face lit up. He bent down because even seated on the desk she was still tiny. His hands found her glorious mass of hair and tangled in it as he drew her closer. He was hard as a rock, pulsing with energy and hunger but he *knew* he shouldn't have his hands on her, shouldn't be that close, only he could not resist the strength of that urge even while he was waiting for her to stop him because, as he had cause to know, Lara was very, *very* efficient at stopping a man in his tracks if she chose to. Only on this occasion she defied his expectations by leaning into him, tilting up her incredibly pretty face, those amazing eyes locked to him. Desire shot through him in an unstoppable surge.

Lara closed her eyes when he kissed her. She had never ever wanted anything so much, aside of the very first time they had made love. One lean hand framed her face, long fingers stroking her smooth freckled skin, and her heart was pounding so hard that she was vaguely surprised that it didn't burst right out of her chest with sheer excitement. His warm firm mouth tasted hers and she kissed him back with fervour, her hands flying up to smooth over his broad shoulders and then lace into his luxuriant black hair. He groaned into her mouth as her tongue met his and eased her closer, pushing his way between her legs until he gained the actual physical contact that both their bodies seemed to be screaming to experience.

She could feel how aroused Gaetano was through the taut fabric of his trousers and a steamy blur of memory almost consumed her as she clenched down deep inside in the place she hadn't thought about since she had last been with him. Her breasts were tight and swollen, her core hot and damp. She wanted more, had never wanted more so badly but the warning voice that screamed the reminder, 'divorce', in the back of her mind refused to be silenced. Stinging regret made her remove her hands from his hair and press them against his chest instead to separate them.

'We can't do this…' she muttered shakily.

Gaetano pushed an unsteady hand through his messy hair and stepped back from her as if he were stepping back from a seriously deep drop on a cliff edge. He knew she was right, and he said nothing because to his mind there was nothing to say. The same attraction that had first drawn them together still lingered but should *not* be acted on, he reminded himself grimly. He was letting his body and his almost overpowering emotional state of mind lead him down the wrong path. His big brother had programmed him from an early age to step away, step back, always cool off before he acted on any emotion and Dario at his elbow was a little like a mini-Vittorio, always urging Gaetano to be practical, sensible, self-disciplined and controlled. As if he had ever been anything else, his entire life through…with the single exception of those crazy weeks with Lara, he acknowledged guiltily.

'We both got upset and there was a bit of a timeslip there,' Lara mumbled, making excuses for them both when what he really wanted from her was a slap or a kick for his having dared to touch her again. Why? Only punishment would have made him feel less culpable for yet another mistake where she was concerned.

She slid off the desk, her head bent, and scooped up the mop.

'Let me take you home now, draw a line under this,' Gaetano muttered tautly.

Fortunately, that gave her something else to think about and she was grateful for it, so grateful not to have to think of how she had surrendered to his lust the instant she was offered the opportunity. The job?

'You can stay home with Freddy until we get all this sorted out,' Gaetano suggested. 'I'd be very grateful.'

He was saying *please* the only way he knew how. Underneath he was still the man she had married, she registered, just a smoother, slicker version, superbly well groomed and with his phenomenal intensity currently muted. And he wasn't happy. He wasn't happy at all that she had let him kiss her—she could tell by the furrow on his brow, the tightness round his mouth, even the veiled darkness of his gaze. There was no triumph and nothing nasty or threatening about his brooding silence. Unfortunately, Lara didn't want to *be* aware of such things, not with a man she had had to learn to get by without, not with a man who was in the process of divorcing her. She had to stiffen her backbone and be…what was that word? That impossible word he had voiced to her the night before?

Impersonal.

Gaetano lowered his mobile phone as she repacked the cleaning trolley. 'Just leave it here. They're sending another cleaning operative out to finish the job.'

'And why would they do that when I'm letting them down?'

'You're not letting anyone down, Lara,' Gaetano sliced back at her grimly. 'I'm paying them to let you go without a fuss just as I paid the guard to let me into the building. That's how I handle problems in my world, and you may be grimacing right now because you see that as immoral but some day you'll be watching our son do the exact same thing.'

Lara reddened that he had read her so accurately and then paled at the thought of her precious Freddy growing into the same kind of man. 'I don't approve,' she admitted stiffly.

'You don't need to approve. It is expected that people of my status pay for their privilege and that if others go that extra mile for our benefit, we reward them. That's my life and it has *always* been that way. Billionaires don't generally get handed something for nothing,' he said gently, borrowing one of the phrases she had once taught him, a phrase her grandmother had taught her.

With that final explanation, he stooped and grasped the hem of the overall she wore to whip it over her head and scrunch it into a ball that he tossed into a waste basket as they waited for the lift. The beanie had already gone missing. Lara was too shocked by what he had just said to react.

'Billionaires? You? Your family?' Lara croaked, shocked almost to silence by that concept, that reminder that they came from totally different worlds. 'You're *that* rich? Seriously?'

A smile broke out on Gaetano's lean darkly handsome face. He didn't bother mentioning that he didn't have a family aside of her and the son he had yet to meet. He simply savoured the shock on her startled face and wished Dario had had the opportunity to both see and hear that little snatch of dialogue. But then, possibly, Dario would never understand that the kind of woman he had married didn't have a mercenary bone in her body. Just like him she had flaws, but that was not one of them.

'I wrecked your hair.' Lara sighed, standing on tiptoe to brush it out of his eyes and smooth it down again and then stilling in mortification at that act of overfamiliarity. 'Sorry, I think I'm too tired to be doing this with you…'

'We'll go and get a bite to eat,' Gaetano announced, urging her into the lift.

'No, let's keep things a little more…detached,' she selected, striving to employ the vocabulary he had used on her. 'I have Alice's car parked outside, so I don't need a lift, and then you can come and see Freddy tomorrow when he's awake.'

It was sensible advice, but Gaetano discovered that he didn't want to hear it. He frowned. 'We have to talk some time.'

'But it doesn't have to be right now this very minute,' she stated calmly, recognising his innate impatience from the past. The more time she spent with Gaetano, the more she caught glimpses of the guy she had married, and she couldn't afford to encourage that painful sense of connection that was now so out of place in their broken relationship.

Alice was in the hall waiting for her the moment she put her key in the front door. 'Are you on your own?' she asked, peering over the top of her diminutive friend and all around her. 'Gaetano is *so* gorgeous, Lara. Not at all surprised that you fell for him like a ton of bricks! I couldn't believe my eyes when he said who he was.'

'He was here?' Lara queried in dismay.

'Yes, looking for you and Freddy. He said he'd forgotten that you worked in the evenings.'

Lara flushed and avoided her friend's gaze. 'He came to see me at work. He's going to visit tomorrow to meet Freddy.'

'That sounds like a keen parent-to-be, at least,' Alice quipped, switching on the kettle as Lara followed her through to the kitchen. 'But I'll be frank… I saw him getting into a limousine out there. Clearly, he's wealthier than the average baby daddy.'

'Yes, Gaetano's not average in any way,' Lara conceded awkwardly, still reluctant to share the entire truth with her friend, especially after Gaetano had referred to his desire for discretion. She loved Alice to death but was painfully conscious that she would talk her head off to everyone she knew if she learned that Gaetano was a royal.

'He's definitely going to pay support for Freddy,' she told the brunette, willing to share other information. 'He asked me to quit my job and stay home with him and, to be honest, while he's this young I would enjoy that. I can't say being a cleaner is so much fun that I will stick with it if I don't have to.'

'And you could study while you're at home, start catching up again,' Alice commented with enthusiasm. 'I still think it's so unfair that your mother was so thoughtless about your education.'

For thoughtless, read selfish, Lara ruminated wryly. Every time her mother, Eliza, had broken up with a boyfriend, she had moved to another city and Lara had been pulled out of school to be changed to another one. Once they had moved abroad, Eliza had pretty much stopped worrying altogether about her daughter receiving an education. After all, Lara had been more useful to her helping out at home or working in a bar kitchen or waitressing.

Alice gave her a warm smile. 'I'm so happy that Gaetano is willing to give you support without making a fight out of it like some men do.'

'No, he's not likely to be difficult in that line.' Lara drained her cup and put it in the dishwasher. 'I'm going to go to bed early. I'm very tired and I want to be fresh for tomorrow.'

She hovered over Freddy's cot. He was fast asleep, stretched out like a little starfish, as good as his father had once been at hogging all the available mattress space. As soon as she thought that she tried to squash such thoughts because looking back in time did her no favours. What was gone was *gone*.

But by the time she was climbing into bed, the weight of memories had grown too heavy to avoid and just as quickly she slid back into that very first week spent with Gaetano.

Right from the start there had been a curious synchronicity between them, an ease as if they had known each other for years. It had probably been the hothouse effect of it being just the two of them in an isolated snowbound house, she reflected now. The day after the first night she had climbed up the hill and found his rucksack, dragging it back to the house and presenting it to him as if she had won the lottery, somehow expecting his every question to be magically answered by what they found within. They had discovered only a passport and an extraordinary amount of cash concealed in a hidden security pocket.

His passport had told them that his name was Gaetano di Santis and he was British, and was twenty-seven years old. It had not occurred to either of them that he might have dual nationality or that the reason he was travelling on his British passport was probably that he had sought that anonymity. The day after that they had gone up the hill together to search for a mobile phone, convinced he must have had one and had lost it as well, but they hadn't found one.

Her friend, Cathy, and her husband had given permission by text for Gaetano to stay on in the house with her. His condition would have condemned him to a homeless shelter but the cash he had would have got him a hotel room. She had cringed at the prospect of Gaetano spending Christmas alone someplace else. And in between Lara teaching him the rudiments of basic cookery and how to chop firewood, Gaetano had taught her algebra and how to play chess. He was a keen reader and, fortunately, Cathy's shelves had been packed with books.

The snow had been gone within days and Dr Beresford had called in, calming Gaetano's concerns and telling him that temporary amnesia was much more common than he might think after a head injury and that it was even possible that some stress in his life prior to the accident could have inhibited his memory to protect him and allow him time to recover his equilibrium.

'The mind is a wonderful thing,' the elderly woman had told him cheerfully. 'Most people with amnesia recover their memory within weeks or months but I must warn you that it doesn't always work that way and that perhaps you should consult a professional in the field.'

Gaetano, however, had baulked at the suggestion that he confide in anyone else, making Lara realise that he was much more reserved than most people she knew. They had been together day after day, and she had taken him everywhere with her. She had taken him to church, introduced him to the local priest and he had discovered with relief that the rituals of worship were familiar to him. She had taken him shopping when he wanted new clothes, amused by his fastidiousness, his awareness of fashion, so unlike the men she was accustomed to meeting. They had gone to the supermarket together, the post office and even the pub, where he'd decided that he didn't like beer very much.

Their relationship had moved at breakneck speed. On the tenth day he had told her that he was falling in love with her, and she had been shattered that a man could be that open and honest with her. That was when she had fully opened her heart to Gaetano to admit that she felt the same. That was also when the barriers had come down and she had stopped saying no when it came to more than a little light petting because of course they had become incredibly close spending so much time as a couple. He was also the first guy she had been with who didn't pressure her for sex and who took no for an answer without making her feel bad about it.

In every sense of the word, it had been a love affair and that constant closeness, sharing and talking, had accelerated the process. Gaetano's passionate nature had made everything run faster than the speed of light.

'I want you. I know I shouldn't say it when I can't prove it for a fact, but I don't believe I could *ever* have wanted a woman as much as I want you, *bambola*.'

And that was it, her defences had crumbled. That same night he had also asked her to marry him.

'I'll never be as sure of anything as I am of my feelings for you,' Gaetano had sworn. 'I want to know you're mine in every way and that means I put a ring on your finger and my own and we do it legally.'

She had said yes straight away, not a single doubt in her head either, and the next day they had gone to see the priest to see if they could get married in time for Christmas. Only Dr Beresford had sounded a note of caution, pointing out that Gaetano still knew next to nothing about himself but, like young lovers everywhere, neither of them had listened because neither of them had had the smallest desire to play it safe. They had wanted to plunge on in their lives and savour every moment to the fullest...

CHAPTER FIVE

THE NEXT DAY, Lara was up at the crack of dawn, tidying the house, making sure everything was presentable, at least, for a man who had grown up in a palace. Thinking that made her roll her eyes and grimace at her own thoughts.

She had nothing in common with Gaetano, absolutely nothing, she told herself firmly. They had been ships that passed, people who, under normal circumstances, would never have met each other. They had had a fling, a foolish fling, that was *all*, she programmed herself. He was *not* the love of her life as she had once fondly believed. In fact, were it not for her son, Gaetano would be the worst mistake she had ever made because *nobody* had ever made her feel as miserably wretched and unhappy as he had.

Sadly, two years earlier, rejection from her nearest and dearest had not been a new experience for Lara. At the age of nine she had gone from being a much-loved daddy's girl to being an often irritating burden and unwelcome expense to her surviving parent. That had been tough. Her grandparents had done much the same thing to her. They had warned her from the outset that when she reached eighteen, they expected her to move out and make her own life. She was grateful they had given her a home when she was desperate for one at sixteen but pretty hurt that, in spite of her warmth towards them, they had never viewed her as more than a nod of respect towards the memory of the adored son who had died after adopting Lara.

Gaetano texted her a time for his arrival. She dressed Freddy in jeans and a sweater, dampened down his riot of black curls and fed him well to keep him in a good mood.

Gaetano asked her if he could pick them up on the road at the rear of the house. Lara winced because she had assumed that Gaetano would see Freddy at their home, but she couldn't come up quickly enough with an argument to protest the idea of them travelling else-where. Perhaps he was thinking of them going to the park, she reckoned with more enthusiasm because Freddy was easier handled outdoors. Putting on coats and tucking her son into his pushchair, she hurried out of the front door to walk round the corner, wondering if this was the kind of 'discreet' that Gaetano had alluded to while looking down an almost empty suburban road and thinking it was a decided overreaction.

A huge limousine idled by the kerb, nothing dis-creet about that in such a neighbourhood, she reckoned with wry amusement, lifting Freddy out and begin-ning to collapse the pushchair before the driver and another man intervened, seemingly shocked that she would think to do such a thing for herself. The passen-ger door was opened. Gaetano was not inside. So, not the park, then. She settled Freddy into the plush car seat already awaiting him and did up the straps.

The car took them straight back to the Victorian mansion and Lara winced, feeling underdressed in her worn jeans, sweatshirt and padded jacket. It was a relief when Gaetano greeted her alone in the hall, nobody to question her about who she was, nobody to judge her appearance with scorn. And her attention was immediately taken by Gaetano, sheathed in jeans and a shirt, looking very much as he had two years earlier.

When Lara walked in, Gaetano's fists clenched. He was on edge because so much was riding on this meeting. And then Lara blew in, fresh as a daisy with her strawberry blonde waves floating back from her face like in some slow-motion scene in a romantic movie, and he was rivetted to the spot, noting the freckles scattered across her nose. Exactly six, he *remembered* that. And those eyes, set below arched brows, the purest breathtaking aquamarine above her soft pink lips. There was nothing honourable about his plan, indeed it was ruthless, although not quite as ruthless as his friend Dario's would have been. And Dario's plan, while strictly necessary in such a dangerous situation, would be cruel and it would frighten her. Whatever Lara might expect from him, she did not deserve any form of a scare.

A tiny noise escaped the large wriggling bundle in her arms, and she set it down and for the first time Gaetano registered that the bundle was actually *his* son and definitely what he should have focused his entire interest on, rather than on his son's mother. Lara knelt down to remove Freddy's coat and the little boy slowly turned round, taking in his unfamiliar surroundings with interest.

Gaetano got down on his level to meet him, but Freddy was already past him, moving at toddler speed, having espied the enormous flower arrangement seated on a low table to the rear of the hall.

Aghast, Lara plunged forward as her son reached up a grasping hand, and she shouted, 'Freddy, *no!*'

Freddy looked back at her with huge chocolate-button eyes, a flush on his cheeks of rage at her rebuke. Before she could even reach him, he had flung himself down in a passion to kick and scream and sob.

Mortification claiming her, Lara stilled beside Gaetano and said in a stifled voice, 'This is Freddy. It's best not to lift him until he gets the worst over with because that only makes him fight and shout louder.'

Involuntarily, Gaetano was fascinated. 'My brother once showed me a photo of me doing the exact same thing,' he told her, disconcerting her when she had expected an admonishment from him and at least a hint of criticism that she might not be the best parent in a disciplinary sense.

'What age were you?'

'About two. It was to teach me what I was capable of when I lost my temper.'

'No wonder you hate getting angry. I think that was brutal,' Lara opined. 'As Freddy learns more words, he will hopefully grow out of the meltdowns. Right now, it's his only way of expressing his frustration.'

While they had been talking and ignoring him, Freddy had sat up, his tear-streaked little face now intent on Gaetano, who was unfamiliar to him.

'*Madonna mia*…he is the picture of me as a child,' Gaetano almost whispered. 'Except for the curls.'

'I don't know where the curls came from. Looks wise he didn't get much of me, either,' Lara framed as Freddy toddled over to Gaetano and grabbed his knees to look up at him. 'As you can see, he's very friendly and outgoing.'

Gaetano startled her by bending down and scooping their son up into his arms with every appearance of enthusiasm. 'Let's go upstairs. This house has a play-room and I brought in more toys and…er, a nanny,' he completed rather stiffly.

'What on earth would you need a nanny for when I'm here?'

'I was thinking of a future visit, when perhaps you might want to leave him,' Gaetano lied, shading that story a second later by adding more convincingly. 'And, of course, if we're going to talk, that wouldn't be easy with a young child around.'

'Good grief…a nanny? How long are you planning to stay here?' Lara asked in astonishment, watching his lean darkly handsome face tense until her attention fell on the huge and fabulous portrait above the landing. 'That is gorgeous,' she whispered, in awe of the beau-tiful brunette and the fabulous blue ball gown and jew-ellery she sported. 'I wonder who she was.'

'My mother,' Gaetano informed her, his tone clipped. 'When he died, my grandfather left this entire estate to me. He had cut off communication with her long before she died. It was a generous legacy but I wish he'd given me the chance to get to know him instead.'

'You never met the man?'

'No. My mother was an only child and she disappointed him, much like she disappointed me. Possibly he feared that I would do something similar, so he never sought me out.'

Lara swallowed hard, aware that she was discussing a sensitive topic because she had done her homework on Gaetano's background as far as was possible with only the Internet as a research tool. 'She left you when you were very young,' she remarked ruefully.

'Walked out on my father and me, divorced him and, only weeks later, married a Swiss billionaire who lived in Brazil,' Gaetano completed unemotionally.

'Did she ever have any more child—?'

'No. I think we can take it as a given that she wasn't the motherly type,' he incised very drily. 'She died three years ago, I believe. Her husband informed me after she had passed, although I can't think why because I have no memory of her whatsoever.'

Lara recognised the coolness of his gaze shielding his enduring pain over that hurtful truth and her heart went out to him because she knew how such a wound lingered in the mind. 'Perhaps the same could be said for my birth mother—I mean, her not being the motherly type. Remember I was adopted,' she reminded him.

'Yes, I recall that. What do you know about your birth parents?'

'Nothing whatsoever. I decided not to look into it—'

'Why not?'

Lara flushed. Two years earlier, she hadn't shared much beyond the barest facts of her life with Gaetano because she had been ashamed of how unprepossessing even her adoptive background was. 'I just wasn't interested,' she said uncomfortably. 'Getting curious could be a mistake, too. I could be a child born after some awful event like rape…who knows?'

'You're too pessimistic. That's not like you,' Gaetano pronounced with a frown as he pushed open a door into an old-fashioned children's nursery. 'You once impressed me as an incurable optimist.'

'Yes…well, we all put our best face on when we think we're falling in love,' Lara countered, lifting her chin.

'Think?' Gaetano echoed with emphasis as he lowered Freddy and their son sped towards the box of brightly coloured toys he had glimpsed.

'Yes,' Lara confirmed with determination. 'I don't think it was real for either of us. You needed something or someone to ground you when you had no memory.'

'Oh, don't stop there,' Gaetano urged sardonically, getting down on the rug beside Freddy to show him how to open the big red bus he was investigating. Of course, she was telling the truth, he acknowledged inwardly and, since he had reached the same conclusion on his own, why exactly was he arguing the point? Or had he only reached that conclusion because it was a coping mechanism to persuade himself that what he had grieved at losing had never been real in the first place?

'What do you think you were feeling if it wasn't love?'

Lara compressed her lips while her cheeks burned. 'I was very attracted to you, and I hadn't felt like that before.'

'Lust, then. How edifying to discover that now about the woman I married.'

Lara wanted to throw something at him. Saving face

around Gaetano was an uphill challenge. She could feel
the heat in her cheeks as though she were boiling alive
because lying didn't come naturally to her. But forcing
herself into that mindset, even when she didn't believe
it, had been a necessary part of her recovery process.
Shoving a smile on her face as she told herself that she
could afford to be the bigger person now that she had
got over him, she removed her coat and got down on the
rug on the other side of her son. 'I was very attached to
you,' she admitted grudgingly.

Somewhat mollified by that admission, Gaetano was
already questioning why he cared and why conversa-
tions with Lara went in directions that they never ever
went with anyone else. And as the answer dawned on
him, his taut expression vanished, and he smiled bril-
liantly at her. 'You're the only person I know who treats
me normally.'

'What's that supposed to mean?'

'The job title gets in the way of normality. Nobody
but Dario ever tells me anything that I don't want to
hear, which is why I value him so highly. I appreciate
that you have a different attitude from him.'

'The first time we met he looked at me as though I
had *conned* you into marrying me.'

'He's inclined to be too protective towards me but
then, basically, protecting me legally is his career. Dario
and I went to the same English boarding school but even
he doesn't speak to me the way you do. Probably because he's from Mosvakia and even he can never quite
forget who I am.'

'I'm sorry I'm so…blunt.' She used the word awkwardly, feeling embarrassed that she just had no idea

how to treat royalty even though she was still married to the man. Freddy chose that moment to crawl into her lap, curl up and close his eyes with a sleepy sigh.

As he watched that display of his son's trust and dependency on his mother, a shimmering smile chased the tension from Gaetano's darkly handsome face and his eyes glittered pure gold below his curling black lashes. Lara's heart skipped a beat and fireworks flared in her stomach as she looked at him. He could light her up like a fire inside herself just with a certain look. And, uneasily aware that she should no longer be reacting that way to Gaetano, Lara scrambled upright slowly because Freddy was quite a weight and said, 'Is there any place I can put him down for a nap?'

'He's that tired *already*?' Gaetano asked in surprise.

'He's been on the go since six-thirty and I usually let him have an hour to nap about now.'

'It's fortunate that I had a new cot delivered. The original was an antique,' Gaetano told her with a chuckle as he vaulted upright and reached out quite naturally to ease his son out of her arms. 'You forget that he's still a baby. He looks older as I did because he's going to be tall.'

He walked over to the cot she hadn't noticed in the corner, and she censured herself for being so wrapped up in Gaetano's presence that she was almost blind to her surroundings. He laid the little boy down on top of the mattress and she leant over to slip off his shoes. 'It's warm here so I won't cover him, but I'll just nip downstairs and collect his bunny in case he wakes up.'

Before Gaetano could intervene, she had flashed out of the room and he stood on the landing, watching her speed downstairs to gather up the bag she had brought with her and return. Breathless, she tucked a shabby bunny into the cot beside their son, brushed his hair back from his face and smiled tenderly down at her child. 'He sleeps like a log. Nothing short of an earthquake would wake him when he's tired.'

And just like that, Gaetano knew he would be doing the right thing, even if most other people, including Dario, would think that what he was about to do was the very worst thing he could do. She was a wonderful mother and, for all their sakes, he would not part her from her son, no, not even for a day. He was praying that she was *still* that naïve woman he had married.

'You said something about us talking…' Lara reminded him.

Gaetano shifted position with the strangest hint of hesitancy. Even without his memory Gaetano had been a very decisive guy. 'I have something very important to say to you,' he announced, burnished dark eyes suddenly homing in on her wide gaze and holding it fast. 'Let's move across the corridor. It's my private suite and we won't be disturbed by the staff there.'

As he pressed a bellpush in the wall, she frowned, everything knocked out of kilter by his statement as she tried to fathom out what he could possibly want to say.

'The nanny knows to come and take care of our son when I ring the bell,' he explained.

'I didn't know big houses still had systems like that in operation,' she confided.

'It's a convenience in a building this size,' Gaetano pointed out pragmatically as he ushered her through a door opposite into a gracious drawing room.

Lara walked over to one of the three windows, which were grandly draped in extravagant curtains. She gazed out at the rolling lawn with its woodland groves and the park beyond where she thought she could see a herd of deer grazing. Gaetano lived in another world and the surroundings inside and out were a distinctly painful reminder.

'I suggest that we forget the divorce idea for the present…'

Lara's eyes rounded and she spun back to him, her throat tightening with nerves and that awful sense of having lost her way in the conversation because she could not think of a single reason why he should propose such an idea. 'Right…' she muttered uncertainly, waiting for him to finish talking, which he seemed to be in no hurry to do.

His high cheekbones were flushed, his dark eyes very level and intent on her, *so* intent that she went rigid with self-consciousness, her small frame bracing as though she were under attack.

'I would like for us to try a reconciliation instead.'

Lara was so shocked and so utterly unprepared for that suggestion that she lost all her colour, her small face turning wan. *'Really?'* she mumbled weakly.

Gaetano didn't feel that her turning as white as a ghost was much encouragement and, that fast, he was wondering if there was another man in her life. He stalked forward, angry destructive feelings tugging at him even as he rammed them back down again, determined to stay in control because so much hung on her answer.

'I don't know what to say. You've really taken me by

surprise,' Lara confided, turning away and then turning back, not wishing to be rude when he had had the courage to make such a proposal.

Gaetano halted mere inches from her, making her extraordinarily conscious of his height and forcing her to turn her face up to look at him. It was a comfort to acknowledge that Gaetano looked every bit as tense as she felt and deadly serious.

'Hear me out at least,' he asked her in a taut undertone. 'I want us to be a family. I didn't have that and neither did you, from what little you have told me. Freddy deserves parents willing to make the effort to be together. But to be frank, I also want *you* back, not just Freddy...'

Lara was so shattered by that assurance that her knees went all wobbly. She blinked rapidly, her heartbeat thundering inside her tight chest, making ordinary breathing a challenge. *I want you back.* Never ever had she even dreamt of hearing such a declaration from Gaetano. She had left everything she felt for him behind her...hadn't she? Wasn't that, for her own sake, all old history not to be revisited under any circumstances?

'And, to be even more frank, I haven't had a single happy moment since you left me,' Gaetano framed in an almost disjointed rush. 'I do the job I'm expected to do and the job is my entire life, which is far from ideal.'

Her soft heart clenched. Why had she always assumed that he would be delighted to take the throne and become King? Not a single *happy* moment? A rush of tears stung the backs of her eyes and she glanced down at the rug beneath their feet, the colours blurring as she struggled to control her emotions, but just then she was feeling more emotions than she could possibly handle all at once. Disbelief, bewilderment, a literal terror of making another mistake but, ultimately, a sense of pure joy. The very first thought that raced through her, shaming her, making her despise herself was that she *wanted* him, wanted him back yesterday for that matter, had probably never stopped wanting him back since she'd first walked away from him.

'I couldn't be a queen,' she declared with pained certainty. 'I haven't got what it would take to be *that*.'

'You don't have to be a queen anywhere but behind closed doors in our private apartments. I'm not expecting you to do anything in public unless you decide that you want to do so…which eventually you might do when you realise that the job's not quite as intimidating as it seems,' he assured her smoothly. 'But here, now at the *beginning*, I would expect nothing from you beyond being my wife and Freddy's mother.'

'OK,' she said hoarsely, that assent falling from her lips before she could even think better of it. 'Let's go for it…we can only try, there's nothing wrong with trying.'

And she stood there in a total daze of incredulity but deciding really *was* that simple, that fast, because for two long years she had been kidding herself that she had got over him and it had all been a lie to save face. She had thought that he had rejected her but now it seemed as though she must have got that wrong. Only, what if they got together again and their marriage fell apart for a second time? It happened, didn't it? People found that good intentions were insufficient to keep a relationship afloat.

Even so, wouldn't trying to be a couple again be the

braver option? At least giving both of them a chance to prove that they could be together? What if Gaetano changed his mind again? What if she got hurt again?

But why was she even thinking such thoughts when he had voiced words that might have described her own feelings?

Not a single happy moment...

CHAPTER SIX

A SENSE OF intense relief ran through Gaetano and crashed over him like a wave: he had got Lara back. He could do it; he could fake *anything* for the sake of the three of them!

And even though he had decidedly fudged the truth, he had not told any direct lies, he reasoned, determined as he was not to see himself as a deceiver or a liar. He would do everything within his power to make her happy and he would offer her every possible support. Above all, the best feature of Lara was that what you saw was what you got. She had none of the unscrupulous personality twists that even *he* rejoiced in. In addition, she had a very small ego in comparison to most people he met. She couldn't lie to save her life and she trusted him. In every way he would prove worthy of that trust, he reassured himself.

While Gaetano was engaged in intense self-examination, Lara was in a dizzy whirl of happiness. Gaetano had *missed* her. He had looked back and accepted how *good* they were together, had evidently only seen that value when it was too late to keep her by his side. In the spirit of newly rediscovered confidence, reminiscent of the Lara she had been with Gaetano two years earlier before his changed attitude had stripped her of such assurance, Lara closed the distance between them and stretched up to wind two slender arms round his neck.

Momentarily, Gaetano was stunned by that forward move on her part but just as quickly, his body reacting with instant visceral hunger, he was on board with the invitation. He stared down at her with scorching dark golden eyes and covered her mouth with his in a breathtakingly urgent kiss. His desire was that immediate, that driven by need. Lara gasped under that onslaught of passion, feeling the instinctive response of her body to his just as she had on that office desk the day before. But now, everything was different, she thought fondly, slender fingers stretching up into his luxuriant hair with that wicked, wanton possessiveness it had taken so long for her to shed after leaving him. She wasn't about to think about the other women he would have been with since, she *wasn't*! New book, clean page, she urged herself.

Without hesitation, Gaetano bent down and swept her up fully into his arms and her slip-on shoes fell off.

As he lifted his mouth from hers to thrust open a door, Lara giggled. 'So, I'm getting the full *Gone with the Wind* experience, am I?'

'No,' Gaetano retorted with a sudden slanting grin of amused appreciation that few Mosvakians would have realised their serious king was even capable of. 'The very last thing I'm about to say right now is, *Frankly, I don't give a damn*—'

'I didn't even realise you were a movie buff…you didn't recognise *Dr Zhivago* when we first met.'

'I'm not but my former sister-in-law, Giulia, is, and as a teenager I watched her favourites with her many times.'

'*Former?* Don't you count her as family any more now that she's a widow?' Lara queried.

'She's remarried and living in Italy now. I'm happy that she's found love with someone new. Her union with my brother was more a marriage of convenience.'

'Oh.' As Gaetano had laid her down on a big bed and was in the process of stripping her with an indecent haste that was insanely seductive, Lara's ability to make rational comments was on the retreat.

Her boots, socks and jeans were gone in a moment, and she sat up to remove her own sweatshirt, marvelling at how her whole world had changed focus since her arrival at the mansion. 'This…*us*, doesn't quite feel real yet.'

Gaetano stared at her sitting there in an unmatched bra and pants of the most ordinary kind of white unadorned lingerie. She was slender and yet just curvy enough in all the right places. Her skin gleamed like a pearl in moonlight while her beautiful hair glowed like the dawn in the wintry shadows of the bedroom. She had the most extraordinary effect on the way he thought, he acknowledged absently, lost in sensual appreciation.

'You look incredibly sexy,' he murmured hoarsely, one hand reaching round his back to haul off the casual shirt he had teamed with designer jeans.

In many ways, the mysterious workings of Gaetano's mind had always been a closed book to Lara. She could see nothing sexy in herself, only flaws like her skinny legs and the faint stretchmarks on her stomach. She glanced down uncomfortably at her serviceable bra and knickers and marvelled that a man of his experience and wealth could still find her so desirable. And she knew that he wasn't saying it for effect when that admiration was openly etched onto his lean darkly handsome face. Yet it was he, Gaetano di Santis, who totally took *her* breath away, poised there, his chest bare, smooth dark olive-tinted shoulders, washboard delineated abs and lean hips on display. He was gorgeous. She was *not*. Even before she'd discovered that he was royalty there had, for her, always been a credibility gap attached to their love and marriage. She had struggled to believe that he could genuinely love her as much as she loved him. With a dexterous wriggle she slid beneath the duvet, hiding her imperfect self.

He peeled off his jeans and boxers with the same careless speed, pushing back the bedding to reach for her. 'I can barely believe that I'm with you again.'

'You're not the only one,' she whispered before his mouth found hers again and that wild, seething sense of excitement started to climb inside her like an unquenchable flame.

Gaetano still wanted her more than any other woman. That was a miraculous fact to Lara and the knowledge strengthened her. She ran her hands down over his chest, loving the feel of the smooth brown skin and the curling black hair smattering the centre of his broad chest.

'Don't stop,' Gaetano groaned, throwing his dark head back on the pillows and resting back like a very willing sacrifice.

She found him with her roaming fingers, already long and thick and pulsing with desire. She shimmied down the bed, the tip of her tongue tracing her path, and his fingers laced tautly into her hair. It was as if some magical clock had turned back time. As she traced that velvety smooth tip, his hips angled up to her and a hoarse sound of pleasure was wrenched from him.

So she was surprised when he stopped her, hauling her back up to him to kiss her with ferocious hunger, rolling her over and tugging off her remaining garments with scant ceremony. 'I'm not likely to last very long,' he warned her gruffly.

'I'll survive,' Lara muttered, amazed that he should worry about something she considered unimportant. She didn't need or expect perfect after so much time had passed, she simply longed for that irreplaceable physical closeness to be renewed.

With his lips he traced the pointed buds of her nipples and a wave of sensitised reaction rippled through her, lighting up the warmth blossoming between her legs. She couldn't stay still as he traced the damp swollen folds there with one skilled hand and used the other to make her quiver and whimper as he sucked hard on the pouting peaks of her breasts.

'What is it about you?' he muttered in a roughened undertone. 'You turn me on faster than anyone else ever did.'

'Stop talking,' she framed shakily, parting her thighs round his lean hips, tugging her knees back to encourage him. 'I can't wait.'

'I'm trying to take this slow, *bambola*,' Gaetano reproved thickly.

Lara uttered a breathy little cry of impatience and shifted against him, quite deliberately sliding her heated core over his jutting erection.

Gaetano bit out a groan and gripped her slender hips to raise her to him. Mere seconds later, he was exactly where she wanted him to be, reintroducing her to sensations she had almost forgotten. The stretching fullness of his invasion, the glorious friction of his retreat and advance. Wound round him like a vine, she moaned in delight, hands skating down his long smooth back in appreciation as she angled up to him for more. With a ragged sound fleeing his parted lips he stared down at her with joy, speeding up, finally pounding into her welcoming body until what she hadn't believed was that important happened anyway, grabbing her up in a great storm of corporeal sensation. The world behind her lowered eyelids flashed white and her slender frame arched for a timeless moment before fireworks flared inside her and she went incandescent, her whole body flooding with blissful pleasure.

With Lara still wrapped round him, Gaetano released a sigh of immense relaxation and snaked out a hand to lift his phone. She listened to him ordering champagne and raised her brows.

'Champagne and strawberries?' she whispered. 'Are we still pretending we're on a movie set?'

'No, we're celebrating. I've got my very hot wife back in my bed,' he told her smoothly, flashing her a triumphant grin. 'Mission accomplished.'

'I suppose I could raise a glass to my even hotter husband,' Lara murmured, clashing with glittering dark eyes that left her breathless.

It was an effort to get out of bed after the champagne and strawberries and she felt more than a little giggly in the aftermath. Only her concern for Freddy and what he might be having for lunch, nanny or not, roused her from the bed, in spite of Gaetano's attempt to keep her there. She felt happy, incredibly, extravagantly happy, and feeling like that after spending so long just bumping along the bottom of life while being a working mother also felt strange. And she almost felt guilty. Why guilt? she questioned herself as she stepped out of the shower that Gaetano had just vacated. Didn't she feel that she deserved to be happy? Or was she just afraid that somehow something or somebody would steal that happiness away from her again?

As she emerged from the bathroom, fully clothed and rather flushed and unsure of herself in the aftermath of the life-changing decision she had reached at the speed of light, she heard male voices, one of them Gaetano's, in the next room because the bedroom door wasn't fully closed. Breathing in deep, she returned to the sitting room to retrieve her shoes. The first thing she noticed was that Gaetano's companion was Dario and he dealt her a shaken look before glancing away, swiftly wiping all expression from his bearded face. Lara reddened because it was very obvious that she and Gaetano must have shared a bed again but, on another level, she was pleased by Dario's astonishment. Close friend Dario might be but, plainly, Gaetano had not confided in his lawyer before asking his estranged wife to reconcile with him. It was a relief to know that there were limits to that friendship.

'I'm just going to check on Freddy,' Lara murmured,

ducking past both men, who appeared to be locked into some sort of serious discussion. 'And then I'll need to see about picking up Iris from school… Iris, my friend Alice's little girl.'

'No, you had better hear this first,' Gaetano countered with compressed lips. 'I'm afraid the press have got the jump on us and are presently besieging the house where you live.'

Lara looked at him in horror. 'Oh, my word…'

'If you give me your keys, my security team will remove your belongings and my son's to bring them here.'

'I can't just walk out of my whole life like that,' Lara began shakily, her eyes huge in her pale face. 'Alice depends on me for childcare, for goodness' sake. I can't leave my best friend in the lurch—'

'It's not a problem, *bambola mia*,' Gaetano cut in smoothly. 'Alice and Iris should come here for tonight at least until the press have given up. They'll be perfectly comfortable here and we have a nanny who is capable of taking on any childcare concerns you may have. *Relax.*'

Inadvertently, Lara glanced at Dario, somewhat comforted by the reality that he had only travelled from shocked to seemingly stunned into silence while Gaetano outlined his solution to their predicament.

Gaetano glanced at Dario. 'Have an announcement of our marriage and Freddy's birth released at home and then here in the UK. What is his birthdate?'

Lara told him and Dario dug out a notebook and made a note of it.

'We no longer have to be discreet,' Gaetano informed his employee.

'Yes, sir. Is there anything else I can do for you?' the other man enquired stiffly, his formality pronounced.

'Lara, give Dario your keys and he will pass them on.'

'I'll go with them.'

'To be engulfed by a scrum of paparazzi when you've never faced that challenge before?' Gaetano prompted drily. 'I don't think that's a good idea.'

'I'll phone Alice, ask her to go home and oversee the removal of our stuff if she can.' Lara crossed the corridor into the nursery where Freddy was sitting at a little table cheerfully eating a lunch of finger foods while the nanny, a youthful smiling brunette, supervised him.

'Prince Freddy is very sociable.' Standing up, the young woman approached her and extended her hand politely. 'I'm Ellie Ross. I'm sorry, I don't know who you are—'

'I'm Freddy's mother, Lara,' Lara admitted in a stifled undertone after hearing her son labelled in such a manner as she dug into the bag she had abandoned to find her phone.

She moved back into the sitting room where Gaetano was now sitting at a desk with Dario still hovering. '*Is* Freddy a prince?'

'Crown Prince and my heir,' Gaetano confirmed succinctly. 'Isn't it obvious?'

'No, not when I believed our marriage might not be legal and I thought that for the whole of the two years we were apart,' Lara told him quietly. 'And I don't know anything about royalty except that here in the UK the family have a lot of rules to follow.'

'Mosvakia is not a large country and it's rather more

laid-back,' Gaetano responded in a tone of apology. 'Sorry I was short with you. I was miles away, reading something.'

'You are also, automatically as the King's wife, our Queen, Your Majesty,' Dario slotted in.

Lara nodded and nodded again and backed away as though she had been threatened by a hot poker. A queen. *Her*, a queen? A woman who had washed dishes and floors and served in run-down bars as a waitress? A woman who had only three pairs of shoes to her name?

'You shouldn't have said that,' she heard Gaetano reprove before she could close the door again. 'Lara's not some social climber, keen to acquire a title. All that nonsense scares her off!'

Unexpectedly, that little overheard snippet, which told her just how well Gaetano understood her more reticent nature, made Lara straighten her spine, square her slender shoulders and smile. Gaetano had explained her for Dario's benefit, taken her side, shown his support. She brought her phone in the corridor and rang Alice.

'A *king*?' Alice almost shrieked when she was told. 'Are you kidding me? Is this an April Fool or something?'

'Of course I can leave early…joys of being my own boss,' Alice quipped a few minutes later. 'Don't worry. I'll pick up Iris—no need to involve some nanny. Oh, Lara, isn't Freddy just going to *love* being a prince and the centre of attention?'

'Without a doubt,' Lara agreed ruefully.

'I can't wait to talk to you,' her friend admitted. 'When I left the house this morning, you were meeting Gaetano to discuss a divorce and now, only a few hours later…my goodness, that guy moves at super-sonic speed!'

'I don't know how I could explain it or explain why I didn't tell you.'

'I'm a complete blabbermouth,' Alice filled in chirpily. 'Always have been, always will be. No explanation required. As for why you're reconciling. Well, no surprise there on your side of the fence.'

'Am I really that predictable?'

'Where he's concerned? I'm afraid so. Look, I'd better run if you've already handed over the keys and you don't want your vast wardrobe stuffed disrespectfully into bin bags,' Alice teased, because they both knew that Lara owned very little. 'See you later.'

Lara joined Freddy in the nursery. Gaetano joined them for Freddy's bath, dive-bombing little boats and ducks with an aeroplane while Freddy screamed with excitement. After a quick supper, her son was ready only for his cot.

'Your friend has arrived and will be joining us for dinner,' Gaetano informed her. 'I gather you hadn't told her who I was.'

'Why would I?' Lara parried ruefully. 'I was Cinderella, but I didn't get my prince.'

Gaetano's eyes flared fiery gold. 'I married you! What greater faith in you and what we had could I have demonstrated?' he demanded in a raw undertone of condemnation that told her she had touched a nerve. 'But you were too weak to seize the moment and you ran away!'

Slowly, Lara straightened. 'That's not how it happened. I wasn't weak and I didn't run away. It's interest-

ing how reality gets massaged and twisted out of shape
when people are apart. People develop their own story.'

But once again, Lara was being reminded of what
a risk she was taking in trusting Gaetano again. Their
unsuccessful past together still hung over them like a
dark cloud and could still catapult them into conflict.
She could get hurt again, badly hurt, if their marriage
failed a second time and that still filled her with fear
and insecurity.

Gaetano flexed long brown fingers that had briefly
clenched with the force of his emotions and breathed in
slow and deep, calming himself down as he recognised
the tripwire that had almost entrapped him and dam-
aged what he had gained. 'No doubt we'll talk about
it some day but *not* any day soon,' he murmured with
smooth emphasis. 'Re-establishing our relationship is
more important than dwelling on our past mistakes.'

Having been taken aback by that sudden flash of
anger, Lara turned away, as pale and shaken as though
a shark had leapt out of a tranquil pond in front of her.
She had been ridiculously naïve, she thought painfully,
to think that all was forgotten and forgiven. Evidently,
he had put the blame on her, and she was tempted to
round on him and give him her frank opinion of what
he had done and said to drive her from his side. But
Gaetano had been quite correct in that this was neither
the time nor the place to dive into the swamp of the past.
Everything was too new and fresh between them, and it
would be wiser to concentrate on the present than risk
destructive recriminations.

That afternoon, a stylist arrived to take her clothing measurements, Gaetano having pointed out that

she would require what he described as a 'more flex-ible wardrobe'. By the time the stylist had moved on from measurements to requesting her colour and fash-ion preferences, even Gaetano's subtle approach had warned Lara that she was really receiving a makeover. She joined Gaetano, Alice and Dario for dinner in a lofty-ceilinged formal dining room where they were waited on as if they were…well, royalty.

She learned from a question that Alice asked that this was Gaetano's very first visit to the house he had inher-ited three years earlier. As her friend raised her brows in her direction, Lara knew exactly what Alice was think-ing. Who on earth inherited a giant house from their grandfather, unknown or otherwise, and waited three years to visit it? And only then because it was conve-nient to where he wanted to be? Someone who might well own a lot of property, someone from a world en-tirely removed from theirs in every way…

Alice studied Lara when she accompanied her back to her bedroom where Iris already slept in one of the twin beds. 'You really have jumped in with both feet again with him, haven't you?'

'Yes, there's just something about Gaetano which blasts all common sense right out of my head,' Lara conceded wryly. 'I'm still insanely attached to him.'

Alice laughed. 'Well, I'm not sure I would call it insane. He's filthy rich, devastatingly handsome, very entertaining and he's a king. He does also seem incred-ibly keen to be married to you again.'

'It feels a bit too much like a fairy tale,' Lara whis-pered worriedly.

'You really do *deserve* the fairy tale,' her friend told her softly.

Gaetano wasn't there when she got ready for bed in the grand bedroom that they had shared that afternoon. He had mentioned having allowed work to pile up while he came to England to visit her. She felt alone, though, and scolded herself for it. Of course, Gaetano, the monarch, had many more responsibilities than the guy with amnesia she had first met, who had been able to devote himself unreservedly to her. My goodness, without even appreciating that truth, she had been spoilt by him!

The acknowledgement made her buck up and accept reality. He would give her and Freddy what time he had to give, and she would make the best of it for the sake of their marriage. She fell asleep feeling lonely but comforted by the pious reminder that there was no such thing as perfect in any marriage…

CHAPTER SEVEN

THE FOLLOWING AFTERNOON, Gaetano, Lara and Freddy flew to Mosvakia. She barely recognised her own reflection in the luxury washroom on the private jet. Her glamorous powder-blue knee-length dress and light matching coat teamed with toning shoes looked incredibly elegant, although nothing could have prepared Lara for the pomp and ceremony that greeted their arrival.

'Why didn't you warn me?' she gasped, as Gaetano urged her down the steps from the jet to the crowds awaiting them.

Some people were waving with enthusiasm. Many were wielding cameras. Yet more were arranged in a formal line to greet them. Off to one side a regimental band was playing an upbeat thundering tune. The smiles and the music went some way towards banishing her immediate attack of stage fright. It was a celebration, not something to fear, she registered, the tightness in her chest receding and her breath coming a little easier.

A wave of introductions followed on the tarmac, the prime minister, the chief of staff of the army and that of the police force. Those were just some of the people she met. An eye-catchingly beautiful woman with long black hair and bright blue eyes disconcerted Lara by immediately mentioning that she was an ex-girlfriend of Gaetano's.

'Although I'm afraid there are all too many of us in *that* category!' she joked with such wide-eyed amusement that Lara could only admire her good nature. Her name was Antonella. 'I'm so happy that Gaetano has found a wife and now he has a son as well. How wonderful! I currently have an intern position at the palace, so you'll see me again. I do hope we can be friends.'

'I don't see why not,' Lara responded, charmed by that frank speech as Gaetano's hand at her spine urged her on down the line.

'What did Antonella have to say to you that took so long?' Gaetano enquired.

In surprise, Lara glanced up at him and immediately recognised the faint tension etched in his lean darkly handsome features, tightening his high cheekbones and bracketing his narrowed golden gaze. 'Nothing much. She seemed charming.'

'Oh, she is,' Gaetano agreed calmly. 'She's the prime minister's daughter, quite a privileged young woman.'

Someone else grabbed his attention and that was the end of the conversation. Lara had wanted to ask when he had dated Antonella but, on reflection, decided that that would be an unwise enquiry. How would she feel if he told her he had been seeing the beautiful woman during their marriage? And that was perfectly possible, wasn't it? She suppressed the sense of insecurity assailing her. She didn't want to turn into an insanely jealous woman, did she?

After all, whether she liked it or not, she had been

the one to walk out on their marriage. It was even possible that she had misread Gaetano's signals that day. She didn't want to think that about herself. She didn't want to think that she could have made such a ghastly mistake about *his* feelings for her. Even so, the anger he had revealed about her disappearance from his life only a day earlier had forced her to wonder whether she had misinterpreted his reaction to their marriage after he had regained his memory.

'You're very quiet. There won't usually be this amount of interest in us, but the marriage announcement two years after the event and Freddy's existence were bound to attract attention,' Gaetano pointed out in an effort to be soothing, because at the back of his mind he still had the fear that if Lara was thrust too fast and too deep into the limelight, which she didn't want in the first place, she might vanish on him again. It was foolish, he told himself, but, nonetheless, that fear was alive and well just about every time he looked at her. He needed to put that anxiety behind him. He didn't fuss over women; he didn't normally worry about them either. Why was she so different?

'So, why did you call Antonella "privileged"?' Lara heard herself ask, although she had promised herself that she would not ask Gaetano a single question about his ex-girlfriend. Her curiosity betrayed her, however.

'Her sense of entitlement and confidence have ruffled feathers on the household staff,' Gaetano confided. 'But to be fair to her, the staff *are* behind the times. My brother preferred the old ways in every sphere but I'm of the younger generation. Antonella does all the PR and she's the first in that position.'

Lara let the subject drop, relieved of any further concern by Gaetano's relaxed response and explanation.

The limousine was driving now at a slower stately pace down a long steep driveway surrounded by trees. When the trees finally parted, she saw an elegant white building on a hill. Adorned with castellated towers, it bore a remarkable resemblance to a jigsaw of a fairy-tale castle she had once done as a child. Several different storeys climbed the slope. Beautifully manicured terraced gardens surrounded Gaetano's home.

As her nerves began to nibble at her composure, she breathed in deep. Freddy, who was in top form after meeting so many strangers and receiving smiles and appreciation from them all, squealed with excitement. Gaetano dismissed the offer of assistance from one of the half-dozen hovering staff eager to help and reached in to lift his son out of the limousine himself. As Freddy squirmed in the grip of one arm, he closed his free arm round Lara's small trembling frame with all the firmness of a prison guard.

'No need to glad-hand anyone here. This is our home and we're heading straight to our private apartments,' he intoned half under his breath before he fixed a polite smile to his darkly handsome face and forged a path through the gathering crowd to take them indoors.

Lara's eyes glazed over in the vast echoing hall where towering, majestic mirrors and chandeliers offered a myriad reflections of people awaiting their arrival.

'My wife is very tired.' Gaetano excused them smoothly, urging her across the hall into a lift while signalling their nanny.

'I'm not that tired,' Lara muttered apologetically as Gaetano lowered Freddy to the floor in the corridor they stepped into.

Gaetano stepped round her to speak to the nanny and suggest that she take their son to the nursery.

'Gaetano, I was planning—' she began uncomfortably.

He closed a hand over hers in a gesture that brooked no argument and urged her down the corridor and into a room with giant double doors. 'Our bedroom,' he told her. 'Be grateful for the modern furniture. When my brother was alive, it was the same as it was in my great-grandfather's day with a massive four-poster. It gave me the creeps. Giulia refurnished it for me. She did a lot of redecoration after losing Vittorio. It gave her something to do. However, you are free to change anything and everything in this wing of the palace. It is now *our* home.'

'That's good to know,' Lara mumbled, still shaken by a bedroom the size of a football pitch with numerous connecting doors. It was exquisitely decorated in shades of soft blue and green with touches of white. 'But I shouldn't think I'd want to change anything in here. It's stunning as it is.'

'It's a shame that Giulia has moved abroad. You would have liked her.'

'You must miss her too.'

'Yes, but now I have a family again,' he reminded her, his lean hands lifting to curve to her shoulders, long brown fingers flexing against her slender bones in a caressing motion.

'I was going to spend time with Freddy,' she murmured.

'You've been with Freddy all day, now *I* want a piece of your time,' Gaetano husked as he gazed down at her with mesmeric golden eyes under a canopy of lush black lashes. 'Freddy has an entire nursery staff at his disposal and it's not as though our son is shy or clingy, is it?'

'No, it's not. He's like you…full of himself,' she teased with a sudden helpless smile because when Gaetano looked at her in a certain way, the rest of the world just vanished along with every other concern.

'And I'm allowed the occasional piece of you too,' Gaetano reasoned huskily, tipping the coat off her shoulders and turning her around to run down the zip on the dress. 'When I came to bed last night you were asleep and I had an early morning phone call I had to rise to take. That happens a lot in my life: I can't do what I want to do.'

'I suppose it goes with the job,' Lara mused as her dress hit the splendid woven rug below her feet.

'But now I have a private life and a good reason to free myself up more often,' Gaetano pointed out.

'I'm quite sure you had a private social life *before* you found out where I was living,' Lara returned quietly, wanting there to be no secrets between them and that included topics that she might feel that she preferred to avoid.

Gaetano straightened as he scooped her up and laid her down on the wide bed. 'I haven't had a single social engagement outside what I consider to be work.'

Lara's brows knitted. It worried her that he didn't feel he could be honest with her. 'I did walk out on our marriage but then I did assume that, as Dario had said, it couldn't have been legal for you to marry me without your brother's consent.'

'I have to admit that I don't even recall Dario saying anything of that nature,' Gaetano admitted as he wrenched off his tie and then paused to reflect on her words. 'I was so devastated to hear of my brother's sudden death that I barely recollect anything that anyone said that morning. I knew his illness was terminal, but I assumed he would be with us for many months more. Vittorio was virtually my father, and I had no other family. And the realisation that I was to become King without any warning…well, to be brutally honest, it *overwhelmed* me.'

It was a moment of truth for Lara. She had been too busy that day seeing her own cosy little world with Gaetano destroyed to acknowledge the traumatic news that Gaetano had received at the same time. Although she had had all the facts, she had not put them together then, or afterwards, she conceded with regret. The sad truth was that both she and Gaetano had been too preoccupied with their separate concerns to think sensibly about their marriage.

'And *I* was overwhelmed by who you really were,' she confided belatedly, sliding off the bed to brush his stilled fingers away and efficiently unbutton his shirt. 'Realising that you were rich and royal, and that you had this whole other important life in another country, scared the life out of me.'

'But you're not so scared now, are you?'

Lara fumbled with his cufflinks. 'I'm working on it. I'm a bit gutsier now than I was back then.'

'Stronger,' Gaetano agreed with a smile. 'I like that.'

'You may not like it so much if I ever dare to use it against you,' Lara contended with a glint in her aqua-marine eyes.

'Would you?' he asked, shedding his shirt, toeing off his shoes, bending to peel off his socks. 'Because two years ago, you wouldn't have.'

'Without you, I toughened up.'

Gaetano tugged her into his arms. 'I like strong, in-dependent women,' he declared, crushing her parted lips hungrily with his, his breath fanning her cheek as he slid her back onto the bed with single-minded pur-pose.

'I'm talking too much,' she guessed.

Gaetano laughed and grinned down at her. 'I missed your honesty but I'm not quite sure I like the fact that you can read me so well. I've never met anyone else with that ability and occasionally, it's unnerving.'

'You said it, Your Majesty,' Lara whispered, running her hands down the sides of his lean thighs and then sending them up to rove across his hard stomach and his firm pectorals as she sat up and claimed his mouth again for herself. Every nerve in her body thrilled to that connection.

He groaned into her mouth, momentarily rigid with sexual hunger against her and it whisked her back in time because his response to her had not changed in the slightest. With impatient hands he removed the silk and lace lingerie she still wore. 'I can't get enough of you now, *bambola*,' he assured her feverishly.

'I think I can live with frequent ravishment.' She laughed.

Gaetano spread her out on the bed as though she

were a feast to be savoured. Expert hands traced her slender ribcage up to the pouting fullness of her breasts and tugged on the delicate peaks. He lowered his mouth there to toy with her until her hips began to shift and rise, the liquid heat at her core making her restless. She wanted more…oh, *how* she wanted more, she reflected, helpless in the grip of the craving he was awakening inside her. He traced the delicate folds between her thighs and used his carnal mouth and fingers to incite a fire of need. For a long time, he teased her until her whole body was trembling on the sharp edge of delight. When a climax engulfed her in a blaze of intense pleasure she writhed and moaned.

'You are the hottest, sexiest woman on this earth,' Gaetano groaned into her hair, sliding over her and into her in one sleek, hard thrust of power.

A surge of renewed hunger washed through her as he pushed her knees back to deepen his invasion. Her body jolted with the driving power of his possession. Every nerve ending reacted, firing her response with an immediacy that was incredibly exciting. Her heart was racing, her blood rushing in her veins and then the excitement peaked for her, drowning her in blissful sensation until she lay limp.

As Gaetano released her Lara rolled onto him, determined to retain that intimacy. 'I want a hug,' she told him saucily.

And his immediate smile chased all the gravity from his lean darkly handsome face, his dark eyes tawny gold with satisfaction below the tousled black hair on his brow. My word, he was beautiful, she thought abstract-

edly, tracing the fullness of his pink lower lip, emphasised by the black veil of stubble beginning to frame it.

He closed his arms round her and she felt safe and
secure the way only he had ever made her feel. She
wanted to tell him that she still loved him, but she held
the words back because she felt that it was far too soon
to be that honest.

The next day she explored their enormous private
wing, amused to discover that it spanned three floors
and countless rooms as well as enjoying access to a
private garden. Certainly, space was unlikely to be a
problem for them. Gaetano had an office in the top of
one of the towers, a book-lined refuge. She popped her
head round the door, saw Dario was with him and went
into instant retreat.

'No, join us for coffee,' Gaetano insisted, yanking
open the door again before she could escape.

Dario pulled out a chair for her and she sat down, a
diminutive figure clad in a green sweater and leggings.
Gaetano laughed. 'You look like an elf in that colour.
We have to fill in some forms to apply to have Freddy's
birth certificate altered and brought up to date.'

As the forms were settled in front of her, Lara
scrawled her signature, a guilty grimace etched on her
face. 'I wish I had named you on the certificate and
owned up to our marriage.'

'We'll get it sorted out eventually,' Gaetano said
bracingly, squeezing her shoulder and urging her back
into her seat. 'Don't worry about it.'

'You'll have a fabulous time in Morocco,' Dario remarked.

Gaetano frowned at his friend. 'Thank you, Dario, for breaking the news.'

Lara's eyes had widened. 'Morocco?'

'A belated honeymoon, the least of what I owe you,' Gaetano told her with a slow smile. 'We leave at the end of the week.'

'Freddy—?'

'He's my son too. I wasn't planning to leave him behind.' Gaetano studied her with amusement as she poured the coffee.

A knock sounded on the door and a tall blond man strode in, greeting Gaetano with enthusiasm. For a couple of minutes they spoke in French and then Gaetano swung him round with a smile and introduced him. 'Lara, meet Olivier Laurent. He's a renowned photographer and a good friend from my schooldays. I invited him here to take some photographs of you and Freddy. If we release official photos, it gives the paparazzi less reason to sneak up on us,' he explained.

Lara stood up to be kissed French fashion on either cheek. Olivier didn't have a reserved bone in his body, it seemed, as he grabbed her hands, set her back from him and looked her over with a professional eye that had a flirty twinkle. 'You've done very well, Gaetano. I work with models who would kill for that glowing complexion and that combination of hair and eyes.'

'Thanks.' Lara straightened her shoulders.

'You said to make it an informal session,' Olivier reminded Gaetano. 'I like your wife dressed just as she is but she may want to gild the lily first.'

'You want to do this now?' Lara asked, because as far as gilding the lily went she had already applied

make-up from the giant box of cosmetics she had received along with her new and vast wardrobe, which
contained outfits to cover every possible occasion. 'Because I'm fine as I am.'

'Put on your rings or earrings at least,' Olivier advised.

'We'll be back in a few minutes,' Gaetano murmured, his high cheekbones scored with colour as he
closed a hand to hers and urged her out of the room.

'Where are we going?'

'I've been very remiss. I haven't even *given* you any
jewellery!' Gaetano ground out in a guilt-stricken undertone. 'What sort of a husband am I?'

'Well, you were only a husband for six weeks and I
wouldn't let you spend what you had on stuff we didn't
truly need, then we had the break and I've only been
back in your life for a few days. Luckily, I kept my
wedding ring even if I didn't wear it until this week,'
Lara pointed out soothingly. 'Let's not fuss about the
little things.'

Gaetano took her into another room and opened a
safe, carting out a towering pile of jewellery boxes while
Lara looked on in wonderment. 'The trouble is that all
this is antique and family stuff.'

'I don't need to wear your family's jewellery, for
goodness' sake,' Lara protested in embarrassment.

'All of this is yours to wear as my wife. I'll buy you
your own pieces when we have the time but Olivier's
right…it would look odd in the photos if you wore no
jewellery at all.'

'I don't care if I look like a bargain-basement bride,'
Lara told him with a chuckle.

'But *I do*,' Gaetano shot back at her in a raw undertone. 'In marrying me, you lost out every step of the way. You had to borrow your wedding dress because you wouldn't agree to me buying you one. You had no party, no engagement ring, no honeymoon, not one single thing that other brides take for granted!'

'Things like that are not important to me. It's feelings that matter. Our wedding was very romantic,' she reminded him softly. 'Snow on the ground, just you and me and Dr Beresford and her husband. I *loved* my borrowed dress. I thought the whole day was magical.'

Gaetano stared back at her in amazement, his stunning dark golden eyes still troubled. 'Honestly?'

'Honestly,' Lara confirmed with a smile. 'I didn't have a family to invite and the only close friends I had weren't available. We were together. That was all that mattered.'

With visible difficulty, Gaetano dragged his eyes back from her lovely face and began snapping open several ring boxes. 'Pick a couple…' he invited.

'Oh, that's gorgeous!' Lara prised a beautiful solitaire diamond out of a box and tried it on her finger beside the wedding ring. 'And as it fits it was obviously meant to be!'

'It was my grandmother's… I believe. She was gone before my birth, but Vittorio and Giulia once sat me down to talk me through all this stuff and its provenance. Somewhere there is an official catalogue. Try another ring and some earrings,' he encouraged.

Lara slid a square-cut sapphire dress ring on her other hand.

All the earrings he unveiled were either too fancy or

for pierced ears and her ears were unpierced, so Gaetano had to be satisfied with the rings now adorning her fingers.

Lara collected Freddy from the nursery. Like her, he had enjoyed a wardrobe refresh and he looked adorable in embroidered dungarees and a matching sweater. Olivier met them at the foot of the stairs and said to Gaetano, 'I can take it from here and you can go back to work. I've been using the palace as a backdrop for portraits for long enough to know all the best locations.'

'I'll stay. I haven't seen much of Freddy today,' Gaetano announced.

Olivier definitely seemed to know what he was doing behind a camera, giving her detailed instructions of how to pose, where to look, with slick directions and amusing comments that made her relax and laugh more than once. They had to be a little more active to please Freddy and keep him in one place long enough to be photographed.

'I'm really enjoying winding Gaetano up,' Olivier murmured quietly after an hour as he bent down to Freddy's level and play-fought the little boy to make him chuckle. 'I've never seen him so gone on a woman that he would stand around watching just to make sure I don't get *too* friendly with her!' Laughing with satisfaction, he backed away from mother and son again.

It was frustrating for Lara not to be able to look around right at that moment to see if Gaetano really was there watching. Olivier was an old friend and his frank words lifted her to a height. The idea that Gaetano could be recapturing some of the emotion she had once inspired in him was extremely appealing now that she had accepted that she was as much in love with him today as she had been two years earlier.

The main difference between then and now was that she understood how much more complex a character Gaetano was than she had once assumed. And how volatile he could be, she acknowledged ruefully, beneath the hard shell of equable cool that his royal role had imposed on him. Without knowing who and what he really was, she hadn't grasped what that conflict in his nature meant, nor had she been aware that she and Freddy saw a side of him that few other people, if any, had had the benefit of experiencing.

Gaetano had a flinty darkness to his gaze when he gathered her up after the session ended and Freddy was borne off to have his supper by his nanny. 'You should have told Olivier to back off,' he breathed unreasonably.

Lara lifted a brow. 'He's a happily married man with two kids. You can't be serious. He was winding you up deliberately.'

Gaetano frowned and stiffened. '*Stai scherzando...* are you kidding me? I felt that he was being disrespectful.'

'No, not at all,' Lara disagreed. 'He's a friend and he was teasing you.'

Gaetano gritted his teeth and said nothing more. Seeing Olivier, one of the worst womanisers in Europe before his marriage, getting that close to Lara had inflamed him. Clearly, Lara liked Olivier—well, most women did, he conceded grudgingly. But the more she had laughed and responded to Olivier's undoubted charms, the angrier Gaetano had felt. Obviously, he was a rather territorial man, who preferred that other men respect clear boundaries rather than flirt with his wife in front of him. There was nothing wrong with that. Olivier had been in the wrong, *not* him.

'Oh, yes, Dario's wife, Carla, is dying to meet you and I said we'd drop in on them later for supper,' Gaetano imparted. 'She's very friendly and warm. I think you'll like her.'

'Would you have a minute?' Antonella asked Lara as she was walking through the big hall towards the lift, intending to join Freddy in the nursery.

'There's some ideas I wanted to run by you. Mosvakia needs to meet their new queen properly,' she told Lara cheerfully as she invited her into one of the offices on the ground floor.

Lara swallowed hard, recalling how Gaetano had promised her that she only had to be a queen behind closed doors. 'Is it really important? I don't want to put myself out there if I don't have to.'

'You and Gaetano are a double act. How could you not appreciate that he needs your support?' Antonella asked in almost exaggerated surprise. 'Charities and other organisations, not to mention the government's scheduled events, require more time than the King has in his day. You could relieve some of the pressure on him by taking on some of those duties.'

Lara had paled. She levelled her shoulders, trying to stand taller because, although she was accustomed to being smaller than most of the people around her, inexplicably Antonella made her feel like a small person on the inside as well as the outside. 'Of course, I'll help if I can,' she murmured limply, terrified that she was being selfish and determined to make Gaetano proud of her. Antonella's surprise made it obvious that skulking behind closed doors was not going to impress anyone. 'I didn't appreciate that Gaetano was under so much pressure. This is early days for us.'

'The King works very hard. When I was with him... oh, forgive me.' Antonella studied her with an apologetic grimace. 'I meant not to remind you of that. It just slid off my tongue.'

'Don't worry about it. I'm well aware that I'm not the only woman whom Gaetano has had in his life,' Lara managed to respond in an upbeat tone, resolute, as she was, not to be oversensitive, but perhaps it *was* time for her to talk to Gaetano more honestly about the time they had spent apart rather than dancing round the sticky subject and avoiding it. In some cases, such as right there at that very moment, ignorance was not bliss.

'Well, of course, I knew the King before you entered his life,' Antonella began in a remorseful tone.

'Before?' Lara queried, her spine snapping rigid with sudden fierce tension. *'Before?'* she repeated helplessly.

'I'm sorry. I assumed he would have mentioned it by now. We were dating before he disappeared the way he did.' Antonella had lowered her voice. 'I only know about *that* episode because my father is Prime Minister. For obvious reasons, it's been kept very quiet. He forgot that he already had a girlfriend, but I can hardly complain when he had a medical reason for doing so.'

'My goodness,' Lara exclaimed in response to that revelation. She contrived a stiff smile and struggled to maintain her composure when, in actuality, she felt as though she had received a hard punch in the stomach.

'That must have been very difficult for you. Do you mind me asking how close you were?'

Already regretting asking such an intimate question, Lara watched Antonella bend her head, her face colouring. 'I don't think we should get into that, but I was like any other woman in a relationship with a man of the King's standing... I did hope that it was a lasting bond, of course I did. And unfortunately, nothing was explained when he first came back, and he stayed away from me. *Nobody* knew that the King had married—well, possibly Dario did, but the rest of us didn't. That was a very well-kept secret.'

'I'm so sorry you had that experience,' Lara murmured tightly. 'Look, Freddy's waiting on me. Could we discuss those events you mentioned on some other day?'

'Of course, Your Majesty. Get back to me when you have a free moment,' Antonella urged with a pleasant smile.

She's a nice person, Lara reasoned, why do I feel as if I hate her? Why do I feel as if she has destroyed me?

But it wasn't Antonella's fault that she had brought something to light that neither Gaetano nor Lara had considered two years earlier. Why hadn't they considered that he might have another woman in his life? Indeed, that he might even be in a relationship with someone else? On the only occasion when Lara *had* mentioned that possibility, Gaetano had outright laughed at the suggestion, insisting that he could never ever have forgotten someone that important to him. And she had believed that, hadn't she? Because it had suited her to do so, her conscience pointed out. Madly in love as she had been and Gaetano had *seemed* to be, the idea that he might owe loyalty to another woman would have been a devastating blow to her warmest hopes and prayers.

But for Gaetano, how much worse would it have been had he remembered that he *loved* that other woman the moment he regained his memory?

And wasn't that, bearing in mind his tension when he had seen her talking to Antonella, the more likely scenario?

After all, Antonella was absolutely gorgeous, like one of those supermodels you saw and lingered on in a glossy magazine. She was well educated, Mosvakian and from a good background. In short, Antonella was everything that Lara was not, and she was painfully conscious of the differences between them.

Gaetano had said he had not enjoyed a single happy moment since she had left their marriage, she reminded herself in desperation. But hadn't Gaetano originally approached her looking for a divorce? And hadn't his attitude only changed after Freddy entered their relationship and he accepted him? Freddy, the Crown Prince, their son, who was so much more important in Mosvakia than Lara in her naivety had ever appreciated. Freddy was treated in the palace like a precious jewel. Young though he was, Freddy was viewed as a future king. Here in the palace his outgoing nature was much admired. Freddy was a vital element in their marriage. Without *his* existence would Gaetano still have wanted her back?

Such damaging fears would normally have sent Lara to bed early but instead she had to head out with Gaetano to visit Dario and Carla's town house. Engulfed by Carla's lively tribe of pet dogs, however, there was no time to brood. Carla was much more outgoing and casual than her husband and, not being a Mosvakian by birth, she didn't have his reverent attitude to the monarchy. To her surprise, Lara thoroughly enjoyed the evening and noticed how much more relaxed and likeable Dario was in his wife's company.

Lara was remembering the last time her trust in Gaetano had been tested, two years earlier, and she had run away sooner than stand her ground like an adult. She was no longer that immature and insecure, she reasoned with herself. He deserved the benefit of the doubt this time around.

She might want to confront Gaetano about Antonella, but how could she confront a man who might well have done nothing wrong? Who had had every *right* to be in love with another woman when he first met Lara even if he couldn't remember the fact? That worrying question kept her lips sealed for the following two days while she struggled to behave normally.

CHAPTER EIGHT

FLYING ON HIS private jet to Morocco with his family, Gaetano was brimming with dissatisfaction.

He had accepted the ugly truth that in the husband stakes he had been a disaster. He was proud that he had the humility to acknowledge that reality and he was fully committed to rectifying his mistakes. Sadly, for him, however, Lara was no longer on the same wavelength. For the very first time in his life, he was at a loss with a woman and his recently awakened conscience did not prevent him from seething with angry frustration when his attempts to improve the situation met a solid brick wall of indifference.

For the past forty-eight hours, Lara had been more distant than the Himalayas. She emanated an invisible but highly effective forcefield that repelled him. Even in bed, surely the ultimate insult, he reflected grimly, thinking of how she had muttered about how tired she was before taking refuge at the farthest edge of the bed as though he were some kind of sex fiend she was desperate to avoid.

Lara's real problem, however, was that she was hopeless at hiding anything from him. Her smiles were stiff, her voice expressionless, her eyes unwilling to meet his. That something had gone wrong pretty much screamed from Lara. Unfortunately, she was married to a guy who was too clever by far to *ever* ask a woman what was wrong and receive some bitten off passive-aggressive 'Fine' in response.

But slowly and steadily, nonetheless, Lara was driving Gaetano up the wall. Worse still, her behaviour had *shocked* him. Gaetano, who had fondly believed that he was shockproof with women. And yet here was Lara, whom he had truly believed was above such games, and she was shocking him with her detachment. *Shutting him out.* He couldn't stand it; he genuinely couldn't stand it. And it didn't help that he didn't know why, didn't understand why such a change in her attitude could affect him to such an extent when no woman before her had had the ability to affect his mood.

Of course, he was accustomed to her warmth and her acceptance, and no woman had ever had the power to make him relax the way Lara did. When that was suddenly withdrawn without explanation, naturally he would feel troubled. While he had been taught to suppress his emotions, he still couldn't manage that feat around Lara, and when one distant glance from Lara bothered him, his own overreaction made him feel out of control because he wasn't accustomed to handling the turmoil inside him.

Maybe she had somehow got him hooked on all that touchy-feely cuddling she was so keen on. Certainly, he wasn't stupid. He was aware that he had never had that sort of warmth from any other woman, not that it hadn't been offered, only that he had once had the good sense

to refuse that kind of empty, inappropriate affection.
But Lara's affection hadn't felt empty or inappropriate
or fake. And weirdly, he *missed* it. All of it: the hand
slipping into his, the hugs, the appreciative smiles, the
laughter like liquid sunshine that revitalised him. His
shapely mouth flattened and compressed. The awareness and the thought that had led to it only increased
his annoyance. *Madre di Dio*…she now had him ago-
nising over stuff as if he were a teenage girl!

As they climbed into an SUV at Marrakech Menara air-
port, Lara was painfully aware that she was handling
what she had learned from Antonella very badly. Sadly,
Antonella had struck a killing blow because Lara deeply
cherished her memories of that first six weeks with
Gaetano during which she had fallen in love with and
married him. Antonella had struck at the very roots of
that precious emotional history and squashed her flat.
If the other woman was telling the truth, Gaetano had
never been Lara's except by default and his love had
never been real even at the beginning, indeed, could
only have been an infatuation caused by circumstance.
And that hurt, good grief, that *really* hurt, Lara acknowledged unhappily.

'Where are we staying?' she enquired to break the
awful silence that had fallen between her and Gaetano
long before they left the palace.

'At the Palais des Roses property my grandfather
built in the swinging sixties. The estate lies on the out-
skirts of the city. As a child I came here for regular
holidays with Vittorio.'

'Not Giulia?'

'I was already an adult by the time my brother married Giulia. Her parents were family friends, though, and often visited the palace when I was a teenager. That's when I watched movies with her. Vittorio had several ill-fated relationships with women and, with everyone keen to see him marry and carry on the family line, he finally settled on Giulia because she was a safe choice—'

'That's sad.'

Gaetano frowned. 'It would have been even sadder if Vittorio had made the mistake of choosing a bride who only wanted him for his wealth and status. My mother married my father for his position and Vittorio watched that car crash happen. It made him very wary. Once my mother established that Mosvakia was not *the* most fashionable place to be, she spent her time socialising in London with her friends. I was born there because she didn't want to return to Mosvakia.'

Having left the buzzing, busy city behind, their convoy of cars was driving through olive groves. Soon enough they were surrounded on all sides by a plantation of soaring date palms and Lara carefully confined her attention to the view from the car windows. The SUV only slowed down when an impossibly long expanse of tall white wall appeared. The wall was divided by massive wrought-iron gates, which were swung open by two beaming older men.

A glorious wash of exquisite pastel-coloured roses in brimming beds encircled the driveway and she stepped out into the sunshine. A horseshoe arch led into a courtyard with pillars and a tiled floor sprinkled with rose petals to welcome their arrival. Water was running somewhere nearby, and a healthy collection of ever-green shrubs and small trees vied for her attention in the flower beds.

She was ushered straight into a room so packed with striking colourful features that she simply stared, taking in intricate kilim-upholstered seating, elaborate plaster-work, a carved wooden painted ceiling, and spectacular mosaic tiles applied to shoulder height on the walls. 'My word, it's like some *Arabian Nights* fantasy.'

'It's a house of curiosities,' Gaetano said wryly, urging her in the direction of the concealed staircase at the rear of the room. 'My grandfather spent years building it with teams of master craftsmen and ran himself deep into debt. Like my father, he was extravagant.'

'There's fireplaces everywhere,' Lara remarked, glancing into another room as they passed it. 'I wasn't expecting that.'

'Desert nights are chilly once the sun goes down.' On the floor above, he walked her out onto a giant roof ter-race that contained a gleaming swimming pool, plants in massive colourful urns and loads of outside seating. 'In summer we lived mostly outdoors here.'

'It sounds idyllic...and the view is out of this world,' Lara remarked as she leant on the retaining wall, gaz-ing out at the snow-capped Atlas Mountain range back-ing the seemingly endless expanse of dense date palms. 'Much more lush and green than I was expecting.'

'When are you planning to tell me what's wrong?' Gaetano shot at her with an unexpectedness that jolted her.

Lara spun round, clashing with scorching dark eyes

that seared her, and she lost colour. 'I don't know what you're talking—'

'Quit while you're ahead. You can't act for peanuts. For the past two days you have been treating me like the invisible man when we're out of bed and a potential degenerate when we're in it!'

Taken aback by that full-frontal attack and his anger, Lara stared back at him, her cheeks red with heat and her chest heaving as she sucked in oxygen to fill her compressed lungs. For a moment she couldn't find her voice.

'Did Olivier say something about me that annoyed or offended you?' Gaetano prompted in a low intense tone. 'I noticed that your attitude to me changed after *his* visit…and if you don't come clean right now, Lara, I intend to phone him.'

'Don't you *dare*!' Lara snapped back at him in dismay. 'It's nothing to do with Olivier. He said not one word out of place about you.'

His lean, strikingly handsome face merely tightened. 'That is good to know, because he's a close friend. But it annoys me that you feel that you cannot speak freely to me. Am I so intimidating? So untrustworthy that you can't simply be frank with me?'

Shame and regret filled Lara and an uneasy silence stretched as a tray of refreshments was brought out to the terrace by a member of the staff.

Gaetano thanked the older woman in French and introduced her to Lara. 'This is our housekeeper, Maryam. Her husband, Ahmed, is our cook.'

The mint tea was poured, and tiny pastries offered. Lara was too overwrought to be capable of eating anything. She sipped the sweet herbal tea and nibbled at the edge of a pastry to pass herself below Maryam's anxious scrutiny while wondering if the older woman had heard their raised voices. Inside herself she was dying a thousand deaths of embarrassment.

'I'm not very good at confrontation, but that doesn't matter because you haven't done *anything* wrong,' she stressed uncomfortably as soon as Maryam had vanished indoors again.

'Then what on earth has caused this change in you?' Gaetano demanded rawly.

'Something Antonella let drop,' she muttered reluctantly.

'Antonella?' Gaetano's mouth took on a sardonic curve and his dark golden eyes hardened. 'Why does that not surprise me?'

Lara sank down on a cushioned seat because her legs felt weak. 'I was a bit shocked because she mentioned that you and she had been dating *before* you had your fall that Christmas with me two years ago.'

'*Dating?* That's news to me,' Gaetano countered thinly, incensed colour lining his hard cheekbones. 'Her father brought us together on a trip to the opera house, and then on another occasion I was invited to a dinner by a friend and discovered that I was expected to partner Antonella. Neither event was a date and, in any case, in my position, I would have to be pretty stupid to get involved with the daughter of a politician. I have always given the daughters of our local dignitaries a wide berth. In fact, I have never had an affair with a woman in Mosvakia. Since I was a teenager, it was easier and safer to enjoy such freedoms abroad.'

'That's quite a speech.'

'Evidently a necessary one,' Gaetano condemned. 'Do you honestly think that I would allow an ex to work in the palace and work closely with my wife? I'm more sensible than that, although I have to say that you seem to be less than sensible on the same topic. What else did Antonella tell you?'

'Well…' Lara floundered. 'It wasn't so much what she said as the impression she gave me…that you and she had been very close.'

'Nonsense,' he dismissed without hesitation. 'I'm skilled at being courteous and nothing more to women keen to attract my attention when I have no intention of reciprocating. That's been an element of my life since school. You're too trusting, Lara. You should have brought this concern straight to me. I'll put Dario onto finding another location for Antonella.'

'Oh, don't do that—not if it's likely to cause offence to her family.'

'I don't like troublemakers, *bambola*…or the streak of spite Antonella has revealed. She lied to you. We weren't dating. There has never been any physical contact between us. What other stories might she weave? There was no *other* woman in my life when I first met you. Plainly, Antonella hit out at you because *I* had injured her ego. I won't have her anywhere near you now that she's shown her true colours.'

A slow smile curved Lara's formerly tense mouth. He was so protective that he made her toes curl. Even two years ago, clueless about his identity, Gaetano had been driven by that same compassionate strength. Not since her father's death had she been able to rely on a man and her experiences as a teen, forced to live with the ever-changing turmoil of her mother's love life, had made her wary and distrustful of men before she met him.

'I should've trusted you, at least given you the benefit of the doubt,' she conceded, pained that she had believed every word that fell from the other woman's lips. 'I've wasted two days fretting about something that never happened.'

Gaetano reached for her hands and held fast to them. 'I don't like it when you close me out.'

'I'm not used to having anyone I can talk to in a crisis,' Lara confided. 'I was never free to honestly talk to Alice about us because she's hopeless at keeping secrets.'

Shimmering dark golden eyes held hers. Her mouth ran dry, and her tummy flipped with the force of her sexual awareness. He wound long fingers slowly into several strands of wavy strawberry hair, watching how the fading sunlight lit it up to a peach shade. 'I'm used to keeping my own counsel, so I have to admit talking is a challenge for me as well.'

Her hand tugged free of his to curve to one lean cheekbone, her fingertips stroking his olive skin. 'In other words, we are both useless at communication.' She sighed.

Gaetano burst out laughing. 'I love the way you find fault with me.'

Black lashes dipping low over piercing eyes, he scooped her up into his arms. 'It is much easier to kiss you lying down, *bambola mia*,' he explained.

'Is that your excuse?' Lara was thinking that Gaetano had never had the smallest problem in communicating his needs. He was innately powerful, persuasive and driven to succeed.

His stunning eyes flared down into hers. 'Do I need one?'

'No.'

Her heart raced as he claimed her parted lips ravenously with his own, his tongue delving deep as he carried her indoors to the blessed cool. That electrifying shock effect lit up every nerve ending in her body. She trembled against him as he rested her down on a bed and joined her there to continue kissing her with driving hunger. Nothing had ever felt so good or so necessary as the restoration of that physical connection.

As they both paused to draw breath, Lara looked up at him anxiously. 'I don't want to be asking you awkward questions about what happened in your life while we were apart. I know I walked out on you...as you see it. I accept that...morally speaking, you felt that you were free to do whatever you liked with other women.'

Gaetano stared down at her with troubled dark eyes. 'I never felt that way. I knew I was married. I knew I wasn't free. I don't cheat, Lara. My mother cheated on my father and a couple of Vittorio's girlfriends cheated on him. It's painful and humiliating. I haven't been with anyone but you since the day we exchanged our vows,' he admitted tautly.

Lara gazed back at him in shock and surprise and a great floodtide of relief washed through her, her aquamarine eyes glazing with the sheen of emotional tears. 'I didn't expect you to be faithful.'

'But I *was*,' he asserted levelly.

'And I was too,' she whispered shakily.

'I wouldn't let myself ask you that question.' Gaetano released his breath on an audible hiss. 'But I thank you for making that choice.'

That quickly, Gaetano felt as though he was *all* hers again. There was no ghost of Antonella or any other woman to come between them and make her wonder about comparisons and feel inadequate. Her arms closed round his lean muscular frame, hands smoothing down over his shirt-clad muscular back. 'I can't really convey in words how much that means to me. I made a false assumption. My expectations were too low.'

'I'm far from perfect.'

'I *know*.'

A faint smile tugged at the corners of his shapely mouth. 'You're supposed to tell me I'm perfect, not agree that I'm not.'

'You value honesty,' she reminded him softly, shifting and flexing every muscle to roll him over. 'So, now I shall tell you that you're wearing far too many clothes…'

Lara sat up and embarked on his shirt buttons, plucking them loose, spreading her hands across his bronzed and muscular torso, shimmying down the bed to let her lips follow that same trail. His fingers laced into the tumble of her hair as she ran down his zip and then, without warning, he lifted up again from his prone position and settled her back from him.

'I can't wait,' he groaned. 'I'm like a teenager with you, always frantic to be inside you…'

His frank admission sent a surge of need hurtling through her at storm-force potency and reawakened memories. Gaetano grabbing her in the middle of the day, powered by that simmering passion she couldn't resist, confessing his impatience, apologising, almost embarrassed by the strength of his desire for her and then taking her to orgasmic heaven at record speed.

He was wrenching his jeans down and she helped him, sitting up then too to peel her sundress over her head, laugh as he detached her bra to lift appreciative hands towards her freed breasts and then, with a groan of regret, abandon them to remove the last item that blocked her body from his. That feverish frantic pace was achingly familiar. In the midst of it, she kissed him with joy bubbling up through her.

He flattened her to the pillows with the power of his response, a hungry growl rippling through his chest as he rearranged her to his satisfaction. 'I even messed up in bed with you,' he husked half under his breath. 'You never got the cool version of me.'

'Did you hear me object?'

She angled her hips up to him as he leant back from her to don protection. She lay back against the pillows, her body throbbing with readiness. He entered her fast and deep and her body jerked at the rush of pure pleasure. His raw passion, his innate intensity, was one of the things she loved most about him. He drove her out of her mind with desire and broke through her every inhibition with ease. Excitement climbed as fast as his lethally effective pace and energy. She reached her peak equally fast, clenching and convulsing around him before breaking into a thousand pieces and floating back to earth, winded and shaken by the power of the experience.

Gaetano hugged her so tightly without being

prompted to do so that she almost yelped and then he relaxed his hold and released her from his weight while retaining an arm round her to keep her close. Her very bones hummed with contentment.

'The worst thing was not being able to find you,' he admitted abruptly, disconcerting her by raising that particular topic. 'It wasn't until you were gone that I realised how very little you had ever told me about yourself. I knew your father died when you were nine and that you were adopted and that your mother moved around a lot but that was literally it. And it wasn't enough, anywhere near enough, to track you down.'

'My background felt kind of sleazy in comparison to yours.'

'But you didn't know my background when we first met.'

'Your accent, the obvious level of your education, those things gave it away for you and I had my educational years basically stolen from me,' she volunteered ruefully. 'I had a good childhood and great parents until Dad died and then everything I took for granted just disintegrated. Mum couldn't seem to cope without Dad. Every time Mum broke up with her latest man, we had to make a fresh start. And every time I was dragged out of school and put into a new one, which was incredibly disruptive.'

'I had no idea.'

'I was ashamed of it, so I played it down with you.'

'There's plenty of skeletons in my family cupboard.'

'Mum married Alice and Jack's dad and life was stable while she was with him, but she got bored after a year and asked for a divorce,' Lara related uncomfortably, still nervous of sharing that part of her past with him. 'She had a friend in Spain who owned a bar and things only got seriously bad after we moved abroad.'

Gaetano gazed down at her with frowning dark golden eyes. 'Tell me about it…'

'We never had a home of our own. She moved in with her boyfriends and a couple of them took too much interest in me and if I talked to Mum about it, she went crazy with me and accused me of trying to steal them from her. I was only fourteen and more a late starter on the boys front than anything else.'

'*Madonna mia*…how the hell did you cope with that? That must have been terrifying for you!' Gaetano grated with heat. 'Your adoptive mother was very irresponsible and selfish to subject you to a life of that sort at such a young age.'

'Well, the last guy she was with when I was still there was the worst. He owned his own bar, and I was always helping in the kitchen or clearing tables. I hardly went to school, and it suited them because I was free labour. But when Mum was behind the bar he'd come upstairs and he'd open my bedroom door and stand there staring in and saying, "Just checking on you…" It was the creepiest, scariest thing,' she confessed, drawing in a shallow breath as she shuddered in recollection. 'The way he looked at me, the way he spoke to me, it wasn't right and, eventually, I wrote to my grandparents, Dad's parents, and asked them if I could come home and live with them and go to school. I was lucky they agreed.'

'And what did your mother think of that?'

Lara grimaced. 'I think relief would be the best word to describe her reaction when I told her that I could return to the UK. They even sent me the money for the ticket. Mum couldn't be bothered with me. She was a good mother while Dad was alive, but I think he must have been the one who wanted to adopt the most because once he was gone, she didn't seem to have any real interest in me.'

'I would have understood your situation if you'd confided in me,' Gaetano told her fiercely. 'There was no need to pretty anything up for my benefit.'

'It was more of a matter of personal pride,' she admitted ruefully. 'I didn't want it to seem like there was a huge gulf between us…and then you had to go and turn out to be a prince on the brink of becoming a king. Everything just fell apart then.'

Gaetano wrapped another arm round her. 'That's not going to happen again. It fell apart for both of us that day. We should have had more faith in ourselves and in what we had found with each other.'

She rested her brow down on a smooth brown shoulder and sighed. There was much she could have thrown at him, not least his horrified disbelief when he had realised that he had married her. Only she didn't want to step back into the dangerous ground of the past when the future and the present seemed so much more inviting.

She was on the very edge of a doze when she heard a gong reverberate through the house, the deep boom vibrating through the walls. 'What on earth is that?'

'The dinner warning. Very effective. You can hear it inside and outside,' Gaetano imparted, thrusting back the sheet and lifting her out of bed to settle her bare-

LYNNE GRAHAM

143

foot into the biggest, most colourful bathroom she had ever seen.

Twin showers with moulded basins stood side by side. A copper bath was situated beside the window. A huge, tiled vanity with two sinks took up most of the final wall. It was just as Gaetano had said—a house of curiosities—but it was luxurious and full of art and handicrafts.

Dinner was served in the courtyard. Freddy would only pick at his meal. Too many treats, his nanny admitted with a guilty grimace. Lara soothed her concerns, having already noted that the star guest in the Palais des Roses was her son as far as the staff were concerned. They took Freddy out into the beautiful gardens to run around before bedtime. He emerged giggling from under a large shrub and ran to her. She scooped him and his toy rabbit up with an 'oomph' of effort, because he was no lightweight, and cuddled him. He rested his head down drowsily on her shoulder.

'He's getting tired,' she commented.

Gaetano extended his arms and gathered Freddy into them. 'You're a fabulous mother. When I see you with our son, I realise how much I missed out on. He's friendly and very confident because he knows he's loved. I was much more suspicious of new faces and quite lonely,' he admitted as they strolled back towards the house. 'Some day—it doesn't have to be soon—I'd be really happy if you would consider having a second child.'

'Yes,' Lara agreed with a smile. 'I'd like Freddy to have a sibling. I always wanted one myself.'

'At least I had Vittorio.'

'But he was more like a father than a brother. A sibling would be different…someone to play with,' she mused, thinking that Gaetano's big brother had looked like a very serious man in the couple of photos she had seen of him, not the type of parental figure to get into the rough and tumble games that Freddy revelled in.

Gaetano, on the other hand, loved that sort of stuff and didn't object to getting his clothes dirty.

'I'll take him into the pool tomorrow,' Gaetano announced. 'I have a great toddler swimming ring waiting for him. I planned ahead.'

It was a conversation that Lara recalled almost two weeks later as she sat in the shade watching Gaetano entertain their son in the pool. Freddy, safely ensconced in his flamingo ring, chubby little legs kicking, arms waving as he squealed with excitement at his father's antics. Yes, maybe another child was a good idea, Lara thought abstractedly, thinking back with regret of her decision to keep their son a secret on the assumption that their child would be no more welcome to Gaetano than his wife was after he had regained his memory. With hindsight that had been a mistake and perhaps she should have given his recovery from amnesia a few days more before deciding to leave him and their marriage behind her. Only there hadn't been time for her to dally on that decision because Gaetano had been due to fly straight back to Mosvakia.

But Lara didn't want to look back to the past, finding it much more sensible to simply revel in her recent experiences. There had been visits to the souks in the old town of Marrakech. She had bought a pair of soft red leather sliders for Alice, who adored shoes, and a cute wool jacket for Iris. She had even bought a manly leather belt for Alice's brother, Jack, who would be home on leave soon from the army.

And while she was searching for gifts, such as a book on Moroccan history for Dr Beresford, who she remained in contact with, Gaetano had been busy buying gifts for her. There was no stopping him. Anything she liked, Gaetano bought for her. A picture she admired—it became hers. There was a wonderfully shaped and sculpted terracotta urn that would remind her for ever of the colour of the twelfth-century walls surrounding Marrakech when the sun was setting in the early evening.

Nor would she ever forget the vibrant buzz of life and the scent of grilled meat and spices in the air in the Place Jemaa el-Fna. The big square was full of entertainers, dancers, musicians, fortune tellers and snake charmers. Freddy loved snakes, which made his mother shudder. They had toured a lot of public gardens where their son could run free, and their security team could chase after him. They had visited the beach at Agadir where Freddy had paddled in spite of the breeze, and they had driven out into the countryside where they had seen mule trains carrying goods to market and women balancing tall copper jars of water on their heads.

And there had been some extraordinary moments, she recalled with a dreamy smile. Gaetano had presented her with a spectacular blue diamond ring after dinner in a secluded restaurant in the foothills of the mountains. He knew all the best places to visit, and it had been a magical break but none more magical than the presentation of that ring over mint tea served below the flowering almond trees. He was still trying to talk her out of what he had called her 'cheap' wedding ring and into accepting a new and fancier one, but that ring had too much sentimental value for her to consent to a replacement.

Someone had come to the house to pierce her ears and she was never likely to live down the fact that she had fainted, and that Gaetano had panicked and had insisted on a doctor visiting. Her cheeks could still burn reliving that embarrassing morning. But now she owned a beautiful pair of finely worked traditional earrings that, unfortunately, she would only be able to wear once her ear lobes healed. Gaetano had been disappointed by that news.

Surfacing from her daydream at the sound of her name, she realised that Gaetano needed help with Freddy. Standing up, she grabbed a big towel and went to the edge of the pool to gather the dripping, slippery little body of their toddler into its cosy folds. As she knelt down at the edge, Gaetano left the water as well and followed her across to the sunbed where she had stowed Freddy's clothes.

'My phone rang, and you didn't hear it.' He sighed, drying his hands and grabbing it up.

'Sorry,' Lara muttered as she slotted a wriggling Freddy back into his clothes. 'But answering your phone is a risk and I'm risk-averse, especially after answering it and getting the prime minister!'

'Chicken,' Gaetano taunted with amusement as he punched buttons and walked away with that animal grace that never failed to grab her attention. His bronzed physique spattered with drops of water that sparkled in

the sunshine, he still made her tummy turn a somer-
sault and her breath catch in her throat.

She listened to his voice in the distance but tickling
Freddy soon drowned Gaetano's conversation out. She
moved indoors with her son, looking forward to the
cooler evening that would come but decidedly sad that
they would be leaving Morocco in the morning. As
their nanny reclaimed Freddy, Lara wandered into their
bedroom, smiling as she always did when she noticed
the spectacular ornate gold metal crown above the big
bed from which mosquito netting flowed in a great bil-
lowing cascade. Gaetano's grandfather, it seemed, had
never forgotten that he was a king even when he was
on holiday.

'Something unexpected has come up,' Gaetano said
from the doorway. 'Dario is faxing me a copy of the
letter addressed to you and he apologises for opening
it since it falls into the realm of personal correspon-
dence, but you can blame me for that. He's authorised
to open *all* our letters.'

'A letter for me?' Lara frowned. 'But who would
write...*personal*?'

'I'll bring the letter for you to read,' Gaetano declared.

'You should get dressed first,' she reminded him.

He glanced down at his swimming trunks and then
grimaced, peeling them off in a wet heap to stride into
the bathroom.

'Letter?' she queried before he could even turn the
water on.

'From a legal firm. Evidently one of Olivier's photos of you was widely taken up and published round the

world. A woman in Italy believes that you are the living resemblance of her late British mother and she and her brother are asking if you're willing to take a DNA test to see if you are related to them.'

'Good grief,' Lara gasped, dropping down on the carved chair in the corner with her brain swirling in shock.

'Yes, quite a surprise and your two potential connections are rich and well connected so it's highly unlikely to be any form of a scam. Perhaps you would prefer to look into your birth family for yourself first by your own methods… I don't know. It would take longer but it's up to you.'

Lara blinked rapidly, sheer surprise and bewilderment plunging her into a daze. 'I'll think it over,' was all she could say.

'Don't get your hopes up,' Gaetano advised quietly. 'What are the chances that your parentage could be recognised from a photograph? This will most probably come to nothing.'

CHAPTER NINE

THEY FLEW BACK to Mosvakia very early the following morning. During the flight, Lara could only think
about that letter and the truth that if those two people
were related to her, both her birth parents were dead.

It had been a legal letter, short and to the point, re-
vealing the barest facts but also declaring that the two
parties had been looking for their sister, who had been
adopted as a newborn, for several years. And although
Gaetano had pointed out that the possibility that they
could be related to her was a slight one, Lara could only
think how wonderful it would be to be so *wanted* and
so *important* that people would spend years and presumably a lot of money in search of her. Far too often
as she had grown up, she had felt unwanted and tolerated rather than loved. It had often been painful and had
contributed to her loneliness and insecurity and possibly
even the speed at which she had decided that Gaetano
no longer wanted her two years earlier.

'I spent two years searching for you…you didn't give
me any accolades for it,' Gaetano declared drily.

Lara went pink. 'That was different. I wasn't sure

we were legally married, and I assumed you wouldn't want Freddy. But family is a connection I've never had.'

'Except with me and Freddy,' Gaetano informed her with irrefutable logic.

Lara stiffened. 'Until Freddy was born, I had never seen anyone related to me by blood. And Freddy looks exactly like *you*. When I looked up Leah Zanetti online, though, she had black ringlets and I don't look remotely like her or Ari Stefanos.'

Gaetano's shapely mouth curled. 'Don't tear yourself up about this because there's probably nothing in it,' he forecast.

Inexplicably he had realised that he didn't really want Lara to discover long-lost relatives. That would entail sharing her and he wasn't much for sharing any part of her, he acknowledged grudgingly. He quite liked having Lara all to himself. She was the one woman in his entire life who had only ever been his and who focused almost entirely on him. True, he had to share that limelight with Freddy, but he had never enjoyed such closeness in a relationship before. Was he being selfish in not wishing to share Lara? Or was his apprehension more related to the truth that her potential siblings were wealthy enough to provide Lara with an escape hatch should she ever want one from their marriage?

She had walked out on him once. Whether he liked it or not, it could happen again. Lara could be flighty. Hadn't he already learned that? Deep down inside where it was well hidden, Lara had insecurities. She set too low a value on herself. She didn't give her trust easily and she still didn't trust Gaetano. Antonella had only had to hint at a previous relationship with him to cause her very real distress. And in that distress, Lara might have been spooked into leaving him again, Gaetano reasoned worriedly.

Yet he had had to corner her to force her to tell him what was worrying her. Sadly, she had chosen not to trust him with the problem and that problem just created a bigger one. Lara could be vulnerable, and she was very emotional. It was Gaetano's job to protect her and ensure she was happy. But how could he function in that role if she refused to have faith in him?

For possibly the first time he wondered exactly what he had said to Lara the day she walked out on him. In his memory, his recovery from his amnesia, the arrival of Dario and the police and security he had brought with him remained a hopeless blur in which Lara barely featured until she was gone. Only when she had vanished had he appreciated how much of a loss she was to him. So why hadn't he discussed that with her yet? Why, when that one episode was so crucial to the breakdown of their relationship, had he prevented her from even talking about it? Perhaps because even now just remembering that day brought him out in a cold, clammy sweat…

Wondering at Gaetano's unusually quiet mood, Lara accompanied him into Dario's office.

'Have you come to any conclusions?' Dario asked her at the same time as he handed her a glossy magazine folded back to show the relevant page. 'I thought you might want to see the photo that stirred all this up.'

Olivier had sent her digital copies, but Lara wasn't so fond of her image that she had sat down to look at them in any great detail. Now she saw the photo that had attracted Leah Zanetti's interest. It was a close-up and she was smiling, probably laughing at one of Olivier's jokes. She knew from the letter that the other woman believed that she bore a striking resemblance to her late mother, whose newborn baby had been adopted shortly after her death.

'Of course, if the British paps hadn't been so diligently engaged in trying to dig up your background, the fact that you are adopted would never have entered the public domain and it would probably never have occurred to Leah Zanetti that there was a chance that you could be her missing sister,' Gaetano commented. 'Unfortunately, that would make it more difficult for you to check out your birth parentage for yourself because it would be almost impossible to do it discreetly now with the press watching out.'

'Yes,' Lara conceded, wincing because she hadn't thought about that risk, and she was quite sure that her possible siblings wouldn't want that kind of searchlight shed on their family secrets any more than she did.

'The DNA test, however,' Dario imparted as he pulled out a chair for her to sit in, 'would be much more straightforward. It's quick and accurate. You will have an immediate answer, if you're interested.'

'But Lara may *not* be interested in pursuing this further,' Gaetano interposed quietly. 'You once told me that you hadn't enquired into your birth parentage because you were afraid of digging up trouble.'

Her brows pleated at that reminder, and she glanced at his tense profile, wondering why he was so lukewarm, even discouraging, about her researching her background, but before she could speak Dario spoke up for her.

'I don't think that will be an issue. Ari Stefanos has happily acknowledged Leah Zanetti as his half-sister. It seems that his father must have had a long-running affair, which Stefanos only found out about after his father's demise, but nobody would ever have known about that affair if Stefanos hadn't decided to find and acknowledge his sister, Leah,' Dario advanced, his mouth quirking. 'Full marks to him for not caring what anyone said about it.'

Lara had been pondering that warning about press interest, which made her shrink. Now she looked directly at Dario and said, 'I'll agree to the DNA test. It seems the easiest option.'

'Are you sure you've thought it through?' Gaetano prompted.

'Yes, I'd rather know one way or the other, even if it means I'm disappointed.' Lara raised her head high. 'They're both married with children. Do you realise that that could mean that *I* have nieces and nephews?' she murmured in wonderment. 'A sister and a half-brother? It's so exciting!'

'I'll make the arrangements for the test,' Dario announced. 'It can be done today and sent off.'

'Don't forget that this may only be a mirage,' Gaetano breathed, closing an arm round her slender back to guide her out of the office again.

'Why are you so down on me looking into this?' Lara demanded of him in the corridor.

'I'm not down on it. I just don't want you to get hurt,' Gaetano parried, casting a tense look down at her delicate freckled profile. 'You're already investing too much in what may be false hopes.'

Lara spun and tiptoed her fingers down over his lean, muscular midriff in reproach. 'You're such a gloomster sometimes.'

His hand captured her wandering digits. 'I'm more realistic than you, *bambola*. Let's discuss something more practical…perhaps, the party we're holding next week to introduce you to everyone?'

Lara paled. 'You didn't warn me about that.'

'I'm proud of you and I want to show you off. Do you remember that gorgeous ball gown you insisted that you'd never ever wear? It's for this party. I've already organised travel for Alice to attend and I promise I won't leave your side for a moment,' he intoned huskily. 'I'll act as though we're chained together.'

'And then everyone will say, "Look at how trapped he looks with her!"' Lara quipped with amusement.

He gazed down at her, dark golden eyes full of heat and hunger. 'Or, look how much he *enjoys* being trapped with her?'

The DNA test was quickly carried out that same morning. Conscious of Gaetano's warnings, Lara put the whole matter to the back of her mind because she didn't want to build fantasy castles in the air. Shortly before lunch, Gaetano appeared with an air of purpose etched into his lean dark features and walked her into the dining room. With the wine poured and the meal awaiting them, he dismissed the server and tucked her into a seat.

'Where's Dario?'

'He went home to Carla for lunch and plans to return

to that arrangement. Vittorio didn't like staff leaving the palace to eat. He made a lot of rules and I'm changing some of them.'

Lara sipped her wine.

'Now…' Gaetano hesitated, his mouth tightening. 'Something I've been avoiding but which was a major experience for both of us. I'd like to talk about the day I regained my memory.'

Lara glanced at him in surprise. 'I thought that was on the forbidden list.'

'That wasn't one of my wisest decisions,' Gaetano admitted tautly. 'As I've already admitted, I don't remember that day's events very well. I saw Dario on that path and immediately recognised him. But when my two worlds—the one with you and the one I originally came from—merged all of a sudden…*everything* blurred. I got lost between the past and the present.'

Time had already slid back for Lara to that momentous day. She was staring into mid-air while recalling how on edge she had been even before the helicopters landed. 'Cathy's son, Patrick came home unexpectedly the night before his mother had texted to tell me that he'd lost his job and was coming back home for a while—'

'I remember Jamie and how drunk he was when his friend dropped him off.'

'You helped me put him to bed. I was fretting about how much longer we could stay with Patrick in residence. With him there to take care of the pets and everything, we were surplus. And I didn't know where we were going to go at short notice or how we would live when we got there,' she completed weakly.

'We'd only finished breakfast when the helicopters landed in the field on the other side of the road,' Gaetano recalled.

Lara remembered racing upstairs to have a better view of what was happening and when she had seen all those men converging on the farmhouse, some of them clearly policemen, she had started to panic. They had traced Gaetano by a sighting from a local in a neighbouring village. Rushing back downstairs, she had joined Gaetano at the front door as a young, bearded man wearing a troubled expression had come through the gate.

Gaetano's arm had dropped from her shoulders, and he had said slowly, heavily, almost as though he had been drugged, 'Dario...what's happened?'

And the two men had stood there chattering volubly in Italian while she'd hovered like a third wheel, desperate to know what was going on but shut out by the language barrier. It was Dario who had guided Gaetano back indoors and urged him down into a seat. For the first time, Gaetano had recognised someone, and it was obvious that with that recognition his memory had returned just as quickly as he had lost it. Whatever he had learned from Dario had left him looking drawn and devastated. Finally, she had tugged at his sleeve to remind him of her presence.

'Dario, this is my wife, Lara...use English, please.'

'Your *wife*, Your Majesty?' Dario had been stunned almost speechless by that introduction.

'Don't call me that,' Gaetano had urged sickly.

'What else can I call you? You became our King the instant your brother died,' Dario had proclaimed.

'That was the moment,' Gaetano murmured, dragging Lara back to the present after that mutual surge of recollection. 'That was the moment when I realised what a hash I'd made of everything.'

'In marrying me,' Lara completed tightly, pale as milk and pushing her plate away.

'No, in leaving home without my phone, in going off grid and the way I'd married you in *secret*. I was in shock at Vittorio's death and the knowledge that I had to step up to the throne. My brother was terminally ill. That's why he sent me away. He said he wouldn't have me hovering by his deathbed like Giulia and that I had to enjoy what freedom I had left before I was forced to replace him. But he believed he had months of life left,' Gaetano advanced.

'Just before you explained our marriage in Italian to Dario, you looked at me in horror and said, "What the hell have I done?"' Lara swallowed hard and pushed back from the table to rise and move over to the windows. She folded her arms because her hands were shaking. 'And it seemed quite clear to me that the minute that you realised *who* you were, you regretted marrying me.'

'That's not how it was,' Gaetano countered in fierce disagreement. 'I was in a state of disbelief that I had married *anyone*! Lara, I was a hopeless womaniser before I met you and I'd never had a normal relationship with a woman! I had never been in love either. I had sex. I had a lot of sex but not with anyone who mattered to me. You were in a class of your own and I was blown away that I had met you, fallen in love with you and married you that quickly.'

Lara swallowed hard. 'Well, I interpreted your attitude differently. I assumed that you deeply regretted our marriage and Dario's reaction convinced me that you thought you'd made a mistake in marrying me.'

His ebony brows pleated. 'That's not how I felt. But I can see now that I was being selfish that day and only focusing on my own concerns. I was totally blind to how you might be reacting to the news that you had married a royal and… I think *you* panicked.'

Lara breathed in deep and slow to calm herself, ready to snap back at that reading of her behaviour. But she connected with brilliant dark golden eyes fringed by lush black lashes and lifted her chin, unable to lie to him. 'Yes, you're right. Later I couldn't admit that to myself—that I had panicked. But you had also made me feel rejected… I felt I wasn't good enough to be married to you. Add in that I genuinely believed that our marriage might be illegal then and I had no good reason to stay.'

'*I* should have been your reason to stay,' Gaetano told her, setting his empty wine glass down with a snap as he stood up. 'I relied on you. I trusted you. You are the first woman I ever trusted apart from Giulia and yet you walked out on me when I needed you the most!'

Lara was badly shaken by that condemnation. 'You *needed* me?' she whispered.

'Of course, I did when I'd just lost the only family I had. I was grieving for my brother. I had the throne, but I didn't want it… I had never wanted it. I was closer to you than I'd ever been to anyone and when you disappeared, it almost destroyed me. I went through the year that followed like a zombie on autopilot. I wasn't expecting you to walk out on me and disappear. I wasn't prepared for that to happen...and I *still* have this ridiculous fear that you will vanish again!' Gaetano ground out in a raw undertone.

Tears of guilt and discomfiture were lashing Lara's eyes. She closed the distance between them and wrapped her arms tightly round him, gripped by a powerful wave of remorse. 'If I had understood that you needed me, I would never have left you.'

'But you did, and you can't turn back time and change it. It happened. You had your reasons for doubting my commitment to you. I neglected to give you the reassurance you needed, and I have to learn to live with that,' he breathed tautly.

'I had to live without you too,' Lara whispered shakily.

'But you *chose* to do that... I didn't. And I missed out on Freddy as a baby.'

'I can't change those things,' Lara pointed out wretchedly as her arms dropped from him.

'I know.' Gaetano bent his handsome dark head and claimed her lips with a hungry sound of urgency before she could step back from him. 'I'm working on myself,' he declared against her swollen mouth, returning for another taste with intense enthusiasm.

Three days later, Dario entered the nursery to find Lara reading Freddy his favourite storybook complete with all the choo-choo noises that accompanied it and made her son squeal with laughter. He held out an envelope. 'This came marked urgent. I guessed what it was and thought you'd like some privacy to open it.'

Lara smiled at him, marvelling at the change that

had occurred in their relationship. The longer she had known him, the friendlier and warmer Gaetano's right-hand man had become. She had begun to admire his efficiency, his fierce loyalty to Gaetano and his protectiveness towards him. She understood exactly what had caused his more aggressive attitude the first time they had met. His driving motivation was always Gaetano's wellbeing and if Gaetano had got himself into the wrong marriage, Dario would have been the first to help him to get out of it again.

Lara left her son to his nap and wandered off to the sitting room to open the letter. It had to be the DNA results. She tore it open and lifted out the paper within. A little scream of excitement broke from her parted lips. She had a sister, an actual living, breathing sister, which meant that she had a half-brother as well, not to mention a whole host of nieces and nephews! She performed a little happy dance in the middle of the room. She would finally be able to find out the whole story of who she was and where she came from and she could discover it all in private from the brother and sister who had been involved in that same story. She thought that would be wonderful.

She looked for Gaetano and couldn't find him. She headed for Dario's office, hoping he would be able to help her find her sister's email address or phone number, so that she could make the next move. She heard male voices within and hovered, reluctant to walk in on an official meeting of some kind. She smiled as she heard Gaetano speak, his deep dark voice louder than usual.

'I ignored all your advice and it's come back to bite me. I believed I was deceiving Lara! That was the price of getting them *both* home to Mosvakia. I had to make her believe that it was a reconciliation. I couldn't face a court battle for custody or doing anything more un-derhand, like luring her out here and then springing a custody suit on her in a Mosvakian court. And all the time I believed that we were happy because I was a great actor, I was *lying* to myself…in fact I was lying to my-self from the very minute I met her again!'

'You have to be the only person in the palace un-aware of that piece of self-deception.' Dario chuckled. 'In this one field alone, you have no game. I caught on to the true story before we even left England.'

Lara blinked, emerging from her daze, anguish claw-ing at her, destroying her happiness, her confidence, her calm. She couldn't breathe. It was as if someone had cut off her oxygen supply. She stumbled away, in search of a little dark hole to hide in. She had been so stupid, she had been so dreadfully stupid to trust him, particularly where Freddy was concerned.

It was obvious that Freddy, rather than Freddy's mother, had been Gaetano's most desired acquisition. He had wanted custody of his son and the easiest way to accomplish that goal had been to persuade Lara that he wanted a reconciliation. Well, he had got what he wanted. Could it be said that he was simply making the best of a bad job where their marriage was concerned? Since he was stuck with her anyway, he was suggest-ing they consider having another child. But why had he also said that he was afraid of her vanishing again?

Where's your wits, Lara? Of course, Gaetano would be afraid of that development because he knew that if she left, she would be taking his son with her. And there was no deception there, was there? Gaetano indisputably adored his son and enjoyed being a father. He took breaks in the busiest day to spend time with Freddy. And their son was equally attached to his father. Freddy was benefiting from having two parents in a stable relationship. So, an immediate desire to run and keep on running from Gaetano would be a bad, selfish idea, she acknowledged.

She walked into their bedroom, still struggling to catch her breath as she hung onto the door handle for support. She had believed what she wanted to believe: that Gaetano had genuinely missed her and wanted her back. It had been too good to be true, but she hadn't smelled a rat, had she? No, she had jumped back into his arms faster than the speed of light.

When had she forgotten that the guy she loved had been a notorious womaniser before their marriage? A man with loads of experience, practised at persuading women to believe what he wanted them to believe? So, he had given her the fairy story and she had swallowed it whole.

But this time he wasn't going to get away with chewing her up and spitting her out, she thought bitterly. This time, there would be a reckoning…

CHAPTER TEN

GAETANO FINALLY FOUND Lara lying fast asleep on their bed. He had looked everywhere else for her. The staff had been looking too. Her phone had been found in the nursery.

He had expected her to approach him once she'd received the news of the positive DNA test but she had kept her distance. Gaetano, on the other hand, hadn't had that luxury with her siblings. Ari Stefanos had phoned first and, assuming that Gaetano was already aware of that positive test, had asked when he could speak to his newly found sister because he wanted to arrange a visit to Mosvakia as soon as possible. Leah Zanetti had rung next, bubbling with excitement and enthusiasm, every bit as eager to meet Lara.

Gaetano had told them both that they were very welcome to visit and stay at the palace and was only a little taken aback when they announced that they would be arriving the following day. Presumably, Lara would be ecstatic because she would have them with her at the party.

Gaetano stared down at his slumbering wife. Sadly, Lara didn't look ecstatic about the discovery that she

had a new family. Weren't those tear stains on her
cheeks? Maybe it was just the emotional charge of that
new knowledge that had stressed her out and saddened
her. He was also wondering how she would handle the
rather forceful personalities he had recognised on the
phone. Lara was quiet, gentle and vulnerable and even
if she decided that she didn't much like Ari and Leah,
she would pretend otherwise because she was kind and
always thinking about other people's feelings. They
had better not hurt or disappoint her, Gaetano thought
grimly, *or* try to interfere in their marriage.

'Yes, I appreciate that you've been married for two
years but you didn't announce the marriage,' Ari Stefanos had reminded Gaetano sardonically on the phone.
'And from what I understand my sister was on her own
raising your child for those two years. Of course I've
got questions.'

So, no, Gaetano wasn't looking forward to meeting
Lara's brother and sister quite as much as he might have
been. He did not think that his past misunderstandings
with Lara were anyone's business but their own.

Lara came awake slowly and for a moment she
drifted until her brain kicked back into gear and then
she sat up with a start, thoroughly disconcerted to see
Gaetano working on his laptop at the table in the corner
of the room. Pushing her tumbled hair off her brow, she
mumbled, 'Why are you working in here?'

'I wanted to be here when you woke up. I was worried about you. I thought you'd come to tell me about
the positive DNA test but you didn't.'

'I fell asleep…not enough sleep last night,' she
framed, her cheeks warming, but for once she didn't

try to meet his liquid dark golden gaze with the under-standing mutual glow of a couple who were unable to keep their hands off each other for very long.

'My fault. Your brother and your sister will be fly-ing in tomorrow.'

'Tomorrow?' she prompted in shock.

'They're exceptionally keen to meet you. Both of them phoned but we couldn't track you down. You left your phone in the nursery,' he reminded her.

Lara groaned and breathed in slow and deep. Her plan to stage an immediate showdown with Gaetano was now impossible. She didn't want to stage a show of a troubled marriage for her new brother and sister. And naturally that would be a consequence of her tack-ling Gaetano head-on now about the fake reconcilia-tion tactics he had used on her. There would be a huge row. And after that, there would be no hope of hiding the tension and awkwardness between them. So, for the present, she had to hold her fire.

From below her feathery lashes, she studied him. In the well-tailored charcoal-grey suit that outlined his lithe, powerful physique, he was breathtakingly good-looking. Black hair, stunning dark deep-set eyes, per-fect bone structure. And on the surface, he was so courteous, considerate and supportive, but that could only be a smooth, sophisticated façade hiding the real truth of his feelings. Deep down inside he had to resent her for being so necessary to Freddy that she and her son were a package deal.

It was cold consolation that he had never said he loved her, but then she hadn't said those words either. At least he hadn't uttered that lie. It hardly mattered when

Gaetano had sucked her in and spat her out, shredding her heart all over again. What was it about him that got to her every time? No matter what he did, no matter how he behaved? She couldn't allow love to make a fool of her again. There had to be honesty without lies or pretty pretences.

'I thought you'd be more excited about your brother and sister.'

'I am, maybe just a little nervous. Are they bringing their families?'

'They didn't say. And we've plenty of space if they do but I would suspect they'll only bring their partners. I warned them about the party tomorrow night and told them that they're very welcome to join us,' he completed quietly.

As usual he had thought of everything. Her chest felt tight, her throat even tighter. She needed to get a grip on herself again, she told herself angrily. She needed to be the best actor she could be for the next day or so, at least until her siblings had departed again and she had the privacy to confront Gaetano. And what was she going to tell him?

Yes, what was she planning to call him out on? How dare you give me my dream marriage? How dare you make me happy? How dare you convince me that what we have is real when it's *not*? In truth, he might have lied but he had lived up to every one of his promises.

'You don't seem happy. You're not reacting the way I expected.' Gaetano rose with feral grace and dropped down on the side of the bed to curve an arm round her. 'What's worrying you? Are you afraid that they won't like you? Don't be daft. You're a lovely person and they'll see that in you, just as other people do.'

'Gaetano—' she said in embarrassment.

'You know, I used to be the kingpin around here, but I'm afraid Freddy outshines both of us. However, we've got a chef who wants to know how to fatten you up and I told him that there was no chance of doing that. And Dario wants to serve you up first to the Spanish ambassador because you speak Spanish.'

'Only some. Four years in Spain,' she reminded him unnecessarily.

'Your siblings will absolutely love you,' Gaetano asserted with confidence.

Lara felt as if her heart were cracking inside her, as if he had just put a hand inside her chest and squeezed it, because she loved him and almost every time he spoke he reminded her *why* she loved him. How could she still be feeling like that after what she had overheard?

Leah and Gio Zanetti and Ari Stefanos and his wife, Cleo, all flew in on the same flight and arrived at the palace together. Alice had been upset that she was unable to attend the party because an aunt had died suddenly, and she was driving up north to visit the family.

Lara was very nervous, but she need not have been because her sister, Leah, chattered away freely, releasing her from tongue-tied reticence. It was Leah's older brother, Ari, who told Leah to slow down before she frightened Lara off. Leah kept on staring at her and then apologised, digging into her capacious bag to pull out a small photo album. 'This is all I've got, I'm afraid. I went through several foster homes, and I lost stuff. But this is Mum and, although she's older than you here, you can see how much you resemble her and why I was totally knocked back when I saw that picture of you in the magazine.'

Lara stared down at the image and she too recognised the strong similarity in colouring and facial shape.

'You've got her eyes, absolutely her eyes!' Leah carolled. 'They're a very unusual shade.'

'Aquamarine,' Gaetano slotted in. 'The very first thing I noticed about Lara was her eyes.'

'Who's the little boy with you?' Lara asked her sister as she studied the photos.

And Leah told her about her twin brother, Lucas, who had died from an overdose. Lara's eyes swam with tears, and she sniffed, only beginning to regain her composure when Ari told her that Lucas and his girlfriend had left behind a baby, whom he and Cleo had adopted, a little girl they called Lucy.

'My goodness, there's so much I have to catch up on,' Lara exclaimed. 'But that was a wonderful conclusion to a sad story.'

'Twins run through the family. Ari was a twin. We have twins and Ari has a set too,' Leah told her. 'You've been warned.'

It wasn't very long before the three siblings were catching up on family history.

'Now I want to know how on earth you met and married a king!' Leah announced as Lara poured her fresh coffee.

'And why it took two years for Gaetano to bring you and your son back to the palace,' Ari completed more seriously, taking a seat beside Lara.

For the first time, Lara felt comfortable enough to tell other people that story with all its twists and turns and misunderstandings.

'Clearly you love him and if he makes you happy, I'm happy for you, but if you have any doubts, I hope you know that you can always come to Leah or me for support,' Ari completed before going on to tell her about her inheritance from her late father and a few more facts about the paternal half of her background.

Leah was more interested in finding out about Lara's life after the adoption and that took some time to cover and both women got quite emotional during the discussion.

'Mum would never ever have given you up if she'd lived and it would have broken her heart if she'd known what happened to you afterwards. I can't believe that you're not even still in contact with your adoptive mother.'

'She had no wish to stay in touch. I'm not part of her life any more. I'm used to it now.' A rueful smile lit Lara's face as Leah squeezed her shoulder in comfort.

'I want you to come to Italy and stay with us so that I can really get to know you. I've been longing to find my little sister ever since I lost her,' Leah told her evocatively. 'I held you in my arms and helped to feed you when you were only a few days old. But I never expected to find you living in a palace.'

'And I never expected to marry a royal! I'd love to come to Italy and stay with you,' Lara declared as she stood up. 'Now come and meet Freddy. I can't wait to meet your children.'

'I'd love you to visit Cleo and me in Greece as well,' Ari confided quietly.

Gaetano hovered, his lean, darkly handsome features taut and serious. 'I have a business meeting I can't cancel,' he said apologetically. 'But I'll see you all at lunch.'

Lunch went well. Leah opted to join Lara when the beauty stylist, organised for her, arrived to do her nails and hair and immediately called in back-up to look after Leah as well. Lara was more than ready for a little personal grooming help in advance of the party that evening. The number of confidences that her siblings had made had helped Lara to keep her mind busy and her spirits up, but once Leah left her to return to her room that overheard conversation between Gaetano and Dario returned to haunt Lara and it hit her mood hard.

Gaetano had only chosen to be with her for Freddy's sake. She remembered him telling her that his brother's marriage to Giulia had been one of convenience. Possibly that was one reason why he was willing to accept a similar arrangement for himself. But he *had* to feel that he was settling for less than he deserved. Freddy might benefit from having his mother, but Gaetano would be losing out in the personal stakes.

The more she thought about her situation, the angrier Lara became. Lara didn't care how good his intentions might have been. Gaetano hadn't given her a choice about what *she* wanted and needed. What she had learned had made her feel…*less*, decimating her pride and her confidence. She didn't want to be any man's second-best or convenient bride. She didn't want to be merely tolerated because she was Freddy's mother. She wanted to be loved, madly lusted after, *valued*. She didn't want to be the one who loved and lusted alone, always the bridesmaid, never the bride.

Clad in a pretty lingerie set from her new collection, Lara was tweaking her make-up in the en suite bathroom when Gaetano entered the bedroom to get changed. He paused in the doorway, shooting Lara an appreciative scrutiny. Her high full breasts artfully cradled in a strapless pale blue lace bra matched with bikini knickers made him release a low whistle. 'You look incredibly sexy in that get-up.'

Lara whirled round to face him. 'You deceived me!' she heard herself condemn out of hand, inwardly wincing but unable to suppress the angry swell pushing up inside her when she saw him. 'You let me think we were having a real reconciliation when all the time it was just a big fat *empty* fraud!'

Taken aback by that attack, Gaetano stared back at her with stunned intensity. 'Back up a minute…where is this coming from?'

'I heard you talking to Dario in your office.'

His brows pleated. 'Dario hasn't been in my office since yesterday.'

'So?' Lara interrupted aggressively, brows raised, mouth compressed. 'You think you're the only one around here who can pride themselves on their acting ability?'

'You mean you've been sitting on these crazy assumptions of yours since *yesterday*?' Gaetano demanded incredulously. 'All these nasty suspicions were going on below the surface and I had no blasted idea?'

The thundering annoyance in his raised voice only

provoked a shrug of Lara's slight shoulder. 'Not so nice, is it, when you're not the one in the know?' she quipped.

'Are you aware of that saying that eavesdroppers never hear good of themselves?' Gaetano asked grimly as he slid free of his jacket and yanked loose his tie to toss them back into the bedroom.

'Well, I heard the truth.'

'If you'd stayed long enough to hear the truth, you wouldn't be attacking me now!' Gaetano blitzed back with unhidden annoyance. 'And as you didn't stay, you didn't hear the whole conversation and went away with completely the *wrong* impression of what I was talking about.'

Lara shrugged another shoulder, her face tense. 'Of course, you're going to say something like that in circumstances like this. You want to put a lid on this argument before the party. You're going to make some very smooth and practised explanation and try to hang me out to dry and convince me that I didn't hear what I heard. I know how you operate.'

'There are some definite markers requiring further exploration in that speech, *bambola*—'

'Don't call me that now as if you're fond of me!' Lara practically spat at him in her rage. What was infuriating her most was that the angrier she became, the cooler and calmer Gaetano seemed to be.

'You don't think that I could possibly *be* fond of you? *Dio mio.* Evidently, no matter how smooth and practised you believe me to be, I seem to have failed utterly to impress you with my ability to be truthful and sincere.'

'Ha!' Lara snapped, unimpressed, as she pushed past him to return to the bedroom, stalking in her high heels.

'Back in England, you tied me into knots with your cleverly chosen words and I believed you every step of the way...so much for that!'

'And so much for your perception and self-belief,' Gaetano traded with sardonic clarity.

Hands on hips, Lara spun back to him. 'What's that supposed to mean? You implied that you regretted our marriage breakdown and that you wanted us to be a couple again.'

'As far as it goes, that was true. I knew that I had to bring Freddy back to Mosvakia and I didn't want to fight you through the courts for custody of him. I was determined not to frighten or intimidate you with threats of legal action.'

'I could have coped!' Lara slung back at him with determination.

'You didn't deserve that. You're a brilliant mother but Freddy is the heir to the throne, and I couldn't leave him with you in the UK. He needs to grow up here and learn about who he is. That's my duty: to do what's best for the Crown, regardless of how fair or unfair it is,' Gaetano breathed in a raw undertone. 'Freddy belongs with you *and* me and you belong with me as well. We're together. We're a family. No way was I prepared to fight you in court and threaten to take him away from you. He needs you every bit as much as he needs me.'

'So you lied to me by letting me believe that it was *me* you wanted back more than Freddy because you guessed that that would be a winning proposal.'

'Yes,' Gaetano conceded with none of her drama. 'But lying is a harsh description of what I did to get you both back.'

'Sorry if I offended!'

'I had no idea what my feelings for you were at the time,' Gaetano disconcerted her by admitting. 'I knew that I was still hugely attracted to you the instant I saw you again, but I was still at war with what happened when we fell in love two years ago.'

'At war?' she queried with a frown of incomprehension.

'You caused that war, Lara,' Gaetano told her. 'When you walked out and disappeared on me, I couldn't believe or accept that we *had* loved each other. People who love each other don't usually lose faith in each other that suddenly.'

Lara lost colour. 'I don't know what you're talking about.'

'Yes, you do. You just don't want to hear it,' Gaetano incised gravely. 'When you walked out, it made me doubt my feelings for you. The way I saw it, if you could walk away that easily you had never had true feelings for me. That fast I told myself that I'd never been in love with you even to begin with.'

'Two years ago I thought you regretted our marriage. I thought leaving and disappearing was the kindest thing I could do!' Lara shot back at him shakily, all her emotions swelling inside her tight chest.

'That may be true but that's not how it affected me. It wrecked me *and* the trust I had in you. Don't tell me that I didn't feel what I felt,' Gaetano warned her very seriously. 'You're not the only one of us who got badly hurt.'

Lara was trembling and thinking that wasn't it just typical that she confronted Gaetano and all of a sudden he was turning everything round and blaming her for walking out on him in the first place.

'Do you know how I managed without you? I told myself that I hadn't really loved you and that it was an infatuation. Back then, I didn't think I had it in me to fall in love as deeply and as fast as I did with you. So, naturally, it had to be an illusion.'

'I thought stuff like that too,' Lara confessed reluctantly.

'But I was wrong,' Gaetano declared. 'I really do wish you'd heard that whole conversation I had with Dario.'

Lara grimaced. 'I didn't want to listen to you laughing at me.'

'No, the laugh was entirely on me. I was finally admitting that I was as much in love with you as ever and Dario was the one laughing. He pointed out that everyone else in the palace had guessed how I felt about you *weeks* ago,' he confided.

Her aquamarine eyes had widened. 'In love with me?' she echoed blankly.

'You didn't guess?' Gaetano asked in surprise. 'I mean, Dario said I was about as subtle as a thunderstorm. He said I changed so fast from wanting a divorce to announcing our reconciliation that his head was left spinning. He worked out what was happening to me ages before I understood my own feelings.'

'Did he?' Lara whispered, still up in the air without a parachute and barely able to credit what Gaetano was telling her.

'I used Freddy and my desire not to engage in a court battle over him as an excuse to get you back. That approach was a sop to my pride. I wasn't ready to admit how I still felt about you.' Gaetano winced. 'I think I was even a bit scared to put myself out there with you again—'

Tears erupted from Lara's eyes, and she dashed them away with a trembling hand. Could she have been so stupid that she didn't recognise how he felt about her? She remembered Morocco, which had been one long, wonderful, magical honeymoon full of romance and tenderness and passion. She was in shock and yet when she looked back at the amount of daily attention and support he gave her, she was rocked by her own inability to acknowledge the love that he had shown her.

'And I'm still absolutely terrified of losing you again,' Gaetano breathed grimly.

'I need to apologise to you for not having faith in you and for not trusting my own judgement,' Lara whispered unevenly. 'I've suffered a lot of rejection in life from people I cared about, and I think I was much too quick to assume that you were rejecting me two years ago. That's sad because it means we lost out on each other, and you lost out on knowing Freddy from the beginning. But whether you find it hard to believe or not, I have always loved you…practically from the first moment I saw you and right up until now when you've got the courage to share how *you* feel.'

'And make you cry,' Gaetano pointed out ruefully. 'You're not just saying that you love me because you think that's what I need to hear?'

'Don't be silly,' Lara urged as she unbuttoned his shirt, and he took the hint and toed off his shoes. 'I love you to death and back.'

'And even last night when you thought I had deceived you, you *still*—'

Lara turned beet red. 'A good memory on that score is not always appreciated. I'm not very good at saying no to you.'

'Long may it last,' Gaetano husked with fervent appreciation and he lifted her to lay her down on the bed.

'You said you don't believe in it, but it was kind of love at first sight, wasn't it?' Lara prompted on the back of a blissful sigh and then she sat up with a start. 'The party! We can't do this now!'

Gaetano's lips claimed hers with scorching hunger and her spine liquefied, heat arrowing down into her pelvis. He followed her down onto the bed. He told her that he loved her again and she reciprocated with enthusiasm as he made her his again. It was fast and wildly passionate. In the aftermath of immense pleasure, her body feeling pleasantly floaty, she belatedly recalled the party and almost fell out of bed in her haste to get dressed. Gaetano was already out of the shower, and she raced in.

Arrayed in a fresh set of lacy lingerie, she lifted her ball gown. It ranged from a purple shade at the neck and slowly deepened down into the richest violet. Crystals were scattered across the full skirt and narrow diamanté straps crossed her shoulders catching the light. It was a dream of a dress, she thought happily as she eased her feet into her high heels.

'Let me help you with the jewellery,' Gaetano urged, flipping open the boxes stacked in readiness on the dresser and extracting a sapphire necklace to clasp it around her slender throat. 'You look utterly amazing, *bambola mia*.'

Lara donned the sapphire and diamond drop earrings and smiled at him, exhilaration brightening her eyes and lifting the curve of her lips. 'For the first time ever I feel amazing,' she told him honestly. 'I'm afraid we're late.'

'The main guests should make an entrance,' Gaetano teased.

'I love you,' she told him in the lift, a new confidence in her upright carriage.

'I love you even more,' he whispered as they stepped out into the glittering gathering of guests in the palace foyer, smiles on their faces, immense warmth in their hearts and contentment in their eyes.

EPILOGUE

Seven years later

LARA THOUGHT BACK to that wonderful party with Leah and Ari by her side, her brother and sister, who had been so proud to acknowledge their relationship, and she smiled. There had been many parties since then. Christmases, birthdays, christenings and holidays in the UK, Italy, Greece, Morocco and Mosvakia. Internationally based family members made for a lot of travel. And then there were the shopping trips she enjoyed with Leah and Cleo. The Christmas shopping trips were especially enjoyable.

'Why did you once tell me that you didn't like Christmas?' she had asked Gaetano a couple of years earlier as he'd helped her decorate one of the many festive trees in their wing of the palace.

'When I was a child, Vittorio only attended official celebrations and they were boring. By the time I got to eighteen, Christmas was just an endless string of exhausting parties. And *then*,' he had stressed, turning to look down at her possessively, 'I saw you in front of a Christmas tree and fell madly in love and that sort of jolted me out of my dislike of the season. It made Christmas a whole new occasion to appreciate. And then you gave me Freddy and the rest of our little tribe, and I realised Christmas is all about children having fun. I never had that, but I want our children to have it.'

It was their turn to stage the family Christmas this year and the palace was already hopping with children having a whale of a time. Freddy had discovered that his older cousin, Lucy, wasn't impressed when he announced that he was a prince and that he should be in charge even though he was younger. Gaetano had told his son that he should be looking out for his siblings, five-year-old Rosa and three-year-old Tommaso. Freddy had heaved a sigh of disgust, protesting that Tommaso was still a baby who ate with his fingers if he could get away with it, while Rosa insisted on lugging a baby doll and buggy everywhere.

Leah and Gio had three boys and two girls and Ari and Cleo had four boys and a girl, so the games they played could be fairly rough and lively, even with supervision. As far as Lara was concerned their own family was complete but Gaetano was trying to persuade her to consider one more pregnancy. She had said she would think about it while pointing out that they had so far contrived to miss out on a twin arrival, and it might not be wise to tempt providence. Gaetano, however, was very much of the 'more the merrier' persuasion and was willing to take that risk.

Life was good but frantically busy. Lara now had a busy social life. And as her confidence grew, she had ventured out from behind closed doors in the palace to take on a children's charity. Other responsibilities and requests for her presence had quickly followed. She had spread her wings a little but still zealously guarded her time with Gaetano and her children. Time went by so fast, and she didn't want to miss out on the children's early years.

Gaetano joined her in the once formal drawing room, which had all the space they needed to entertain her relatives and friends. Alice was joining them with her husband, Rory, Iris and her little boy, Amos. Dario and Carla, along with their baby, Sofia, would also be part of the festivities.

'You seem thoughtful,' Lara remarked as Gaetano studied her, his dark golden gaze brilliant below the thick canopy of his lashes.

'You look good,' he told her, scanning the short velvet fitted skirt she had teamed with a soft silk shirt, her shapely legs crossed and capped by slender high heels.

It was Christmas Eve and their wedding anniversary, and later, they would be having a special dinner with their family and friends and attending a carol service at midnight. The most beautiful tree took up the whole of one corner. It was the family tree, the one adorned with the children's hand-crafted gifts and ornaments that had been bought to commemorate certain events. Decorating it was an annual exercise of reliving fond memories.

'It scares me to think that I might never have met you,' Gaetano admitted, startling her. 'That bout of amnesia was the best thing that ever happened to me.'

Her aquamarine eyes widened in surprise. 'How can you say that?'

'I didn't know who I was, and the amnesia allowed

the *real* me to emerge…the guy I would have been had I not been born royal and conditioned to be a cold bastard,' he breathed through compressed lips. 'Vittorio did his best with me, but I was taught to suppress every normal emotion.'

'I know, but he was too buttoned up himself to see any other way of handling your temperament,' she told him gently, knowing how guilty he felt if he criticised his late brother.

'I didn't let loose until I met you and the instant I was free of those fetters, what did I do? I fell in love and married you within days and then, when I regained my memory, I thought that I must have been insane to do something like that. But in reality, I was doing what came naturally to me.'

'Only it shocked the life out of you when you recovered your memory and found a wedding ring on your finger,' Lara reminded him.

He stretched out a hand to her. 'Come here…' he urged and as she crossed the room he caught her hand in his and slid a glittering ring onto her finger. 'An eternity ring for our anniversary. Sapphires and emeralds to match your eyes, *bambola*.'

Her eyes shone. 'It's beautiful, Gaetano.'

'I was telling you the truth when I told you that I didn't have a single happy moment without you. I was re-energised the minute I saw you again, although I did try to play it cool,' he murmured with husky amusement. 'You transformed my life, and you gave me the strength to be the man I am now.'

When he looked at her in a certain way, her whole

body lit up like a traffic light and pulsed with sexual energy. 'I love you...'

Gaetano reached down to grasp her waist and hoisted her up against him. 'And I'm about to take advantage.'

'We *can't*!' Lara gasped. 'Our guests?'

Gaetano grinned down at her as he elbowed his way out of the room, taking the shortcut down a former servant's staircase to their bedroom. 'Already organised. Our guests are taking the kids to the Winter Fair to give us some downtime to celebrate our anniversary,' he imparted.

'You don't do that to your guests!' Lara moaned in horror.

'They're family and they understand that we can't help the fact that our anniversary is Christmas Eve and we're usually entertaining or in someone else's house. And thank you for making your family my family as well. Sometimes they come in very useful!' he teased.

Lara punched his shoulder in mock rebuke as he dropped her down on the bed and slipped off her heels, following her down to claim her mouth passionately with his own. Clothes fell away like confetti in a breeze. There was passion and laughter and joy and great tenderness. As usual, Gaetano's sheer intensity blew her away and, in the aftermath, she felt buoyant with happiness.

'I'm insanely in love with you,' he groaned into her tumbled hair, rolling back to keep her with him, both arms still wrapped round her, lean hands smoothing over her slender back with warm affection.

'I'm crazy about you, too,' Lara whispered, sinking deeper into contentment, a drowsy smile on her lips as she rested her head down on his shoulder, her nostrils flaring at the achingly familiar scent of his skin. She had the loving, supportive family that she had always craved and in addition she had Gaetano and their children. Life was better than she had ever believed it could be.

* * * * *

PREGNANT INNOCENT BEHIND THE VEIL

MICHELLE SMART

MILLS & BOON

This is for Mitchell.
I hope life brings you an abundance of joy. xxx

CHAPTER ONE

ALESSIA BERRUTI'S HAND shook as she pressed 'play' on her phone. The scene, one which had already been viewed by over two million people since its upload four hours earlier, was a wedding reception. Hundreds of finely dressed people were celebrating in a stateroom in the castle where the royal family of Ceres lived. The camera zoomed in on two women. The loud music and waves of surrounding conversation faded.

'Your brother looks smitten,' the blonde lady in the video footage said. Her voice, although pitched low, was clearly audible.

'He is.' The tiny, chestnut-haired woman who answered looked over her shoulder. The camera perfectly captured the face of Princess Alessia Berruti.

The blonde's voice dropped even lower. 'I wonder how Dominic's feeling right now, seeing his intended bride marry another man.'

'Who gives a…' A loud beep was dubbed over the princess's scathing retort. 'That man's an obese, sweaty, disgusting monster.'

'Don't hold back,' the blonde said with a laugh. 'Say what you really think.'

The princess laughed too and drank some more champagne before saying, 'Okay, what I *really* think is that King Dominic of Monte Cleure should be locked behind bars and never allowed within three kilometres of any woman ever again.'

The footage ended the moment Alessia's phone buzzed in her hand. It was her eldest brother, Amadeo.

'My quarters,' he said icily. 'Now.'

Four days later, Alessia covered her flaming face and wished for the chair she was sitting on to plunge her into a deep pit.

What had she done?

Trying her hardest not to cry again, she lifted her stare to Amadeo. His features were as taut and un-compromising as she had ever seen them. To his right, their mother, her expression as unyielding as her eldest son's. To their mother's right, their father, the only person in this whole room with a smidgeon of sympathy. She couldn't bring herself to look at the man sat on the other side of Amadeo, the final link in the human chain of disappointment and anger being aimed at her.

'I'm so sorry,' Alessia whispered for the third time. 'I had no idea I was being filmed.'

It was an excuse that cut no ice, not even with her.

One unguarded moment. That's all it had been. Un-guarded or not, she should have known better. She *did* know better. Her whole life had been spent having her basic human desires and reactions restrained so that she was always in total control of herself.

'I'll marry Dominic,' she blurted into the silence.

'I'm the one who's got us into this mess, I'm the one who should be punished. Not you.'

That had been the king's first demand in the Berrutis' valiant efforts to make amends. Marriage to Princess Alessia. It would show the world, so he said, that she had been jesting and that the Berruti royal family respected him. That the world had already got wind that he'd once made overtures about marriage to the princess and been politely rebuffed mattered not a jot to him. King Dominic had thicker skin than a rhinoceros. He also had the vanity of a peacock and the cruelty of a medieval despot. So atrocious was his reputation that not a single eligible female member of any European royal family had agreed to a date, let alone marriage. Dominic's desperation for a blue-blooded bride had seen him trick a very distant relation of the current British monarch to his principality and then hold her hostage until she agreed to marry him. His victim escaped barely an hour before her forced nuptials when Alessia's other brother, Marcelo, rescued her to worldwide amazement and Dominic's fury, and married her for himself. It was at Marcelo and Clara's wedding reception that Alessia had opened her mouth and made the simmering relations between the two nations boil over.

'Don't think I've not been tempted,' Amadeo said grimly at the same moment their father stated, 'Out of the question.'

'But why should Amadeo have to give up his whole life for something that's my fault?' she implored.

'Because, sister,' Amadeo answered, 'tempting though it may be to insist you marry that man, I wouldn't marry someone I hate to him never mind my own sister.'

A tear leaked out and rolled down her cheek. She wiped it away. 'But this is *my* fault. Surely there's a way to make amends and bring peace to our countries without you having to do this?'

The man Alessia had been cursorily introduced to three days ago addressed her directly for the first time. 'This is the one resolution satisfactory to both parties.'

Gabriel Serres. The 'fixer' brought in by her parents and brother to fix the mess and bring peace to Ceres and Monte Cleure, and the most handsome man she'd ever laid eyes on. She'd taken one look at him and, for a few short moments, all her troubles had blown out of her mind.

For three days Gabriel had flown back and forth between their Mediterranean island and the European principality, negotiating between the two parties. Alessia, in disgrace for pouring fuel over the simmering tensions between the two nations, had, to her immense frustration, been cut off from the negotiations. Until now. When the deal was done.

Done deal or not, that didn't stop her arguing against it. 'How can Amadeo marrying a complete stranger be satisfactory?'

'The bride is the king's cousin. Their marriage will unify the two nations, reopen diplomatic ties and prevent a costly trade war,' Gabriel reminded the princess with deliberate indifference.

His indifference was usually effortless. A man did not reach the top of the diplomatic field by getting emotionally involved in the disputes he was paid to resolve, but he'd found himself having to work at maintaining his usual detachment since Alessia had entered the meeting room. Dressed in a pair of tight-fitted, cropped black trousers topped with a loose, white scooped top, her straight dark chestnut hair hung loose around her shoulders. A puffiness to her dark brown eyes suggested she'd been crying, and he could see she was battling to maintain her composure. Like her mother, Queen Isabella, the princess was tiny, more so in the flesh than in the constant ream of photographs the press so loved to publish of her. In the flesh, there was something about her that brought to mind the spinning ballerina in his sister's old musical jewellery box.

Since their introduction three days ago, he'd found his mind wandering to her in ways that could not be classed as professional. The few times he'd spotted her in the distance had made him give double takes, and he'd had to consciously stop himself from staring at her. Yesterday, on a brief visit back to the castle, he'd been getting out of his car when she'd appeared, flanked by her bodyguards, clearly about to head off somewhere. Their eyes had caught and held. Just for a moment. But it had been moment enough for a frisson to race through his veins. It had been moment enough for him to see the mirroring flash of awareness in her eyes.

He supposed any red-blooded man would find the princess attractive but it was a rare occasion Gabriel found himself noticing someone's desirability when working. Single-minded focus and a refusal to accept failure were traits that had helped make him one of the world's leading negotiators. There was not a top agency in the world that hadn't, at some point, called in his services. His services were simple—he acted as a bridge between warring peoples, be they businesses, government agencies or a division of the UN. His skills meant that disputes were resolved without either side losing face.

He charged a hefty fee for those services. A diplomatic Svengali who worked under the radar of the press, he also had a canny eye for start-ups with potential and, as such, his investments had made him rich beyond his wildest dreams. Gabriel Serres was the billionaire no one had heard of. Intensely private and disdaining of the celebrity-fixated world, this anonymity was exactly how he liked it. His affairs—though he disliked calling them affairs when they involved two consenting adults enjoying each other until the time came to move on—were conducted under the same intense bounds of privacy, and never with a client. To find himself attracted to his client's daughter, a woman who lived her life in the glare of a media circus, was disconcerting to say the least. Gabriel's childhood had been one huge media circus, and it was a state of being he'd actively avoided ever since.

'And what of his bride?' the object of his attraction bit out in the husky voice that evoked thoughts of dark, sultry rooms and sensual pleasure. 'Does she get a say in it? Or is she being married against her will and without her consent?'

Her anger and concern was genuine, he recognised. Princess Alessia Berruti, the darling of the European press, a woman who'd mastered the art of social media to display herself and her royal family in the best possible attention-grabbing light, was not as self-centred as he'd presumed.

'She has agreed to the marriage,' he assured her.

Gabriel's expression was indifferent, his smooth, accented voice—an accent Alessia couldn't place—dispassionate, but there was something about the laser of his brown stare and the timbre in his tone that sent a shiver racing up her spine. It was a shiver that managed to be warm and was far from unpleasant. For the beat of an instant, a connection passed between them, sending another warm shiver coiling through her. But then he snapped his eyes shut and when they next locked on hers, the dispassion in his voice was matched in his returning stare.

A man clearly used to being listened to and heeded, Gabriel Serres had a presence that commanded attention even when he wasn't speaking. Alessia had noticed him a number of times since their introduction and, though most of those times he'd been at a distance from her—apart from in the castle's private car park when she'd come close to losing her footing when their eyes had suddenly met—he'd certainly commanded *her* attention. There was something about him she found difficult to tear her gaze from, something that made her belly warm and soften even though she'd come to the conclusion that there was nothing warm or soft about him. Under the impeccably tailored grey suit lay an obviously hard, lean body that perfectly matched a hard, angular face with hooded dark brown eyes that were as warm as a frozen waterfall. Even his thick black hair had been tamed into a quiff she doubted dared escape its confines.

Anger rising that he could be so detached about a situation where a woman was required to give her entire future just to save her family's skin, Alessia eyeballed him and snapped. 'What, like Clara consented?'

'It has been agreed,' her mother said in a voice that brooked no further argument. 'Gabriel has gone to great lengths to bring a rapprochement between our nations. Your brother is in agreement, the king is in agreement and the bride is in agreement. The wedding preparations start now. The pre-wedding party will be held in two weeks, the wedding in six. You will be a bridesmaid and you will smile and show the world how happy you are for the union. We all will.' And with that, her mother rose with the innate grace only a born queen had, and swept out of the room without another look at her youngest child.

Devastated to have caused her mother such disappointment and realising she was in danger of going into a full-blown meltdown in front of her father, brother, Ice Man and the staff, Alessia got to her feet. Casting each of them a withering stare, she left the meeting room with her head as high as she could manage.

Gabriel had a tension headache, caused no doubt by three days of intense negotiations between a despotic king and a rival royal family desperately trying to salvage their own image. Having had little sleep in that period didn't help, and neither did the engine problem with his plane he'd been notified about earlier. His plan to leave the Berrutis' castle and fly home to Spain delayed, he'd accepted King Julius's offer of a bed for the night. After dining with the king and queen and the heir to the throne, he was escorted through the warren of wide corridors to his appointed quarters. Once inside, he rolled his neck and shoulders and took a shower.

As far as royal families went, the Berrutis were relatively decent. Relatively. They inhabited a privileged world where, by virtue of their births, they were exalted and deferred to from their very first breaths, and, as such, took being exalted and deferred to as their due. Compared to King Dominic Fernandes, however, they were modest paragons of virtue. Gabriel cared little either way. His job was to be impartial and broker an agreement both parties could live with and he'd done that. Negotiating a marriage was, however, a first, and had left a bad taste in his mouth, which he unsuccessfully tried to scrub out with his toothbrush. He was quite sure Princess Alessia's outrage about the marriage had contributed to the acrid taste on his tongue.

Despite his exhaustion, Gabriel was too wired to sleep. After twenty minutes of his eyes refusing to close and fighting his mind's desire to conjure the pint-sized princess, he gave up and threw the bedsheets off. Pulling on a pair of trousers, he prowled the quarters he'd been appointed, found a fully stocked bar and helped himself to a bourbon. If he wished, he could lift the receiver on the bar and call the castle kitchen, where an on-duty chef would prepare anything he desired. He would give the Berrutis their due, they were excellent hosts.

Taking the bottle of bourbon with him, he opened the French doors in his bedroom and stepped onto the balcony. The warm air of the night had lost much of the day's humidity, the distant full moon lighting the castle's extensive grounds. With a strong gothic feel, it was an intriguing castle dating back to the medieval period, and full of mysteries and secrets. In the distance he could see the ancient amphitheatre, which divided the castle's two main sections...

His thoughts cut away from him as the strong feeling of being watched made the hairs on the back of his neck rise.

Alessia had been laid in her hammock for hours. Unable to face another meal with her family, unable to bear seeing more of her mother's disappointment, unable to look at the brother whose life she'd ruined, she felt desperately alone, wracked with guilt and so very ashamed. Now, though, her heart was thumping, because a man had emerged through the shadows on the adjoining balcony, and as he turned his head in her direction her heart thumped even harder as recognition kicked in.

It was *him*. The gorgeous Ice Man who made her belly flip.

Under the moonlight, he somehow seemed even more devastatingly attractive, and she sucked in a breath as her gaze drifted over a rampantly masculine bare chest.

For a long, long moment, all the demons in her head flew away in the face of such a divine specimen of manhood.

Suddenly certain her misery had conjured him, she blinked hard to clear his image, but it didn't clear anything. That really was the gorgeous Ice Man.

Impulse took over and before she could stop herself, she called out. 'Having trouble sleeping too?'

Gabriel's heart smashed in instant recognition of the

husky voice. Holding his breath, he rested an arm on the ancient waist-high stone balustrade that adjoined the neighbouring balcony, and peered into the adjoining space. There he found, laid out on a hammock in the moonlight's shadow, the woman whose unguarded words had almost caused a war between two nations and whose image had prevented him from sleeping.

He cursed silently even as his heart clattered harder into his ribs. He'd been unaware his appointed quarters adjoined hers.

'Good evening, Your Highness,' he said politely. 'My apologies for disturbing you.'

Though her spot in the shadows prevented him from seeing her features clearly, he could feel her gaze on him.

'You're not disturbing me… Is that a bottle of scotch you're carrying?'

'Bourbon.'

'Can I have some?'

The silence that fell during his hesitation was absolute. The last thing he should encourage was a late-night conversation with the beautiful princess who'd occupied so much of his thoughts these last few days.

'Please? I could do with a drink.'

What harm could a quick drink with each remaining on their respective sides of the balcony do? He would make sure it was a quick drink. Allow her one nip and then make his excuses and return to his room. 'Of course.'

She climbed off the hammock and padded barefoot to him. As she drew closer and out of the shadows, he barely had time to register that she was wearing pretty,

short pyjamas before she put her hands on the balustrade—she was so short her shoulders barely reached
the top of it—and, with an effortless grace, swung herself over. In seconds she stood before him, the moonlight pouring on her casting her in an ethereal light that
highlighted her delicate beauty and gave the illusion of
her dark velvet eyes being limitless pools.

Spellbound, for perhaps the first time in his life, Gabriel found himself at a loss for words.

CHAPTER TWO

THERE WAS AN intensity in the princess's stare before her chest rose and she indicated the bottle engulfed in Gabriel's hand. 'May I?'

A cloud of soft, fruity scent seeped into his airwaves and darted through his senses.

Dragging himself back to the here and now, he forced a tight smile and passed it to her.

'Thanks.' She unscrewed the cap and placed it to her lips. Her small but perfectly formed mouth was one of the first things he'd noticed about her. It was like a rosebud on the cusp of blooming. She took a long drink and swallowed without so much as a flinch then delicately brushed the residue with a sweep of an elegant finger. Everything about her was elegant. Graceful.

She bestowed him with a small, sad smile that did something funny to his chest. 'May I sit?'

His next forced smile almost made his face crack. 'Of course.'

Carrying the bottle to the balcony's deep L-shaped sofa, the princess sank elegantly onto the L part and stretched her legs out, hooking her ankles together. The shorts of her pale blue pyjamas had risen to the tops of her thighs and he hastily cast his gaze down. The toes at the end of feet that were the smallest he'd ever seen on a grown woman were painted deep blue. It was a colour that complemented her golden skin and set off the delicate shapeliness of legs that appeared almost impossibly smooth.

His veins heating with dangerous awareness, Gabriel dragged his gaze from the princess's feet and looked back in her eyes…only to find himself trapped again in those beguiling orbs.

Her stare fixed on him, she took another drink of bourbon. 'Don't worry, I won't stay long,' she said softly in that husky voice. She pulled another sad smile and shrugged. 'Looks like it's true that misery loves company.'

'You are unhappy?' he asked before he could stop himself.

He shouldn't encourage conversation. The moonlight, the all-pervading silence in the air around them… it lent an intimacy to the balcony setting that made his skin tingle and heightened his senses.

'I…' She cut herself off and closed her eyes. After a mediative breath, she looked back at him, her features showing she'd composed herself. She indicated the space next to her. 'Don't stand on ceremony on my account.'

He inclined his head, thinking hard as to how to extract himself from this situation but coming up with nothing. 'You're a princess. As a commoner, I thought it was my duty to stand on ceremony.'

Her cheeks pulled into a smile fractionally wider than he'd seen from her before, and in a faintly teasing voice, she said, 'Then as a princess of this castle, I invite you to sit on the sofa of your own balcony in your own quarters.'

Alessia looked into the eyes of the man standing so rigidly he could have a pole for a spine. When he finally sat, placing himself far at the other end of the sofa, it was with the same rigidity that he'd stood.

It was nothing but a mad impulse that had made her call out to him. Nothing but a second mad impulse that had made her swing over the balustrade to his balcony. And now she was sat on his balcony sofa. Sat alone with a bare-chested man in the middle of the night where the only living beings observing them were crickets and frogs and the other nocturnal creatures who played and sang and mated when the sun went down.

'I didn't realise you'd stayed,' she said when he made no effort at conversation.

'There is a problem with my plane's engine. It should be fixed by the morning. Your parents kindly invited me to stay the night.'

'That's my parents,' she said with a muted laugh, and drank some more bourbon. 'Kindness personified.'

She saw the raising of a thick, black brow at this but his firm lips stayed closed.

Feeling a stab of disloyalty for her slight on her parents, she changed the subject. Not that he'd allowed himself to be drawn into it. Was that discretion on his part or a lack of interest? She'd seen the way he looked at her, sensed he was attracted to her, but that didn't mean he liked her. After all, he had spent the last three days clearing up the mess she'd made. He probably thought her a vacuous troublemaker who'd brought shame on her family. The latter part was true but the former…? No. Alessia had put duty first her entire life. Maybe that's where the guilt at her disloyalty had come from—the Berrutis did not bad-mouth each other to outsiders. Their loyalty was to the monarchy as an institution first, and then to their people, and then to each other as family. 'Where are you from? I can't place your accent.'

Gabriel breathed in deeply. He wanted to ask her to return to her own quarters but was conscious that this magnificent castle was the princess's home. And conscious that she was a princess used to being deferred to. She would not take kindly to being ordered about by a commoner, and his brain ticked quickly as he tried to work out how he could extract himself from this situation without offending her. A man did not reach the heights Gabriel had in the diplomatic world by offending clients or members of their families.

Those were the reasons he tried to convince himself as to why he'd not already asked her to leave. The pulses throbbing throughout his body proved the lie. Those pulses had been throbbing since the moonlight had bathed her in its silver glow, a shimmering mirage made of flesh and blood.

Alessia Berruti was a princess, yes, but she was also a woman. A highly desirable woman.

He fisted his hands and clenched his jaw.

Alessia Berruti was a highly desirable woman he couldn't touch. Shouldn't touch. Mustn't touch.

'My mother is French, my father is Spanish,' he said in his practised even tone. 'I spent my formative years in Paris but I was raised to be bilingual.'

'You're fluent in both languages?'

'Yes.'

'And you speak Italian like a native too… Impressive.'

He didn't respond. He would not encourage this conversation. Without any encouragement, she would bore of his company and leave.

'Do you speak other languages?'

He wouldn't encourage her but it would be the height of rudeness to ignore a direct question. 'Yes.'

This was like getting blood from a stone, Alessia thought, but instead of deterring her, it only intrigued her. Most people when finding themselves in a private conversation with her fawned and flattered and set out to impress. Others became tongue-tied—it was the cloud of 'celebrity' around her that caused it—but long experience at putting those people at ease usually found them loosening up quickly. Gabriel, though, was neither of those people. He was a man who dealt with powerful people and institutions on a daily basis, and carried an air of power and authority in his own right, and everything about his body language was telling her he wanted her to leave. Which only intrigued her more. Because she'd seen that expression in his eyes which had pulsed with something quite different. 'Which ones?'

'English, German and Portuguese.'

'You're fluent in six languages? That really is impressive.'

Yet more non-response.

'Do languages come naturally to you?'

There was an almost imperceptible sigh before he answered. 'Yes.'

'I speak English fluently, but that's because I went to boarding school there,' she told him. 'I can converse in Spanish as long as it's taken at a slow pace, but my French is pretty basic, my German diabolical and I've never learned any Portuguese.'

She thought she caught a glimmer of humour on Gabriel's poker face.

'I suppose good linguistic skills are essential for your line of work,' she mused into the latest bout of silence, inordinately pleased to have made his face crack into a smile, as tepid as that smile might have been. Gabriel was so serious that she wondered if he ever truly smiled. She wondered if he ever allowed himself to. He was the most intriguing person she'd met in a long, long time. Maybe ever.

'Yes.'

'And what made you choose diplomacy as a career? I don't imagine it came up on a list of career choices when you were at school.'

Another quickly vanishing glimmer of humour. 'I learned at a young age that I had an aptitude for diplomacy.'

'Who discovers something like that?'

'I did.'

'How?'

Those dreamy light brown eyes suddenly fixed on her. A charge laced her spine, even stronger than the shiver she'd experienced when gazing at him earlier. 'Forgive me, Your Highness, but that is personal.'

The sudden flash of steel she caught told her his wish for forgiveness was pure lip service. He was giving her a diplomatic answer that translated into *mind your own business*.

Another charge thrummed through her. This man was no sycophant. This man had a core of steel. That self-containment, coupled with his drop-dead gorgeous looks and tripled with the innate self-confidence that oozed from his bronzed skin, made him the sexiest man she'd ever laid eyes on.

'That's perfectly reasonable,' she assured him although she was perfectly certain he didn't want or care for her assurance. 'And please, call me Alessia.'

His jaw tightened but he inclined his head in acknowledgement.

She took another drink of the bourbon, allowing herself a glance over the sculpturally perfect chest she found so fascinating. The moonlight had turned the bronze silver, and if not for the dark hair covering so much of the chest and forearms, she could believe he'd been cast in it.

'Where do you live?' she asked, passing the bottle to him. 'If that's not considered too personal a question.'

She noticed he made sure not to allow their fingers to touch as he took it from her.

'I travel a lot with my work.' He poured a small measure into a glass she hadn't even noticed him holding.

'I'd already gathered that, but you must have a place you call home.'

She noticed his jaw clenching. 'I consider Spain to be my home.'

'Which part?'

'Madrid.'

'I've visited Madrid many times. It's a beautiful city.'

He took a large sip of the bourbon and swirled it in his mouth a long time before swallowing. His throat was as sculpturally perfect as the rest of him.

'You don't like me, do you?' she said after another bout of lengthy silence.

That strong, perfect throat moved before he answered. 'What makes you think that?'

'Just a feeling. And you didn't deny it.'

'I cannot help how you feel.' He drank the rest of his bourbon.

'Do you blame me for the mess between my family and Dominic?'

'It is not my place to cast blame.' He poured himself another measure. 'My role is only to find solutions all parties can live with.'

'Your role doesn't prevent you forming opinions.'

'It prevents me voicing them.' He extended the bottle to her.

Her fingers brushed against his as she took it from him. The electric shock that flew through her skin was so strong that her eyes widened at the same moment Gabriel yanked his hand back as if he too had felt the burn. It took her a beat to find her voice again. 'So you do have opinions?'

'Everyone has opinions. Not everyone has the sense to know when those opinions should not be voiced.'

'Like when I voiced my opinion on Dominic?'

An extremely thick black eyebrow rose but his answer was a diplomatic, 'If people only voiced their opinions at appropriate times, I would be out of a job.'

She considered this with a small laugh. 'Then you should be grateful to me...' She winced and shook her head. 'Forget I said that. It was crass of me.' She sighed. 'And I owe you an apology too, for the way I spoke to you earlier. My tone was rude. I apologise.'

There was a detectable softening in his stare and in his voice too when he said, 'You were upset.'

'There is never an excuse for rudeness.'

'But there is often a reason for it,' he countered with the ghost of a smile and a glint in his eye that said far more than would come from his mouth, and she realised that he understood.

To Alessia's horror, hot tears welled up. She didn't want to cry. She had no idea why but the last thing she wanted was to appear weak and fragile in Gabriel's eyes. She suspected he had no time for weak and fragile women. She *wasn't* a weak and fragile woman. She wasn't. Not normally. Tiny but Mighty, her brother Marcelo used to call her. But Marcelo wasn't there: the one member of her family she could usually rely on for support was abroad on his honeymoon, and she'd had to suffer days of everyone else's anger and disapproval without any respite, so to have this man of all people offer her a crumb of comfort... It only made all the guilt and anguish she'd been suffering, which had diminished in the excitement of Gabriel's appearance, rise back to the surface.

A tear rolled down her cheek. She wiped it away and tried desperately to compose herself. In that moment it felt like one more blow could shatter her to pieces. 'I just feel so responsible about everything. Not just Amadeo's marriage but everything.'

He gazed at her for the longest time, piercingly intense eyes slightly narrowed, his mouth a straight line, as if he were weighing whether to speak what was on his mind. And then he closed his eyes briefly and inhaled. When his eyes snapped back on hers, he leaned a little closer and said in a low timbre, 'What you said at your brother's wedding was just one piece of a large jigsaw of enmity between your nation and Dominic's. You were not responsible for anything that occurred beforehand. The structural damage between the two nations had already been done.'

Alessia had no idea why this attempt at reassurance made her feel worse, but the tears she'd been fighting burst free and tumbled down her face like a waterfall before she could do anything to stop them.

With a sharp tightening in his chest and guts, Gabriel closed his eyes to the sobbing princess.

His sister had been a master at turning on the tears, using them as a weapon to manipulate their warring parents in her favour. He'd rather admired her for it. Since he'd left home, though, the women he'd chosen to acquaint himself with were women like himself: reserved, stoical and never prone to histrionics. As a result, he had no idea how he was supposed to handle this situation. He couldn't throw money or the promise of clothes or the promise of a specially wanted treat at Alessia as his parents had done when Mariella turned on the waterworks. So, when he opened his eyes and found her knees brought to her chest and her face buried in them, one hand still clinging tightly to the bottle of bourbon, he did the one thing he really didn't want to do, and moved closer to her.

First removing the bottle and placing it on the floor, he then patted her heaving shoulders in what he hoped was a reassuring manner. To his consternation, she twisted into him. A slender arm snaked around his waist, and then she sagged against him and wept into his chest.

'I'm sorry,' she sobbed. 'I don't want to cry but I just feel so bad. One unthinking comment and now Amadeo has to marry a stranger and an unwilling woman is being forced into marriage with him, and it's all my fault.'

Gabriel closed his eyes again and gritted his teeth, trying to block out the sensory overload of having this most beautiful of women crying in his arms. It had been a battle he'd fought since Alessia had joined him, uninvited, on his balcony.

He'd never been in a situation like this before. For sure, there had been women who'd invited themselves into his space through the years—the foreign minister of a Scandinavian country who'd turned up at the door of his hotel room with a bottle of Dom Pérignon came to mind—and he'd been able to disentangle himself from those potentially dangerous situations with no harm done and no hurt feelings. The difference, he knew, was that he'd not been attracted to any of those women. Gabriel was select in his choice of lovers. A celebrity princess who also happened to be a close family member of an existing client—the very reason for his being employed by that client—was as far removed as a choice of lover as he would ever make, and yet there wasn't a cell in his body that hadn't attuned itself to her since she'd called out to him from the shadows in that sexy, husky voice.

The rack of her distress, though, wove through his

veins to penetrate his heart, and the instinct to comfort overrode the last of his self-preservation. Gabriel wrapped an arm around her and held her tightly to him.

Dios, his heart was thumping.

Nothing was said for the longest time as, slowly, Alessia's sobs subsided.

He could feel the heat of her breath against the dampness of her tears on his naked chest.

Swallowing hard, knowing that with every second that passed with his arms around her he was dancing with danger, Gabriel rested his chin on her head and quietly said, 'I know you're concerned for Amadeo's bride, but I assure you, she is willing.'

'How can you know that?' She squeezed her arm even tighter around him, her husky voice muffled. 'Dominic doesn't believe in giving women choices. He held Clara against her will and would have forced her down the aisle if Marcelo hadn't rescued her.'

'I know because I spoke to Elsbeth privately to satisfy myself that she was a willing participant. I do have principles and there is no sum of money on earth that would see me be party to a forced marriage.'

Slowly, the princess lifted her face and gazed into his eyes. 'How can you be so sure? Dominic might have forced her to lie. He might have guessed that you would want to speak with her privately.'

It was staring into those dark, velvet orbs that made it a sudden effort to speak and filled his veins with lava. Just unimaginable depths…

He had to clear his throat to speak. 'The eyes don't lie, Princess. You have to take my word that her eyes showed only excitement. She's glad to be leaving Monte Cleure.'

And his loins were trying to show *their* excitement. They were responding to the princess being pressed so tightly against him, the feel of her small breasts jutting into his naked chest… The telltale tug of arousal battled for supremacy against his willpower and, for the first time in decades, it was winning.

Her brow furrowed. 'Excitement?' she asked doubtfully.

He needed to extract himself from this situation right now. To stay like this would be madness. *Was* madness.

'Think about it,' he murmured roughly, clenching the silk of her pyjama vest top to stop himself from slipping a hand beneath it. 'Why did your family refuse to entertain the notion of you marrying Dominic, even before he kidnapped Clara?'

Understanding glimmered in the warm depths of her brown eyes. 'Because he's a monster,' she whispered.

Unwilling to incriminate himself verbally, Gabriel inclined his head and, for no good reason, inched his face closer to hers. Now he could smell the underlying scent of the princess's skin beneath the soft fruitiness. It was intoxicating. As intoxicating as the sight of those pretty rosebud lips barely inches from his own. 'Now put yourself in her shoes,' he said, his voice so low even he struggled to hear it. 'If you were a member of the Fernandes royal family living under Dominic's rule and the opportunity came for you to marry into another royal family with a more…' So many heady feelings were shooting and weaving through him that he had to grope for the word. '*Benign* reputation, what would you do?'

Dominic's rule over his people was absolute. His rule over his family, especially the female members, was a clenched iron glove.

And this woman, this sexy, beautiful, fragile woman, had wanted to marry him to right the wrong of the mess she'd created.

He could never have been party to negotiations in which Alessia had been the pawn, he realised hazily, soaking in every delicate feature of her face. Not even if she'd been a willing pawn as Amadeo's bride was.

Alessia had become so spellbound by Gabriel's eyes that his words had dissolved into nothing but a caress to her senses. She'd thought he had brown eyes like her own but the irises were so transparent that, this close, it was like looking into golden supernovas ringing around pulsating black holes.

To think she'd thought his eyes cold when they contained such life and colour and fired such warmth that their radiation was heating her insides in a way she'd never felt before. Or was it the warmth of his hard body heating her veins and melting her deep in the secret place no man had touched before?

She supposed she should move her arm from around his waist but right then his solid comfort and the warmth of his flesh seeping through the thin fabric of her pyjamas made her reluctant to do what propriety said she should do.

She'd never been held by a man like this before.

Still staring into his eyes, she whispered, 'I'm sorry for making a scene.'

A finger dragged gently along her cheekbone. 'You haven't.'

She shivered and pressed herself closer.

He was divine, she thought dimly, from the thick black eyebrows to the long straight nose to the angular jaw that had been clean shaven only hours before but was now covered in thick black stubble. That stubble carried on down to his strong neck until it tapered away leaving bronzed skin so smooth that her hand tugged itself from its hold around his back to skim lightly up the hard planes of his chest to gently palm his throat and feel the smoothness for herself.

If someone had told Gabriel that morning that he would end the day in the battle of his life, he would have laughed disdainfully, but now, trapped in the seductive gaze of this incredibly sexy and enthrallingly beautiful woman, the darts of arousal he'd been fighting had turned into flames and his efforts to remember all the reasons he needed to resist these feelings for her were fading. Thoughts themselves had become ephemeral clouds, and when the elegant fingers stroked his neck at the same moment the rosebud lips parted, a jolt of electricity struck that vanquished the clouds leaving only the man in his rawest form.

CHAPTER THREE

ALESSIA HAD BEEN kissed only once. It had been at the leaving ball at her English boarding school at which sixth formers from the twinned boy's school nearby had been invited. Drinks had been spiked and inhibitions, which a born princess like Alessia had in spades, were dismantled. What she remembered most about that kiss was its slobberiness. In the five years that had passed, she'd looked back on that night with a certain wistfulness. If she'd known it would be her only kiss she would have made the most of it, slobberiness or not. It wasn't that Alessia prized her virginity, more that she was acutely aware of her position and that the eyes of the world followed her whenever she left the castle grounds. Many of the eligible men she came across were either sycophants or leeches or brimming with pomposity. Often all three. If she was to be linked to a man, the press would make a huge deal about it, and if she was to put herself under what would be an even greater microscope than the one dealt with on a daily basis then that man needed to be worth it. She wanted to respect the man she gave her heart to, and be confident that he wouldn't sell stories about her or her family. No such man had come into her life.

When Gabriel's firm mouth found hers, the feelings that engulfed her were so incredible that it made her five-year kissing abstinence worthwhile.

Now *this* was a kiss…

Alessia closed her eyes and sank into the headiness of a mouth that sent sensation thrumming through her lips and over her skin and then seeped beneath the flesh to awaken every cell in her body.

Wrapping her arms tightly around his neck, her hunger unleashed and she returned the kiss with all the passion that had hidden dormant for so long inside her. At the first stroke of his tongue against hers, the heat that filled her insides was strong enough to melt bone, and when his hands roamed the planes of her back there was only a dim shock that she had, at some point since their mouths found each other, shifted her body so that she was straddling his lap.

She didn't want to think, she thought dreamily as his mouth broke from hers and dipped down to the sensitive skin of her neck and his hands lifted her silk pyjama vest top up and over her head. If a touch and a kiss could evoke such wonderful pleasure then she wanted to fall into it.

For the first time in her life, she wanted to forget who she was and all the expectations she put on herself for being Princess Alessia, and let all the demons be thrown aside and just *feel*, because she'd had no idea that feeling could be so incredible.

A voice in her head whispered that she should tell Gabriel she was a virgin…

She pushed the voice away.

The moment the pyjama top was discarded, Gabriel cupped her cheeks tightly and kissed her with an ardency that sent more incredible tingles racing through her. Alessia dove her fingers through the thick black hair and moaned when his mouth assaulted her neck again, gladly letting his hands manipulate her into arching her back so he could take one of her breasts into his mouth. At the first flicker of his tongue against her erect nipple, she gasped at the thrill of pleasure, and dug her fingers even harder against his skull, and when she shifted slightly and felt the hard wedge pressing against the apex of her thighs, instinct had her press down and gasp even louder at the pulsing sensations that enflamed her.

Gabriel's arousal was such that when Alessia ground down on him, the barrier of thin clothing separating them was barrier enough to make a grown man weep for release. No woman's skin had ever tasted this good or felt this soft, Gabriel thought as he devoured Alessia's other breast. And what beautiful breasts they were, tiny and high and with dark tips as moreish as her rosebud lips.

He didn't know who was more desperate for him to take possession of her. Alessia ground down on him, cradling his head tightly against her breasts, and when she gave another of the throaty moans that added fuel to his arousal, all he could focus on was his need to be inside her. In an instant, he flipped her round so she was on her back. In an instant, her legs wrapped around his waist and she was grabbing at his buttocks, rosebud mouth finding his and kissing him with the hot sweetness that was as intoxicating as everything else about her. Mouths fused, hands grabbed down low, brushing against each other as they scrambled to undo his trousers and rid Alessia of her pyjama shorts. Without breaking the connection of their mouths, they managed to rid themselves of her shorts and then Gabriel was free from his own confines and Alessia was using her toes to yank them down to his knees. Any idea of kicking his trousers off were forgotten when she arched up with her pelvis and he felt her slickness.

Damn but she was as hot and ready for him as he was for her.

Her hands grabbed his buttocks again, and that was it for him. Spreading her thighs and pushing them up, he thrust deep into the tight, tight heat.

The discomfort was so momentary that Alessia ignored it. How could she do anything else when she was being filled so gloriously and completely?

She'd watched enough sex scenes to know what to expect but this was so much more than she could ever have known and she cried out with every hard drive inside her, Gabriel's each and every thrust filling her so greatly that her mind detached itself from her body and she became nothing but a vessel of sensual ecstasy.

Breathless groans and cries of pleasure mingled between their enjoined mouths, fingers bit into flesh and scraped through hair, the moans between them intensifying as something deep inside her wound tightly, coiling and coiling, *burning*.

Gabriel, lost in a hedonistic cloud, resisted the demand for release building inside him. Never, in all his thirty-five years on this earth, had he experienced anything like this, such complete sensory capitulation. It wasn't just the feel of being inside Alessia's tightness—and Lord, such unbelievable tightness—it was the feel of her flesh compressed so tightly to his, the seductively sweet taste of her mouth, the scent of their coupling... It was mind-blowing, and he didn't want it to end. He spread her thighs even further to reach even deeper penetration—Lord, this was something else—and lifted his face from hers so he could stare at the face of the woman as beautiful as the body he was pounding into, and when he plunged his tongue into her mouth again and heard the throaty groan as she thickened around him, he could hold on no more and, with a roar of ecstasy, Gabriel let go.

Gabriel quietly donned his clothes using the small stream of dusky light through the gap in his curtains to see by. The sun was rising. Soon it would be day. Soon the castle would come to life. He wanted to be gone before that happened.

Before he left, he gazed at the dark hair poking out above the bedsheets, the figure the hair belonged to huddled beneath. His heart clenched into a fist.

He'd never experienced a night like that before.

He'd never lost himself like that before. He'd been cast under a spell, that was the only explanation for it. He usually came right back to himself after sex but with Alessia the spell had remained intact. He'd carried her delectable body to his bedroom and made love to her again. The second time, they'd taken it much slower, the combustible lust that had exploded between them reduced to a simmer that had seen them exploring each other's bodies until every inch had been discovered and worshipped. His climax had been every bit as powerful as the first time. They'd finally fallen into slumber hours after the rest of Ceres had gone to sleep. And then he'd woken up and the spell had been lifted.

All he wanted now was to leave before Alessia stirred. Self-recriminations about bedding a client's family member—a princess, no less—could wait until he was in the privacy of his own home.

She stirred beneath the sheets. He held his breath as a throb of desire stirred in his loins and closed his eyes tightly. He would not return to that bed, however deep his craving.

Only when satisfied that she was still safely asleep did he slip out of the room.

Not wishing to see any member of the Berruti family, uncertain he'd be able to look any of them in the eye, he called the driver he'd been appointed, left a note for Queen Isabella, King Julius and Prince Amadeo thanking them for their hospitality and, ten minutes later, left the castle grounds.

For the first time in Alessia's life, she didn't fight waking up. Even before her eyes opened, she thrilled to be awake, the magic of the previous night flashing through her.

For the first time in her life, Alessia had thrown propriety, duty and decorum to the wind and allowed the woman beneath the princess skin to take control. It had been sublime. If she closed her eyes she could still feel the echo of the fulfilment throbbing deep between her legs.

Joy filled her and she laughed softly as she opened her eyes, fully expecting to find Gabriel's gorgeous face on the pillow beside hers.

His side of the bed was empty.

Holding the bedsheets to her naked form, she sat up. 'Gabriel?'

No response.

Climbing out of bed, she quickly yanked her pyjama bottoms off the floor—when had *they* been brought in from the balcony?—and pulled them on and padded to the bathroom. She knocked on the door. No answer. A quick look behind the door found it empty.

Slipping the pyjama vest top over her head and, trying hard to fight against the coldness filling her veins, Alessia left the bedroom calling out his name again.

The guest quarters Gabriel had been appointed, usually given to family members like her parents' siblings, were nearly a mirror image of her own. Laid out like an apartment, it had a bedroom and adjoining bathroom, a guest room with its own bathroom, a dayroom, a dining room, a reception room and an unused kitchen. Gabriel was nowhere to be seen. Nor were his clothes.

The quarters being on the second floor, a set of iron steps ran off the balcony and led down to the private gardens. She hurried down the steps barefoot.

Although brimming with early-morning birdsong, the garden was empty of human life.

Her heart thumping, she checked each room of his quarters a second time and then a third, her calls of his name gradually weakening to a choked whisper. Back in the bedroom, she stared at the bed. It was the very first time she'd shared a bed with another human being. She could still smell Gabriel. Could still feel his touch on her skin.

In a daze, she stepped back onto the balcony and stared at the plump sofa she'd lost her virginity on. Limbs now feeling all watery, she somehow managed to climb over the balustrade and back onto her private abode. Inside, she called the family's head of house-keeping, not even bothering to think of an excuse to explain why she was enquiring about the whereabouts of the negotiator who'd saved the Berrutis from almost certain destruction.

The answer, although expected, still landed as a blow.

Gabriel had gone.

He hadn't even left her a note of goodbye.

Alessia closed her eyes and resisted pulling at her just-done hair. She felt sick. After a few minutes spent doing breathing exercises, she felt no better, and briefly considered calling her mother and telling her she felt too ill to attend Amadeo and Elsbeth's pre-wedding party.

She couldn't miss the party. A royal princess did not bow out of engagements from something as pathetic as illness, not unless she was at death's door, which a bout of nausea did not class as. Not that it was a royal engagement as the public would recognise it. As far as the public were concerned, the party was a private affair although the carefully selected members of the press corps who'd be in attendance to document the evening—and it was a momentous occasion and not just because the heir to the throne would be showing off his new bride-to-be—would publish the usual photos and video clips to allow the public to feel a part of the event. So, a private event with as much privacy as the animals in London Zoo had. And Alessia had to smile and dance with that horrible monster King Dominic Fernandez of Monte Cleure to prove to the world that there was no bad feeling between them. She'd bet that was the cause of her nausea.

There was a knock on her bedroom door.

Opening her eyes, she stared at her reflection and brought her practised smile to her face before calling out, 'Come in.'

Rather than a member of her domestic staff, her visitor was her new sister-in-law. Immediately, Alessia's spirits lifted. Clara was the woman Marcelo had rescued from King Dominic's evil clutches. It was that rescue, photographed and leaked to the world, which had started the diplomatic war between the two countries. The fallout from the rescue had compelled Marcelo to marry Clara himself and, as a result, Alessia had a brand-new sister-in-law. What made it even better was that Marcelo and Clara had fallen madly in love for real.

There was an acute pang in her chest as Alessia wondered if a man would ever look at her the way Marcelo looked at Clara, a pang made sharper as Gabriel Serres's handsome face floated in her eyes. She willed the image away.

She'd not heard even a whisper from him since he'd snuck out of the bed they'd made love in.

For days she'd drifted around the palace in a fugue of disbelief. Disbelief that she'd fallen head over heels in lust with a man she barely knew, falling so hard and so fast that she'd given her virginity without any thought, too wrapped up in the moment to care about anything but the wonder of what they were sharing. Disbelief that Gabriel had left without a word of goodbye when they'd shared such an incredible night together. Disbelief at Gabriel's subsequent silence.

And then she'd made the fatal mistake of making excuses for his silence. After three days of this fugue-like drifting, she'd convinced herself an emergency had taken him from their bed and that he'd left without waking her because he wanted her to have more sleep. She'd convinced herself too that the only reason he hadn't called was because he didn't have her personal number and that to ask her brother or parents or any of their staff for it would lead to too many questions. Gabriel was experienced enough in her world to know a man didn't just casually ask for a princess's personal number. And so she'd decided to put them both out of their misery—because *surely* he was in as big a flux as she was after what they'd shared—and call him, asking her private secretary to obtain his number for her.

It was a business number answered by an efficient-sounding woman. Alessia left a message. For days she'd waited on tenterhooks, her heart leaping every time her phone buzzed. There had been no call back.

Her pride wouldn't let her ask her secretary to go one further and obtain his personal number, and even if it wasn't out of the question for Alessia to obtain it from her parents or brother, she finally opened her eyes and let reality sink in. It simply wasn't possible that Gabriel's assistant hadn't passed the message on. Gabriel had simply ignored it.

He'd deliberately crept out of their bed without waking her.

He hadn't called her because he didn't want to.

Despite everything they'd shared, he didn't want to see her again and didn't think her worthy of a two-minute call to tell her this.

Alessia had given her virginity to a man who was treating her like a worthless one-night stand. Now, just over two weeks on, she was well and truly done with hoping and moping.

Gabriel Serres could go to hell.

'Hi, sis,' Clara said chirpily, bounding over to the dressing table and bringing out the first smile on Alessia's face in two weeks. 'You look fantastic! That dress is amazing! Gosh, I am so envious.'

'You can talk,' Alessia laughed, rising from her seat to embrace her tightly. Where she had chosen an elegant deep red strapless ballgown for the party, Clara had gone for a toga-style shimmering silver dress that accentuated the bust Alessia would give her left kidney for. 'You look beautiful.'

Clara beamed. 'Thank you. Call me petty but I really want to look my best tonight for King Pig. Rub his face in it a bit more.'

'You're not worried about seeing him?'

'If anyone should be worried, it's *him*. Marcelo has promised Amadeo not to make a scene and I think it's going to kill him to keep that promise. I have to keep reminding him that he got his revenge on the monster when he rescued me from him.'

'Did Amadeo make you promise not to cause a scene too?'

'I promised that voluntarily. After all, I'm trying to be the perfect princess and the perfect princess doesn't

karate chop guests at a grand social function, does she?'
She actually looked a touch woebegone at not being
able to do this.

Alessia giggled then changed the subject. 'How did
the honeymoon go?' This was the first time the two old
friends had had a chance for a private catch-up since
Clara and Marcelo's return from their honeymoon.
'Were the Seychelles as pretty as you hoped?'

'It was amazing! Not that we saw all that much of it
as we spent most of our time in bed—'

'Hold it right there,' she interrupted before Clara
could start giving details. 'I'm feeling sick enough as
it is without having to listen to details about my brother's sex life.'

Clara cackled but then her brow furrowed. 'You're
feeling sick? What's wrong?'

'I've just been feeling a bit off for a couple of days.
Probably something I ate.'

She looked even more closely at her. 'Any other
symptoms?'

'No.'

But Clara continued to scrutinise her. 'Are you wearing a padded bra?'

'I'm not wearing a bra. Why?'

'Your boobs have grown. If I didn't know better, I'd
ask if you were pregnant.'

Those words set off an instantaneous reaction in
Alessia. Cold white noise filled her head, cold dread
prickled her skin. Instinctively, she put her hand to her
abdomen and breathed hard.

'Alessia? Are you okay? Your face has gone a funny
colour.'

But Clara's voice had become distant and Alessia had to lean into her dressing table to support her weak frame as the room began to spin wildly around her.

Gabriel dispassionately watched the previous evening's footage of Prince Amadeo and Lady Elsbeth's pre-wedding party in his hotel room in Rome. Italy, a country that shared a language and much cultural history with Ceres, was enthralled by the wedding between the glamorous heir to the throne and his pretty bride-to-be. The breakfast television channel he was watching as he prepared for the day's meetings with his newest client had so far devoted over two minutes to it.

He'd been invited to the party but politely declined. He had no wish to be part of a montage such as the one being televised.

His stomach clenched when the footage came to its star turn, the attendee its viewers would have been waiting for a glimpse of above all others: Europe's premiere princess, Princess Alessia. The clenching sharpened as he watched her laughing with a member of the British royal family before the camera cut to her dancing with the King of Monte Cleure. The smile on her face belied what he knew would be crawling beneath her skin to be held in the arms of a man she so despised, and Gabriel felt a stab of anger at her family for forcing this dance on her.

'I think we can safely agree that the animosity between these two nations is now a thing of the past,' a gushing reporter was saying as the cameras panned back to the studio.

Gabriel turned the television off and pinched the bridge of his nose.

A trade and diplomatic war had been averted. Any popular uprising against their royal family from the Ceresian people, who would surely have blamed them if the situation had deteriorated further and hit them economically, had been avoided. Dominic felt valued as a 'player' again. Everyone was happy.

This should be a moment of quiet satisfaction at a job well done but the discontent at seeing Alessia again was too strong. Truth was, Gabriel was furious with himself for what had happened between them and time had not abated that fury an iota. He'd had a few one-night stands over the years—he wasn't a saint—but this was the only one he truly regretted. And the only one he couldn't erase from his head.

Couldn't erase *her* from his head. He still felt the weight of his arousal for her as a memory in his loins.

He still had her number in his wallet from when she'd called the business line. His heart had thumped so hard when his PA passed Alessia's message to him that he wouldn't have been surprised if it had smashed straight through his ribcage.

The message had been brief, inviting him to call her if he wished. He'd read it a number of times, his heart deflating as the meaning had become clear.

Alessia wanted to see him again.

It was out of the question.

He should have called her back and politely made his excuses.

What he should have done before that was say goodbye and explain that as great as their night together had been, it was a one-night-only thing.

What he should have done before any of those things was rewind even further and not sleep with her in the first place.

But he should have called her back.

He'd never treated a woman so callously before. But then, he'd never reacted so strongly to a woman before or felt such a strong reaction towards him from a woman before. Or lost his mind the way he had with her.

Despite everything, he removed the folded Post-it note from his wallet and stared at the number he'd committed to memory at the first reading. It was the strength of his desire to call her back that had stopped him doing just that. Look at him now—twenty seconds of footage of her had distracted him from his preparations as effectively as a tornado hitting his hotel room.

Alessia Berruti was a princess. She was Europe's most photographed woman. She was the antithesis of what he wanted in a partner. Gabriel's childhood had been destroyed by press intrusion and he had no wish to experience the media spotlight again under any circumstance. It would be a disaster for his career too—anonymity was essential for him to be effective. Even a casual affair with the princess who seemingly loved the spotlight would bring press intrusion of unimaginable levels.

As scalding…as *fantastic*…as their lovemaking had been, he could never see or speak to Alessia Berruti again.

He had to forget her.

Another burst of unwelcome fury raged through him

and he crushed the note into a tight ball. Before he could throw it in the bin—maybe burn it to ash first for good measure—his phone rang.

He gritted his teeth and took a deep breath before reaching for it. Anger was the most futile of emotions, one he rarely succumbed to. He'd suffered more of it these last two weeks than he had the whole of his life and needed to rid himself of it.

His heart managed to jolt and sink at the same time when Prince Amadeo's name flashed on the screen.

'Good morning, Your Highness,' he said smoothly, refusing to allow a trace of his emotions show in his voice. 'This is an unexpected pleasure. What can I do for you?'

'You can explain to me how the—' an expletive was shot into Gabriel's ear '—you managed to get my sister pregnant.'

CHAPTER FOUR

'How do I look?' Alessia asked as she checked her reflection one last time. She'd selected a pair of deep blue fitted trousers, a simple short-sleeved, high-necked silk top a shade lighter, and a thick satin band separating the two items around her waist. After much deliberation, she'd left her hair loose. She'd originally tied it into a severe bun but Clara had said it made it look like she was trying too hard. According to Clara, the bun sent the message of 'this is me *proving* that seeing you again doesn't affect me in the slightest,' instead of the 'seeing you doesn't affect me in the slightest' look Alessia was aiming for.

Clara looked her up and down and nodded approvingly. 'Perfect.'

Alessia swallowed. Her world had been thrown into chaos but she could always rely on her sister-in-law's honesty. Clara's 'perfect' answer meant Alessia had achieved what she set out to. To get through the meeting that would bring her face to face with the man who'd slipped out of her life without a goodbye and which would determine the rest of her life, she needed to look as perfect on the outside as she could. God knew she was a shambles inside.

It was Clara's comment that she could believe Alessia to be pregnant that had started it all. Alessia must have had her head in the sand because until that point, she hadn't put together the dots of a late period, tender breasts and nausea. Until that point, she hadn't registered that she had no memory of Gabriel using contraception.

What fateful naivety. What brainless stupidity.

She still had no idea how she'd got through Amadeo's party. If Clara hadn't stayed so close throughout the evening, she probably wouldn't have. Clara had come to the rescue when it came to the pregnancy test too. Knowing how difficult it would be for Alessia to buy one without detection, she'd popped to a pharmacist the next morning with her security detail. Let them think the test was for her! she'd said. She'd then sneaked it over to Alessia and sat holding her hand while they waited for the result to show, and hugged her and stroked her hair for an hour while Alessia sobbed over the positive result. Unfortunately, Clara was incapable of telling a lie, and when she'd returned to her quarters and Marcelo asked what she and Alessia had been doing, she'd felt compelled to tell him the truth. Even more unfortunately, their father happened to be there too.

There had been no time at all for Alessia to come to terms with her situation before her whole family and the majority of the palace staff knew about the pregnancy. Within two hours of the positive result an emergency family meeting was convened. For the second time in less than a month, Alessia was the subject behind said meeting.

Barely a day had passed since that positive result and she still hadn't fully come to terms with it, not on an emotional level. Her family had gone straight to damage limitation mode and she'd been carried by the panicking swell with them.

If she'd thought her mother's disappointment at her unguarded comment about Dominic had hurt, it had nothing on the cold anger she'd been hit with over the pregnancy, wounding far more deeply than Amadeo's furious diatribe.

She checked her eyes one last time to ensure the drops she'd put in them that magically disappeared redness from all the crying she'd done were still working, then slipped her feet into a pair of silver heels, dabbed some perfume to her neck and wrists and left her quarters.

If not for a lifetime of poise, just one of the many things drilled into her from the moment she could walk, her first glimpse of Gabriel in the meeting room of her mother's private offices would have knocked her off her feet. Her heart thumped so hard she couldn't breathe but she kept her back straight and her head high and strolled with all the nonchalance in the world to the empty chair.

Whatever happened in this meeting, her eyes would stay dry. She was a princess and she would remember her breeding and remain regal if it killed her.

Above all else, she would not let Gabriel know that seeing him again made her feel more violently sick than any pregnancy sickness.

She'd been nothing but a night of fun for him, quickly discarded and even more quickly forgotten.

It would be too humiliating if he guessed how deeply their night together had affected her. She could still feel the whisper of his touch on her skin. Still caught phantom whiffs of his cologne. Still felt her insides clench to remember how wonderful his lovemaking had been.

A member of staff held the chair out for her and she sat with a nod of thanks and cast her gaze around every person sat at the large oval table. Her family—her parents and two brothers, who Alessia was sandwiched between—and the family lawyer, sat at one end. At the other end sat Gabriel and a woman she assumed was his lawyer. The only person her eyes skimmed over rather than meeting their stare head-on was Gabriel. She'd intended to but at the very last second been unable to go through with it. She didn't think she could bear to see the expression in his eyes.

Skimming her eyes didn't stop the blood pumping through her body as she still somehow managed to soak in every last detail about him, from the impossibly uncreased white shirt he wore to the perfectly positioned quiff of the black hair she'd thrilled to run her fingers through.

Jutting her chin, she rested her hands flat on the table, praying no one could see the tremor in them, and purposefully faced Amadeo. Channelling their long-dead grandmother, who'd taken regal haughtiness to heights that deserved to be acknowledged as an art, she said, 'Has he agreed to accept his responsibility?'

Gabriel had watched Alessia make her grand entrance with his heart in his mouth.

Feelings he couldn't begin to describe had clawed and fisted his guts and heart since Amadeo's bombshell. When he'd driven through the castle gates, the usual photographers on duty hoping to get a shot of a Berruti family member or newsworthy associate bound for disappointment by his blacked-out windows, the clawing and fisting had reached a pinnacle. Damn it, unless he treaded very carefully, this would be his life again.

The woman he'd never wanted to see again was pregnant with his child, and it enraged him that the blame for it was going to be laid on his shoulders by Alessia as well as her family. He'd thought better of her.

He'd thought better of himself too. But they'd both been there. They'd both got carried away and failed to use protection. After their first failure there had been little point in bothering with it, and truth was, the first time had been so damn glorious that he'd wanted to experience every single aspect of it again. Maybe that's why it had felt so good, he thought darkly. That was the first time he'd made love without a barrier. He was clean. He'd assumed the princess was too, something else that weighed on his mind—since when did he give the benefit of the doubt to anyone about anything, especially with regards to his sexual health? Keeping himself safe, aka Contraception, was his responsibility. This had the added benefit of him never having to worry that there might be miniature Gabriel Serres roaming the earth, and, as all these thoughts flashed through his mind, he found himself wondering if this had been her plan all along, to seduce him and get impregnated by him. Because she sure as hell hadn't mentioned that she wasn't on the pill. He could forgive the first time they'd made love—the madness had trapped them both—but allowing him to make love to her a second time knowing there was nothing to stop an accidental conception? Not taking action to stop any conception when there *was* still time? Unforgiveable.

Intentional or accidental, he was there, about to negotiate for his life and the life of his unborn child. He could play hardball and insist they wait until the birth for a DNA test but knew it would do nothing but delay the inevitable. He knew in his heart the child was his, but if Alessia wanted him to go along with her family's demands then she'd damned well better start showing him some respect or he would walk out of there and make the whole damn family wait until the birth for fresh negotiations.

He exhaled the anger that had spiked through him at Alessia's contemptuous tone as well as her unjustified blame. He would not allow *any* emotion to show. He needed to treat this like every negotiation he'd taken control of since he was a teenage boy negotiating his warring parents' divorce.

'I am more than willing to accept responsibility,' he informed the side of her head icily, before her brother could speak. 'The extent of that responsibility is still to be decided, but whatever the outcome of these negotiations, I will support my child and be a father to it.'

'What is there to negotiate?' Marcelo asked, his eyes blazing. 'You've got my sister pregnant. You have to marry her.'

Gabriel folded his arms across his chest. 'Actually, I don't.'

'You took advantage of her,' Amadeo spat.

'I took advantage of a twenty-three-year-old woman?' he drawled with a hint of disdain.

Angry colour stained the heir's cheeks. He would have said something else had Queen Isabella not placed her hand lightly on his. 'You have to see things from our position,' she said.

'I do,' Gabriel countered, 'and as I understand it, you fear news of the princess's pregnancy will cause a scandal in your country which, coming so close to the recent scandals, will dent your already waning popularity and lead to more voices joining the chorus for Ceres to become a republic. Is that the measure of it?'

Barely a flicker of emotion crossed the monarch's face. 'Yes.'

'Then allow me to state my position. I will marry your daughter, and I will marry her for one reason only—to enable my child to be raised with a parent who prioritises their emotional wellbeing rather than leave them to the mercy of a family who cares more about duty and public perception than what's best for them.'

There was a sharp intake of breath from every member of the royal family. With the exception of Alessia, who didn't react at all.

He failed to understand why they should be shocked at his observation. After all, Amadeo was marrying to salvage the public's perception of the Berrutis and head off talks of republicanism. Marcelo, however happy his marriage appeared to be, had married for the same reason. And now Alessia was being asked to do the same—and so was he. Three marriages to save a monarchy.

'However, before I commit myself to a loveless marriage, I have conditions that must be agreed in writing.'

There was a long beat of silence before the queen asked, 'And those conditions are?'

'That Alessia and I do not live in the castle but in a suitable dwelling elsewhere on the estate. I will not have my life dictated by protocol within my own home. I will not have my life dictated by any means. So there are no ambiguities between us or things that can be left open to interpretation, let me be clear—I will not be a working member of your family. I will not attend palace functions that have the press corps in attendance, and that includes family functions like Prince Amadeo's wedding. I will not undertake royal engagements. I will never do anything intentionally that will cause harm to your family but I will live out of the spotlight and remain autonomous in how I conduct my life.' Ignoring the latest collective intake of breath, he continued with his demands. 'My word as my child's father will be absolute. Alessia and I will raise him how we see fit and there will be no argument or interference from any of you.'

At this, Alessia's eyes finally met his. He caught the surprise in them and…was that admiration? Whatever it was, one blink and it was gone, replaced by an indifference that bordered on contempt.

'Anything else?' Amadeo asked through gritted teeth.

'Yes. If we marry, it will be a private affair, and by private I mean immediate family only. No guests, no photographers, no press, just a simple statement after the deed has been done in which you can clarify my intention to live as a private person, and which brings me to my final condition—I will only marry Alessia if I have her personal assurance that she is in agreement and, as such, I ask you all to leave the room so we can discuss the matter in private.' He deliberately held Amadeo's stare. 'I need to be satisfied that she gives her consent freely, so if you will excuse us…'

He let his words hang in the air. He doubted any member of this family had ever been spoken to in such a manner before. He wasn't being deliberately provocative or disrespectful but he knew perfectly well that he needed to set his stall out early so there could be no misunderstandings.

The queen was the first to react. Rising to her feet—she was so short that even standing while the rest remained seated she barely reached her husband's and sons' heads—she looked him in the eye. 'Speak to my daughter privately, by all means, but as you have spoken so freely, allow me the same courtesy. Whatever you think, I love my daughter. Whether you marry her or not, I will support her. We all will. And we will weather any storm that comes our way in the same way we always do—as a family.'

With only the briefest inclination of her head, she summoned the men of her family to their feet. In silence, they followed her out, the two princes towering over their mother and throwing daggers of loathing at Gabriel, and were quickly followed by the lawyers and other assorted staff.

And then it was just him and Alessia.

Huge, painful thumps in his chest made it suddenly hard to breathe but he fought through it to try and read the beautiful face of the woman he'd shared the best night of his life with.

Gabriel was excellent at reading body language. While they'd waited in tense silence for Alessia to arrive, he'd read the body language of all the Berrutis. Both princes were mountains of barely concealed rage. He sensed Amadeo's fury was at the situation as a whole. Marcelo's, he suspected, was directed entirely at him, Gabriel. The queen was steely concerned only with damage limitation. The king's body language told him that he would, once again, be the family peacemaker. It was a role Gabriel understood all too well—it was the role within his own family that had propelled him into a making a career out of peace negotiations. The reasons for needing those peace negotiations were the same reasons he kept such tight control of his emotions and had always selected his lovers from a pool of reserved, emotionally austere women. That he was on the cusp of marrying a woman who had passion embedded in her DNA and who guaranteed the press intrusion he so despised were things he must learn to handle, and quickly.

Alessia was the only Berruti who'd kept her feelings in check during their talk. Other than that flicker of surprise when he'd informed the family in no uncertain terms that they would raise their child as *they* saw fit, she'd revealed nothing of her inner feelings. Even now, when it was just the two of them at opposing ends of the large, teak table, she simply sat in her chair, back straight, hands folded neatly on the table, eyes on him, giving nothing away other than haughty disdain.

He knew though, that her haughty façade was just that—a façade.

Born princess she might be, but it wasn't possible that the woman who'd sobbed in his arms and then come undone in them, who'd exploded with a passion so strong it had to be a fundamental part of her nature, could be as cold on the inside as she was showing on the outside. And he shouldn't be wishing her to reveal it.

Alessia willed herself to hold Gabriel's hard stare. The vast space between them had shrunk to nothing and it was a struggle to think over the blood rushing through her head to console herself that he was too far away to see the thuds of her heart beating so hard and fast through her chest.

She willed even harder for the tears to stay away.

She would not let the hurt he'd put her through leech out. He would never know how his early- morning disappearing act had devastated her.

'I have to say, this feels a rather extreme method of forcing you to see me again,' she said with airy nonchalance when the silence finally became too much, and was gratified to see his jaw clench. Allowing herself a tight smile, she got down to business. 'I am grateful that you have agreed to marry me and save my family from further scandal, and grateful for your concern about whether I consent freely to us marrying. As I'm sure you remember from the night we conceived our child, when we spoke of Amadeo's marriage, consent and free will are important to me. You have my assurance that I do consent.'

One of the thick black eyebrows that had so fascinated her that night rose. 'You consent to a loveless marriage?'

'Of course.' She smiled and added with a touch of sarcastic bite, 'After all, I'm from a family that puts duty before personal feelings. In that respect, I think it can only be a good thing to marry a man who will put our child's emotional needs first because I, like the rest of my family, am far too repressed to know how to do that. What a great example you'll be able to set to him or her.' Her smile widened. 'A *great* example. One day in the future, I must remember to tell them of the time when Daddy sneaked out of the castle after spending the night having sex with Mummy and then cold-shouldered her until he came riding in to rescue the conceived child from the horrors of a family without any mercy in them.' She mock shuddered before bestowing him with another, even brighter smile. 'Let me know when it's your birthday—I'll buy you a superhero cape with *SV* for Super Virtuous emblazoned on it.'

Fearing her charade was on the verge of cracking, Alessia rose and strode to the door, opened it and invited her anxious, waiting family back inside before Gabriel could find a response.

Alessia entered 'the zone,' a place she inhabited during certain interminably boring royal engagements. Being in the zone enabled her to put her happy face on and speak brightly and clearly while a pre-marriage contract was drawn up, read through, redrafted, read through again, more clauses removed, others added... And so it went on, and on, and on, the monotony broken by a regular supply of refreshment that she made sure to consume even though her stomach was so tightly cramped she had to force the food down her throat and into it.

Occasionally a stunned voice played in her ear: *You're planning a marriage to Gabriel Serres*, but she ignored it. Everything was too fantastical and happening too fast for it to actually feel real.

She was going to have to live with him and she couldn't even begin to dissect the swell of emotions that rose in her to think of what this would mean.

Time passed in a strange alchemy of speed and slowness. Though Alessia kept strictly to her side of the table, her awareness of Gabriel's presence within these four walls was as acute as if he were standing right beside her. He was too far from her to be able to smell him but she kept catching whiffs of cologne that made her abdomen clench and her pulses soar. She fought not to gaze at him. She also fought to not march over and slap his face, which frightened her as much as the yearning to stare.

Only when Gabriel was satisfied that it protected him from actually having to be a royal did he sign the contract, and then it was her turn. She wanted to fix him with another icy stare, prove her indifferent disdain, but by then her emotions were so heightened that it was all she could do to hold the pen. She added her signature to the document without the flourish she'd so wanted to make it with. Their respective lawyers acted as witnesses and made their marks too, and then it was done.

Her composure in severe danger of unravelling, Alessia left immediately, using the excuse that she wished to rest before dinner. Leaving before anyone else, she hurried out of the room avoiding Gabriel's attempt to catch her eye.

Her nausea had returned with a vengeance and she hurried along the wide corridors to her private quarters. She climbed the stairs, closed her bedroom door and ran into the bathroom, where she threw up straight into the toilet.

It seemed to take for ever before her stomach felt settled enough for her to crawl off the floor and brush her teeth, and then she staggered back into the bedroom and collapsed on her bed.

Closing her eyes, she pressed a hand to her belly and breathed deeply, in and out. Having inherited her mother's petite figure and danced for exercise and enjoyment most days of her life, her stomach had always been flat. Early though the pregnancy was, there was a noticeable swelling, just as her breasts had swollen. As dream-like as everything had felt these last few days, one thing had made itself felt with concrete certainty. She was pregnant. Her body was doing what it needed to do to bring her baby safely into this world. And Alessia would do what was needed too, and that meant marrying Gabriel.

She'd expected coming face to face with him to be hard but she hadn't expected it to be that hard. She hadn't expected to feel so *much*.

Being a good, dutiful princess…that was Alessia's role in this world, her purpose, her reason for being.

Her comments about Dominic had been one unguarded moment but her night with Gabriel was a different matter entirely. That night, she had broken free from the bonds of duty and freed the real woman inside, and it was terrifying how strongly seeing Gabriel again relit that passionate fire inside her.

She was a *princess*.

There was a rap on her door.

Wishing the world would leave her alone, she sighed and closed her eyes tightly before calling out. 'I'm resting. Please come back in thirty minutes.'

The door opened.

Surprised, she lifted her head, but any mild rebuke to whoever had taken it on themselves to disturb her solitude fell from her lips when Gabriel marched into her bedroom.

CHAPTER FIVE

GABRIEL NOTED THE shock at his intrusion on Alessia's flushed face as she scrambled to sit up, gripping one of the four-poster bed's posts and pressing herself into it. He'd taken her by surprise in the one room in the whole castle she could expect privacy.

Too bad, he thought grimly. They were going to be married soon. Two strangers who'd spent one perfect night together were going to be tied together for life.

'Who let you in?' she whispered, pressing her cheek to the post. 'What do you want?'

'Your staff let me in—they know that they will soon be my staff too. As for what I want…?'

Did it matter what he wanted? No, was the concise answer. He'd envisaged his child's entire future in half a minute and known at the end of that flash into the future that his or her best chance of growing into a functional adult was with Gabriel a permanent, constant part of their life. That his own life would be uprooted and upended was irrelevant. He'd failed to use protection. His child had not chosen to be conceived. Therefore his wants were unimportant.

One want that was important, though, was a want

for a cordial relationship with Alessia. He had no wish for a wife who despised him. He knew first-hand from his own parents' toxic hatred of each other the damage warring parents could do to a child.

He headed to a pale blue velvet armchair placed close to the bed. It was an elaborate piece of furniture that fitted in perfectly with the feminine vibes of the princess-perfect room. His sister, he thought, would have gladly killed for a bedroom like this. Although long used to riches, he had a feeling this castle would still blow Mariella's mind.

He could take only a small crumb of solace that Alessia's room, as with the brief impression he'd obtained of the rest of her quarters, had a warmer feel to it than her parents' quarters.

'I want to talk before I leave Ceres to sort my affairs,' he said.

'Why?'

He sat down and gazed at her steadily, trying his best to block the feminine scents of this most feminine of rooms much as he was trying to block the surging of his pulses. 'Why do you think? We've pledged to spend our lives together with only cursory words exchanged between us.'

'What else is there to say?' Bitterness seeped into her husky voice. 'We've agreed to marry and raise our child together. End of story.'

'Our story is only beginning. I had hoped to discuss things properly with you when we had that time alone together earlier but you used it to take cheap shots at me and then invited your family straight back in before I could give a rebuttal.'

The burn of her angry eyes blazed enough to penetrate his skin.

Gabriel took a deep breath. He'd made his point. Time to move on to what he'd sought her out for in the first place—to diffuse tensions. 'I never meant to imply that you and your family are incapable of loving a child.'

She released her hold on the bed post and straightened, her chin jutting. Her shock at his appearance was rapidly diminishing, the regal princess remerging from the vulnerable woman who'd scrambled with shock at his appearance in her room. With a glimmer of her earlier haughty disdain, she said, 'You didn't imply it. You were explicit about it.'

'If I offended you, I apologise.' He'd spoken the truth to make his point to Alessia and her family but, he conceded, it was a point he would have softened if he hadn't reacted so strongly to seeing her again. Those same feelings were rampaging through him now but he'd prepared for it before entering her room and that mental preparation made it possible for him to choose his words with his usual care. He could look at the rosebud lips and sultry dark velvet eyes, and temper the awareness coursing through him so that it became nothing but a distant thrum.

'Apology accepted,' she said curtly, wriggling elegantly to press her back against the velvet headboard. 'Now please leave. I'm tired and wish to rest.'

'Not yet.' He rested his elbows on his thighs. 'We marry in three days and—'

The composure Alessia had only just found shattered. 'What are you talking about? I thought the wedding would be in a few weeks?'

'If you hadn't run away from the meeting, you would know this.'

'I didn't run away—I thought everything had been agreed.'

'Only the basics. Everything else is to be decided between you and me, which is why I am here.'

'Everything like what?'

'Our marriage. How we're going to make it work so that we can live together and raise a child together.'

Icy panic clutched her chest. Three days was nothing. How was she supposed to prepare herself in that time? It was impossible. Three days! Three days until she became the wife of the man who'd ghosted her? It was too soon! She'd thought she had weeks! 'Who decided we'd marry in three days?' she demanded to know, unable to keep the agitation from her voice.

'It was a collective decision. Your family worry that news of our marriage will take the spotlight from Amadeo's wedding. We marry on Thursday and release the news on Friday. The press then have over a month to milk it until it curdles before Amadeo's wedding takes place.'

'And you agreed to this?'

He shrugged. 'Your family agreed to all my conditions. It was only fair I give them a concession in return.'

'How magnanimous of you,' she spat, hating that his composure was as assured as ever while all her turmoil was showing itself, feelings heightened by him sitting close enough to her that it wasn't the ghost of his cologne seeping into her senses as it had been during the meeting but his actual cologne, splashed on his cheeks and neck after he'd shaved that morning. It made her remember how she'd buried her face in his neck and inhaled his scent so greedily, which only made the feelings heighten. She didn't want to feel anything for this man or to show anything but the deserved contempt she'd managed earlier, but everything she'd had drilled in her the entirety of her life had slipped out of reach. They could be talking about the weather for all the emotion Gabriel was showing and she hated him for it. 'How truly *benevolent*.'

Gabriel recognised that Alessia's cool façade from earlier had been well and truly stripped away. He'd been right—it *had* all been a façade. Beneath the haughty exterior, she'd seethed with emotion. For whose benefit had she chosen to hide it? His or her family's?

He stared deep into those blazing velvet eyes again, the thrum of awareness heightening. She wanted an argument, he realised. Gabriel did not fight, physically or verbally, and never would. His parents' marriage had been too volatile even in the supposedly happy years for him to ever allow himself to follow in their shoes and lose his calm, and it was unnerving to find himself responding to the passionate emotions Alessia was brimming with.

With a sickening jolt, he realised it was this passion that had sang to him that night.

Making love with Alessia was the only time in his adult life he'd lost control of himself, and the thrumming of awareness thickened to fully realise for the first time that marriage meant he no longer had to bury his desire for her.

Closing his eyes briefly, he inhaled to control the

tightening in his loins. To regain control of his thoughts. To regain control of the biting emotions.

He shifted his chair forwards and locked back onto Alessia's fiery stare. Making sure to pitch his voice at its usual modulated tone, he said, 'Considering that marrying you means I have to give up the career I excel at and move to a new country, I would say my conditions were reasonable and justified.'

'No one asked you to give up your job.'

'Once news of our marriage hits the press it will be impossible for me to continue. My clients employ me because I guarantee results and my discretion is guaranteed. Once I become a public figure, the anonymity I rely on to do my job effectively is gone.'

She pulled her knees to her chest and rested her chin on them in the same way she'd done when he'd first found himself falling under her spell. 'I'm sure you'll find a way to adapt it to the new circumstances.'

'Adaptation is always possible, of course, but continuing the business as it is will not.'

'You don't have to marry me. No one's putting a gun to your head.'

'I've put a metaphorical gun to my own head. Secrets don't stay secret. Even if we didn't marry, as soon as the pregnancy starts to show speculation about the father will start and sooner or later my name will leak, and I'll still be thrust into the spotlight I never wanted. Either way, my life as it is is over, which leaves me only two choices—marry you and be a permanent feature in my child's life, or don't and leave everything about my child's upbringing to chance. If there is one thing you will learn about me it is that I do not leave anything to chance.'

'And you don't think I'll be a loving mother,' she stated, tremulously. The implication had wounded her. Alessia had only known she was pregnant a few days but, once the tears had dried, her heart had swollen with an emotion she struggled to define, a combination of excitement and fear and love. Love for a fledging being that probably didn't as yet have a heartbeat.

Many times over the years she'd wondered what kind of mother she would be. The only conclusion she'd reached was that she'd be a different mother to her own, but she couldn't say that to Gabriel. It wasn't just a matter of disloyalty but because he wouldn't understand. How could he? A monarch wasn't an ordinary person and, even with the best will in the world, they couldn't be an ordinary parent. Their number one priority had to be to the monarchy. Alessia, though, would never be a monarch, and she thanked the good Lord every day for that.

Gabriel's eyes had narrowed but when he answered, his words were measured. 'I think you're capable of it but you're from a world where duty comes first and often to the detriment of the individual. Look at you and your brothers—all of you marrying for one reason or other to save the monarchy. I will not have our child feel forced to make those same choices.'

'It's a choice *you're* making too.'

'For their sake,' he replied in the same measured tone. 'And it is up to you and me to make the best of it and create a stable home for them. It will take many compromises and concessions on both our parts but if we are both willing, then it is achievable.'

'Will you compromise on coming to Amadeo's wedding with me?' she retorted, already knowing how humiliating it would be to attend Ceres's biggest state event in decades without her new husband by her side. People would understand someone wanting to remain private and not wanting to be a working royal, but family events, even when they were state occasions, were different. Gabriel's refusal to attend could only be interpreted as personal.

'My conditions have already been agreed but everything else is open to negotiation. The question is, are *you* willing to make the compromises and concessions necessary for our child?'

How could this be the same man who'd made love to her with such frenzied passion? Alessia wondered, gazing at him in disbelief. From the expression on Gabriel's face and the tone of his voice, he could be conducting an ordinary business meeting, not discussing the upturning of both their worlds; and his world was being upturned far more than her own.

On paper, he was everything she'd ever wanted in a husband. He was everything she'd waited for—a man she could respect, who made her feel and who wouldn't sell her out. Gabriel commanded respect just by walking in a room, and there was no denying he made her feel. In the short hours they'd spent together, he'd made her feel more intensely than she'd ever felt in her life, more than she'd believed it was possible to feel. Even now, after he'd cold-shouldered her for two weeks, the intensity of her awareness for him hadn't diminished at all. Watching his mouth as he spoke, taking in the stubble thickening on his jaw, catching those whiffs of his cologne…it all did something to her. Meeting his eye was even worse, and now she was stuck on her bed with her veins buzzing, her heart a pulsating mess, hugging her legs as tightly as she could so he couldn't see the tremors wracking her. So yes, as much as she wished he didn't, it was undeniable that he made her feel.

She knew too that he would never sell her out. His clients' loss was her gain; Gabriel's discretion was assured. And he'd made it clear he took fatherhood seriously. She should be rejoicing that he ticked all the husband boxes.

But he felt nothing for her. He wouldn't be her prince. He'd left her sleeping and disappeared from her life as if what they'd shared had never been… But it had been. The tiny life in her belly was proof of that.

She breathed in deeply and kneaded the back of her neck. It scared her how badly she wanted the man who'd created that life with her, who'd made love to her with such intense passion, who'd brought the woman out in her, to resurface.

'Alessia?' he said, one of his thick black eyebrows raising at her silence.

She blinked her thoughts away and took a deep breath before meeting his gaze. 'Yes,' she said. 'I am willing to make compromises and concessions for the sake of our child.'

'That is good to hear. It will make life easier for all concerned if we always strive for common ground.'

Unable to speak about her marriage—an event she'd always looked forward to with rose-coloured lenses—

any further in such an emotionless way, Alessia changed the subject. 'Was anything else agreed while my back was turned?'

'Yes. The converted stable block is going to be our home here. Your father tells me it is in need of modernising. Once we have agreed what we want from the renovations, the work on it will begin immediately.'

The stable block in question sat apart from the two main turreted mishmash of buildings that constituted the castle, and had initially been converted for Alessia's widowed grandmother to live in when her daughter took the throne on her husband's death. The dowager queen had been a cantankerous old boot who'd loathed living in the castle surrounded by the thing she hated most: people. And so the stable block had been converted into a seven-bedroom dwelling which she'd taken great delight in not admitting anyone into. Alessia had been terrified of her but also secretly fascinated. It had been this grandmother whose haughty spirit she'd channelled earlier to get her through seeing Gabriel again without falling to pieces. She'd tried hard to reach for that spirit again since he'd barged his way into her room but she couldn't find it any more. Knowing her grandmother, she'd probably hidden from her out of spite from her perch in heaven.

Knowing her grandmother, she would have adored Gabriel. A man who seemingly disdained the monarchy as much as she had marrying into the family would have thrilled her. The difference was that her grandmother had been from the old Greek royal family and had played her public part as queen consort until her husband's death magnificently. For all his talk about compromise, Gabriel had been very clear that when it came to royal life, he would have nothing to do with it and that there would be no compromise on this, not even for Amadeo's wedding. Alessia would be a princess with a husband but without a prince for the rest of her life.

Fearing the swelling of emotions filling back up in her, Alessia straightened her legs and spine, and lifted her chin. 'Anything else?'

'That's everything that was discussed.'

'Good. Then I would be grateful if you would leave. I'm tired and wish to rest before dinner.'

He eyed her meditatively. 'Before I go, I would like to apologise.'

'You've already apologised.'

'This is a different matter. I wish to apologise for not returning your call.'

It felt like he'd plunged an icy hand into her heart. The impulse to draw her knees back to her chest was strong, but she fought it. 'Oh. That,' she said with an airiness she had no idea how she achieved. 'Don't worry about it—it was a mere whim. I just thought if you ever came back to Ceres and was at a loose end then we could go out for drinks. I'd forgotten I even made the call.'

'Whatever your reasons for calling, it was unforgivably rude of me to not return it. I will not insult your intelligence by making up excuses. A great part of me did want to call you back but the reason I didn't is because I knew that nothing could happen between us. You're a princess and I'm a man who values my privacy and anonymity. The two are not compatible.'

How she managed to meet his stare after those words, she would never know. But she did. She forced herself to, and she forced herself to hold it. What she couldn't do was stop the tremor that came into her voice. 'Then you will have to agree it's ironic that you're being forced to marry a woman you're not compatible with.'

There was a long moment of stillness before Gabriel got to his feet. Slowly, he stepped to the bed and leaned his face down to hers.

His eyes were ringing with that beautiful supernova of golden colour she'd seen the night they'd made love and, though she tried hard to fight it, a tingle of electricity raced up her spine and tightened her skin.

His firm lips tugged into something that nearly resembled a smile but there was nothing ambiguous about the pulsating of his eyes. 'No one is forcing me to marry you, Alessia.' His face was so close to hers his hot breath caressed her face just as his tone caressed the rest of her senses. 'Our lives are not compatible and it is unlikely we have compatibility in our interests... But there is one area where we *know* we are compatible.'

The flush that crawled through her was the deepest and hottest she had ever known. She felt it crawl through every cell in her body, burning her from the inside out, and when his face moved even closer, she could no longer draw breath.

'We can have a successful marriage,' he whispered, the tips of their noses touching. 'And we can have a fulfilling one too.'

Her lips were buzzing manically even before Gabriel's mouth brushed lightly to them, but still that first touch landed like a thrill that filled her mouth with moisture and made her pelvis contract into a tight pulse.

She hadn't even realised she'd closed her eyes until the delicious pressure against her lips vanished and she opened them to find Gabriel upright and gazing down at her with that sensual, hooded expression she remembered so well.

She couldn't open her throat to speak.

His shoulders rose as he breathed in deeply, then, wordlessly, he reached into his back pocket and pulled out his wallet. From it, he plucked a business card. Eyes still boring intently into hers, he handed it to her.

She still couldn't open her throat to speak, could barely raise an eyebrow in question.

'My personal number,' he said with the hint of wry smile. 'Call me at any time. If I don't answer, I will call you back. I give you my word.'

At the door he gave one last inclination of his head. 'Until our wedding day.'

Gabriel took a moment to compose himself before going back downstairs.

The thrills racing through his loins stretched the moment to an age.

Only when certain his arousal was contained did he take the steps down.

As he left the castle, acknowledging a dozen members of staff along the way, he acknowledged too the satisfaction of a job well done.

The sexiest woman in the world was carrying his child and he'd successfully negotiated a marriage to her in which he would not be tainted by the celebrity of monarchy or controlled by her family, and in which he could continue living his life as a private man. Undeniably, he had to wind down the business that had been the biggest part of his life for such a long time, but at the end of negotiations, it was the gains you made that counted, not the losses, and his gains were ones he could live with.

He was certain too that soon Alessia would appreciate the gains *she'd* made in the negotiations. A husband and protector for their child.

And a lover for herself.

Two a.m. and Alessia was still wide awake. There was so much going through her head, so much to process, that sleep was impossible.

What a day. What a month. Part of her wished desperately that she could wind back time to Marcelo and Clara's wedding reception and gag her own mouth. But that was only a small part of her because wishing to reverse time meant wishing the life in her belly out of existence and she could never wish for that. That fledgling life was already a part of her and a growing part of her heart had already attached itself to it.

Switching her bedside light on, she reached for the business card she'd laid by her book. Her heart in her mouth, she lightly traced a finger over the numbers printed on it.

Impulse, much like the ones that had made her call out to him and swing herself over the balustrade into his balcony, had her grab her phone and dial the number.

It was answered on the third ring.

'Alessia?' His voice was thick with sleep.

Blinking with surprise that he'd guessed it was her, all she could say was, 'Yes.'

'Are you okay?'

She closed her eyes as the deep, smooth timbre poured into her ear and sent tingles racing through her, and gave a long, soft inhale. 'Gabriel...?'

'Yes?' he said quietly into the silence.

She drew her knees to her chest and took a deeper breath. 'You do know it's a huge risk that you're taking?'

'What is?'

'Marrying me. The pregnancy is at such an early stage...the most dangerous stage.' Her voice dropped even lower. 'My mother had three miscarriages between me and Marcelo. It's why there's such a big age gap between us. I'll do everything I can to bring our child safely into the world but sometimes nature has other ideas. Are you prepared for that? That our marriage might be for nothing?'

This time the silence came from him. When he answered, his voice was the gentlest she'd ever heard it. 'I am marrying you for our child's sake, Alessia, but it is you I am committing myself to. Whatever the future holds for us, it is a commitment I am making for the rest of my life.'

Tears filled her eyes, and she had to squeeze them tightly to stop them falling. 'I'm sorry for waking you.'

'Don't be.'

Her voice was barely a whisper as she wished him a goodnight.

CHAPTER SIX

ALESSIA'S WEDDING DAY arrived in a blaze of glorious sunshine. Wearing only skimpy silk pyjamas, she stepped onto her balcony and welcomed the rays sinking into skin that had felt so cold when she'd pulled herself out of the earlier nightmare.

'Good morning, Alessia.'

Startled, she whipped her head to the adjoining balcony. Gabriel emerged to stand at the balustrade, coffee in hand. Her stomach flipped, her heart setting off at a canter at the sight of him. All he wore was a pair of low-slung black shorts that perfectly showed off his taut abdomen and snake hips, his bronzed, muscular chest bare and gleaming under the sun, hair mussed and the stubble on his face grown so thick it should rightly be called a beard.

'What are you doing here?' she asked dumbly, unable to scramble the wits together to stop herself from staring. She swore he grew more devastatingly handsome each time she saw him.

A faint curve of a smile. 'I flew in last night.'

'No one told me.'

He raised a hefty shoulder and took a sip of his coffee. 'I dislike being late. My immediate affairs were all in order so I thought it prudent to arrive early. It meant there were less things that could go wrong today. You'd already retired for the night when the decision was made.' His eyes narrowed, deep lines forming in his brow. 'You look tired. Are you still not sleeping?'

With the memory of that awful dream, which had come after it had taken her hours to fall back to sleep after the previous one, still fresh in her mind, she shook her head. 'Bad dreams.'

She'd been chasing her mother through the castle screaming for her, but her mother had been deaf to her cries. Then she'd found herself in the old, disused banqueting hall. Gabriel and Amadeo had been in there, dining together, but they'd been deaf and blind to her too.

She'd had much worse dreams before but this was the only one she'd woken from sobbing.

There was a brief flare of concern. 'Anything you wish to share?'

'It's bad luck to share a dream before midday unless you want it to come true.'

'You don't believe that superstitious nonsense, do you?'

'No. But just in case, I'm not going to risk it by telling you.'

His firm lips curved into the first real smile he'd bestowed on her. It transformed his face into something that made her already weak legs go all watery and a deep throb pulse inside her, somehow managing to make him look a decade younger despite the crinkles around his eyes and the grooves that appeared down the sides of his mouth.

Her returning smile didn't falter when a glamorous woman of around thirty dressed in a kimono-style robe and with her dark hair piled messily but artfully on top of her head appeared on his balcony and padded like a panther to stand beside him.

'Buenos días,' the woman said, rising on her toes to plant a kiss on Gabriel's cheek.

The violence of the nausea that caught hold of Alessia at this was so strong she pressed both hands to her abdomen. So loud was the roaring in her head that she almost missed Gabriel's introduction.

'Alessia, this is my sister, Mariella.'

His sister?

There hadn't been time for her to think about who this woman could be, but the spinning sensation that had her clutching the balustrade was undoubtedly relief, and she only realised Gabriel had introduced her in Spanish when Mariella's eyes widened and she dropped into a deep curtsey.

'You don't have to do that,' Alessia croaked. 'Please, Gabriel,' she added when his sister lifted her head and looked at her non-comprehendingly, and her own proficiency in Spanish had deserted her, 'tell her not to do that.'

Not taking his eyes off Alessia's flushed face, Gabriel translated while his mind whirled with what could have caused the strange turn she'd just had. Pregnancy hormones? Whatever the cause, the same needle of concern that had fired in his blood when she'd called him in the middle of the night pierced him again.

She'd sounded so vulnerable that night. He'd laid awake a long time after that call wondering whether he should fly back to Ceres. It still disturbed him how strong the pull had been.

It disturbed him too how hard a thump his heart had made when he'd recognised the number flashing on his phone and how deep the prickles that had covered his skin when her voice first seeped into his ear.

Having no need to fight himself from thinking about her any more, Alessia had unleashed in his mind a permanent vision that must have blurred because, looking at her now, she was more impossibly beautiful than his mind's eye had remembered. As his thoughts now skipped forwards to their wedding night, anticipation let loose in his blood and he came to the realisation that there was nothing disturbing in his reactions to her. Quite the opposite. He should be celebrating that he was pledging his life to a woman who aroused him more than any woman before her.

Yes, he thought thickly. Much better that he felt the pull to be with her than the alternative.

Mariella pushed herself up off the floor, and pulled Gabriel's thoughts away from the sensual delights the evening promised.

'Please,' Alessia said in that same strange croaky voice, placing a hand on the balustrade next to his, 'tell her we don't stand on ceremony.'

Unable to resist, he covered it with his own and was gratified when, though her eyes widened and more colour saturated her cheeks, she made no effort to move it. Pressing his abdomen against the cold stone, he leaned his face closer to hers and dropped his voice. 'You wish for me to lie to her?'

'But we don't,' she protested, her indignation making her sound a fraction more like her usual self.

'Perhaps not compared to your ancestors,' he agreed lightly. The compulsion to reach over the balustrade, grip her handspan waist and lift her over it and to him sent a throb rippling through his loins. She was so tiny, well over a foot shorter than him and roughly half his weight, and yet they had fit together so well. *Perfectly* well, he recalled with another throb in his loins. Like two pieces of a two-piece jigsaw...

'We don't,' she insisted, bringing *her* face closer to *his* with a piqued glare. 'Please tell your sister that I'm delighted to meet her and that I look forward to getting to know her.'

An unexpected zip of humour tugged at him at her formal tone but, remembering they had an audience, he reluctantly moved his hand, took a step back and made the translation.

The Berrutis did not expect commoners to bow and scrape to them any more, he conceded, but there was an absolute expectation of deference. From the expression on Alessia's face, this expectation was so deeply ingrained that she likely didn't realise it was there. In fairness to her, there was nothing he'd seen of her behaviour to indicate she thought herself better than anyone else. She didn't parade on her royal dignity like so many royal people were wont to do, Amadeo, her eldest brother, being one of them. But she was oblivious to how elegant and regal her bearing was, even when dishevelled, wearing pyjama shorts that perfectly displayed her toned, golden legs and a strappy pyjama top her small breasts jutted against. Her perfect breasts, he remembered thickly as he slowly swept his gaze over her again. They'd tasted so sweet. Fitted in the palms of his hands. And as he feasted his eyes on her, another flush of colour crept over her face, and the tips of those perfect breasts became visible through the silk of her pyjama top.

She was extraordinary. As desirable a creature as he had ever seen. Her dark, velvet eyes were locked on his, an expression in them he recognised: it had lodged itself in his retinas in that breath of a moment before their lips had first fused together. Unfiltered want. Want for him.

Mariella tugged at his arm, pulling him out of the strange, heady trance-for-two he'd become frozen in. Dragging his gaze from Alessia's, he stooped down a little so his sister could whisper in his ear.

He cleared his throat and translated for Alessia. 'Mariella says it's bad luck for us to see each other before the wedding.'

She blinked before responding. Then blinked again. The heightened colour still stained her cheeks but she pulled—and he swore he saw the effort it took to achieve it—a smile to her face. Taking a step back, she said lightly, 'You don't believe in that superstitious nonsense, do you?'

'I don't believe in superstition.'

'Neither to do I, but as with my dream, I don't want to take risks so I'm going to use your sister's reminder as an excuse to go back inside. I'll see you at the chapel.' Then she turned to Mariella and, in almost perfect Spanish, said, 'It was a pleasure to meet you,' before she padded into the quarters he'd be sharing with her before the night was out.

* * *

Alessia reached for the glass of water on her dressing table and tried to quench her parched mouth, but her hand trembled so hard more water ended up spilling down her chin than down her throat. A drop splashed on her wedding dress. It felt like a portent.

She'd chosen a simple white silk dress with spaghetti straps that formed a V at the cleavage and a short train that splayed behind her. The royal beauty team had worked their magic, pulling her hair into a loose knot with white flowers carefully entwined into it and loose tendrils framing her face. Subtle makeup and a subtly elegant diamond tiara placed on top of the sheer veil completed the look. The simplicity of the dress had felt fitting for the simplicity of the wedding when she'd chosen it, but looking at it now, all she felt was an unbearable sadness. The dress, like everything, was the opposite of what she'd envisaged whenever she'd daydreamed about her perfect wedding day.

Her father entered the room. Placing his hands on her arms, he kissed her temple, then stepped back to take a proper look at her. 'You look beautiful.'

She tried to smile but couldn't make her mouth work.

He looked at her awhile longer then sighed and said heavily, 'You don't have to do this.'

She met his eyes. 'I do.'

'No.' He sighed again. 'It feels wrong. No one will blame you if you change your mind.'

She thought again of the barely suppressed fury in her mother's eyes when the family had confronted her about the pregnancy. It was a look she'd never seen from her before, worse than the reproach from her unguarded comments about Dominic, and she prayed she'd never see it again. The angry censure had been in all her blood family's eyes. But not Marcelo, she remembered wistfully. His eyes had been full of sympathy. He'd known exactly how she was feeling because he'd been there himself, trying to fix a mess of his own making.

Their family, though, had never looked at him with the same disappointment they'd looked at Alessia. Their reproval had been laced with understanding of his nature. Their forgiveness for him had come easily.

'*I'll* blame me,' she told her father, whose troubled eyes told her he, at least, had forgiven her. 'I wouldn't be able to live with myself if my actions led to the destruction of the monarchy.' The smile she'd tried to conjure finally came, small though it was, and she took her father's hand and gave it a reassuring squeeze. 'This is for the best. We can trust Gabriel with our family. If we honour our side of the deal, he'll honour his.' Of that, she was certain.

It was the only certainty she had about him.

Shortly, she would leave her quarters and marry a man she knew so little of that when a woman had appeared on his balcony on her wedding morning, Alessia's automatic assumption was that the woman had been his lover.

She knew so little about him that she didn't know if he did have a lover tucked away somewhere. She didn't know if Mariella was his only sibling.

But there was one more thing she did know, and it frightened her badly. That brief moment earlier on the balcony when she'd automatically assumed Mariella to be his lover...it had felt like she'd been hit by a truck.

The relief to learn she was his sister had been dizzying, and then she'd found herself trapped in Gabriel's stare…

She'd seen the desire in his eyes. She'd seen it and been helpless to stop herself from reacting to it, no more than she'd been unable to stop the swelling of her heart when he'd smiled and his face had lit up into something heartbreaking.

So that's the one more thing she knew—how he made her feel. Like a giddy, jealous schoolgirl. And it's what frightened her so badly too.

She didn't want to feel like that for him, full stop. She believed in the commitment he was about to make to her as his wife but she couldn't forget how he'd ignored her. If not for their baby, she would never have seen him again because he didn't think her worth the bother due to their supposed incompatibility. He'd never given her a chance to find out if they could be compatible in ways that didn't involve sex for the simple reason that he hadn't wanted to.

And she couldn't forget how devastated she'd been when she woke up to find him gone.

The Berrutis royal chapel was much bigger than Gabriel had envisaged and so ancient he could feel its history seeping through the high, stone walls and dome ceiling. He could feel his sister's awe at it all as she stood next to him while they waited for the bride to arrive. He could feel the Berruti family's bemusement at his choice of a woman for a best man and that the glamorous best man had donned a feminine tuxedo to match his own. Clara, the newest family member, had clapped her hands in glee at Mariella's outfit.

Gabriel had few friends. He could travel to almost any country in the world and find hospitality from friendly acquaintances, but true friends were rare. Partly this was because of his nomadic lifestyle, always basing himself wherever his current job was located. Partly it was because he liked his own company and would much rather spend a rare evening off sipping a large bourbon and watching a film noir or reading a good thriller. The only person he was close to was his sister. Two years younger than him, they'd been as close as siblings could be since before Mariella was out of nappies. Living in their family's war zone had cemented their closeness. Trusting her implicitly, he'd confided the entire Alessia and baby situation. There had been no judgement or efforts to tell him he was being a fool to throw his life away by marrying a stranger. She knew him well enough not to bother wasting her breath like that.

'Mum would wet herself if she could see this,' Mariella murmured. 'You, marrying a princess in a royal chapel.'

He gave a subtle mock shudder. 'I can well believe it.' Their mother was the most horrendous social climber, a born attention seeker and the root cause of his media hatred. The only thing that stopped her exposing Gabriel as her son to her countless social media followers was the hefty monthly allowance he paid her. A royal wedding, though, no matter how small, would be a temptation too far for her and so he'd made the decision not to invite her. This was his last event as a private person. The circus his life was going to turn into, one that made his guts twist to imagine, could wait a few days longer.

Movement broke the stillness of the chapel and jolted his heart. The bride had arrived. His bride.

Clutching her father's arm, she walked towards him. The closer she came, the clearer she became and the greater his heart swelled.

When she reached him, he carefully lifted the sheer veil. Her eyes locked with his. The swelling in his heart stopped and his chest tightened, crushing it. His jaw locked. Alessia was simply breathtaking. He'd never imagined such beauty existed.

For a long moment she stared at him, then her shoulders rose and she jutted her chin. 'Ready?'

He nodded.

'Good.' She smiled tightly. 'Then let's do this.'

Had there ever been a more miserable excuse for a wedding? Alessia wondered morosely. No wedding march. Only six guests and a priest. She signed her name to the certificate and thought of her large, extended family. They would have loved to be here. She would have loved for them to be here. The only moment that had matched her dreams had been the wedding kiss to seal their vows. Gabriel's eyes had pulsed with a heady sensuality and the promise of more before his warm lips had brushed hers, but even that had been tainted because she couldn't forget that she wasn't his choice for a bride. He wanted her, that was obvious, and he'd said as much in words and body language, but he'd never wanted to want her.

She wished she didn't want him. She wished the woman he'd unlocked in her would go back into hiding.

The ring he'd slid on her finger felt too weighty. She wished she could wrench it off.

Once Marcelo and Clara had signed their parts of the certificate as witnesses, they all left the chapel, cutting through the chapel garden to return to the castle, where a mockery of a banquet had been prepared for them.

'Where's the photographer?' Clara asked as they walked the winding footpath.

'There isn't one,' Gabriel informed her.

'Then can I take a picture of you both? For posterity?'

'That would be nice,' Alessia said at the exact same moment Gabriel politely said, 'The agreement was no photos, but thank you for the offer.'

It was seeing the disbelief on her sister-in-law's face that made Alessia crack and, suddenly frightened she was going to burst into tears, she sped off.

She would not cry in front of Gabriel again.

A hand caught her wrist.

'What's wrong?' Gabriel asked.

'Nothing,' she muttered, loosening her arm from him and setting off again. His legs being much longer than hers, he caught her in seconds and stood before her, blocking her path.

'Clearly something is wrong.' Not an auspicious start to married life, Gabriel thought wryly. 'If I have upset you, you must tell me, else how can I fix it?'

Velvet eyes snapped onto his. 'I don't understand why you don't want pictures taken.'

He strove for patience. 'It was one of my conditions for marrying you. If you had a problem with it you should have said when you had the chance.'

'You made it very clear they were take it or leave it conditions.' She twisted as if to barge past him but then stopped and folded her arms tightly around her chest and raised her chin to meet his stare again. 'You got your way about everything with this wedding.'

'Not the date,' he said lightly, trying to defuse the head of steam she was clearly building up.

'No, that came from my family. Not from me. In fact, not once did you or any of my family ask what *I* wanted from our wedding day.'

'And what did you want?'

'It's a bit late to ask me that now, isn't it?' she suddenly shouted, before kneading the back of her neck and making a visible effort to calm herself. 'I apologise. You were upfront about your conditions and the only thing that really bothered me about them at the time was your refusal to attend Amadeo's wedding and other family events the press will be at, but I didn't really think about our wedding in emotional terms until I put my dress on this morning. I chose this dress because it fitted the simple wedding we were having but my dream was always to wear an elaborate fairy-tale dress with a twelve-foot train and to have a dozen bridesmaids. I always envisaged my entire family and all my friends being there, and a truckload of confetti being tipped over my and the groom's heads, and a huge party afterwards that went on until the sun came up, but I didn't have any of that. So many people I love forbidden to be here, and now I'm not even allowed one photo as a reminder of my wedding day.'

Gabriel stared at the hurt on her face, the same hurt that had sounded in her husky voice, and wondered if she'd been given lessons on how to make a man feel like a heel. He had nothing to feel bad about, he knew that. He'd been upfront and open, unlike his bride, who'd clearly festered about the wedding day she believed her due and which she felt had been denied her. But she'd agreed to this. As she would say, he hadn't put a gun to her head. She'd agreed to this marriage of her own free will and agreed to his conditions, so it was a bit rich to start complaining once the deed was done.

Closing her eyes, she kneaded the back of her neck again and breathed deeply. Then her eyes fluttered open and fixed back on his. 'Ignore me. I'm just feeling a little more emotional than I expected and it's making me unreasonable.'

With an apologetic smile, she set off back down the path.

Gabriel watched her. The sun high above her seemed to cast her in a golden glow. For a moment he could believe she'd been conjured by an enchantment.

'You're not being unreasonable,' he called out, speaking through a boulder that had lodged in his throat.

She turned her head.

He breached the distance between them and gazed down at the pretty heart-shaped face and those sultry velvet eyes. A wave of desire sliced through him. Whether they could ever find common ground to build a successful marriage or not, she was now his wife, and she was breathtaking. There was not a man alive who wouldn't ache to share a bed with her.

Her chest rose, lifting those perfect, pert breasts. The desire tightened, making his skin tauten.

Colour rose on her cheeks. The tips of her breasts strained through the silk of her dress. He leaned his face closer. Her lips parted and her breath quickened. Whatever his wife's personal feelings about him, she wanted him. He could practically smell the desire radiating from her.

'And you're right,' he finally added. 'This is our wedding day. We should have photos to remember it by.' Then he placed his lips to a pretty, delicate ear and whispered thickly, 'And then, tonight, I will give you something else to remember this day by.'

The wedding banquet was as sorry an affair as the wedding itself but Alessia dragged it out as long as she could, eating at the same pace she'd done as a child when she'd wanted to annoy her brothers, who'd been forbidden from leaving the table until everyone had finished. She'd perfected the art of nibbling then and she brought those skills back out now. However, if Gabriel was annoyed at this, he hid it well, eating and drinking and conversing as if it were any meal for any occasion while she was filled with so many emotions that she didn't know how her knotted stomach was admitting food into it. All she could think was that once this banquet was done, the 'celebrations' would be over, and then she and Gabriel would go to her quarters. *Their* quarters.

As much as she tried to block them, his seductive words before he'd called Clara over to take photos of them kept ringing in her head. Every time she recalled them, heat flushed through her, a powerful throb deep in her pelvis sucking the air from her lungs. The same things happened every time she met his eye and caught the anticipatory gleam in them. Frightened at the strength of her desire for him, she tried hard not to look at him, but it was like Gabriel were a magnet her eyes were drawn to.

There were so many knots forming inside her that she couldn't work out if it was dread or excitement causing them. Or a mixture of both. Their night together had been so wonderful that the thought of experiencing it all again was almost too tantalising to bear, but the way Gabriel had left her the next morning and then ghosted her… Her new husband had hurt her badly, and if she didn't protect herself, she feared he would hurt her again.

She hated that her body and her head, the woman and the princess, were at such odds. Until she found a way to marry the two, she didn't know how she could dare risk letting him touch her and risk losing her head like she'd done the first time with him.

'Have you decided when you're going on honeymoon?' Clara asked from across the table.

Alessia had a drink of her water, wishing it was wine. 'We're not having one.'

Clara looked like she had something to say about this but Marcelo whispered in her ear and she clamped her lips together.

A honeymoon was something else Alessia would miss out on. And being carried across a threshold… She'd fantasised about that many times, being swept into her hunky husband's arms and carried through the door and laid lovingly on their marital bed…

She grabbed her spoon and stabbed it into her ricotta and cinnamon trifle, and gritted her teeth. She needed to stop these foolish thoughts. It was done. She'd married him.

As her old headmistress had loved to espouse, she'd made her bed and now she had to lie in it. What her old headmistress had not espoused was how this was supposed to be achieved when one had to share that bed with a man it was imperative she protect her heart against.

CHAPTER SEVEN

THE BEATS OF Gabriel's heart were heavy as he followed Alessia into what was now their shared quarters, at least until the renovations of the converted stable block were completed. When he'd visited her after their marriage had been agreed, he hadn't taken much notice of any of it other than her bedroom but now he craned his neck around the high walls to take in the sumptuous furnishings, many of which he suspected were family heirlooms centuries old and much of which were too large for the rooms that were, surprisingly, the same size as the ones in the quarters he'd stayed in. They could never be described as small but in comparison to her parents' and brother's quarters, they were as pint-sized as the princess who lived in them. But there was plenty of modernity there too, the new blending perfectly with the old to create an eclectic apartment that was feminine and chic and regal all rolled into one. Although not to his taste, it was an apartment that suited Alessia perfectly and he couldn't deny the throb in his loins to know that soon—very soon—they would share that princess bed.

His new wife, who'd walked silently with her hands

clasped together from the banquet room to their quarters, kicked her shoes off and hovered in the day room doorway, not looking at him. 'I need to shower so I'll leave you to familiarise yourself with the place. It's virtually the same as the quarters you stayed in so you shouldn't get lost.'

'Where has my stuff been put?' He'd been told his suitcases would be moved to his new quarters and his possessions unpacked for him.

She swallowed. 'In my dressing room. Come, I'll show you.'

He followed her up the stairs and caught the brief hesitation before she opened the bedroom door.

She padded across the room and opened the dressing room door. 'I've made as much room for you as I can but I'm afraid it's quite small—this section of the castle is four hundred years old, so relatively modern compared to other parts, and was once lodgings for courtiers until my great-grandparents had them all fiddled about with to create family apartments. This one and the one you stayed in are by far the smallest and were intended for visiting family but it was always my favourite, I don't know why, and when I came of age, I asked to have it rather than move into the one earmarked for me. The only thing missing from it was a dressing room so they stole space from the guest bedroom to create one for me.'

She paused for breath, a sheepish expression crossing her face. 'A very long-winded way of telling you that there isn't much space for your things. I'm sorry. I had all my ball gowns moved into the guest room, so if you find it all too cramped, you can put some of your stuff in there too. I hope that's okay?'

Leaning against the arch of the door beside her, Gabriel gazed at his bride.

Anticipation for what the night would bring had tortured him since he'd seen her on the balcony that morning, and now they were finally alone and all the fantasies that had sustained him through the long wedding banquet, of peeling that sheer dress from her perfect body and then kissing every inch of her soft skin before burying himself in her tight sweetness, could be acted on.

But he would keep his desire in check awhile longer. Even through his fantasies he'd sensed Alessia's nerves growing as the banquet had gone on and guessed the anticipation of their wedding night had got the better of her. It was up to him to help her relax.

'I didn't bring much with me so I'm sure it's all fine,' he assured her with a slow smile. The dressing room, long though it was, *was* small but cleverly designed to maximise every available inch of space. The left-hand side bulged with feminine colour. The right-hand side— his side—had barely a third of the available space taken. 'See, plenty of room.'

She rubbed her arm. 'When will you bring the rest of your stuff?'

'When we move into the stables. In the meantime, I'll be spending my working weeks in Madrid so will keep the majority of my stuff in my home there.'

Her eyes met his, perfectly plucked eyebrows drawing together. 'I thought you were giving up your business? You said you'd got your affairs in order.'

'No, only my affairs concerning the client I was supposed to start with this week. I will be winding my main business down but I have many other business interests too. There isn't the space for me to work here.'

A flintiness came into the velvet eyes, an edge appearing in her voice. 'I know my quarters are cramped but it's a castle with over three hundred rooms. An office can be created for you without any problem, and it can be as big as you want.'

'It's more convenient to base myself in Madrid—it's easier to travel to the countries I do business in from there,' he explained. 'By the time we move into the stables and the baby's born, my affairs will be much more straightforward and my need to travel much reduced.' Having their child and not having to live in the castle itself should hopefully make living in this royal goldfish bowl more bearable.

The flintiness sharpened. 'That sounds like an excuse to me.'

'It's a truth. The other truth is that I have no wish to live in this castle full-time. There are too many staff to have any real privacy and I suspect that being under this roof means your family and their personal staff will be incentivised to try and change my mind about being a working member of the family. If I'm out of sight then I'm more likely to be out of mind.'

'Is being a working member such an intolerable idea to you?'

'Yes.'

'And you don't think having a husband who spends his working weeks away is an intolerable idea to me?'

'It is only until the renovations are complete.'

'Which could take months.' She raised her chin and gave a smile as flinty as the expression in her eyes. 'I shall come to Madrid with you.'

'That isn't necessary,' he stated as smoothly as he could in an effort to diffuse what his antennae was warning him: that Alessia was spoiling for an argument.

'Why not? Do you have a woman stashed in Madrid waiting for you?'

Surprised at both the question and the tone in which she asked it, he narrowed his eyes. 'Of course not.'

'Then you can have no objection to me travelling there with you.'

Gabriel closed his eyes and inhaled deeply before staring back at the face that now brimmed with what he was coming to recognise as temper. He had no choice but to add fuel to it. 'I'm afraid it's out of the question.'

'Why?'

'Because a circus follows wherever you go, and I have no wish to be a part of it. I've already made that clear.'

'The media circus is not my fault.'

'I am simply stating my reasons.'

'The moment the announcement of our marriage is made public the circus will be on you.'

'But your presence will make it more. The media love you.'

'I don't encourage that.'

'I never said you did, only that I wish to avoid it as much as I can.'

'Then you shouldn't have agreed to marry me. I'm sorry you find the thought of media intrusion so abhorrent but it is possible to have a life as a royal that isn't always accompanied by the flash of cameras, as you will learn for yourself when I accompany you on your travels.'

For the first time, visible anger darkened Gabriel's features but Alessia was too angry at his insinuations about her character and hurt at his readiness to spend the majority of his time apart from her to care about it. 'It's bad enough that I'll be humiliated by a husband who refuses to be my prince even at my own brother's wedding, but I will not be humiliated by a husband who marries me one minute then flies off without me the next too, especially when that wasn't a pre-condition of our marriage, so get used to the idea of having me by your side. If you do have any lovers stashed anywhere, warn them now that you can no longer see them because your wife refuses to be separated from you.' And with that, Alessia snatched a pair of pyjamas off a shelf and stalked into the bathroom, locking the door firmly behind her.

Alessia had never appreciated how greatly the presence of another could change an atmosphere. Her quarters, her bedroom especially, had been her favourite place in the castle since she was a little girl and would make Marcelo go exploring with her. She truly didn't know what it was that she loved so much about it other than its warm atmosphere—lots of the castle's rooms were cold and unwelcoming to a little girl—but she'd gladly foregone the much larger apartment that could have been hers for it. Gabriel's presence had changed its atmosphere markedly.

They danced cordially around each other as they

readied for bed, taking it in turns to use the bathroom, giving each other privacy to undress, and all with fixed, polite smiles that brimmed with a seething undercurrent.

How many brides and grooms argued on their wedding night? she wondered bitterly. Not that they'd argued as such. She doubted Gabriel ever raised his voice. No, Gabriel preferred to make his arguments behind a smooth cordiality she was growing to detest. But she'd seen the anger in his eyes when she'd stood her ground and refused to accept being treated like a chattel. Well, tough. He'd married her. If she had to live in the bed they'd both made then so should he.

Climbing into the bed she'd never shared before, wearing long silk pyjamas with buttons running the length of the top, Alessia leaned her back against the headboard and reached for her book. She always read in bed but tonight was painfully aware she was using her novel as a prop. She imagined that, for Gabriel, sharing a bed with a woman was no big deal. She wished it wasn't a big deal for her too, but apart from the one night they'd shared, this was her first time and her nerves had grown so big that she wasn't sure if they were causing the nausea rampaging in her stomach or if baby hormones were to blame.

When he finally left the bathroom, she took one look at him and her heart juddered, the ripples spreading through her like wildfire. Wearing only a pair of snug black briefs that bulged at the front and accentuated the rugged athleticism of his physique, she doubted Adonis himself could have made a greater impact. She'd seen him entirely naked, of course, but they'd spent that night entwined, and she'd seen him in shorts on the balcony that morning, but the balustrade had hidden much of him. She hadn't had the opportunity to take in everything about him with one sweep of her eyes. All the disparate parts had come together and as he stalked to the bed, eyes softer…and yet more alive…than they'd been when she'd last looked into them, her most intimate parts became molten liquid, and all she could think was that he was the sexiest man to roam the earth or heavens.

The mattress made only the slightest movement as he slipped between the bedsheets but it was movement enough to stop her from breathing. His whispered words from the chapel garden rang in her ear again. *'Tonight, I will give you something else to remember this day by.'*

She gripped her book harder and pressed the top of her thighs together as if that could stop the pulsing heat that was spreading from down low in her pelvis.

The thuds of her heart were suddenly deafening.

She sensed his gaze turn to her. Alessia's lungs squeezed so tightly there was no chance of getting air into them even if she could breathe.

This must be the moment that he reached for her and took her in his arms…

A hard scrub of his body had finally cleansed Gabriel of the unwelcome anger inflamed by Alessia's stubborn insistence that she accompany him to Madrid.

Every time she left the castle it was under the flash of camera lenses. He accepted that those flashes and having the press on her heels—having to smile politely and answer their questions—was something she considered a normal part of her life, but she had to accept too that it was not the kind of life he was willing to live.

He'd been upfront about it and it was not something he was prepared to compromise on.

But he did accept that he would have to get used to a degree of press intrusion, at least for a short period. As Alessia had rightly pointed out, the moment their marriage was made public, the circus would begin. That didn't mean he had to feed the vultures. A refusal to engage with them or give them anything remotely newsworthy would make the press quickly bore of him.

He doubted the press would ever bore with Alessia. On top of being breathtakingly beautiful and photogenic, she was a style icon to millions. She sold magazines and generated social media clicks by doing nothing but be herself, and, he had to admit, raised great awareness for the charities she patronised as a result.

Staring at her now, he could see from the rigid way she held herself, her clenched jaw and the whites of her knuckles where she held her book, that her anger still lingered. And there was something else in her body language too, there in the tiny tremors of her body... Alessia was as aware of him as he was of her.

Having had enough of the game of silence, Gabriel plucked the book from her hand, then leaned over her to place it on her antique bedside table. He caught the intake of her breath at the same moment the soft fruity scent of Alessia hit his senses.

Had any woman ever smelt so good? Not in his lifetime.

With his back propped against the velvet headboard, he kept his gaze on her until she finally turned her face and those amazing dark velvet eyes locked onto him.

'Let me put your mind at ease,' he said. 'I don't have

a lover stashed in Madrid or anywhere. My last relationship ended months ago. I'm strictly monogamous.'

He was rewarded with continued silence.

'And you?' he prompted when she did nothing but gaze into his eyes as if searching for something. 'Are you monogamous too?'

Her teeth grazed her bottom lip. 'I suppose.'

Surprised at her equivocation, he raised a brow. 'Suppose? Surely it's a question that requires only a yes or no answer.'

'Then… Yes.'

Something dark coiled inside him, as unexpected as it was disarming, but he controlled it. 'You don't look certain.'

'I am.'

He stared hard into her brown eyes. His expertise at reading people meant Gabriel knew when someone was lying to him. Alessa was not being truthful. He was certain of it. Which begged the question of why she was lying. As far as he was aware, she'd never been linked to a man so she was discreet in her affairs, probably conducting them all within the castle or in the homes of trusted friends. When it came to cheating, though, he imagined things would get trickier. There were tabloids he knew who would pay a small fortune for a story of Princess Alessia being a love cheat.

If she wasn't a love cheat then why the hesitation about being monogamous? Whatever the answer, the darkness thickened and coiled tighter, and tightened his vocal chords too, and it was a real struggle to keep his voice moderate. 'I don't care what you got up to in your past but I will not accept you taking lovers.' He bore his gaze into hers so there could be no misunderstanding. 'You don't wish to be humiliated by me travelling without you, and I will not suffer the humiliation of being cuckolded. We're married now which means it's you and me, and only you and me. Is that clear?'

Alessia fought the very real urge to laugh. She was quite sure it would come out sounding hysterical.

What would he say if she told him the truth, that he'd been her first? Which incidentally meant he would also be her last.

But how could she tell him that now when she should have told him weeks ago, before things had gone too far between them? How could he forgive her for it? If she hadn't been so inexperienced she would have realised he hadn't put a condom on, but as it was, she'd made the fatal assumption that he'd taken care of things while she'd been in a blissful bubble of sensual feeling. If she'd told him she was a virgin then the subject of contraception would definitely have come up—one thing she knew about her new husband was that he did not leave anything to chance.

If she'd told him she was a virgin he would never have made love to her…

'Are you not going to say anything?' he asked curtly.

Pushing the bedsheets off her lap, she crossed her legs as she twisted to face him. The Ice Man stared back at her, his handsome face expressionless, large hands folded loosely against his taut abdomen. For the beat of a moment the temptation to drag her fingers through the dark hair covering his muscular chest and press down where his heart beat made her skin tingle.

'What do you want me to say?' she asked.

His eyes flashed, but other than that, his expression remained unreadable. 'Whatever's going on in your pretty head would be a start.'

She felt a flare of pleasure at the compliment.

'Trust me, you don't want to know what's in my head.' She linked her fingers together to stop herself, again, from dragging them over his supremely masculine chest. 'But let me put *your* mind at ease—I didn't take my vows lightly. I knew that making them meant I was committing myself to you for the rest of my life, and *only* you.'

His nostrils flared. 'Good.'

'But so we are clear, I am now your wife but that doesn't make me your possession.'

His wife…

'I never said you were.'

'I just wanted to make that clear.'

He leaned forwards, closer to her, a wry expression on his face. 'You did.'

Alessia had no idea why the knots in her belly had loosened so much. If she didn't know better, she would say Gabriel had sounded jealous, but then she reminded herself that if he were, it would only be from a proprietorial sense and not from a place of emotion like her own bout of jealousy had come from that morning.

Grazing her bottom lip, she suddenly blurted out, 'Do you really think I'm pretty?'

He stared at her as if she'd asked the most stupid question in the world. 'Yes.'

'Really?'

He pulled a cynical face. 'I can't be the first man to have told you that.'

'Oh, I've been told I'm pretty by lots of people but I never know whether to believe them or not.' She shrugged. 'My family are biased, and people like to ingratiate themselves with me. Then there are all the trolls out there who like to tell me that I'm pig ugly, so who knows what I should believe.'

The cynicism vanished. 'You have trolls?'

'Everyone in the public eye has trolls.' She tried not to sound too downbeat about it. If trolls were the worst thing she had to deal with in her privileged life then she had nothing to complain about. 'Nowadays, it comes with the job.'

'Who are these people?'

'Mostly anonymous. It doesn't matter.'

'Of course it matters,' Gabriel disputed roughly. The thought of anyone sitting in front of their phone or computer and targeting Alessia for their poison... He clasped her hand and leaned closer to her, staring straight into the velvet depths. 'Anyone who tells you that you're ugly needs to seek help because you're more than pretty. You're beautiful.'

She stilled, the only movement the widening of her eyes and the parting of her lips as she took a sharp intake of breath. A crawl of colour suffused her cheeks. 'Do you really mean that?' she whispered.

He drew even closer so the tips of their noses almost touched. 'You're beautiful,' he repeated. 'So beautiful that sometimes I look at you and think you must have been created by an enchantment.' And then he did what he'd been aching to do for so long, and tilted his head, brushed his lips to hers and breathed her in.

For the longest time he did nothing but allow his

senses to fill with the delicate scent of Alessia's skin. Then he kissed her, gentle sweeping movements that slowly deepened until their lips parted in unison and their tongues entwined in a private dance that sent sensation shooting through him like an electric current through his veins.

All these weeks, Alessia's scent and taste had haunted him, memories so strong he'd come to believe he'd imagined just how intoxicating they were. His memories hadn't lied. Hooking an arm around her waist and pulling her to him, he fed himself on kisses that were as headily addictive and as potent as the strongest aphrodisiac could be.

With a soft sigh, she sank fully into him, returning his hunger with a ravenousness that only fed his burning arousal even more. Tightly she wrapped her arms around his neck, hands and fingers clasping the back of his head, her perfect breasts pressed against his chest, as the passion that had caught them in its grips all those weeks ago cast its tendrils back around them.

From the first whisper of his breath against her lips, Alessia had been reduced to nothing but sensation. The dark taste of Gabriel and the burning thrills of his touch raged through her flesh and veins, feeding the craving for him that she'd carried in every cell of her body since the night they'd...

'No!'

CHAPTER EIGHT

ALESSIA'S MOUTH SHOUTED the word and wrenched away from him before her brain caught up.

Her heart thumping madly, her skin and loins practically screaming their outrage at the severing of such dazzling pleasure, she disentangled herself from his arms and scrambled backwards out of reach.

Stunned eyes followed her movements, Gabriel's breaths coming in short, ragged bursts. 'What's wrong?' he asked hoarsely.

Trying hard to control her own breathing, trying even harder to control the wails of disappointment from her body, Alessia shakily shook her head. 'I can't do this. I'm sorry, but I can't. It's too soon.'

He stared at her in disbelief. 'What are you talking about? How can you say it's too soon when we've just got married?'

'It just is!' she cried, before her lips clamped together and she crossed her arms to hold her biceps, gripping them tightly as protection, not from him but from herself because like the rest of her furious body, her hands were howling to clasp themselves to his cheeks so her equally furious lips could attach themselves back to his mouth, and the whole of her could revel again in the heady delights of Gabriel. Her pelvis felt like it was on fire. Her blood burned. *Everything* burned.

His face contorted and he cursed under his breath before his chest rose as he inhaled deeply, visibly composing himself. 'You have to talk to me,' he said. She could take little comfort that the smoothly controlled voice had a ragged tone to it. 'Tell me what's on your mind. I'm trying to make sense of what you mean about it being too soon when we already know how good we are together. The night we made our child is proof of that.'

'And you walked out the next day without a word of goodbye or even a note,' she retorted tremulously, because it was remembering that little fact that had snapped her out of the sensual haze she'd been caught in.

This time his curse was more audible, and he closed his eyes.

'Are you not going to say anything?' she asked in an attempt to mimic the curt tone he'd used on her earlier, but the upset in her voice was just too strong for it to be successful.

Nausea churned heavily in Gabriel's guts. He'd apologised for not returning her call but the fact of him leaving her sleeping while he slipped out of the room had been left unsaid. He should have known this conversation would one day come.

Arousal still coursed like fire through his loins and veins, and he closed his eyes again and concentrated on tempering it. Then he locked his stare back on her. 'I left without saying goodbye because when I woke next to you, I felt like the biggest jerk in the world.'

Her chin wobbled but she didn't look away. 'Why?'

'Because your family were generous enough to give me a bed for the night when my plane was grounded and I repaid that generosity by sleeping with their daughter.'

'I'm a twenty-three-year-old woman.'

'But you're not an ordinary woman. You're a princess.'

'I'm also a woman. A woman with feelings, not some mythical creature that can't be hurt.'

'I behaved terribly. I know that. When I woke up... Alessia, I was sickened with myself, not just because of who you are and the abuse of your parents' hospitality but because I never mix business with pleasure. Never.'

Her eyes continued to search his until her neck straightened and something that almost resembled a smile played on her lips. 'You mean I was your first? Mixing of business with pleasure, I mean?'

'Yes.'

Her gaze searched his for a moment more before the smile widened a touch. 'Should I be flattered?'

'If you like.'

'I do like.' Then the smile faded and she stilled again. 'I can understand why you felt bad about yourself for what happened. But, Gabriel, that doesn't excuse or explain your behaviour towards me.'

'It's the truth of it all.'

'Maybe, but it doesn't excuse it. It doesn't. I had the best night of my life with you and then I woke up and you were gone. Do you know how that made me feel?'

He took a long inhale.

'Dirty. I've never...' She swallowed, and drew her knees to her chest and wrapped her arms around them.

'I've never had a one-night stand before. Don't misunderstand me, I didn't fall into your arms expecting any of this—' she waved a hand absently '—to happen, but finding you gone… It hurt. To feel unworthy of even a minute of your time after what we'd shared.'

'I'm sorry,' he said, speaking through a throat that felt like it had razors in it. 'It was never my intention to make you feel like that.'

'Then what was your intention?'

'To get out of Ceres. It felt like I'd woken from a spell and all I could do was kick myself for losing my head the way I did.'

An astuteness came into her stare. 'You don't like losing control of yourself, do you?'

'No,' he agreed.

'Why is that?'

'It's just the way I am.'

She gave a grimacing smile and rubbed her chin against her knees. 'I think we can both agree that what we shared was…madness. A child was created through it and here we are. But I'm sorry, Gabriel, I can't forget how I felt when I realised you'd gone. I kept hoping you sneaked out because you were worried about making love with a princess and my family's reaction if they found out—I guess I was partially right there—so I decided to be a modern woman and call you. I hoped you'd see my message and realise I was just a woman like any other and that there was nothing to stop us seeing each other again, but you blanked me there too, and I can't forget that. I can't forget how cheap you made me feel. I want to put it behind me—I've married you so we're stuck together now—but I've got nothing to replace those feelings with because you're still a stranger to me, and until you start opening up about who you really are, you'll continue to be a stranger.'

Alessia's heart was beating hard. Her body was still furious with her for severing the passionate connection with Gabriel and, though she knew she'd done the right thing in not letting things go any further, the ache deep inside was a taunt that she was being a prideful fool.

She didn't think she'd ever been so honest about her feelings before. 'Never complain and never explain' was a creed many royal families lived by and it was a creed she'd taken to heart at a very young age. The only person she'd ever felt able to open up to was her brother Marcelo, and even then she'd often held back because he'd suffered for being who he was born to be far more than she ever had. Alessia had never yearned to be someone else like him.

In many ways, laying her cards on the table was liberating, and she experienced a little jolt to realise that there was something in Gabriel that put her at ease enough to say what was on her mind and in her heart without sanitising or editing. There was another jolt to realise that when she was with him, she didn't have to *be* a princess. And it wasn't just about him bringing out the woman beneath the princess mask—for Gabriel, the mask dropped itself of its own accord.

And then she remembered, again, keeping her virginity from him and another spasm of guilt cut through her.

It shouldn't matter, she knew that. Her sexual history— or lack of it—was no one's business but her own. It shouldn't matter, but she suspected that for Gabriel it would.

After the longest passage of silence had passed, hands more than twice the size of hers wrapped around her fingers.

'I can see I have much to do to make amends,' he said, his expression as serious as his tone, 'and I will do my best to do that. There is much to learn about each other, but I should warn you, I'm not one for baring my soul. I have always been a private person.'

'Would you believe it, but I'm not one for baring my soul either?' She gave a rueful shrug. 'Not usually, in any case.' And then she shook her head as if disbelieving. 'And yet I cried in your arms and told you everything I was feeling that night because on some level I must have trusted you.'

It was the first time Alessia had considered that. Though there had been no forethought behind it, she'd trusted Gabriel with her feelings as well as with her body that night. She'd unbuttoned herself to him like she'd never done with anyone else on this earth, and then he'd left her life as if he'd never been in it. Was it any wonder she was so scared of getting close to him again?

The look on Gabriel's face as another long stretch of time passed told her he was thinking the same thoughts.

'Yes,' he finally said. 'I think I do believe that, and I will do whatever it takes to rebuild your trust in me.' Then he released her hands and lifted the bedsheet for her. In a softer tone, he said, 'It is late. We should get some sleep.'

She hesitated. Should she sleep in the guest room? Insist he sleep in it?

But the expression in his gaze was steady. Reassuring. And it made her mind up for her.

Her heart in her throat, Alessia slipped back under the sheets while Gabriel leaned over to turn out the lights, then her heart almost shot out of her ribs when he reached for her.

'I'm just going to hold you,' he murmured, and pulled her rigid body to him. Then, having manoeuvred her as easily as if he were manipulating play dough so that her cheek was pressed into his chest and their arms wrapped around each other, he dropped a kiss into her hair. 'Goodnight, wife.'

'Goodnight, husband,' she whispered.

The moment Alessia awoke, her eyes pinged open. There was an arm draped over her waist, the attached hand loose against her belly. A knee rested in the back of her calf.

The duskiness of the room told her the sun had already risen.

From Gabriel's steady, rhythmic breathing, he was in deep sleep.

She had no idea how long she lay there, afraid to move so much as a muscle. Afraid of the feelings swirling inside her. The deep yearn to wriggle back into his solid body and press herself to him. To wake him…

Holding her breath, she slowly inched herself out from under his arm. Once she'd inched herself off the bed too, she carefully picked up her book and her phone, and crept out of the room. Only when the door was closed behind her was she able to breathe.

Downstairs, she padded into the kitchen and fixed herself a coffee. It was the one thing she liked to do for herself, and when she had days without any engagements, she relished the solitude and independence the early mornings gave her. The days she had engagements, staff surrounded her before she'd even climbed out of bed.

Her hand clenched around her favourite coffee mug, and she squeezed her eyes shut. Hurt and anger had made her tell Gabriel she would accompany him to Madrid. She wondered if he would even pretend not to be relieved when she told him that wouldn't be possible after all?

Rolling her neck, she pulled herself together and took her coffee into the day room, opened the curtains, snuggled into her reading chair and opened the book.

Ten minutes later and she was still on the same page. It didn't matter how many times she read the same passage, the words refused to penetrate. Or should that be, her brain refused to concentrate?

With a sigh, she closed her eyes.

Her brain refused to concentrate because it wanted to think about Gabriel, and nothing but Gabriel.

Wasn't it enough that her stupid brain had taken for ever to go to sleep because Gabriel's arms had been around her and her every inhalation had breathed in the divine scent of his skin? Wasn't it enough that her body had also taken for ever to relax itself into sleep for the exact same reason? She swore it had taken at least an hour before she'd even been able to breathe properly. And then there were all the thoughts that had crowded her already frazzled mind, every single one about Gabriel, never mind the battle between her mind and her rigid yet aching body. That had been the worst of it. That yearning ache deep inside her that had spent hours begging her to wake him with a kiss.

'You're up early.'

If Alessia hadn't already finished her coffee she would have spilt the contents of her mug, which was still in her hand, all over herself.

Snapping her eyes open, she turned her head and found Gabriel in the doorway looking at her with an expression that made her heart inflate and her belly flip.

Black hair mussed, his jaw and neck thick with stubble, all he wore was a pair of low-slung black jeans that perfectly showed off the muscular chest her face had spent half the night pressed against, and the yearning that had kept her awake for hours hit her with its full force.

The hint of a smile played on his mouth. 'What does a man do for coffee here?'

Her certainty that he could sense or see the effect he was having on her sent a flush of heat thrashing through her, and she had to clear her throat to speak. 'There's a pot made in the kitchen.' Trying not to cringe at the overt croak in her voice, she straightened her back and added, 'If you're hungry, press three on any landline and it will connect you to the palace kitchen. The chefs will make you anything you want.'

The only thing I want is you, Gabriel thought. Although the angle of Alessia's armchair hid much of her from his sight, the little he could see was enough to make his chest tighten and his pulses surge. That his appearance had such a visible effect on her only heightened the sensations, and he ground his feet into the carpet and filled his lungs slowly before speaking again. 'Have you eaten?'

She tucked a strand of her silky dark hair behind an ear. 'Not yet. I'll order something later, but please, don't wait for me. The chefs are used to preparing dishes any time of the day or night.'

'I'll wait until you eat. Did you want another coffee?'

'No, thank you. I'm limiting myself to one a day.' She pressed her belly as explanation.

The tightness in his chest loosened and expanded, and he nodded his understanding. 'Can I get you anything else?'

'No. But thank you.'

Gabriel nodded again and turned down the corridor that led to the kitchen. The aroma of freshly ground coffee greeted him, and he poured himself a cup and added a heaped spoonful of sugar while taking a moment to gather himself together.

He'd fallen asleep surprisingly easily considering everything, but had woken with a weighty feeling in the pit of his stomach. He'd felt Alessia's absence from the bed at the same moment everything that had occurred between them on their wedding night had flashed through his mind. The weighty feeling had spread to his chest as, for the first time, he had an insight into how she must have felt that morning to find him gone.

Why had he never allowed himself to think of that before? He didn't have the answer. He'd always acknowledged to himself that his behaviour that morning had been abhorrent but all the justifications he'd heaped on himself had smothered his ability to think of how it must have been for Alessia.

He wished he could say that she was overreacting. One-night stands happened all the time. Alessia wasn't his first and, princess though she was, she was a modern woman so he doubted he was hers either—although her reaction to his question about monogamy and his reaction to that reaction told him previous relationships were a subject best avoided between them—but what they'd shared did *not* happen all the time. The chemistry between them had been off the charts.

It still was.

That Alessia refused to act on the chemistry was a situation of his own making. It was on him to make things right.

Carrying his coffee back to the main living area, he took a seat on the armchair closest to her. Her eyes flickered up from the book she was reading, colour rising on her cheeks.

'I would like us to take a visit to the stables at some point this weekend,' he said. 'We need to start thinking about how we want it to be renovated.'

'Sure.' She closed her book. 'I'll ask Ena—my private secretary—to find the keys for us. She'll be at her desk in an hour.'

'What about your domestic staff? What time do they start?' All the times he'd been at the castle, whatever the time, the stone walls had contained a hive of activity, worker bees efficiently getting on with their individual tasks, unobtrusive but always in the background.

'This is an official day off for me so they won't come until I call for them.'

'Do you have many free days?'

'My weekends are normally free, but sometimes I have engagements to attend, sometimes issues crop up that need to be dealt with—my role within the family isn't something I can turn on and off. None of us can.'

'How many engagements do you go to each week?'

'It varies.'

'What do you like to do in your free time?'

Alessia studied him warily before answering. All this talk about engagements made her think there was a real irony in Gabriel making the effort to engage with her as he was currently doing when she'd been the driving force on their night together, forcing him to engage in conversation with her. She remembered thinking that he didn't seem to like her. Clearly he'd wanted her but that was physical desire. It was the liking of *her*, her personality, she'd had doubts about. She still had them. For all his excuses about ghosting her, she couldn't help but think that if he'd liked her more, he would have returned her call.

She wished she didn't feel so resentful that he was only making this effort to engage and get to know her now as part of his efforts to build trust between them so they could have some kind of harmony in their marriage rather than because he wanted to know her for her own sake as she'd so longed to know him.

But there was no point thinking like this. She had to think of their marriage as being like her headmistress's proverbial bed and imagine it having a lumpy mattress. Alessia had no choice but to lie on it and play her part in flattening those lumps, and as she thought that, she was helpless to stop the image of them naked, entwined together on a real bed, and helpless to stop another wave of longing.

She expelled a slow breath and forced herself to answer. 'Sometimes I see friends. Sometimes I go shopping. Sometimes I'll spend a whole day reading or watching boxsets. It depends.' And then, because she knew she *had* to get over her resentment and find a way to deal with her hurt otherwise she'd be condemning them both to a lifetime of misery, added, 'What about you? What do you do on your days off?'

'I don't take many days off but when I have free time I like to unwind with a bourbon and a good film or a book.' He nodded at the book on her lap. 'What are you reading?'

Bracing herself for a cutting comment, Alessia showed him the cover. It was a historical romance, the kind of book her brothers had always laughed at her for enjoying.

Gabriel didn't seem to find anything amusing about her literary choice, pulling a musing face and asking, 'Any good?'

'So far.'

'Do you read only historical books?'

'I'll read anything.'

'Me too, although I tend to lean towards thrillers and biographies. I have a library at my home in Madrid. I'm sure you'll find something on the shelves you'll enjoy.'

Caution made her reluctant to jump to conclusions. 'Does that mean you're going to let me come with you?'

'I don't remember you giving me any choice in the

matter,' he said dryly. 'But you're right, I didn't make it a precondition of our marriage and, having thought about it, it would be good for you to see the place I call home. All I ask is that your presence there is kept from the press. I am serious about my privacy, Alessia, and would like any press intrusion to be kept to an absolute minimum.'

So he didn't actually want her to come. Like this whole conversation, it was a sop to her.

She lifted her chin, determined not to show the hurt. 'Our press office only notifies the press about my movements for official engagements so that won't be a problem.'

'Good.'

'But if it does become a problem, I'm sure you'll be glad to know I'll only be able to travel with you next week. After that, I'm afraid my engagement diary's full, so you will get your wish to have me out of your hair Mondays to Fridays after all. Now, if you'll excuse me, I'm going to do my dance exercises and take a shower.' Already regretting the flash of bitterness she'd had no control over, Alessia rose from her chair and, in a softer tone, added, 'Order yourself some breakfast—please, don't go hungry on my account.'

Before she could walk away, though, he said, 'Have you heard of Monica Binoche?'

She turned her face back to him. 'The French actress?' Monica Binoche was the actress Marcelo had had a crush on in his early teenage years. Alessia distinctly remembered him asking their father if she could be invited to castle so he could meet her, and their father laughing and replying with something along the lines of 'If only.'

'Yes.' Gabriel took a deep breath, and watched her reaction closely as he said, 'She's my mother.'

CHAPTER NINE

ALESSIA'S MOUTH DROPPED OPEN, her eyes widening in shock.

'Monica Binoche is my mother and the reason I value my privacy so highly,' Gabriel explained evenly. 'My father was Pedro Gonzalez. You probably haven't heard of him but he was a well-respected acting agent. He died in his sleep five years ago. Heart failure.'

She sat back on her armchair, her face expressing nothing but compassion. 'That's awful. I'm so sorry.'

He smiled grimly. 'Thank you. It was not unexpected. He was seventy-eight and not in good health. I loved him, I miss him, but it's my mother I want to talk to you about.'

He'd never discussed either of his parents with anyone but his sister in his entire adult life other than in generic terms, but Alessia wanted to know who he was and why, and until she knew, she would never trust him. He could see too that she deserved to know his past so she could understand that his refusal to play the royal media game was not anything personal or a slight against her or her family.

'There is nothing my mother enjoys more than attention,' he said. 'It's what feeds her. As children, my sister and I were accessories to her. I don't mean to paint her as a bad mother—she tried her best—but she thought nothing of using Mariella and I as props for photo opportunities. For my mother, it's a terrible day if she leaves the house and there isn't a swarm of paparazzi waiting on the doorstep. I used to have to fight my way through them just to go to school. On quiet celebrity news days, they would sometimes wait outside the school gate for us.'

'But I thought France had strict privacy laws?'

'It does. Much stricter than what you have here in Ceres. What you're not taking into consideration is that my mother encouraged it. She wanted her privacy invaded. It's how she found validation—how she still finds it.'

'That must have been rough for you,' she said softly.

'It was infuriating. And it was the reason I didn't invite her to our wedding. She hasn't used me as an accessory in twenty years, not since I gave her the ultimatum, but I didn't want to put temptation in her way. Inviting her to a royal wedding, no matter how small it was, and expecting her not to put it on her social media feeds would be like locking a recovering alcoholic in a fully stocked English pub.'

Her eyes hadn't left his face since he'd started his explanation. 'What was the ultimatum you gave her?'

'That either she stopped using Mariella and me as props for her ego or we'd move in full-time with our father.' He gave a wry smile. 'See? She does love us in her own way because it all stopped right then.'

'Your parents divorced?'

'They separated when I was twelve.'

'Because of your mother's behaviour?'

He laughed. 'His behaviour wasn't much better. My father was her agent and credited himself with ensuring her big break. As her fame grew, his jealousy grew and he started having affairs, I think to validate himself and to humiliate her. He wasn't very discreet about it. He was thirty years older than her screwing around like a teenager. She was an aging ingenue terrified of the aging process and being thought irrelevant. It was a toxic combination that eventually turned into warfare between them. Both of them blamed the other for the destruction of their marriage and both refused to move out of the marital home or give an inch on custody of me and Mariella. Neither of them was prepared to give an inch on anything.'

Alessia's head was reeling. Whatever could be said about her own childhood and upbringing, the security of her parents' marriage had never been in doubt. She'd rarely heard them exchange a cross word. 'That must have been tough to live with.'

'It was. They both tried hard to be good parents to us but there were a few years when they were too wrapped up in their mutual loathing to notice the damage they were doing.'

'What made them see sense?'

'Me.'

'You?'

He inclined his head. 'I'd listened to so many of their screaming matches that I knew exactly what their issues with each other were and what they both wanted, so I sat them down individually and brokered peace negotiations.'

'You did? When you were *twelve*?' At twelve, the only brokering Alessia had done was when trying, unsuccessfully, to negotiate the right to read books with rather more salacious material than her Enid Blyton's.

'I was fourteen at this point. It took a couple of weeks of negotiating between them but eventually they agreed to sell the house and split the profits.' He flashed a quick grin. 'That way, neither of them "won." I also got them to agree to buy a new home each within a mile of mine and Mariella's school, and drew up a custody plan that gave them equal access to us.'

'How did that work?'

'There's fifty-two weeks in a year. We spent twenty-six with each parent, with each year carefully planned to cater for their individual work schedules. We alternated Christmases and birthdays.'

'A fair compromise to them both,' she mused dubiously.

'Exactly. Neither won. Neither lost.'

'What about you and your sister, though? Wasn't it hard carving up your time between them and never being settled in one home?'

'That brought its own challenges but it was easier than living in a war zone. I also had it written into the contracts that they were forbidden from bad-mouthing each other to us.'

She rubbed the back of her head. 'You were one mature teenager.'

'My mother used to say I was born serious.'

Her eyes were searching. 'Do you agree with her? Or was it circumstances that made you that way?'

He considered this. 'A combination of both, perhaps. The circumstances certainly made me the man I am today. Pursuing a career in diplomacy felt natural after negotiating their divorce and custody arrangements.'

'And the circumstances gave you a pathological loathing of the press?' And, Alessia suspected, a loathing for conflict and a need to always be firmly in control of himself and his surroundings.

He nodded. 'I changed my surname legally when I turned eighteen—my father's name isn't as well-known as my mother's but their marriage made him a celebrity in his own right. I value my privacy because I never had it when I was a child.'

'And now you've married a princess,' she said quietly, now understanding why he was so adamant in his refusal to be a 'proper' royal. 'A life you never wanted.'

He shifted forwards in his seat and stared deep into her eyes. 'I married *you*, Alessia, and I need you to understand that though I don't want the princess, I do want the woman. I want *you*.'

So many emotions filled her at the sincerely delivered words that she couldn't even begin to dissect them. It frightened her how desperately she longed to believe him, believe that he did want her, but even that longing was fraught because she didn't know if he meant he wanted her, body, heart and soul, or just the first part, and she couldn't bring herself to ask because she didn't know if she'd be able to take the answer.

She was saved from her tortured thoughts by the ringing of the bell and the simultaneous trilling of both their phones, but there was no relief in the interruption, only a plunge in her heart as she immediately understood what it meant. It meant the media circus Gabriel so despised and had spent his adult life avoiding had come for him.

She closed her eyes briefly and sighed. 'I think the announcement of our marriage has just gone out.'

It took three days before Gabriel and Alessia were able to inspect the place that was going to be their marital home. Gabriel had expected news of their marriage to cause a sensation but, when it broke, sensation was an understatement. The east side of the castle, the half open to tourists, was so besieged by press that it had to close to visitors. The rotors of helicopters ignoring the no-fly zone above the castle was a constant noise for hours until the Ceres military put a stop to their illegality. Gabriel's phones, business and personal, didn't stop ringing. It seemed that everyone he'd ever been acquainted with felt the need to call and congratulate him. Once the press obtained his number, he'd had enough and turned it off, but not before his mother, furious not to have been invited to the wedding, cried and wailed down the phone like the good actress she was for an hour before ringing off so she could call his sister, who'd stayed for the wedding night in the castle's guest quarters, and sob theatrically down the phone to her. Alessia's phone rang non-stop too, her private secretary and other clerical staff rushing in and out of their quarters with updates and messages, the usual buzz of activity within the castle walls having turned into a loud hum.

He'd not needed to step foot out of the castle grounds to feel the impact of the circus.

Gabriel knew the stables, which had once housed hundreds of horses, had initially been converted for the reigning queen's mother to live in, but it was still much, *much* bigger than he'd expected. U-shaped with a bell tower in its centre, it was built with the same sand-coloured stone as the rest of the castle, its roof the same terracotta hue that topped the castle's turrets, and was situated close to the side of the castle where the Berruti family lived and worked but far enough from it to feel entirely separate. Even before Alessia unlocked the grand front door, he knew this would make the perfect home for them.

And then he stepped inside and knew it would only make the perfect home if the entire thing was stripped to bare walls and started again. The high-ceilinged reception room they'd stepped into glowered—there was no other word for it—with faded glamour. It was a glamour that would have held no appeal even if it wasn't faded. Nothing had been done to mitigate the lack of natural light coming in from the small windows. If anything, the décor had been chosen to enhance the shadows. Even the exquisite paintings that lined the reception walls seemed to have been selected for the menace they exuded, and he recognised a variation of Judith with the severed head of Holofernes.

Not wanting to insult Alessia, he kept his initial impression to himself and indicated the tall archway in front of them. 'Do you want to lead the way?'

Having been staring wordlessly at a painting of the

medusa turning naked men into stone, Alessia faced him, her brow creased in confusion.

'Do you want to give me the grand tour?' he elaborated.

'But I can't—I've never been in here before.'

He gazed into her velvet eyes, convinced she was joking. 'You never visited your grandmother, who lived on the same estate as you? But I thought she only died eight years ago?'

'She did but she was a miserable witch who hated people and *really* hated children.'

'That explains the décor then,' he murmured.

A glint of humour flickered over her face and then she put a hand to her mouth and giggled. 'It's *awful*, isn't it?' She shook her head, her giggles turning into a peal of laughter. 'Marcelo told me it was bad but I never guessed it was this bad. I'm glad she never let me visit. This would have given me nightmares.'

The weight in his chest lifting at the sight of Alessia with glee etched over her beautiful face and the sound of her husky laughter ringing in his ears, Gabriel couldn't stop his own amusement escaping. In his laughter was a huge dose of relief.

Since the statement had been released, Alessia had carried herself with a careful deportment around him. She was unerringly polite but meticulous about not touching him… Not until they went to bed. The moment the light went out, she would wrap her arms around him under the bedsheets and press her face to his bare chest just as they'd done on their wedding night. But, as on their wedding night, she held herself rigidly, barely drawing a breath. He could feel the fight she was waging with herself, the rapid beats of her heart a pulse against his skin, but knew better than to do anything more than hold her. As painful as it was to accept, he'd hurt her deeply. He couldn't wipe that hurt out with confidences about his childhood. She needed to learn to trust him.

And so he would lie there with her, under the sheets, her beautiful body entwined with his, holding himself back from even stroking her hair, hardly able to breathe himself with the pain of his desire cramping his lungs, having to push out the memories of the first time they'd laid entwined, both naked, fitting together like a jigsaw. When he did manage to push aside images that only fired the desire he was having to suppress, his thoughts never strayed from her. The more time he spent with her, the greater his thirst to know everything there was to know about the woman behind the always smiling, dutiful princess who so rarely smiled for him.

So to see her now, her face alight with the joy of shared absurdity, her laughter still filling his senses…

'Do you think she put these paintings here to repel people from going any further than the front door?' he asked, ramming his hands into his pockets to stop them from reaching for her.

God knew how badly he longed to reach for her.

'I'd put money on it.'

'She hated people that much?'

'More.'

'How on earth did she cope with royal life if she hated people?'

'By drinking copious amounts of gin. As soon as my mother took the throne after my grandfather's death, my grandmother announced she never wanted to endure another royal engagement or the company of another human ever again and insisted the stables be converted into a home for her. When she moved in she demanded—in all seriousness—that her new household be staffed only by mutes.' But relating this only set Alessia's laughter off again as the ridiculousness of her grandmother's behaviour really hit home, which in turn set Gabriel's laughter off again too.

Feeling lighter than she'd done in a long time—it *was* true that laughter was good for the soul—Alessia wiped the tears from her eyes. 'Come on,' she said, 'let's go and see if we can find her potion room.'

The pair of them were still sniggering when they went under the arch and entered a rectangular room with cantilevered stairs ascending from the centre. The posts at the bottom of each gold railing were topped with a gargoyle's head.

'They can go,' Alessia said, shuddering at the ugly things.

'The whole lot can go. Shall we start from the top or the bottom?'

'Let's start at the top and then we can save the dungeon for a treat at the end of it all.'

He laughed again.

He had a great laugh, she thought dreamily, a great rumble that came from deep inside him and was expelled with the whole of his body. When he laughed... Just as when he smiled, creases appeared around his eyes, deep lines grooving along the sides his mouth... Just as when he smiled, it did something to her.

She hadn't laughed like that with anyone since her school days.

'Did you have much to do with her?' he asked.

'Not really, thank God. I was six when my grandfather died so I don't have many solid memories of her before that. She would terrorise us at Christmas, Easter and family birthdays when my mother forced her to join us for celebration meals but that was the extent of my interaction with her…apart from the time when Marcelo and I were playing tennis and the ball went into what was considered to be her garden, and she chased me off like I was trespasser.'

Stepping through the first door they came to on the landing, Alessia was relieved that the worst thing about the bedroom was the blood-red wallpaper. It was replicated in all the other rooms, including the master bedroom. As she peered into the adjoining dressing room, a walled mirror reflected the four-poster bed back at her and her heart jolted to know that this suite would be the room she would share with Gabriel for the rest of her life, and as she thought this, he appeared in the reflection and their eyes met.

He stood stock-still.

The force of the jolt her heart made this time almost punched it out of her.

For a long moment, they did nothing but stare at each other. The longer she gazed at his reflection, the more the deep reds and shadows of the room reflected in the angles of his handsome face and the black clothes he wore, giving him a vampiric quality that sent a thrill rushing through her veins and dissolved the lingering humour that had bound them together in a way she had never expected.

She wanted him so badly…

Oh, why was she still resisting? Gabriel was her husband and she was his wife and that meant something.

Because you're still frightened.

Gabriel's confiding in her about his childhood and his parents' divorce had helped Alessia understand him better but it hadn't changed the deep-rooted instinct to protect herself. If anything it had made it stronger because sympathy and empathy had softened her even more towards him.

He took a step towards her.

A pulse throbbed deep in her pelvis.

The battle between her head, her heart and her body, between the princess and the woman, had been an impossible war to manage since they'd agreed to marry.

With each hour that passed, her longing for him grew stronger. When the lights went out, her weakness for him almost gobbled her up, and she would lay enveloped in his arms, breathing in his glorious scent, desire filling her from the roots of her hair to the tips of her toes, torturing herself; torturing them both because she could feel Gabriel's suppressed desire as deeply as she felt her own, which only made things worse.

She was torturing them both.

He took another step closer.

Blood roared in her head.

One more step.

She blinked and there he was, right behind her, towering over her just like a vampire from the films.

The beats of her heart tripled in an instant.

Not an inch of his body touched hers but he stood close enough for her skin to tingle with sensation.

'I don't know about you,' he murmured, 'but I think we should knock through the adjoining room. Create another dressing room and double the size of the bathroom.'

It was only when Alessia snatched a breath to answer that she realised she'd been holding it. 'That… Sorry, what did you say?'

His lips twitched but those amazing kaleidoscopic eyes didn't leave hers. He placed his mouth to the back of her ear. 'That we should double the size of our bathroom.'

His mouth didn't make contact but his breath did. It danced through her hair and over her lobe, and then entered her skin like a pulse of electricity that almost knocked her off her feet.

His eyes glimmered. 'Let's see what delights the ground floor has for us.' And then he turned and strolled out of the dressing room as if nothing had just passed between them.

It took a few beats for Alessia to pull her weak legs together.

Where she had to hold the banister to support her wobbly frame, Gabriel sauntered down the stairs with such nonchalance that she wondered if she'd just imagined the hooded pulse in his eyes and the sensuality in his voice.

And then he reached the bottom of the stairs and turned his gaze back to her, and she saw it again. His unashamed hunger for her.

CHAPTER TEN

LATER THAT EVENING, having showered and changed for dinner, Alessia found Gabriel in the dining room. The table had been set for their meal but he was sat at the other end surrounded by sheets of paper.

He looked up as she entered the room. His gaze flickered over her and she caught again that flash of desire as another smile that creased his eyes lit his handsome face.

The longing that had caught her in her grandmother's dressing room flooded her limbs again, weakening them, and it took a beat before she could close the door and cross the room to stand beside him.

'What are you doing?' she asked, glad that her voice, at least, still sounded normal. The rest of her had felt decidedly abnormal since her grandmother's dressing room, like electricity had replaced the blood in her veins. She'd been aware of every movement and every sensation her body made, from the lace knickers she'd pulled up her legs and over her thighs, to the lipstick she'd held between her fingers and applied to lips that tingled, to the perfume she'd dabbed to the pulses on her neck and wrists. Every whisper of sound she heard outside the bedroom had made her heart leap.

It was pounding now, as hard as she'd ever known it.

Why was she standing so close to him?

He looked her up and down again, this time much more slowly. His nostrils flared. 'Getting some ideas down about what we can do with the stables while the ideas are fresh in my mind. I'd like to have my office facing the garden on the ground floor.'

Her arm brushing against his, Alessia peered at the sheets. He'd sketched the floor plan in remarkable detail. How could he remember it so clearly? she wondered, awed too at how well he'd recalled the proportions of each room.

Why this should make her heart swell and ripple even more she couldn't begin to guess.

And why she'd leaned so close into him she couldn't begin to guess either.

Trying hard to cover the emotions thrashing through her, Alessia shifted away from him then turned round so her back was to the table, raised herself onto her toes and used her hands as purchase to lift herself onto it.

They were almost eye level.

If she moved her foot an inch to the left, it would brush against the calf of his leg.

'You are keen to get out of the castle,' she managed to tease. Or tried. She couldn't seem to breathe properly.

His eyes locked onto hers. 'I don't like my business belonging to everyone else.'

Somewhere in the dim recess of her mind, she understood what he meant. The family's personal wing of the castle was busy. Alessia had her own offices but they tended to blur with her private quarters, clerical as well as domestic staff in and out, her family's clerical staff often popping in to ask her questions or get her input. Everything was fluid, communication between the family's respective teams high, everyone working and pulling together for the same aim—the monarchy's success.

Right then, she couldn't have cared less about the monarchy's success. Right then, the only thing Alessia could focus on was the hooded desire flowing from Gabriel's eyes, entwining with the buzz in her veins, and the feel of his calf beneath her toes...

Large hands gripped the bottom of her thighs just above the knees. Jaw clenched, Gabriel brought his face close to hers and bore his gaze into her. 'What are you doing, Lessie?'

'I don't know,' she whispered, staring right back at him.

Had *she* kicked her shoes off so she could rub her toes against his leg?

Her head was swimming. She knew she should push his hands away but the sensations and heat licking her from the outside in were too strong. Erotic fantasies were filling her, a yearn for Gabriel's strong fingers to dip below the hem of her white, floaty skirt and slide up her thighs to where the heat throbbed the most.

Another image filled her: Gabriel lifting the strawberry-coloured bandeau top she'd paired the skirt with over her breasts and taking her nipples into his mouth.

Was that why she'd chosen to wear a top that needed no bra? she wondered hazily.

'Alessia, talk to me.'

His voice was thick, and as she gazed helplessly into

his eyes, the pupils swirled and pulsed into black holes she could feel herself being pulled into.

'I… I don't want to talk,' she whispered hoarsely, unable to stop herself falling into the limitless depths.

Gabriel tightened his grip on Alessia's thighs and tried his damnedest to tighten his control. He could feel her desire with all of his senses, feeding the thick arousal that had become a living part of him, unleashing unbound since she'd walked into the dining room, as beautiful and as sexy a sight as he had ever seen. The heat of her quivering skin burned into his flesh, its scent sinking into his airwaves. Hunger, pure, unfiltered, flashed from her melting velvet eyes into his. It was there too in the breathless pitch of her husky voice. Smouldering.

God, he wanted her, with every fibre of his being, but he would not be the one to make the first move. It had to come from her.

He drew his face even closer to hers and forced the words out. 'Alessia, what do you want?'

Her hands suddenly clasped his cheeks. Her breaths coming in short, ragged bursts, the minty taste of her warm breath flowed into his senses, making him grip even tighter as desire throbbed and burned its way relentlessly through him.

It was the control she could see him hanging onto by a thread that unlocked the last of Alessia's mental chain. She could feel Gabriel's hunger for her as deeply as she felt her own but he chose to starve than do anything without her explicit, wholehearted consent because he knew the mental agonies she'd been going through and, more importantly, he understood them.

He would rather put himself through the agony of denial than risk hurting her again, and her heart filled with such emotion it felt like it could burst out of her.

It was impossible to secure her heart against him. *Impossible.* Her heart and her body were intricately linked when it came to Gabriel and if she couldn't give one without the other then so be it. She'd committed herself to him for life, and the feelings he evoked in her were never going to subside.

What was the point in fighting the woman inside her any longer?

She was crazy for him.

Gazing deep into his eyes, she whispered, 'I want you.'

He breathed in deeply and shuddered.

'I want you,' she repeated, and then she could hold back no more and, digging the tips of her fingers into his cheeks, she kissed him with every ounce of the passion she'd been denying them.

The groan that came with his response could have been a roar.

In seconds he was off his seat, holding her tightly to him and kissing her back with a ferocity that sent her head spinning.

As if he'd looked inside her head and read her fantasies, long fingers dipped under her skirt and dragged up her thigh, and round to clasp her bottom.

Arms entwined around his neck, she closed off the world and sank into her senses…senses which were receptacles for Gabriel, for his taste, his touch… All of him.

Lips moving together, tongues duelling, fingers

scraped over flesh and ripped and pulled at the intrusive fabric separating them. Grabbing his shirt to loosen it, she fumbled with the buttons before giving up and slipping her hand beneath it, flattening her palm against his hard abdomen, thrilling at the heat of his skin, the soft hair covering the smoothness. Up her hands splayed, ruching his shirt as her fingers rose until he broke the connection of their mouths to undo the top few buttons himself and yank it over his head.

Gabriel would not have believed it possible for his arousal to deepen any further but then he saw the drugged ringing of Alessia's eyes as she wantonly grazed her stare over his chest. When she put her mouth to his nipple and scraped her nails over his back, the charge that fired through his veins...

Never had he responded with such violent fever...

Apart from with Alessia.

Time had dimmed the intensity of the pleasure they'd shared that night but now, with her rosebud lips worshipping him and her hands stroking and scraping over his burning flesh, he knew that dimming had been an essential defence mechanism in him because the force of his desire was too savage and greedy to be unleashed again.

But it was unleashed now. Unleashed and frenzied and as essential as the air he breathed. *She* was as essential to him as the air he breathed, and he wanted to taste every part of her and consume her into his being.

Clasping her hair he used every ounce of his control to gently pull her head back.

Those drugged velvet eyes met his. Colour slashed her cheeks, her lips, lipstick kissed off, the darkest he'd ever seen them. He kissed them again. Hard. Thoroughly. And then he buried his mouth into her neck and pressed her down so she was laid on the table, her legs hooked around his waist, and set about consuming her.

Alessia was lost in a world of delirious pleasure. Her flesh burned and, deep inside her, pulses were converging and thickening, an urgency building that Gabriel's slavish assault only added fuel to. Her bandeau top yanked down, she cried out when his hot mouth covered her breast: sucking, biting, licking, sending her spinning until she cried out again and arched her back when he moved to the other.

The assault of his mouth continued down to her belly, his hands clasping her skirt and pushing it up to her hips. Raising his face to look at her with hooded, passion-ridden eyes, he bared his teeth with a growl and clasped her knickers. With another growl, he tugged them down her thighs and off her legs, and in moments he was on his knees with his face buried in the most feminine part of her.

This was a pleasure like no other, an all-consuming barrage of stimulation, and, closing her eyes tightly, Alessia lost herself in the flames.

The musky scent and taste of Alessia's swollen sex was the most potent aphrodisiac to Gabriel's senses. She opened herself to him like a flower in full bloom, her thighs around his neck, and with a greed he'd never known he possessed, he devoured the sweet nectar of her desire, moving his tongue rhythmically over the core of her pleasure until she stiffened beneath him and then, with shudders that rippled through her entire body, and the heels of her feet kicking him, cried her pleasure in one long, continuous moan.

Close to losing his head with the strength of his

arousal, Gabriel only just managed to hold onto his control until the shudders wracking her had subsided and her moans turned into a breathless sigh of fulfilment.

Rising back to his feet, he gazed down at her pleasure-saturated face and then he could hold on no more. Working quickly at his trousers, he tugged them down with his underwear and finally let his erection spring free. The urgency to be inside her had him gripping her hips so her bottom was at the edge of the table, and then he guided himself to the place he most desperately wanted to be. And then with one long drive, he buried himself deep inside her slick tightness.

It was Gabriel's groan as he drove himself inside her that added a spark to the kindling of Alessia's spent desire. Her climax had been so powerful it had sapped all the energy that had driven her to that most glorious of peaks. It was the way his glazed eyes fixed on her as he thrust into her a second time that added fuel to the steadily increasing heat. And it was when he raised her thighs for deeper penetration and his groin rubbed against her still-throbbing nub that the flames caught all over again.

Oh, my God…

It wasn't Gabriel making love to her. It was an animal who pinned her hands to the sides of her head and laced his fingers through hers, an animal who drove so hard and so furiously into her, feeding the flames of her desire… And yet Gabriel *was* there too. He was there, behind those glazed eyes.

This animal…this beast…this was Gabriel in all his raw beauty.

She could see him. And he could see her. See right to her core.

Alessia was so taken by the animalistic beauty of the man making love to her with such ferocious passion that she was hardly conscious of her second climax building inside her until it exploded like a pulsating firework that throbbed and sparkled through her entire being and carried her away to the stars.

It was the ringing of the bell that brought Alessia crashing back down to earth.

Eyes flying open, they locked onto Gabriel's. The dazed expression she found in them perfectly matched what she was feeling inside.

'That's our dinner,' she whispered.

His brow creased as if he'd never heard of dinner before. The surround of his mouth was smeared red with her lipstick.

She laughed for absolutely no discernible reason. Maybe she was delirious? She didn't care. She felt like she could spring onto a cloud and float into the stratosphere. 'The staff will be bringing our dinner in at any second.'

Firm lips crushed against hers, teeth capturing her bottom lip as he pulled away from her with a growl.

Hastily, they scrambled to make themselves presentable. Alessia had a much easier time of it seeing as she still had her skirt and top on, and she tried to help Gabriel button his shirt but it buttoned differently to what she was used to and she was more a hindrance than a help.

She opened the dining room door and took her seat exactly ten seconds before the servers arrived.

Three days later, the paparazzi were waiting in their usual spot outside the castle grounds. That they pursued them all the way to the airfield where Gabriel's jet awaited them reinforced the impact the release of the wedding statement had had. The royal family always travelled in official cars and were always followed, but the times Gabriel had come and gone from the castle before had evoked only cursory interest from the vultures. Now, even though they were in the back of a non-official car, the paparazzi were clearly taking no chances that their cash cow might be inside it.

When they arrived at his home a few miles north of Madrid a few hours later, his heart sank to find another pack of paparazzi staked outside his estate. Fortunately, they preferred to move out of the way than get run over by his driver.

'I'm sorry,' Alessia whispered, squeezing his hand.

He gave a rueful smile. 'You have nothing to be sorry for. They will get bored soon.'

'I'll only be encroaching your space for a few days. Once I'm back home, they'll leave you alone here.'

His next smile was grim. Bringing her hand to his mouth, he kissed it and inhaled heavily. Alessia's birth and the resultant attention it brought her was not her fault. She played the media game because it went hand in glove with her role but she didn't court publicity for personal vanity like his mother did. He should never have made her feel bad for something that was beyond her control.

'You are my wife and what's mine is yours, which means this is your home too,' he told her seriously. 'Don't ever think you're not wanted here or not wanted by me.'

Her eyes held his. Her chest rising as slowly as the smile on her face, she placed a palm to his cheek and a dreamy kiss to his mouth. 'Thank you,' she said when she pulled her mouth away. 'I needed to hear that.'

He kissed her. 'And I needed to say it.'

It astounded him how quickly things could change. Opinions. Feelings. Desires.

Before their wedding a week ago, the thought of Alessia in his home had made his chest tight. Now, it was knowing that on Sunday she would fly back to Ceres without him that made it tighten.

Before their wedding, he'd known he wanted to be a good husband and a good father but they had been driven by the circumstances of their child's conception. His own father had been a good father—those two years of warfare with his mother not withstanding—and Gabriel wanted to give the same feeling of love and security to his own child. As he knew how damaging it could be for a child to witness parents at war, he knew the best way to achieve love and security for his child was by being a good husband.

The more time he'd spent with Alessia and the more he'd got to know the woman behind the princess mask, though, the more he wanted to be a good husband for her sake too. He wanted to make her happy for her own sake. Nothing made his heart lighter than to see her smile and hear her laugh.

Was he falling in love with her? It was a question he'd asked himself more and more since they'd become lovers.

Three days, that's all it had been. Three days of hedonistic bliss that had blown his mind, but it had been a hedonism that had to be rationed to the evenings and nights. Here, in his Madrid home, there was nothing to stop them spending their entire days and nights making love, and he imagined all the places they could...

'Oh, my, your *house*!'

For the first time in three days, Alessia found her attention grabbed by something that wasn't entirely Gabriel. They'd driven past the security gates and now she was trying to stop her mouth gaping open. Surrounded by high, thick trees for privacy, white-edged cubes infilled with glass were cleverly 'stacked' to create a postmodern structure like nothing she'd seen before. Where the castle her family had called home for five hundred years was believed to have had the first wing built around a thousand years ago, this home could be set a thousand years into the future.

Driven into a subterranean car park with a fleet of gleaming supercars lined up, a glass elevator took them up to the next level. A butler was there to greet them. Other than shaking his hand at the introduction, Alessia was still too dazed about the futuristic world she'd just landed in to summon her Spanish and follow the conversation.

'Are you okay?' Gabriel asked, an amused smile on his face, once the butler had left them in a vast white living area that looked as if it would repel dust from fifty paces.

She shook her head, noticing an abstract bronze sculpture taller than Gabriel that she was sure was the one that had made the news earlier in the year by breaking records when it had been sold at auction. 'I'm just trying to take everything in. I've never seen anything like your home before...' Movement caught her eye and she turned her head and did a double take. 'Is that a *waterfall*?'

She hurried over to the wall of windows the water

was pouring down outside of, but before she'd reached it, the glass began to slide open. Still shaking her head, she stepped out into a vast outdoor area with plentiful seating and plentiful sun loungers that lined a long swimming pool the waterfall was falling into. Craning her neck, she gave a squeal to find there was another glass swimming pool jutting out over her.

'It's a trio of infinity pools,' Gabriel explained, standing beside her. 'The one above us extends from the private balcony in our bedroom.'

Walking to the edge of the decking area, Alessia looked down over the glass perimeter railing and saw the third swimming pool.

'That one extends from the spa,' Gabriel told her. 'There's an indoor one too, for when the weather is cooler.'

'Amazing,' she breathed, still craning her neck up and down to take the three infinity pools in. The top one was the shortest and narrowest, the bottom the longest and widest, which she guessed meant the swimmer could swim in the sun or the shade on the lower two levels. 'I've spent twenty-three years begging my parents to have an outdoor swimming pool put in but they always say no because they fear it will ruin the picture-perfect architecture of the castle. And you've got three!'

'I like to swim.'

Now she gave him all of her attention and happily let her gaze soak him in. 'I can tell.' It felt amazing to be able to do that, to let her eyes run over him whenever she wanted and say whatever was on her mind which, admittedly, had mostly been sex these last few days. It felt even more amazing that the heady feelings that had become such an intrinsic part of her were reciprocated.

Alessia had fallen headfirst into lust with her own husband and it was the best feeling in the world. 'I wish you'd told me. I'd have brought a swimming costume with me.'

A lascivious gleam appeared in his eyes. 'Who needs a swimming costume when we have all this privacy?'

The mere thought made her legs go weak. 'What about your staff?' she asked, suddenly breathless.

'All chores are done in the morning. Gregor—the butler—has a self-contained apartment at the back of the kitchen that he shares with the chefs. They don't come into the main house unless I call for them.' He dipped his head and ran his tongue over the rim of her ear. 'We have complete privacy.'

Stepping onto her tiptoes, she hooked her arms around his neck and rubbed her nose into his neck, filling her senses with the scent of his skin she was rapidly becoming addicted to. 'Complete privacy?'

He clasped her bottom and pulled her to him. 'I could take you now and no one would know.'

The outline of his excitement pressed against her abdomen almost flooded her with an urgent, sticky heat.

'Then do it,' she whispered, grazing her teeth into his skin. 'Take me now.'

Minutes later, lifted and pressed against the wall, her legs wrapped tightly around Gabriel's waist as he pounded into her and the pulses of a climax thickened inside her, Alessia dreamily wondered who this wanton woman who'd taken possession of her body was.

CHAPTER ELEVEN

LATER THAT AFTERNOON, when Gabriel had to drag himself away from making love to return some of the calls he'd neglected these last few days, Alessia took herself off exploring. There was so much to see! To her delight, by the time she'd finished exploring the villa's interior, Gabriel was sitting on the balcony having a drink.

'Your home is amazing,' she said, sinking into the seat next to his and twisting round to face him, unable to keep the smile from her face. As well as the huge living area, there was a smaller, cosier living room, a cinema room with sofas so deep and wide a party of people could sleep on them, a games room with a bar, other bars inside and out, a full-blown gym and a spa area bigger than the ground floor of her quarters. On top of all that were the eight bedrooms, eleven bathrooms, an upper floor entertainment area... It was endless! Oh, and Gabriel's office, which she'd only peeked into to blow a kiss at him as he was on a call. Oh, and there were two kitchens too, an indoor one which looked like it belonged on a spaceship, and an outdoor one. She hadn't even thought of exploring the grounds yet!

His eyes crinkled. 'I'm glad you like it,' he said as he poured her a glass of iced water and passed it to her.

She thought of the intricate sketches he'd made of the stables. 'Did you design it yourself?'

'I had the vision of what I wanted but an architect put those visions into something workable.'

'It's the polar opposite of the castle. And I can't get over how quiet it is.' She closed her eyes and listened hard. The castle was quiet at night but by day, it being a place of work as well as her family's home, it bustled with the burr of people's voices, footsteps and general movement.

Large hands wrapped around her ankles and pulled her feet onto his lap. 'How would you feel about us turning the stables into something like this?'

She met his stare with a mournful sigh that turned into a sigh of pleasure when he began rubbing his thumbs over her left calf. 'We'd never be allowed—can you imagine this there? Much as I love this, it wouldn't fit in with the surroundings.'

'Agreed, but with some clever architecture, we can get a lot more light into it.'

Relaxing under his strong, manipulating fingers, she sighed again. 'That would be nice. I've never really considered how little natural light there is in the castle. I don't suppose anyone thought about natural light when they converted the stables either. They probably thought my grandmother's personality suited living in darkness,' she added with a cackle of laughter.

'I'm still astounded by what you told me of her.'

'That she hated being a royal?'

'No, I understand that; but that she seemed to hate people including her own family.'

'She didn't *seem* to, she *did* hate people.'

'Including your mother?'

'I suppose she must have loved her,' she said doubtfully. 'That's what mother's do, isn't it? Love their children.'

His fingers were still working their magic on her legs, now massaging the muscles of her right calf. 'You don't sound sure.'

'I'm not. It's not something we really talk about. I know my grandmother was hard on my mother but she was hard on everyone. She wasn't a woman for drying a child's tears, but she knew her duty and she was the perfect queen consort. She never let my grandfather down.'

'Not until he died.'

'But when he died my mother took the throne and my father became consort. My grandmother was relegated to dowager queen. She gave forty years of her life to our monarchy so I don't blame her for wanting to retire from the public eye and wanting some privacy away from the castle.'

'You sound like you admire her.'

'I do in a way. And I feel sorry for her too. She must have really hated being a royal to go to those extremes once her duty was over.'

'And how do you feel about being a royal?'

She shrugged. 'It's just my life, isn't it? I never had a choice about it and I don't know anything different.'

'Have you ever wished for anything different?'

'Not for a long time.'

'But you used to?'

She nodded. 'When I was small.' She gave a quick smile. '*Smaller.* I used to wish my mother wasn't queen.'

'Really?'

'Really. I was six when my grandfather died and everything changed overnight. My mother took the throne but it felt to me that the throne took her. Before, when she was just heir to the throne, she had many responsibilities but she was still able to be a mother to us…in her own way. She never bathed me or read me bedtime stories—my father read me stories, though; he was always much more present, even after she took the throne—but she did take an interest in me. I remember she wanted to see my schoolwork every day—this was when I had a governess, before I went to boarding school—and see for herself that my handwriting was developing properly and that I was learning my sums. Sometimes she made me read to her. Once she took the throne, that all stopped as she just didn't have the time. There were always more important things that needed her attention.'

'That must have been tough for you.'

'It was but it's how royal life works. In our royal family, in any case. Like your mother, she did the best she could. You have to remember who *her* mother was and the upbringing she'd had. She tried hard to create a more loving environment for us in comparison to what she'd endured but there were times when it was very hard. The toughest time was when she went to Australia and New Zealand for two months with my father on a state tour. I was only seven, and it was the first time I'd been properly separated from them. I can't tell you how sick I felt from missing them. It was awful.'

'What would you do if you were asked to do the same thing?'

'Leave our child on a state tour?'

He nodded.

'I wouldn't do it.'

'Why not? They'd be at home with me so they wouldn't be separated from both their parents like you were.'

'But they'd still be without their mother. Do you remember what you said that day about putting our child's wellbeing before duty?'

His eyes narrowed slightly in remembrance.

'Gabriel… I have always put my duty to my family and the monarchy first, above everything. Everything I've ever done has always been with duty and what's expected of me at the forefront of my mind.'

'And wanting approval from your mother?' he asked astutely.

'Maybe… Probably…' She grimaced. 'When I was a child I lived for my mother's attention because I got so little of it.'

'Was being a good princess a way to get it?'

'Yes. She always noticed…complimented me on my deportment and manners.' She expelled a long breath. 'I'd never allowed myself to step out of line before, and it hurts my heart that she's still angry with me about my Dominic comments and the circumstances of the pregnancy. That night… It's the only time I have ever, *ever* put my own desires first. The consequences were so great I thought I would never be able to do anything like that again but I feel the changes happening inside me and think of the child growing in my womb and the *feelings* I have for it...' She shook her head, unable to put into words how strong the emotions were. 'Our child's emotional wellbeing is more important to me than anything. My feelings are the same as yours in that regard—when you've experienced pain, the last thing you want is to put your own child through the same, and I will not make them go through what I went through. If I was asked to go on tour, I would only accept if our child could come with me.'

His hands had stopped working their magic, his stare fixed on her. There was a long pause before his shoulders relaxed and he lightly said, 'But then I would be left at home alone.'

She swallowed. On Sunday night Alessia would fly back to the castle without him, returning to her dutiful place for a full week of royal engagements. Five whole days without him.

Until the stables renovations were complete, this would be her life, only seeing him at weekends. And those precious weekends would be interrupted too, she thought with an ache, when she attended one of her frequent weekend engagements.

Would things be better when they moved into the stables and Gabriel was in a position to work from home? She would still be a princess going about her duty without her prince by her side.

For the first time, the prince of her dreams had a face. Gabriel's.

'You wouldn't have to be alone,' she whispered. 'Any time you change your mind and decide to be my prince—'

'It isn't going to happen,' he said, cutting her off. But

there was no malice in his voice, just a simple matter-of-factness with a tinge of ruefulness in it.

'I know.'

'I will not be your prince but I will be your husband.'

She nodded, almost too choked to speak, but she forced herself to say what was on her mind and in her heart. 'I'd love for you to be my prince, I really would.'

Carefully placing her feet back on the floor, Gabriel gripped the sides of her chair and pulled her to him. Once their knees were touching, he ran his fingers through her hair, then gently rubbed his thumb under her chin. 'I know our marriage is not what you grew up expecting your marriage to be. It isn't what I wanted or expected of a marriage either, but we can make it work and we can be happy.'

'I want to believe that.'

Palming her cheeks, a fervour came into his voice. 'Think about it, Lessie. When we move into the stables, we can make it a real home, a real distinction between the princess and the woman. We can make it a home without any intrusion from royal life and all its demands, and our child can have the semblance of a normal life. And so can we.'

The following weekend, Alessia walked out of the bathroom after her shower with the robe wrapped around her, and stepped into the dressing room, where Gabriel had made space for her clothes. He was taking her out, something that thrilled her, just as it thrilled her to be back in his arms after five nights apart. She'd arrived in Madrid late last night and they'd gone straight to bed, making love until the sun had come up. Only when they'd finally woken at midday did he lazily announce that he would be taking her out that night. She'd assumed his aversion to publicity meant she would spend her entire marriage without a single date with her husband.

She wished she dared hope that he would one day change his mind and be her prince as well as her husband, even if it was only for those important family occasions like Amadeo's wedding. She wished so hard he would come with her, a wish that no longer had anything to do with not wanting to be humiliated. Alessia just wanted the man she was falling in love with to be a real part of her family, not the royal side of it but the human side, and to hold her hand and create the same memories of those special occasions together.

But it wasn't going to happen and there was no point upsetting herself over it. Their time together was short and she didn't want to waste it by moping.

Choosing a white, strapless jumpsuit, she happily dressed and set to work on her hair and face. It felt strange to be doing her own beauty care for a night out. Normally the castle beauty team would set to work and turn her into the princess the world expected to see. Gabriel had offered to bring in Madrid's top beautician and hair stylist for her but she'd wanted to try it herself. Here, in Madrid, she could just be Alessia, and it was a novelty that showed no sign of abating.

The thought of returning to the castle without him again sent an even stronger pang through her than it had last weekend.

The five days without him had passed quickly and yet somehow with excruciating slowness. She'd had a couple of engagements each day and one on Wednesday evening, so in that respect, the time had flown, and yet, every time she'd sneaked a peek at her watch, she'd found the time until seeing Gabriel again still very far away.

Never mind, she told herself brightly. She was here now. Make the most of the time with him while she had him, and as she thought that, he strolled into the bedroom.

She beamed, unable and unwilling to contain her delight even though it had been less than an hour since he'd crawled out of bed after making love to her again. 'How's your sister?' she asked.

Gabriel, who'd just spent an hour on the phone to Mariella, tugged his T-shirt up. 'She's doing great. She'll be back next week.' He whipped the T-shirt over his head. Mariella was currently doing a sightseeing tour of Japan with her on-off lover. 'It's her birthday next Saturday so I've invited her to join us for dinner to celebrate.'

About to drop his shorts, he noticed Alessia's falling face in her reflection at the dressing table.

'What's wrong?' He'd thought Alessia liked his sister. Not that she knew her properly yet, but he wanted her to. Nothing would make him happier than for his wife and his sister to get along and enjoy each other's company.

'I don't think I'll be here next weekend,' she said, reaching for her phone. Swiping, she began to type, saying, 'I'm sure I've got an engagement next Saturday night at the royal theatre. It's an annual variety night raising money for cancer research. I'm just checking now, but I'm sure it's next weekend.'

'If you've got an engagement then you've got an engagement,' he said evenly, even though his heart had sunk at the news. It meant he would have to spend the weekend at the castle, and without Alessia for a large chunk of it. 'It can't be helped.' Striding over to her, he dropped a kiss into her neck. 'I'm going to take a shower and have a shave.'

'Where are we going?'

'Club Giroud.'

'The private members' club?'

'You've been?'

'Not to the one in Madrid, but some friends and I went to the one in Rome last year... You do know it's owned by King Dominic's brother-in-law?'

'I've known Nathaniel Giroud for years.'

She blinked her shock. 'You've never mentioned it.'

He shrugged. 'We're acquaintances. His clubs are a good place to do business.'

Her phone buzzed. She swiped again then lifted her stare back to him and shrugged apologetically. 'Sorry. The theatre engagement is next Saturday.'

'It can't be helped. I'll rearrange Mariella for another weekend.'

'But it's her birthday,' she said, clearly upset about it. Then her face brightened. 'I know! She can come and stay with us at the castle. If she wants, I can arrange a ticket to the show for her.'

'I will ask her.'

She hesitated before quietly saying, 'And you can come too, if you'd like? You wouldn't have to sit with me. I can get you tickets to sit with your sister.'

'You already know the answer to that,' he said

evenly. Then, placing another kiss to her neck, Gabriel went into the bathroom and stood under the shower, turning the heat up as high as he could endure.

Away from Alessia's alert eyes he took some deep breaths and willed the bilious resentment out of him.

This was the life he'd signed up for. Alessia's job was a princess. He shouldn't resent that it took her away from him on the few nights they had together.

The seductive glamour of Madrid's Club Giroud was everything Alessia had expected and more. Situated in an ordinary street with an ordinary façade, having shaken their tail of paparazzi off they entered through an unobtrusive, ultra-discreet yet heavily guarded underground car park.

An elevator took them up to the club proper and then the night began.

First they had a meal in the swish restaurant, dining on the kind of food served up at the castle when honoured guests of state were in attendance, then they explored the rooms, each with its own vibe. In some, business-suited men and women were clearly discussing business but everyone else was there to dance or gamble or sip cocktails with other members of the ultra-rich and powerful, confident that whatever took place within the club's walls stayed there. Having been in existence for almost two decades, the press still hadn't got wind of it and it remained one of the few places a man like Gabriel could let his hair down and relax.

There were many faces Alessia recognised and, as she sipped a glass of fizzy grape juice in the poker room—no alcohol for her during the pregnancy—an elegant figure caught her eye and she elbowed Gabriel. 'Look,' she hissed. 'It's Princess Catalina and her husband.'

Gabriel, about to lay a card down, followed her stare.

As if they could feel their eyes on them, Nathaniel and Catalina Giroud turned their heads in unison. In an instant, smiles of recognition lit their faces and they weaved through the crowds to them.

Rising to his feet, Gabriel shook Nathaniel's hand and, after being introduced, exchanged kisses with Catalina, who then turned her attention to Alessia and smiled widely. 'Little Alessia Berruti! Look at you all grown up...' A flare of mischief crossed her face. 'Although not much taller than I remember.'

'You two have met?' Gabriel asked.

Alessia shrugged sheepishly. 'The royal world is a small world. But it's been a long time,' she added to Catalina. 'I think I was ten when we last met.'

Almost a decade older than Alessia, Catalina took her hand. 'Yes, I remember. It was at your parents' anniversary party. I remember being sorry for you when you were sent to bed. You tried so hard to keep a brave smile on your face and not show your disappointment.'

'I guess I didn't try hard enough if you noticed it,' she laughed.

'I only noticed because I'd once been in your shoes. You carried it off far more successfully than I ever did.'

Agreeing to join them for a drink, Gabriel finished his game and then they set off to the piano room, where a session musician was playing in the corner.

After a fresh round of drinks were served, the conversation soon turned to the one subject he would prefer not to speak of. Amadeo's wedding. Catalina was cousin to the bride. Though it was doubtful she would know of Gabriel's involvement in the setting up of the marriage, his chest still tightened.

'I'm looking forward to it,' Catalina surprised them by saying.

'You're going?' Alessia asked.

'I wouldn't miss it for the world.'

'But Dominic will be there.'

It was no secret in their circle that Dominic used to hit and tyrannise his sister and that he was the principal reason she'd fled Monte Cleure with Nathaniel.

'Forgive me, but I was under the impression you wouldn't step foot in the same country as Dominic.'

Catalina's face clouded. 'I won't ever return to Monte Cleure, not while Dominic's on the throne.' Then she brightened and looked adoringly at her husband, who gave her a meaningful look that only Catalina could understand. 'But I want to see Elspeth married and safely away from him with my own eyes. She was always a sweet little thing, and the wedding's in Ceres and Dominic can't touch me there. If he tried, Nathaniel would kill him.'

Alessia had no doubt Catalina spoke the truth. The love this couple had for each other was as strong as the love she felt emanating from Marcelo and Clara, and she couldn't help herself from glancing at Gabriel, whose hand was wrapped tightly around hers.

Her heart sighed.

Would Gabriel ever feel such a deep-rooted, protective, possessive devotion to her?

She knew he was as crazy for her as she was for him but that was a physical, chemistry-led craziness. She knew too that the personal dislike he'd once felt for her had gone and that he did like her, very much, and that he intended to be a faithful husband to her.

But love? The kind of love that meant you would do anything for the one you loved, cherish them, and put the other's happiness before your own...?

As she thought this, Catalina said, 'I understand you're a bridesmaid, Alessia.'

Forcing a practiced smile to her face, she nodded. 'Yes. There are five of us altogether.'

'And you, Gabriel?' Catalina asked. 'What role are you playing for the wedding?'

'I'm not,' he replied smoothly. 'I won't be there.'

Even Nathaniel raised a brow at this.

'It was agreed when Alessia and I married that I would remain a private person.'

'But this is your brother-in-law's wedding...' Catalina's voice tailed off, and she took a quick drink of her champagne to cover the awkwardness.

'I'd like you to be there,' Alessia said softly before she could stop herself.

Gabriel's eyes zoomed straight onto hers. For the first time in a long time, the expression on his face was unreadable.

Already regretting her unguarded words, she gave a rueful shrug and squeezed his hand. 'It's okay. I understand why you can't be.'

And she did understand.

But she understood too that Gabriel already knew perfectly well how much she longed for him to be the prince on her arm, especially for that one day.

That he wouldn't even entertain the idea of accompanying her for that one special day told her more than any words that he didn't love her and that, for all his talk about finding happiness and harmony together, her needs could never trump his own.

The burgeoning love growing in her heart was unlikely to ever be reciprocated.

Gabriel prowled the empty quarters of the castle he doubted he would ever feel like a home to him. The silence was more acute than usual for this early in the evening. Normally there would be background noise until around ten p.m.

With his sister having turned down Alessia's theatre offer to take a trip to Ibiza, and unable to get into his book, he remembered Alessia saying the variety show was being televised and figured that as he couldn't be with her in person, he could try and catch a glimpse of her in the crowd.

He got his wish almost immediately. An act had just finished, the three members bowing to the audience. The camera panned to the reaction in the royal box, and he understood why the castle was so quiet. The whole family, even Clara, were in attendance.

As he attempted to digest this, his phone vibrated. When he read the message, his mood went from bad to worse.

'What's wrong?' Alessia asked as she slipped her shoes off. After an evening she'd started with such high hopes that her mother would finally show signs of forgiveness, her hopes had been dashed when all Alessia's attempts at conversation were met with terse replies and a turned cheek. Her lifted spirits at returning home to Gabriel had sunk back down before she made it over the threshold of the dayroom where he was holed up. She could practically smell the foulness of his mood. She could certainly smell the scent of bourbon in the air.

The ardent lover who could strip her naked with a look took a long time to respond. When he finally turned his face to her, the only thing his stare would strip was acid.

Wordlessly, he held his phone out to her.

She looked at the page he'd saved on his screen and silently cursed.

Gabriel's mother had sold her story to the press. The whole world now knew the reluctant prince was the son of Monica Binoche. There was no doubt the media circus that had left him alone during the weeks when Alessia was in Ceres without him would now renew its focus. The privacy he cherished could be kissed goodbye for the foreseeable future. And all because his mother had sold him out again. She'd put her need for validation and the spotlight above her son's emotional wellbeing.

He sighed heavily. 'I should have guessed the temptation would be too much for her.'

Feeling wretched for him, she climbed onto the sofa and wrapped her arms around him.

There was a stiffness in his frame she'd not felt since the night she'd wept on his chest, right before the passion had taken them in its grip.

'I'm sorry,' she whispered, stroking his back. 'I know how hard this must be for you.'

Do you? Gabriel wanted to bite. *Then why did you*

give me those puppy eyes and tell me you wanted me at Amadeo's wedding? Was it to guilt me?

But he wouldn't bite. He would never bite. His parents had always bitten at each other, the early passion of their marriage turning into passionate hatred that rained misery on everyone.

Instead, he filled his lungs with all the air he could fit in them and rested his chin on the top of her head, and waited for Alessia's soft fruity scent to work its magic on him.

It didn't.

The fury inside him refused to diminish, his mother's betrayal a scalding wound, and then there was Alessia too, failing to tell him her whole damn family were going to the theatre engagement. She wanted him to break the conditions of their marriage and attend Amadeo's wedding but refused to renege on an engagement for his sister's birthday. As a result, Gabriel had blown his sister out on her birthday so he could snatch a few hours with his wife when it turned out the engagement she 'couldn't' miss was one she actually could have missed because the rest of the damned Berruti royal family, including the queen and her heir, had been there. Alessia's absence would have been minimised.

Duty would always come first to her, he thought bitterly, and disentangled himself from her arms so he could pour himself another bourbon.

CHAPTER TWELVE

GABRIEL'S MOOD HADN'T improved the next day, and when the invitation came to dine with the queen and king in their quarters that evening for a family meal, he bit back yet another cutting remark and reminded himself that these weren't just monarchs, they were his in-laws and the grandparents of the child growing in his wife's belly.

There was a snake alive in *his* belly, a cobra fighting to rise up his throat and strike.

He would not let it out.

He was conscious from the way Alessia was walking on eggshells around him that she was aware of the darkness. Conscious too that his tone was curter than he would like, he tried hard to moderate it and respond to the affection she continued to show him.

Tomorrow morning he was flying back to Madrid. His departure couldn't come soon enough. Some time alone, away from this damn castle, would give him his perspective back. He tried to find some perspective now too.

So his mother had sold him out? Hadn't he been expecting it? Even his sister, when she'd called to commiserate, had been indulgent in her reaction to their mother's actions. But then, Mariella had never hated the media circus that had followed their childhood and adolescence. She'd hated the fights as much as him and, like him, refused to be drawn into arguments that led to raised voices, but the media didn't bother her in the slightest.

And so Alessia had attended an engagement with her family she could easily have cancelled to spend an evening with his sister for her birthday? In Madrid, Alessia was free to be Alessia. Here, in the ancient castle, she rarely removed her princess skin. It would be easier for the woman to emerge fully when they were living together full-time, and she wouldn't need or want him to be anything more than her husband.

Despite his pep talk to himself, it was with a great deal of trepidation that Gabriel set off with Alessia to her parents' quarters.

He'd dined with the queen and king in their quarters once before, the night his plane was grounded. Then, the meal had been formal, the food and wine as exquisite as anything he'd been served in a Michelin-starred restaurant. That night the food, although served with the usual ceremony, was a lot more homely, slow roasted lamb and ratatouille. The whole atmosphere was much more welcoming and light-hearted, the conversation, too, relaxed.

The only person not relaxing into the atmosphere was Alessia. Seated across from him, she held herself with a straight-backed deportment that would be fitting if it were a state occasion and not a family meal. She wasn't speaking much either, he noted, and every time he caught her eye, her smile seemed forced. The queen, he noted too, wasn't engaging her daughter in conversation, and he thought back to Alessia's comment about her mother still being angry with her over the circumstances of the pregnancy. It was a comment he'd mulled on a number of times as there was something about that whole conversation nagging at him, a feeling that there was something about it he was missing. Something important.

'How are the wedding preparations going?' Clara asked Amadeo.

The heir to the throne pulled a disgruntled face. 'Very well.'

'The whole of Ceres has gone wedding mad,' she said with glee. 'I can't wait! It's a shame I'm not a bridesmaid but I get why I can't be—best not to antagonise King Pig!'

To Gabriel's amusement, even the queen looked like she was trying not to laugh.

'What a shame that despot had to be invited but then it would kind of defeat the purpose of the wedding not to have him there,' Clara continued before whipping her attention to Gabriel. 'Is it true you're not coming?'

'I'm afraid it is true.'

'No *way*? Why's that?'

'Because I wish to remain a private person,' he said tightly, his muscles bunching together. He took a sip of his wine. Why must he continually explain himself?

'I know that, but this is a wedding. How can anyone not love a good wedding? And this will be the wedding of the century. And Elsbeth seems really sweet,' Clara added, looking again at Amadeo, who pulled another disgruntled face. She stuck her tongue out at him, which, to Gabriel's amazement, made everyone, including the perpetually stiff-necked Amadeo, laugh.

Laughing along with them, Gabriel drank some more wine to drown the poised cobra.

'You were quiet tonight,' Gabriel said when they were back in their quarters and finally alone. 'Want to tell me what's on your mind?'

Alessia sank onto the nearest sofa and sighed forlornly. 'Just my mother's attitude towards me. I keep hoping she'll forgive me but there's still no sign of it.'

She kneaded her aching forehead. Alessia's insides had felt knotted from the moment she'd woken. For the first time since they'd become lovers, Gabriel had shared a bed with her and not made love to her. She sensed the demons working their darkness in him and longed for him to open up to her, but she knew what the cause was: his mother's treachery in selling him out. He'd been open with her about that.

But Gabriel was not a man to spill his guts. He'd told her everything about his childhood but had relayed it matter-of-factly. He freely admitted it had made him the man he was but he never spoke about how it had made him feel or how it still made him feel.

She couldn't force it. He would tell her if and when he was ready. But she'd gone to her parents' quarters feeling knotted in her stomach for her husband, and her mother's welcoming embrace had been delivered in such a detached manner that the knots had tightened so she could hardly breathe, and suddenly she could hold it back no longer.

A jumble of words came rushing out. 'Do you know,

my mother has never been angry with Marcelo before, not like she's being with me, and he's the one who started this whole mess. He dangled out of a helicopter to rescue Clara from Dominic's palace, and he was understood and forgiven even before he put things right by marrying her. I made one mistake…okay, two…and I've paid the price for it. I've done everything I can to make amends and even Amadeo's forgiven me, but I can still feel her anger. Marcelo has got away with murder— not literally—over the years, whereas I've always been the good one. I've always been dutiful, always known my place in the family and in the pecking order, never given a hint of trouble, but there's no forgiveness from her for me. She can hardly bring herself to look at me.'

Gabriel listened to her unloading in silence. When she'd got it all out, he sat next to her and took her hand. 'Do you want to know what I think?'

A tear fell down her cheek. She wiped it away and nodded.

'Your mother—all your family—have spent years learning how to temper themselves when Marcelo falls out of line, but you've never stepped out of line before. You've never disappointed them. You've always done your best to live up to your birthright. You've followed in your mother's footsteps and put duty first, above your own wants and feelings.'

'Not as much as Amadeo has.'

'We're not talking about Amadeo, we're talking about you. I don't know if you're fully aware of the impact you have on people—you, more than anyone else in your family, have carried your monarchy into the twenty-first century. You've navigated being a princess with being a modern woman in the age of social media and all without putting a foot wrong and never with a word of complaint, even when you're abused by trolls. Your mother is the queen, Amadeo the heir to the throne, but it is you who captures the public's imagination, and you who the public sees as a princess to her core. I think your family, especially your mother, see you like that too, and so when your human side was revealed so publicly, they did what they always do when the monarchy comes under threat and went straight into damage limitation mode.'

'I don't think my mother likes my human side,' she admitted with a whisper.

'Only because you've never shown it to her before. When we're living in the stables and you have breathing space to remove the princess mask you've always forced yourself to wear, your mother will learn that Alessia the woman is worth a hundred of Alessia the princess. For now, though, your mother doesn't know how to react to you about it on a personal level because...'

A strand of thought jumped at him, cutting Gabriel's words off from his tongue.

He tried to blink the thought away but then the conversation that had been nagging at him interplayed with the stray thought, and his heart began to race.

'Because?' she prompted.

Certain he must be making two plus two into five, he stared at Alessia closely.

Her eyebrows drew together. 'What's wrong?'

'You've never put a foot wrong,' he said slowly. 'Ever. You've never been linked to another man... You told me yourself that the only time you've ever put your own desires first was the night we conceived our child.' His stomach roiling, he hardened his stare. 'Alessia… Was I your first?'

It was the deep crimson that flooded her neck and face that answered Gabriel's question and sent blood pounding to his head.

Letting go of her hand, he rose unsteadily to his feet. 'Why didn't you tell me?'

Her shoulders rose before she gave a deep sigh and shook her head ruefully. 'I'm sorry. I should have told you, I know that, but at the time I was so wrapped up in the moment and all the things you were making me feel…'

Alessia shook her head again from the sheer relief that it was finally out in the open. She hadn't realised how heavily it had weighed on her conscience until now it had lifted.

Whatever had she been afraid of? Gabriel was her husband. He might not love her but he was committed to her. The truth should never be something to be feared. 'I knew if I told you I was a virgin, you would stop.'

One eyebrow rose, his stare searching. 'You're saying you *knew* I would stop?'

'Not consciously at the time. In the moment… I wasn't thinking. I remember I didn't *want* to think.' She closed her eyes as memories of their first night together flooded her. For the first time in a long time, there was no bitterness at the aftermath. At some point, she didn't know when, she'd forgiven him for that. 'You touched me and I exploded. It was the first time in my whole life that I ever threw off the shackles of Princess Alessia and became just Alessia.'

There was a long pause of silence.

'Then it's a real shame you won't throw the princess shackles off for me now, isn't it?'

It was the underlying bite beneath the smooth veneer of his voice that made her gaze fly back to him. 'What do you mean by that?'

Jaw clenched, he stared at her for an age before giving a curt shake of his head. 'It doesn't matter.'

'You wouldn't have said it if it didn't.'

'It's nothing. Excuse me but I have an early start. I'm going to bed.'

And then, to her bewilderment, he walked straight out of the room. Moments later his footsteps treaded up the stairs.

Her heart thumping, her head reeling, Alessia palmed the back of her neck wondering what on earth had just happened and what he'd just meant.

There was only one way to find out.

She entered their room as the bathroom door locked.

Gabriel brushed his teeth furiously.

The darkness he'd been fighting had tightened its grip on him, the cobra winding its way to the base of his throat.

This was unbelievable. All this time.

There had been nothing—*nothing*—to indicate Alessia was a virgin.

But you weren't thinking clearly that night, a voice whispered. *Not with your head…*

Teeth done, he took stock of his reflection, breathed deeply and gave himself another pep talk.

The past was the past. Alessia was his wife and his future…

Acrid bile flooded his mouth. He swallowed it away but the bitterness remained.

Closing his eyes, he took one more deep breath and stepped back into the bedroom.

He took one look at his wife perched on the side of the bed facing the bathroom door and all the efforts he'd made to get a grip on his emotions were overturned.

Her stare was steady. 'I need you to tell me what you meant.'

He clenched his jaw. 'Now is not the time.'

'Now *is* the time. I must have done something to warrant that remark, and as a wise half-Spanish, half-French man once said, if you don't tell me what's wrong, how can I fix it?'

The look he gave her could freeze boiling water.

'I know things are tough for you right now,' Alessia said, somehow managing to keep the steadiness in her voice through the thrashing of her heart. 'I know your mother's actions feel like a betrayal, but if I've done something to add to it then you need to tell me so I can put things right. Is it because I didn't tell you I was a virgin? Or is there something else at play?'

His chest rose and fell sharply. A contortion of emotions splayed over his face.

Gabriel gritted his teeth so hard it felt like his molars could snap into pieces. The scalding fury…he could feel it infecting every part of him.

'Did I hurt you that night?' he asked roughly.

Eyes widening, she shook her head violently. '*No.* It was wonderful. You know it was.'

'Sorry,' he bit out, 'but this little revelation has made me rethink the whole night. I suppose it explains why you weren't on the pill. Or is that another false assumption?' Somehow Gabriel was hanging onto his temper but the thread of it he clung to was fraying and the control he'd always taken with his speech was slipping out of his reach.

She closed her eyes briefly. 'No, I wasn't on the pill. But you already know that.'

'But you didn't think to tell me that then? In the moment? Before we got carried away?'

'I thought you'd taken care of it.'

'How? By wearing an invisible condom?'

There was a flash of indignancy. 'I didn't know and I didn't think to ask. I was stupid and naïve, I know that, but I wasn't thinking that night and neither were you, and you have no right to be angry with me about it because it's on you just as much as it's on me.'

The thread snapped.

'If you'd told me you were a virgin then none of this would have happened!' he snarled. 'Don't you understand that? Do you not know what you've done? I would never have touched you if I'd known! You've trapped me into a damned marriage I never wanted!'

The colour drained from her face. For the longest time she just stared at him, her mouth opening and closing but nothing coming out.

And then something in her demeanour shifted.

She got to her feet.

Somehow she stood taller than he'd ever seen her.

Padding slowly to him, her words had the same cadence as her pace but her quiet tone was scathing. 'I haven't trapped you into anything. We created a child *together*.'

'You think I don't know that? You think I don't know the blame lies with me too? You pushed aside the fact of your virginity and I pushed aside the fact you were a princess and not a mere flesh and blood woman, and I didn't have the sense to think about contraception, and now I'm trapped in a marriage to a woman I would never have married under any other circumstance. I've given up everything for this, my career, my privacy, my whole damn life!'

'You gave all that up for our child,' she snapped back. 'Remember? If you're trapped then it's in a web of your own making. You married me because you didn't trust me to put our child's wellbeing first.'

He crossed his arms tightly around his chest and leaned down into her face. 'You married me for your damn monarchy.'

'No, I married you for my family because the monarchy means everything to *them*, and so that my child could have its father in its life.'

'You married me so you could continue being the perfect princess and redeem yourself in your mother's eyes because being a princess is all you'll allow yourself to be.'

'Being a princess is who I *am*!'

'No, Alessia, you're my wife too, but you wouldn't even take one night off from your duties for my sister's birthday when no one would have missed you at that show.'

'I'd already committed to it, and how you have the nerve to say that when I gladly offered to have Mariella stay with us…' Pacing the room, she threw her hands in the air. 'You talk about everything you've had to give up, but what about all the things I've had to give up, like a whole future spent being a princess without ever having a prince on my arm? You won't even come to my brother's wedding!'

'You knew my conditions before you agreed to our marriage,' Gabriel raged. His unleashed fury and Alessia's passionate defence of herself had his blood pumping through him in a way that seemed to be feeding his anger.

'Conditions without compromise, that's what they were, and I wasn't allowed to impose any of my own, was I? As with our wedding and the home we live in, I wasn't given a say. I had no choice because you gave me no choice. You talk a good talk about compromise but you won't compromise on Amadeo's wedding, will you, even when you know how much it would mean to me to have you there.'

'I will not feed those vultures and I will not set a precedent. I don't know how many times I have to say that.'

'A precedent?' she cried. 'You call me a flesh and blood woman and then talk about precedents as if I'm nothing but some business contract?'

'The woman I made love to that night was Alessia Berruti. *She's* the woman I committed myself to, the woman I made clear to you that I was marrying, but she's not the woman I find myself married to, not when we're here. The minute you step foot on Ceres your princess mask slips back on and everything becomes about duty, but I have committed myself and so I'm condemned to spend the rest of my life on this damned island hoping every day for a glimpse of the woman I thought I'd married. But you won't throw those princess shackles off again, will you? Not if it means disappointing your mother again. I will always come second to your damned monarchy and your need to always be Princess Perfect so that you can bask in your mother's approval.'

'It's not just for her! It's who I am!'

'It doesn't have to be! Look how good things are between us when we're away from this place. If you step away from your royal duties we can have that all the time.'

She stopped pacing and stared at him with shock. 'Step away from being a princess?'

'Why not?' The thought of his wife quitting her royal duties was not something Gabriel had ever given serious consideration to, but now that the words were out, he grasped at them, for in that moment they made perfect sense. 'You've played your part for your family. Marcelo's married. Amadeo's marrying soon. That's two new beautiful Berruti princesses for the public to fall in love with, and soon no doubt new royal babies. You and I can build a new life away from here where you can be whoever you want to be.'

Alessia's early pregnancy sickness had ebbed and flowed since the hormones of conception had kicked in. The nausea in her belly was the strongest she'd known it since the day they'd agreed the contract for their marriage. 'Are you serious?'

'Yes. You, me and our baby, away from this castle building our own private life together. You can take that princess mask off for ever and just be the woman I adore. What do you say?'

Eyes not leaving his face, she slowly wrapped her arms across her stomach. 'If I consider it, will you consider coming to Amadeo's wedding?'

He laughed. 'If you come round to my way of thinking, neither of us will have to attend his wedding. I know you still feel guilty for your part in its being.'

She held his stare for a long time, tightening her hold around her abdomen. 'But I want to go. It's my brother's wedding. And I want you to be there too, as my husband, to hold my hand and support me, because yes, I do still feel some guilt for it. But it's not just about guilt. I want you there for *my* sake, as my prince, for the biggest celebration our island's had since my mother's coronation.' She took a long breath and quietly added, 'Come with me, please. Be my husband and my prince for just that one day.'

She held her breath.

For a long time nothing was said between them. Not verbally. The flickering in his eyes told her more than words could ever say.

Now Alessia was the one to laugh, although there was no humour in it. 'You accuse me of putting you second but I wouldn't have to if you'd meet me halfway and just be my prince for family functions. I can't help that there's always press there too, but you knew it before you imposed that condition. I have no choice but to keep a huge chunk of my life separate from you because I *am* a princess, and this is the situation you've created, not me, and now you want me to give up who I am without meeting me even a fraction of the way.' She shook her head. 'You set me up for a fall right from the beginning. You engineered things in our marriage so I have no choice but to put you second.'

A flare of anger crossed his features. 'That is ridiculous.'

'Your mother always put you second, didn't she, until you gave her that final ultimatum.' Strangely, the more she spoke, the calmer she was feeling and the clearer she was seeing. 'Is that what I can expect from you as the next step? An ultimatum that you'll divorce me or take our child from me if I don't agree to step back from the world I was born into?'

'Absolutely not!' he refuted angrily.

'Maybe not consciously,' she accepted with a shrug. No, she didn't believe this had been done at a conscious level any more than she'd not told him of her virginity at the time. 'What you engineered with your conditions, intentionally or not, has become a self-fulfilling prophecy for you and an excellent excuse to keep me at a distance.'

'Do you have any idea how insane that sounds?' he sneered. But the pulse throbbing on his jaw told a different story.

'Is it? Do you realise this is the first time I've heard you raise your voice or lose your temper? You always have to be in control, don't you? The only time you let your emotions out is in the bedroom. What are you afraid of, Gabriel? That the toxicity of your parents' marriage will somehow be ours? Well, I guess that's become a self-fulfilling prophecy for us too. I don't think you're afraid of the press or that you even hate them. I think your refusal to engage with them is your way of

punishing your mother because you ended the war between your parents but never dealt with its casualties—
you and Mariella. You never dealt with the neglect you
were put through, and you were neglected, Gabriel. You
and Mariella both. So you punish your mother by refusing to play the game you hate her for but you can't hate
her, can you? Not when you love her. So you punish me
instead, only committing part of yourself to me, and
condemning me to a life with a husband who refuses
to be my husband in public, and then you dress it up to
salve your conscience by trying to convince yourself
that our marriage will be happy once we separate the
woman from the princess…'

Alessia took another breath for the strength to continue. 'But the woman and the princess cannot be separated. The woman and the princess are one and the same
thing. We cannot be separated because we are one. Iron-
ically, you're the one who brought that woman out in
me and it's through our time together that I've learned
I *can* embrace both those sides of me. Maybe one day
my mother will learn to embrace them too and start accepting my human side. I don't know. I don't think it
even matters any more. If she loves me then she must
love all of me. I am a princess. I was born a princess.
I will die a princess. A princess. Woman. Human. All
I have done my entire life is put everyone else's needs
and feelings above my own. But for once, today, I will
put myself above duty. I will not live with a man who
wants to split me in two. I deserve someone who can
love all of me… And that someone isn't you.'

Feeling herself in danger of crumbling, needing to
keep a tight hold of her falling strength, Alessia moved

her folded arms up so they covered her chest, and held his now ashen stare. 'Do you know who you remind me of? My grandmother. She hated the royal game and that twisted her and turned into hate for everyone associated with it, so let me save you a life of misery and free you from the trappings of a marriage you detest. Get in your jet and fly back to Madrid, and never come back.'

The last bit of colour in his face drained away.

'You don't need to be here any more. You know perfectly well that I will put our baby's emotional needs first even without your influence. I'm sure we can come up with a good "compromise" about custody but that's in the future. Right now, I'm going to Marcelo's quarters so you can pack your things and go.'

Marcelo, his domestic staff dismissed for the evening, opened the door to his quarters. Alessia looked into the eyes of the only member of her blood family who'd even tried to understand her and collapsed onto the floor in tears.

CHAPTER THIRTEEN

HIS BUTLER'S VOICE telling him that his sister had turned up at his home unannounced made Gabriel close his eyes and breathe deeply. He returned the phone receiver to the cradle and refocused on the documents sent by his lawyer for him to read through.

Mariella let herself into his office without bothering to knock.

'I did tell you I was too busy to see you,' he said, pre-empting her.

'You did,' she agreed cheerfully, draping herself on his office armchair. 'But seeing as it's Friday evening and you're here in Madrid and not in Ceres, and you've been avoiding me all week, I decided to put off my dinner date and ignore your edict. Going to tell me what's going on?'

'There is nothing going on.' He dropped his gaze back to his paperwork and made a point of crossing a line out in heavy black marker pen.

'Then why aren't you in Ceres? The wedding's tomorrow.'

'Yes, and as I told you and everyone else, I will not be attending.'

She was silent for such a long time that Gabriel felt compelled to look back up at her. Hunched forwards, elbows on her thighs, chin in the palms of her hands, her stare was speculative.

'What?' he asked tersely.

Her eyes narrowed. 'I know you're a stubborn thing, but I did think on this one occasion you would change your mind.'

'Then you thought wrong.'

'And what about Alessia?'

'What about her?'

'Don't play dumb, Gabriel. It doesn't suit you.'

He struck another black line through the document. He didn't even know what clause he'd just struck out. 'Alessia and I have agreed to part ways,' he told her, and blacked out another line.

His sister's unnatural silence made him look at her again.

'It's for the best,' he told her. 'Our lives are not compatible. We will agree to custody arrangements for our child nearer the—'

His words were cut off when Mariella jumped up from her seat and snatched the documents off his desk. Seconds later, she'd thrown them out of the window.

'What in hell do you think you're doing?' she raged before he could ask that very same question of her. 'What is *wrong* with you? The woman you love is thousands of miles away preparing for one of the biggest days of her life—the coverage of the wedding is *everywhere*. I know you can't stand the media but how can you let her go through that alone?'

Completely unnerved to witness his sister lose her

temper, something he could never remember seeing her do before, he said, 'I just told you, we've separated.'

'Then get yourself back to Ceres and un-separate yourselves before it's too late!'

'It's already too late. She's made her mind up and I agree with her. We are not compatible. Alessia's life is one of duty and that is not—'

'And what about your duty to her as a husband?' Mariella demanded, stamping her foot for emphasis. 'What happened to your conviction that you could make your marriage work?'

'I was wrong.'

She stamped her foot again. Gabriel had the strong feeling she wished it was his head under it. 'Since when have you told lies and since when have you quit at anything? You have succeeded at everything you've ever set out to achieve and more—if you'd wanted to make your marriage work then you would have done.'

'I *did* want it to work.'

'Then why are you sitting here pretending to work while your marriage falls apart, you idiot?' Slamming her hands on his desk, she leaned over so her face was right in his. 'I have never seen you as happy as you were with her. I could even hear it in your voice. I was so *happy* for you. It gave me hope that maybe there might be someone out there prepared to take on the screw-up that is me. You found the happiness that I would *kill* for and now you're throwing it away? You married a princess, Gabriel. You knew what the deal was. Either you accept that fully and embrace it or you can look forward to a life as miserable as the one our mother leads.'

'Our mother's life is not miserable.'

'Of course it is! She has two children who both love her and have always forgiven her, and still she can only find succour from the adulation of strangers. If that's not a miserable life then what is it?'

'A selfish one.'

'That too, yes! And the path you're heading right now is going to be just as selfish and lonely and miserable as hers is.'

Gabriel couldn't stop thinking of Mariella's loss of temper. The quarter bottle of bourbon he'd drunk since she'd stormed out of his villa had done nothing to numb his brain.

As much as he wished to plead ignorance and deny any of what she'd said, he knew it was her perception that he was throwing happiness away that had made her see red. Mariella's life revolved around finding her personal Holy Grail. Happiness.

His sister's imagination was as overactive as his wife's.

His estranged wife.

His guts clenched painfully. He had another swig of bourbon.

He'd felt no need to argue back with his sister. He'd felt a little like a spectator watching a usually passive animal in a zoo suddenly start behaving irrationally. Not like it had been with Alessia.

He closed his eyes as their ferocious argument replayed itself. His blood pumped harder to remember how that had felt.

After decades spent containing and controlling his emotions, he'd finally met his match. He couldn't hide himself from Alessia. God knew he'd tried. God knew it was impossible.

Alessia brought the full spectrum of human emotion out in him...

He straightened sharply, jerking his crystal glass so bourbon spilled over his lap. As the liquid soaked into his trousers, his mind cleared.

His sister's perception that he was throwing away happiness had been no view. It had been a fact.

And Alessia's view that he'd sabotaged their marriage had been a fact too. Her reasoning, though, was only partly right.

He'd sabotaged it because Alessia made him feel too damn much, and she had from the moment she'd stepped out of the shadows and into the moonlight on the balcony. She'd broken down every inch of barrier he'd installed to protect himself with, and slipped under his skin.

He had no reason to put those barriers back up. He didn't need to protect himself any more. Not from Alessia. She would never use him as a prop or put her needs ahead of his. He doubted she'd ever put her needs above anyone else's in her entire life. She didn't *want* him as a prop. She only wanted him for himself.

He'd been too scared to let go and give her what she needed from him: the whole of himself. She'd offered him the whole of herself, and instead of getting down on his knees and worshipping the goddess in her entirety as she deserved, he'd selfishly demanded she throw the biggest part of herself away.

Ice licked his skin as the magnitude of what he'd

done crawled through him like an approaching tsunami coming to drown him.

He'd pushed away the best thing that had ever happened to him.

He'd pushed away the woman he loved.

He'd pushed away the princess he loved.

With a guttural roar that came from somewhere unknown deep inside him, Gabriel threw the glass as hard as he could. It smashed against the wall and rained down thousands of crystal fragments. His tear-stained image reflected in every shard.

Amadeo's wedding was the first of the three Berruti siblings not to be held in the royal chapel. As heir to the throne, it had been decided with input from the Ceresian government that his position warranted a wedding in the capital city's cathedral. The whole nation had been given a day's holiday to celebrate, and they were out in force, old and young alike lining the entire route from the castle to the cathedral, many wearing the national costume that resembled a brightly coloured poncho, most waving the national flag, and all cheering.

Alessia and the four supremely excited small cousins who made up the other bridesmaids followed the horse-drawn carriage carrying the bride and the man giving her away: the King of Monte Cleure. Alessia and Clara had privately agreed earlier that morning—and Alessia made sure their conversation was entirely private—that Elsbeth would probably run down the aisle to get away from him. Any nagging fears that Elsbeth was being forced into this marriage were dispelled by the excitement shining in her eyes and all over her pretty face.

On that, Gabriel had been right.

She pushed thoughts of him away and continued waving to the cheering crowd.

Today was a day of celebration. Having spent a little time with the bride, she'd become increasingly convinced that she was a woman her brother could fall in love with…if he allowed himself to. Amadeo had a strong streak of stubbornness in him and was quite capable of denying himself happiness if it meant he didn't have to admit he was wrong.

Whether Amadeo fell in love with her or not, Alessia was determined to welcome Elsbeth into the Berruti family and make her feel that she belonged.

Gabriel could have belonged too if he'd allowed it.

Gabriel could go to hell.

The spineless coward hadn't called her. After the way he'd ghosted her before, she shouldn't be surprised. She'd sent him a message giving him the date, place and time of their baby's first scan next week. He hadn't responded. It was on him if he wanted to be there.

Little Carolina, five years old and adorable with a thick mane of black corkscrew hair, spotted someone in the crowd she knew and would have jumped out of the carriage to greet them if Alessia's reflexes hadn't been so good.

Pulling the excitable child onto her lap, she hugged her close and blinked back a hot stab of tears.

No crying today.

It didn't matter how often she told herself that he wasn't worth her tears, they still flooded her face and soaked her pillow every night.

Oh, please don't let him ghost me again. Let him

come to the scan, she prayed. *As painful as it is, I can live without him, but my baby shouldn't have to live without him in its life too. That wouldn't be fair. My baby deserves its father.*

The only light in the dark that had become Alessia's life was that her mother had been markedly warmer to her, her maternal compassion roused by the sudden implosion of Alessia's marriage. For once, there had been no talk about damage limitation. Alessia suspected that was Marcelo's doing.

Her relationship with her mother felt like a fresh start.

Her marriage hadn't lasted long enough for its ending to be stale.

She missed him as desperately as if she'd spent her whole life with him.

The carriages arrived in the piazza the cathedral opened onto.

Placing a kiss on the top of her little cousin's head, she fixed a great smile onto her face and herded the other bridesmaids off the carriage, the driver helping them down one by one.

The flash of cameras was so great that it blurred into one mass of light.

Organising the bridesmaids, Alessia directed them to wave at the screaming, excited crowd and then it was time to follow the bride and King Pig into the cathedral.

The packed congregation got to its feet.

As the bridal party began its long march, Alessia's smile turned into something real as she noticed the spring in Elsbeth's feet. The bride really was fighting the urge to run to Amadeo and demand the bishop get straight to the 'I do's.

Alessia was halfway down the aisle when a tall figure in the family section at the front made her heart thump and then pump ice in her veins.

The cathedral began to sway beneath her feet. If not for the small hands clasped in hers, she would have stumbled.

It took everything she had to keep putting one shaking foot in front of the other. The closer she got, the clearer his features became.

His eyes were fixed directly on her.

The ice in her veins melted and began to heat rapidly. By the time Elsbeth took Amadeo's hand and the bridesmaids' mothers beckoned them to their seats, her whole body was burning, her heart beating like a hummingbird in her chest.

That was her family in their pride of place, the women in the perfect royal attire for a wedding, the men in identical long-tailed charcoal morning suits. Her father. Her mother. Her brother Marcelo. Her sister-in-law, Clara. Her husband…

He held a hand out to her. His features were tight but his eyes were an explosion of gold.

Her hand slipped into his without any input from her brain.

The service began.

Alessia didn't hear a word of it.

Her body went into autopilot, standing and sitting as directed, singing the hymns, clapping politely when the groom kissed the bride. It stayed on autopilot as they filed out of the cathedral, tipped confetti and rice over the happy-ish couple, smiled for the numerous photos that were taken. And it remained in autopilot in the carriage she shared with Gabriel, Marcelo and Clara, all waving at the cheering crowds, back to the castle and throughout the entire wedding banquet.

Gabriel could see Alessia was in shock and was working entirely in princess mode. She ate and conversed, laughed when appropriate, but she'd shut something off in herself. Even when he spoke directly to her she answered politely but there was a dazed quality to her eyes and no real engagement. It was as if he were a not particularly interesting stranger she'd been paired with for the day.

The banquet ended. The five hundred guests moved into the adjoining stateroom where the evening party was being held. Decorated in golds and silvers that shimmered and glittered from floor to ceiling, the round tables with no official place- settings quickly filled. He followed Alessia to the one she joined Marcelo and Clara at. They exchanged a significant look and then Marcelo fixed his stare on Gabriel.

The look clearly said, 'Fix things now or I will do what I would have done if my wife hadn't taken pity on you and made me help you today: I will throw you out of a window.'

He wouldn't blame him. It was nothing less than he deserved.

The bride and groom took to the dance floor.

Alessia's knuckles whitened around her glass of water.

Gabriel's heart splintered.

The first dance finished.

Gabriel got to his feet and tapped Alessia's shoulder. She looked at him expressionlessly.

His heart beating fast, he extended his palm to her. 'May I have this dance?'

She continued to stare at him. With no movement on her face, she looked slowly down to his hand then back to his eyes. But still not seeing. Not seeing him.

By now convinced that she wasn't even going to dignify him with an answer, electricity jolted through him when she pressed her fingers into his palm and rose gracefully to her feet.

He closed his fingers around hers before she could change her mind.

Leading her to the slowly filling dance floor, cameras flashing all around them, he slid his hands around her slender waist.

There was a too-long hesitation before she looped her hands loosely around his neck and turned her cheek so that she wasn't looking at him. Other than her hands, not an inch of her body touched his.

But she was there with him. Dancing with him.

Swaying softly to the music, he spoke in a low voice so only she could hear him. 'I love you, Princess Alessia Berruti. I love all of you, the passionate woman and the dignified princess. I love your sense of duty. I love your loyalty. I love your laugh and your sense of the absurd. I love that you can make me laugh. I love that I can make you laugh. I love your voice. I love your eyes. I love your lips and your smile. I love how it feels when I touch you and how it feels when you touch me. I love that you're carrying my child...'

Still swaying, her face slowly lifted. Her eyes locked

onto his. The dazed sheen had gone but there was still no expression.

Another splinter broke off his heart and he sucked in a breath before continuing. 'But there are things I hate too. I hate that I left you sleeping that morning. I hate that I never called you back. I hate the conditions I put on our marriage. I hate that I didn't consider your feelings when I imposed them. I hate that our wedding was tiny and sparse. I hate that I was arrogant enough to think that you could ever be anything but the woman you are, and I *hate* that I let you believe you would suit me better as anything other than the woman you are.'

A tear rolled down her cheek.

'I hate that my selfish insecurities tried to hoard you all to myself. I hate that I'm a blind, pig-headed fool who pushed away the best thing that ever happened to him.'

Still holding her waist with one hand, Gabriel reached into his back pocket and pulled out a scrap of paper. Taking one of her hands in his, he placed the paper in it.

She dipped her gaze to it before closing it tightly in her fingers then locked back on him, another tear falling.

'My PA gave me this within minutes of you calling me,' he told her, staring deep into her shining eyes. 'I've kept it in my wallet ever since. I tried to destroy it once. Scrunched it up and threw it in the bin. I went back to the hotel room for it. Alessia…' A sharp lump had formed in his throat and he had to close his eyes and swallow it away before he could continue. 'Lessie, I don't know if love at first sight exists but the first time I looked at you it felt like I'd been struck by lightning. You were everything I thought I didn't want but the truth is you're everything I need. All of you. The princess and the woman. The whole of you. I can't live without you.'

His voice caught and he had to take another moment to compose himself enough to speak. 'I can't live without you,' he repeated, choking and now completely unable to control it. 'Please, Alessia, forgive me. Take me back. Please, I beg you. I am nothing without you. I can't go on like this. You are everything to me. I beg you, give me a chance to put things right. Give me a chance to prove that I can be the husband you deserve and the prince you need…'

'Shh.' A delicate finger was placed on his lips.

It took a beat for him to register that Alessia had closed the gap between them, another beat to register that her tear-filled face was shining at him.

'Oh, Gabriel.' Alessia gazed at the man she'd fallen in love with long before she'd even known it, feeling like she could choke on the emotions that had cracked through her frozen heart and were erupting inside her.

The eyes boring into hers… What she saw in them…

Oh, but it filled her with the glowing warmth of his love.

Dropping the slip of paper, she rose onto her toes, wound her arms around his neck and pressed her nose into the base of his strong throat.

He loved her.

With her lungs filled with that wonderful Gabriel scent she loved so much, she tilted her head back so she could look again into the eyes that always glistened with such wonderful colour.

She would look into them every day for the rest of her life.

'I love you,' she whispered. 'With all my heart.'

He closed his eyes as if in prayer.

Loosening one of her hands from his neck, she slid her fingers down his arm and clasped them around his hand.

She smiled up at him. 'Kiss me,' she whispered dreamily. 'Kiss me, dance with me and love me for ever.'

Then she closed her eyes as the heat of his breath filled her senses.

His lips brushing tenderly against hers, Gabriel held her in his arms on the dance floor until the music stopped. And then he loved her for ever.

EPILOGUE

BEAMING SO HARD she thought her face might split in two, Alessia gripped tightly to Gabriel's hand as they walked back up the aisle, their vows renewed. The young bridesmaids who'd carried the twelve-foot train of her wedding dress grinned with varying degrees of gappiness. A heavily pregnant Clara, who'd been tasked with keeping the young bridesmaids in order as part of her chief bridesmaid role, looked like she was only just controlling her urge to jump over the nearest congregants and enthusiastically throw herself into Alessia's arms.

Outside in the royal chapel gardens, the sun shone down on the happy couple and their two hundred guests. To Alessia's glee, the sun's rays were diffused by the avalanche of confetti that was tipped over them, started by Gabriel's best man, his sister, Mariella. The only guest who didn't join in was Alessia's mother, but that was only because she had Alessia and Gabriel's three-month-old daughter, Mari, in her arms. The queen's happiness radiated so strongly Alessia felt its waves on her skin every bit as much as the sun's.

After the professional photographer, who'd been paid

a small fortune and made to sign a secrecy order so as to keep this special day entirely private, had finished herding them all into varying orders for the pictures, they all headed inside for the wedding banquet and after-party. When she caught Gabriel's mother surreptitiously taking photos of the party on her phone and realised he'd clocked her too, their eyes met. He shrugged in a 'what else can we expect?' way, and then burst out laughing. Her husband still loathed the press but had become far more adept at tolerating them. Once, he'd even given them a smile that didn't look completely like a grimace.

When the early hours came and the time for dancing and celebrating was over, an exhausted Alessia walked the lit path back to the stables, holding tightly to her husband's hand. Every single person she loved had been there to celebrate the love she and Gabriel had found together.

When they reached their huge oak front door, she was about to take the first step up to it when the ground moved beneath her feet and she found herself swept up into Gabriel's arms.

'I do believe it's traditional for the groom to carry the bride over the threshold,' he murmured, nuzzling his nose into her cheek.

She smiled dreamily at him. 'Thank you, Prince Gabriel.'

'No, Princess Alessia. Thank you.'

She tightened her hold around his neck and pressed her cheek against his. 'Take me to bed.'

'With pleasure.'

* * * * *

MILLS & BOON®

Coming next month

HER CHRISTMAS BABY CONFESSION
Sharon Kendrick

His words were as emotionless as his expression and Bianca couldn't deny a twist of pain as their coldness washed over her.

But what else had she expected? Joy? Excitement? Surely she hadn't anticipated Xanthos would behave in the way would-be fathers were supposed to behave. Get real, Bianca.

"You're not suggesting I planned this?"

"I have no idea," he drawled, dark eyebrows shooting upwards. "Did you?"

"Please don't insult me!"

He nodded, as if her anger and indignation were in some way reassuring. His gaze rested upon her face. "What do you intend to do?"

"I'm k-keeping my baby, of course!"

"Good."

The word took the wind right out of her sails and she blinked at him in confusion, before reminding herself that she didn't need his approval. But that didn't prevent the sliver of hope which shot through her, like sunlight breaking through a dark cloud. "I know you never intended to be a father—"

"No, you're right, I didn't." His words effectively killed off that brief flash of optimism. "So what do you want from me, Bianca?"

Continue reading
HER CHRISTMAS BABY CONFESSION
Sharon Kendrick

Available next month
www.millsandboon.co.uk

MILLS & BOON

THE HEART OF ROMANCE

A ROMANCE FOR EVERY READER

MODERN

Prepare to be swept off your feet by sophisticated, sexy and seductive heroes, in some of the world's most glamourous and romantic locations, where power and passion collide.

HISTORICAL

Escape with historical heroes from time gone by. Whether your passion is for wicked Regency Rakes, muscled Vikings or rugged Highlanders, awaken the romance of the past.

MEDICAL

Set your pulse racing with dedicated, delectable doctors in the high-pressure world of medicine, where emotions run high and passion, comfort and love are the best medicine.

True Love

Celebrate true love with tender stories of heartfelt romance, from the rush of falling in love to the joy a new baby can bring, and a focus on the emotional heart of a relationship.

Desire

Indulge in secrets and scandal, intense drama and plenty of sizzling hot action with powerful and passionate heroes who have it all: wealth, status, good looks…everything but the right woman.

HEROES

Experience all the excitement of a gripping thriller, with an intense romance at its heart. Resourceful, true-to-life women and strong, fearless men face danger and desire - a killer combination!

To see which titles are coming soon, please visit

millsandboon.co.uk/nextmonth

LET'S TALK

Romance

For exclusive extracts, competitions
and special offers, find us online:

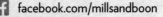

f facebook.com/millsandboon

🐦 @MillsandBoon

📷 @MillsandBoonUK

Get in touch on 01413 063232